Vaetra Untrained

Book Two of the Vaetra Chronicles

Daniel R. Marvello

Published by Magic Fur Press
An imprint of Logical Expressions, Inc.
311 Fox Glen Road, Sandpoint, Idaho 83864, USA

VAETRA UNTRAINED

ISBN: 978-1-61038-017-1 (paperback)
       978-1-61038-018-8 (EPUB)

Vaetra Untrained is dedicated to my wife's mother, Margot Daffron, who lost a long battle with cancer this summer. We will miss the fun times and laughter we shared with her. Margot was a kind and generous soul who helped us through some difficult times.

This book is also dedicated to everyone who has lost a loved one or favorite pet to cancer. I hope that one day, science will find a way to put an end to this horrible disease and the physical, emotional, and financial devastation it leaves in its wake.

THUNDERHEAD COLLEGE
RIVERVIEW
THE ARCHIVES
DUSK
NORTHSHORE
DUNVER
DELTA
PLAINS END
CASSANDRIA

CHAPTER 1

SHORT DETOUR

Jaylan ~ The Archives

I woke from a dreamless and restful sleep, but when I sat up in bed and opened my eyes, it was absolutely dark. I blinked hard a couple of times to assure myself that my eyes were open. I turned my head in search of even the faintest glimmer of light. *Why can't I see? Have I gone blind?*

My racing heart calmed as memories of the past week seeped back into my conscious mind. I wasn't at my home in Northshore. I was at the Archives, the largest and oldest sanctuary for sorcerers in the Tanes Empire, possibly in all of Mundia. My recently assigned chamber was one of many that sorcerer-engineers had centuries ago carved out of the mountain ridge that enveloped the facility.

Today was my first day of learning how to become a sorcerer.

I reached over toward the small table next to my bed, and my fingers fumbled around until they found the base of the lamp. Focusing my attention, I channeled vaetra into the lamp's metal base the way Sulana had shown me the night before. I said the trigger word, "Light," and was rewarded with a tiny squeak and a spark from the igniter crystal that sat next to the wick. It took a second try before the wick caught and settled into a steady flame.

I squinted against the sudden light and my residual fear faded as the features of my room emerged from the darkness. My chamber was small and simple. It had a bed, a tiny square table for the lamp, a larger round table with two chairs over in one corner, and a plain chest of drawers. The walls were solid, grey stone and completely bare of decoration. I didn't expect to spend much time here, but I definitely needed to hang up something colorful to relieve the starkness of these walls.

After living in an apartment that shared a wall with a busy inn in the middle of a bustling town, I wasn't used to the sensory deprivation of a room deep underground or walking subterranean hallways surrounded by sorcerers. Everything here was new and strange. Adjusting to life at the Archives might take a while.

I slipped out of bed and padded over to the chest of drawers. I dressed quickly in the long, grey, one-piece robe Sulana had given me yesterday. "You're a sorcerer now, so you might as well dress like one," she had said with a smile when she held it out to me.

Sulana was the person who had suggested that I come to the Archives and develop my ability to manipulate magic, or "vaetra" as sorcerers preferred to call it. At the time, I considered her suggestion unthinkable. I would have to leave my mundane life behind and potentially alienate all of my friends and family. However, fate conspired to show me that I truly had little choice in the matter; I was a sorcerer, whether I wanted to be or not. During our subsequent adventures together, a friendship, and possibly something more, had grown between us.

After I pulled on the robe, I stopped with a frown. The unfamiliar weight and fit of the garment settled around me like some kind of costume. I might be dressed like a sorcerer, but I didn't feel like one. A tingle of panic shot down my neck as I thought back on the life I had abandoned. For the thousandth time, I wondered if coming here was the right decision. Would my friends and family be able to forgive me for becoming a practitioner of magic? Even a month ago,

I would have counted myself among those who feared and shunned sorcerers.

My thoughts were interrupted by a soft knock on my chamber door. I opened the door to find Sword Sorceress Sulana Delano standing on the other side. The hallway illuminator behind her made a halo of her blonde hair and cast her face in shadow. In addition to the light, I could hear a high-pitched whine from the illuminator, and the combined effect on Sulana's presence was rather eerie.

That was another thing I was going to have to get used to. Being a Sound Sensitive, I was able to hear magical activities or "vaetric manifestations" as Sulana would call them. Living at the Archives was going to be a noisy experience.

Sulana wore tight leggings and a loose, green shirt that hung nearly to her knees. A thin, brown, leather belt gathered the shirt at her waist, emphasizing her petite but shapely form. I invited her in, and she sat down at the end of the bed. Seeing her sitting there comfortably on my bed gave me ideas that I immediately suppressed. She seemed to know what I was thinking and raised an eyebrow as she ran her hand across the surface of the mattress.

"Did you sleep well?" she asked.

"Like a rock," I replied. "Which seems appropriate down here," I added, looking around the room.

She giggled. "Good. You'll want to be alert for your first day of lessons. I hear your instructor is a real task master."

I sat next to her on the bed and pulled on a pair of soft grey boots. Then we both stood together and faced each other.

"Are you ready?" she asked me. Her question seemed to encompass more than just my impending lessons in sorcery. I looked down into her wide blue eyes and suddenly felt much better about coming here. My interest in Sulana had played no small part in that decision.

"As ready as I'll ever be," I said with a sigh. I went over to the lamp and blew it out as Sulana went back into the hallway. When she stepped across the threshold, the hallway illuminator came back on, giving me enough light to exit my chamber without tripping over anything.

I closed my door and we started walking toward the main hallway. I looked up at the illuminator as we passed under it. The light seemed to come from a crystal or a piece of glass held by a bell-shaped metal setting. The bell was attached to a metal rod that was embedded into the wall. "What powers the illuminators?" I asked.

"They draw vaetra from the walls. The entire castle is one enormous vaetric well. The stem of the illuminator is driven into the stone, and the glass focus bead draws vaetra through it to manifest light."

The illuminators were vaetric implements, just like the amulets we had recovered from the villagers of Buckwoods. A manipulative sorcerer named Paeter Thoron had virtually enslaved the villagers with the decorative but insidious devices. But the mind-control magic of the amulets only worked when a sorcerer enabled them. "How do they activate? I thought implements had to be activated by a trigger word before vaetra would flow through them."

She shrugged and responded, "I don't know much about the enchantment that drives them. From what I understand, they are active all the time, but they only emit light when someone moves near them."

"So, you can create an enchantment that loops back on itself?"

She answered with an impatient edge to her voice. "I guess so. I'm not a smith. The illuminators keep me from walking into the walls. That's all I really need to know."

"Sorry. I just like to know how things work." I curbed my desire to ask more questions. Sulana was not the first person to be exasperated by my persistent questioning when something caught my interest.

However, in this case, my curiosity was more than casual. Paeter Thoron had left a trap behind for Sulana's team when he fled Buckwoods. That trap had blown up a small building, and it had nearly blown up Wizard Ebnik Vlastorus and me with it. I wanted to know how the vaetra-driven trap could have been triggered with no one there to activate it, but I had never gotten around to asking Ebnik about it. This looping concept seemed to fit the circumstances. I hoped I would eventually meet a "smith," a sorcerer who created vaetric implements, and I'd be able to ask my questions then.

Sulana and I continued down the narrow hallway in uncomfortable silence. I tentatively reached over and touched her hand. She looked up at me, smiled, and took my hand in hers. We walked hand-in-hand out to the main hall and turned toward the stairwell that would take us up to the level where the classrooms were.

We encountered a few other residents along the way, all of whom nodded and smiled at Sulana as they swished past us in their sorcerer's robes. I was pleased she didn't feel compelled to free her hand from mine in the presence of others, although I was certain our display of affection would cause whispers. *Who is that man with the Sword Sorceress?*

"How do you feel about a short detour?" Sulana asked.

"Do we have time?"

"We have plenty of time." She nudged me with her elbow. "Since you're so interested in how things work, I was thinking you might like to see how we keep this place warm and dry."

That did sound interesting. "Are you sure? I might ask questions, you know."

She laughed. "That's okay. I guess I'll just have to get used to it."

Sulana led the way to the stairwell at the "deep" end of the hall, the end that was farthest away from the front of the castle. We descended the stairs to the next hallway landing, but Sulana kept going. "The convectors are on the utility level," she explained. "That's the next one down."

"How many levels does this place have?"

"Six total. Three above ground and three below."

"It seems to me that they are all underground."

She snorted. "I guess that's true. The only real difference is that the above-ground levels have windows along the front wall. The castle's main doors open into the ground level. The training level is above that, and the council level is at the top. Going down from ground level, we have residence level where your room is, library level, and utility level." She spoke the last words with a sweep of her arm as we stepped out of the stairwell into a dark and dank hall.

Illuminators came on as we emerged from the stairwell, emphasizing the fact that we were completely alone down here. One of the illuminators flickered annoyingly, intermittently casting part of the hallway back into darkness.

"Do those things wear out?" I asked.

Sulana shook her head, staring at the misbehaving illuminator. "Not that I know of. But this level gets the least airflow and almost no heat. Maybe something in it corroded."

The stairwell was at the T-intersection of a wide main access hallway that receded away from us and a narrower corridor that went to our left and right. Sulana led me to the left and stopped at a wide wooden door. She glanced at me and smiled. "You'll like this."

She released my hand, got a firm grip on the door handle, and slid the heavy latch bolt with her other hand. The door immediately pulled away from her and air from the hallway was sucked into the opening. She stepped into the room and I followed, helping her push the door closed against the rushing airflow.

Turning around, I discovered that we were in a long, narrow room with a low ceiling. Our clothes and hair fluttered around us as a chill wind circled around the room. The floor practically vibrated from a deep hum that permeated the space. I folded my arms around my middle. "It's nippy in here," I said, raising my voice over the wind.

Sulana pointed at the far end of the room to our left. A large door made of metal grating seemed to be the source of the inflow. "That door leads into the base of the tower. Cool outside air flows down the tower stairwell into this room." She then pointed up. "The convectors use vaetra to heat the air, and the warmed air flows up through vent tubes between each floor, heating and drying the rooms as it goes. It exhausts through vents along the face of the castle under the eaves."

I moved to the center of the room and looked up into one of the convectors. Set into a cavity behind a ceiling grate, the convector was a set of three metal rods about four feet long held between stone insulators. Heat radiating from the rods warmed my face, and I realized the humming sound was probably the manifestation noise of the convectors at work. I could not see into the darkness beyond the rods, where the cavity presumably split into the vent tubes Sulana mentioned.

"What controls the temperature?"

"I don't think it varies. Being underground, the interior temperature of the Archives doesn't change that much. The convectors keep the air fresh and dry more than anything. In the winter, when the incoming air is really cold, the temperature in the castle drops too."

"This would be a bad place to annoy a skunk," I observed wryly, and Sulana laughed.

"You joke, but according to legend it has happened. That grated door wasn't always there, and the tower used to have a door to the outside. Someone left it open and a skunk *did* get down here. When they chased it out, the skunk did what skunks do. It rendered the entire place uninhabitable for a couple of days while they scrubbed the odor out of the stone."

I shuddered at the thought of the entire castle being flooded by skunk stink. Taking a last look around, I said, "I guess we should get going."

Sulana nodded and let me open the door for her. Once we were outside, I pulled the door shut against the suction of the convector room, and Sulana slammed the bolt into place for me. It occurred to me that the room should probably be locked, but then it wasn't unusual for me to be overly security conscious.

"Thanks for showing that to me. I'm looking forward to learning more about the Archives. All this stuff is probably normal to you, but to me it's amazing."

Sulana took my hand again and we started up the stairs to the training level. "You're welcome. Showing you around is giving me a new appreciation for the things I've been taking for granted. I've got lots more to show you."

I smiled at her and wiggled an eyebrow. "I'll just bet you do."

She rolled her eyes and poked me in the side with a stiff finger. "Let's get you to your class."

CHAPTER 2

PROFESSOR OF SORCERY

Jaylan - Incantation Class, The Archives

Sulana let go of my hand when we reached the doorway to the classroom and stepped inside. The room was long and narrow, with a half-dozen long tables and bench seats. Only three students were present. Two teenage students, a boy and a girl, sat together at one table. The third student was a man who appeared to be about my age, in his mid-twenties. He sat alone at a separate table.

The girl and boy were in their mid-to-late teens and obviously related. They had similar features and the same fair coloring. The girl had fine strawberry blond hair, light blue eyes, and a small, pointed nose. The boy's hair was a darker blond and he had a heavier, wiry build, but he had the identical ice blue eyes and pointed nose.

The older student had the guarded look of someone who was not comfortable in his surroundings. I imagined that I probably had the same look. He had watched Sulana and I enter with narrowed eyes, but relaxed his face and nodded politely when my eyes met his. I estimated that he was a little taller than I was. His dark, stringy hair fell to his shoulders, and his brown eyes were in constant motion. The man's long, thin face was a wedge of wide forehead narrowing to a sharply pointed chin.

Three adults stood at the head of the class near the door. With a nod, I acknowledged Talon, the one person of the trio that I knew. He was a member of the team that Sulana had led to confront Sorcerer Thoron at Buckwoods.

Talon was speaking to a lovely woman of slightly less than average height. She wore a thick white robe with gold and red embroidery along the bottom hem and around the bell-shaped sleeves. Her blonde hair was looped up behind her head in thin braids. She smiled at Sulana and me as we entered. The woman seemed to own the room, and I assumed from her air of comfort and confidence that she would be my instructor. She didn't look much like the taskmaster Sulana had warned me about, but I knew looks could be deceiving.

The last person in the group was a young woman. She was strikingly beautiful with long, dark brown hair and dark blue eyes. Her forest green dress was exquisitely tailored to show off her well-developed figure. The dress had a v-neck that showed just enough cleavage to be interesting. She gave me a brief look of appraisal and then her eyes settled on Sulana. With a grin, she skipped over to give Sulana a hug.

"Oh, Lana, I'm so happy you're home again," she said as she released Sulana and stepped back. She looked me up and down rather brazenly and asked, "So, this must be Jaylan. I've been hearing rumors that you brought a man back with you." She made it sound like Sulana had found me on the side of the road and decided to adopt me.

Sulana laughed and introduced us. "Jaylan, this is my best friend Lissy. She teaches alchemy, so you'll probably be seeing a lot more of her."

Throughout the exchange, my eyes had not left Lissy. Her round face, with its small, upturned nose, deep blue eyes, and dimpled cheeks framed by lustrous dark hair was captivating. I didn't think I had ever met a more beautiful woman in person. My mind froze as I realized Sulana was staring at me, waiting for me to respond. Reacting to her last words, I stammered out "I look forward to it!"

Sulana frowned at me and rolled her eyes at Lissy. "Men," she said, and Lissy giggled.

I tore my attention from Lissy when I saw Talon give the instructor a quick kiss on the cheek before turning and walking our way. He stopped next to Lissy and addressed Sulana. "Are you ready to get back onto a regular training schedule?" he asked her. "We can put it off for another day or so if you want to spend some extra time with your mother," he said, tilting his head toward the instructor.

Sulana shook her head. "No, that's okay. We have plenty of time to catch up, and I wasn't gone *that* long."

"All right, I'll see you later then," Talon said. His parting look included Lissy and me in his comment.

I was busy processing the fact that my instructor was Sulana's mother. And she apparently had a relationship with Talon. "Talon is your step-father?" I asked Sulana. Talon overheard me as he left the room and winked at Sulana over his shoulder.

"Not yet," she answered with a smirk at Talon's retreating back, eliciting another giggle from Lissy.

Sulana's mother came over to join us and stood where Talon had been. She held out her hand to me. "Welcome to the Archives, Jaylan. I'm Professor Marlene Delano. I'd like to thank you for helping my daughter on her last couple of missions."

I shook her hand, although her perfect posture and confident bearing made me feel like I should perhaps kneel and kiss it instead. "It was my pleasure, Professor Delano. Sulana didn't really need my help, but I'm glad I was able to contribute."

She shook her head. "Nonsense. As I understand it, if you hadn't been there my daughter might have been blown to pieces. For that, I am in your debt."

Sulana rolled her eyes. "No one can know how things would have turned out if Jaylan hadn't been there. The circumstances would have been completely different."

Professor Delano looked at Sulana, but pressed her lips together and didn't say anything more. I guessed that this was well-covered territory between them. It appeared that Sulana's mother didn't entirely support Sulana's role as Sword Sorceress.

"Well, I need to go see if I can help Ebnik with the amulets we retrieved from Buckwoods," Sulana said. She turned to me and added, "Good luck on your first day of training."

Lissy took a step closer to me and slid her arm into mine. She smiled at Sulana and said, "Don't worry. We'll take good care of him for you."

Sulana froze in place for a second and narrowed her eyes at Lissy. She looked at our interlocked arms and then into my face. I kept my expression neutral and lifted my arm slightly so Lissy would take the hint and let go, which she did. Sulana took a step closer so she was standing directly in front of me and put her hand on my shoulder. She stretched up to give me a kiss on the lips and settled back onto her heels, looking directly into my eyes.

"Try to stay out of trouble," she told me, and then she quickly turned and fled the room.

That was our first kiss, and it had not gone at all as I had planned. I had been hoping for a tender, lingering, and private experience. When her lips touched mine, I wanted to wrap my arms around her and kiss her back in a way that would show her how I felt about her, but I couldn't exactly do that in front of her mother and best friend. It was an important milestone in our relationship, and I felt robbed.

After Sulana left, Lissy nudged me with her elbow and said, "I think she likes you."

Chapter 3
Disappointing Report

Dumont - Thunderhead College

Headmaster Dumont Fortenz moved swiftly down the hallway to his office at Thunderhead College, his fine maroon cloak billowing out behind him. A cluster of young students quickly moved to the sides of the hall as he passed, parting like a tear in a sail. One nodded to him in respect, but the others looked down at the floor. Dumont ignored them all.

Dumont was in no particular hurry. A quick and purposeful stride was normal for him. Once he decided on a course of action, he let nothing get in his way. He knew that most people found his height and tavern-bouncer build to be intimidating, and he used that reaction to his advantage.

The headmaster noted with satisfaction the new wood trim that had been added to this wing. He was proud of his college. He had taken a run-down manor and turned it into a training facility for sorcerers that rivaled the sorcery school at the Archives.

And rivals they were. The Archives attracted students who supported the conservative tradition of separating sorcerers from the mundane population. This separation was based on the ridiculous fear of repeating a centuries-old conflict dramatically named the Wizard Wars. Known politically as Isolationists, most of the sorcerers at the Archives opposed

Dumont's Integrationist vision of unifying the sorcerers and the mundane.

His students believed that sorcery would one day benefit all of humankind, not just the few who were capable of practicing it. Once the mundane appreciated the value of what he proposed, he was confident that they would set aside their fear and distrust of sorcery and welcome sorcerers back into society with full privileges, including the right to rule.

This morning's course of action was to meet with Paeter Thoron. Paeter had returned from his journey among the mundane, and Dumont was eager to hear how it went. Paeter's success or failure would determine the next step in their plans.

Dumont reached the end of the hallway and pushed open the large door to his office without breaking stride. Grabbing the edge of the door as he passed, he threw it behind him with a practiced back-hand shove that closed it with a quiet thump. He continued around his desk and stood behind it, looking down into the face of the man who sat in the visitor's chair on the opposite side.

Paeter Thoron was in obvious need of a bath and some rest. The lines on his face had deepened during his recent journey, and dark circles underscored hazel eyes that rose sluggishly to look back at Dumont. Paeter's blue robe was smudged with dirt and torn along one sleeve. It was an uncommon look for a man who normally dressed impeccably. Paeter started to get up, but Dumont waved at him to remain seated.

"You look like you've been run over by a caravan, Paeter," Dumont said with chuckle.

"Please forgive my appearance, Master, but I thought I should report to you as soon as I arrived," Paeter responded. He coughed into his hand to clear his throat.

Dumont sat down and folded his hands in front of him on the desk. He had once tried to discourage the use of the old term "Master" in his followers as it had an uncomfortable association with a time when sorcerers ruled the land and battles between Master Sorcerers exacted a horrible toll on humanity and the environment. However, he enjoyed the respect and subservience it demonstrated, so he had convinced himself that it was a harmless indulgence for his loyal followers.

He shook his head and said, "Don't worry about it. How did your trip go? Did you get the Portal Key? Is the amulet ready?"

Paeter removed an amulet from a pocket of his robe and laid it on the desk in front of Dumont's hands. "I made great progress on the amulet. I found an excellent location to work on it."

Dumont picked up the amulet and examined it. Paeter's craftsmanship was meticulous and nearly flawless, as always. The amulet had a smooth, convex glass centerpiece set in a thin, brass-colored base. A ring securely connected the base to a neck chain. The amulet was as fine a vaetric implement as Dumont had ever seen. "Very nice," he commented. "Anyone would be pleased to receive such a lovely gift," he added with a sly grin.

Paeter nodded, and then sighed. "The news on the Portal Key is not as promising. A team of Archives agents arrived before I could take delivery of the key. But the delivery was running late anyway, and I'm certain the agents had something to do with that. We should be prepared for the possibility that the Archives Council knows that I was behind the theft of the Portal Key. They certainly know about the existence of the amulets."

Dumont set the amulet back down on his desk and sat back in his chair. "That's unfortunate. But don't concern yourself. The Archives Council doesn't have the imagination necessary to anticipate our plans. Besides, we'll hear about it if the Council decides to take any kind of action."

Paeter's lips twisted into a sneer. "There's nothing like a well-placed spy," he said.

A well-placed spy indeed, thought Dumont. It had been pitifully easy to infiltrate the Archives and place a disciple on their Council. All it had taken was patience and perseverance.

Dumont continued, "As for the Portal Key, I have other plans to acquire one. It would have been nice if the thieves we hired in Plains End had succeeded in delivering the key to you. The misdirection of using mundanes for the theft should have kept the Archives guessing for a while, but we knew that plan had many opportunities for failure. We'll just have to take a more direct approach."

Dumont picked up the amulet again and squinted through the glass center at the runes etched into its base. "How close are you to being done with the amulets?"

"I'd like some more time with them. I won't be able to work as quickly here at the college, but we only have one chance at getting the enchantment just right," Paeter answered.

Dumont put the amulet down and narrowed his eyes at Paeter. "Don't let your perfectionism stretch this out longer than necessary. We have a window of opportunity that will not last indefinitely. We have to accept certain risks if we are to take action while the time is right. You have until we acquire a Portal Key. Then we must strike with whatever you have."

Paeter tilted his head down and lowered his eyes to the desktop. "As you wish, Master. I'll make sure the amulet is ready."

Dumont smiled. "I know you will, Paeter. But first, go get yourself cleaned up and get some sleep. You'll work better with a clear mind and a rested body."

Paeter levered himself up from the chair and shuffled his way out of the room.

Dumont stared at the amulet Paeter had left on his desktop and idly spun it around. He didn't like resorting to such crude methods for moving his plans forward. The amulets were too easily detected and could be traced directly back to Paeter, and therefore himself. But time was limited and so were his options.

It was time for sorcerers to receive the respect and authority they deserved. The Archives and the emperor were obstacles to natural progress. They were obstacles that he intended to remove.

CHAPTER 4
REFINEMENT CONCLUSION

Sulana rotated her shoulder as she trudged stiffly down the main hall away from the combat practice room on the Archives training level. Her muscles were sore and tired from her session with Weaponsmaster Talon Destry. Working herself to exhaustion was something she hadn't done in a while. She looked forward to getting back to her chamber and changing out of her sweaty and heavily-padded sword practice clothes into something dry and more comfortable.

The illuminators along the hall lit in succession as she approached them. Just as she reached the intersection that would take her to her room, the illuminators at the far end of the main hallway started coming on as well. She stopped when Ebnik glided around the corner and moved toward her in a rustle of long robes.

Wizard Ebnik Vlastorus dominated every room he entered, although he often had to stoop to do so. His imposing height and his long, flowing white hair were his defining physical characteristics. A long conversation with Ebnik often resulted in a stiff neck for Sulana, who at barely five feet, two inches, stood nearly a foot-and-a-half shorter than the wizard.

"I was just looking for you," Ebnik said as he came to a stop in front of her. He held a familiar object in his left hand; it was a small glass amulet attached to a silvery metal chain.

Sulana frowned when she saw the amulet. This particular amulet was one of several that she and her team of agents had confiscated from a small fishing village called Buckwoods a little over two weeks ago. Ebnik had been working with Senior Councilor Gregor Rissik to understand more about their purpose.

"Have you learned something about the amulets?" she asked.

"We have. And I don't think you will like our discovery," he replied. "As you know, all of the amulets have the same basic functions. They give the wearer a sense of belonging and an awareness of everyone else who has an amulet. They also impose a strong desire to protect the other wearers, as well as the surrounding location, from anyone who does not have an amulet."

Sulana nodded. Using the enchantment of the amulets, Paeter had convinced the people of Buckwoods that they were all Guardians of the Lake, and that they were responsible for protecting the fishing village from outsiders. The purpose of his deception was to create more amulets with the help of the villagers and their ice house, which was a natural vaetric well of tremendous capacity. But no one at the Archives could guess what Paeter was going to *do* with all of the devices he created at the village.

Ebnik went on. "While we were evaluating the amulets, Gregor noticed that they aren't all the same. Unfortunately, we didn't keep track of who was wearing which amulet, but the ones that appear to be newest have a noticeably different enchantment from the ones that appear the most worn." He looked into her eyes and waited for her to speak.

Sulana shrugged and responded, "Okay...so they aren't all the same. Maybe he just wanted to use a stronger enchantment on the Raven Company men." Paeter had redirected a shipment of glass, which was essential to his work in creating the amulets, from the town of Delta to Buckwoods. That shipment was accompanied by the wagon driver and two mercenary guardsmen from Raven Company. With the help of the charmed villagers, Paeter captured the three men and put amulets on them as well.

"The amulets he used on those men were *already made*," Ebnik pointed out. "Gregor and I are fairly certain that Paeter wasn't trying to mass-produce the amulets as we initially guessed. He was trying to *refine* them. As far as we can tell, he wasn't making them stronger; he was making them more subtle."

Sulana looked at the amulet again and thought about Ebnik's discovery. "The only reason I can think of to make them more subtle would be to make them less detectable."

Ebnik smiled at her and nodded once. "That's precisely the conclusion Gregor and I reached. Paeter is up to something, but we don't think it involves the mass control of mundane victims. It involves the surreptitious control of one or more *specific* victims."

Sulana's eyebrows shot up. "But who? Who does Paeter need to influence?"

Ebnik leaned toward her and said, "That is what we need to find out."

She smirked up at him and said, "And by *we*, you mean *me*."

Ebnik straightened up and waved his hand toward her. "Well, you are the Sword Sorceress, after all. Investigating potential threats to the mundane populace and maintaining sorcerer compliance with the Sorcery Accords are your responsibility."

Accustomed to his teasing, Sulana rolled her eyes. "I'll see what I can do. Do we have any reports on Paeter's current location yet?"

Ebnik shook his head. "Not that I've heard. But it hasn't been very long, and Paeter could still be on the move. He knows we are looking for him, so he'll be traveling cautiously."

"You're probably right. In the meantime, I'll see what I can learn about Paeter from some of the people who worked with him while he was here. His past might contain clues about his plans for the future."

"Good thinking," Ebnik agreed. "I'll ask Gregor to remind our contacts around the empire to remain vigilant."

They wished each other good luck, and Sulana turned down the narrow corridor to her room, thinking about what Ebnik had said about her responsibilities. She was convinced that Paeter represented a threat of some kind, either to the Archives or to the mundane population; possibly both. Her determination to remove that threat sharpened when she thought about the mind control amulets he had created.

Sulana was indeed a Sword Sorceress, and she had worked hard to achieve that title, in spite of those who doubted her. Here at the Archives, she was surrounded by people who had watched her grow up and struggle to convince the Council to give her the appointment. Her own mother had opposed her dream of being confirmed one day, but Sulana told herself it was just because her mother was concerned about her safety. She thought her first missions would give her the chance to prove herself.

But her first two missions into the mundane world had met with mixed success. On her first trip, she had recovered a stolen artifact from the thieves who took it, but she fatally wounded the thief who could have answered her questions. The man died before she learned why he and his partner took the artifact. On her second journey, she had stopped Paeter Thoron from subjugating an innocent group of mundane villagers, but the wily sorcerer escaped and left a trap behind that nearly killed Ebnik and Jaylan.

She bowed her head and felt her face grow hot as she thought back on those missions. The Archives Council had assured her that she had done as well as could be expected given the circumstances, but the unspoken criticism that a more experienced agent might have done better hung in the air. She had to complete more missions to earn that experience. All she needed was more chances to prove herself.

Sulana opened the door to her chamber and took advantage of the hallway illuminator's light to ignite her bedside lantern. She closed her door once the wick gave off a steady flame and the lantern's warm glow filled the room.

Stripping off her practice gear, she paused and looked up at the tapestry on her wall. It depicted Horace Gaunt mounted atop a magnificent horse with his sword raised into the air. Horace Gaunt was the first Sword Sorcerer and a founder of the Archives. The tapestry artist managed to convey a look of sincerity and determination in his expression. She longed to have the confidence his image projected.

While Sword Sorcerer Gaunt had lived, no sorcerer who threatened the peace imposed by the Sorcery Accords had gone unpunished. Most people thought the accords just protected the mundane world from sorcery, but the reverse was true as well. When the mundane arose in outrage and put an end to the violent and destructive Wizard Wars, many were inclined to eradicate sorcery entirely. The mundane representatives who helped draft the accords were placated by the assurance that sorcerers would never again try to rule over mundane affairs, and that sorcerers would police themselves to uphold that promise. Sorcery could be used to serve the mundane, but never again to control the mundane.

Now the responsibility for maintaining the accords rested heavily on Sulana. She stood straight and rolled back her shoulders under the unseen weight. She was a Sword Sorceress of the Archives. She would do her duty well and prove to the Council, herself, and everyone else, that she was worthy of the title.

CHAPTER 5
RESISTANCE TEST

Jaylan ~ Incantations Class, The Archives

My first few weeks of sorcery training went by in a blur of mind-numbing information. I was embarrassingly ignorant of many concepts, and the two younger students never missed a chance to snicker at my mistakes.

The teenagers were twins as it turned out. Ben and Daisy Morrison had been at the Archives for a few months, and they had already moved on to more advanced training while I struggled with the basics. On most days, the twins were thankfully gone for part of the afternoon. They attended alchemy class in another room with Lissy, who I learned was Professor Delano's teaching assistant.

The other adult student, Lohan, was in a similar situation to mine. He had arrived at the Archives only about a week before I did and was a beginning student as well. He seemed to have a better grasp of things, however, and rarely made the same mistakes I did. We had formed a tentative friendship based on our mutual annoyance with the obnoxious twins.

This morning I was working on refining my control over my vaetra channeling ability.

Three devices of similar design sat on the table in front of me. Each device, or "implement" as sorcerers usually termed them, was a cylindrical cage. They had a solid top and base separated by vertical rods made of a silvery metal. A stone sphere rested on the bottom of the cage. The only differentiating characteristic between the implements was their size. The leftmost and largest of the "levitators" held a sphere the size of an infant's head, while the rightmost and smallest had a sphere the size of a plum. The sphere in the middle one was apple-sized.

My task was to power the levitator with just enough vaetra to lift the sphere into the center of the cage and keep it there. I touched the base of the middle implement and tapped into my internal well of vaetra. This was my first assignment of the day, so I was brimming with power. I willed the magical energy to flow through my arm and into the base of the device. An invisible connection snapped into place, linking my arm to the base of the levitator.

I spoke the word "rise" and felt the levitator begin to draw vaetra through the link. At the same time, the device emitted a low hum that told me it was manifesting its effect, although not enough to lift the sphere just yet.

I chuckled to myself as I remembered my embarrassing first attempt at using the levitators. Professor Delano had told me to try activating the largest device.

"Shouldn't I start with the small one?" I had asked her.

"No, the small one is the most challenging because it requires the finest degree of control. The big one is designed to withstand students who have not yet gained control," she explained. "Most implements draw a fixed amount of vaetra. Once you open a channel and trigger them, they siphon the exact amount of vaetra they need to power their enchantment. They are basically either on or off. These training levitators are different because they let *you* control how much vaetra goes into the levitation enchantment."

I had touched the base of the large levitator and opened a channel to it as I would with the other implements I'd used. But the other implements only took what vaetra they needed, like the lamp on my bedside table, which required very little. This experience was completely different.

With the other implements, channeling vaetra into them was like pouring water into a funnel. No matter how much water I poured into the top, only a certain amount came out the bottom. The training levitator had no funnel. It took whatever I poured into it, and with my lack of control, that meant a torrent.

The stone sphere within the levitator had shot to the top and bounced the entire device right out of my hand. It fell over on its side and started to roll away while I sat there with my mouth open. In that brief moment, the levitator had pulled a tremendous amount of vaetra through the channel I'd opened, and the sensation was like having the wind knocked out of me. Professor Delano caught the Levitator deftly as it started to roll off the table in her direction.

The twins laughed and whispered to each other while I sat there in shock. Lohan, who was sitting next to me, glared at them until they subsided.

I looked up at Professor Delano. "I'm sorry. I didn't mean to do that."

"Of course you didn't," she replied with a smile. "That is the point of the levitators. They teach you how to do exactly what you mean to do."

I thought back on her words now as I worked the medium-sized levitator. I had since mastered the large one.

The levitator's hum increased in volume as I fed it more vaetra, but it still didn't have enough energy to lift the sphere. I envisioned my internal pool of vaetra as having a dam with a floodgate. In the past, the gate was either fully open or fully closed. The levitators were teaching me how to open the gate a little bit at a time.

I fed a bit more vaetra into the device, and the sphere finally lifted off the bottom. It rose a little faster than I wanted and neared the top of the Levitator before I could cut back on the flow. The stone then dropped quickly and bounced off the bottom before I was finally able to settle it into position about half-way up the cage with a steady stream of vaetra.

"Nice work," Lohan said from my side. He was way ahead of me on this exercise, as he seemed to be with most of the things we were learning. He was a week ahead of me in training, but I was starting to suspect there was more to it than that. He either had previous experience with some of these things or, I had to admit, he might simply be better at it.

"Thanks. I think I'm almost ready to move on to the smallest one," I said.

Professor Delano walked over to our table and watched as I slowly reduced my flow of vaetra to the levitator and it gently lowered the sphere onto the bottom of the cage. I cut the channel entirely and the device fell silent.

"You both are doing well with your control," Professor Delano commented. "Some students take twice as long to acquire the level of mastery you've attained."

I was pleasantly surprised to hear that I was doing well. From my perspective, my training was progressing too slowly. I've never been terribly patient with knowledge gaps. Once I set my mind to learning something, I want to master it as quickly as possible.

This time, another factor was driving me to learn quickly; Paeter Thoron was still out there somewhere moving forward with his plans. If I was going to help bring him to justice, I needed to learn about sorcery as quickly as possible.

"What I want you to do today won't require control, however," said Professor Delano. "Today we are giving you a test you can't fail. We call it a Resistance Test. Come over here with me for a moment." She turned to the twins. "You too.

I'd like you to demonstrate how the resistance meter works." Both twins groaned in complaint, but got up to follow.

Professor Delano led us all to the back of the room and removed a cover cloth from a device that resembled a scale. It was a wooden stand with a pair of arms that extended to either side. Sitting at the end of each arm was a grey stone block, perhaps ten inches square. A column of wood rose between the arms from the center of the device. Small, sparkling jewels of different colors were embedded one above the other along the vertical center column. A flat wooden tongue that supported a small metal plate extended forward from the assembly.

The twins jostled one another as they came to the back of the room. "You resist everything," Ben teased his sister with a push at her shoulder.

"And you resist nothing," she said as she shoved him back.

I rolled my eyes at Lohan and he shook his head. Professor Delano just smiled.

"Let's start with you, Daisy." Professor Delano guided the girl forward.

Daisy took a couple of hesitant steps and then stopped. "Do I have to? I don't like this test."

Professor Delano looked her in the eyes. "You don't have to participate, Daisy, but I would appreciate it if you would. Seeing how everyone gets different results is part of the lesson."

Daisy flipped her hair over her shoulder and sniffed at Lohan and me. "Okay. I guess I should help out the late bloomers." Daisy and her brother had taken to calling us "late bloomers" because we were older than most students who began the study of sorcery. Neither Lohan nor I cared for the term, and the twins knew it, which naturally meant they used it at every opportunity.

As Daisy moved to stand in front of the device, Professor Delano explained what she was doing.

"The Resistance Test measures your internal resistance to the flow of vaetra," she said. "The way it works is you place one hand on the isolated well stone and the other on the receptacle." She pointed at the metal plate on the front of the device. "You then channel the vaetra that is stored within the well stone into the receptacle, powering the resistance meter on the center column. The excess vaetra flows into the empty well stone which is connected to the meter."

Taking a closer look, I could see what she meant by "isolated" and "connected." A metal inlay ran through the arms that held the stone blocks. At the center of each arm the inlay had a gap with metal pins sticking up on either side. On the right arm, the gap was bridged by a metal clip, but the pins were bare on the left side.

One thing that stood out about the resistance meter was how relatively new it looked. Most of the implements I'd seen around the Archives since I arrived appeared to be rather ancient. The wood on the resistance meter still had a shiny finish, and the well stones were unworn and lacked the dark sheen of skin oil that was common to other stone components that received regular handling.

"Is the resistance meter a recent innovation?" I asked Professor Delano.

Her eyebrows rose as she answered, "Why yes, it is. The resistance meter is only about ten years old. You actually know the designer. Ebnik conceived it and one of our scholars researched the runes necessary to build it. Councilor Rissik himself was the smith who assembled it."

I had learned that not all sorcerers could become a smith. The process required tremendous concentration, a great deal of vaetra, and a solid understanding of the runes that were used to form enchantments. In addition to all that, a smith needed to learn basic metal-crafting, jewelry making, and glass-working skills.

Daisy placed her left hand on the disconnected well stone and her right on the receptacle plate. She took a deep breath.

"Now link to the well and channel all of the vaetra out of it into the meter as quickly as you can," Professor Delano instructed Daisy.

Daisy nodded, took another breath, and held it. The meter howled loudly and several of the gems lit up brightly in sequence, starting from the bottom. The two lowest gems were red in color, the next two were amber, the third set was green, and the fourth was blue. The fifth and final pair were clear. Daisy lit up both of the red gems, both amber gems, and one green one.

When the meter howled, my hands covered my ears automatically, although the reaction was mostly futile. Solid stone seemed to be the only effective material for blocking the noise of vaetric manifestation. No one else in the room was a Sound Sensitive, so everyone but Daisy, who had her back to me, was distracted by my reaction. "Sorry. It's loud," I said.

Daisy sighed and stepped back as the resistance meter went dark again. She returned to her brother's side with her arms folded. She glared at him, daring him to say something. He grinned back at her, but said nothing, and then he stepped forward to take her place in front of the meter.

Professor Delano reached around Ben and moved the metal clip from the right arm of the device to the left, so the right-hand stone block was now isolated from the meter. "The meter itself doesn't consume much vaetra," she explained. "We can go back and forth between the well stones several times before we have to replenish the device." She stepped back and said, "Go ahead, Ben."

Ben put his right hand on the Well stone and his left on the receptacle plate. I was prepared this time when the meter howled, but couldn't help myself from wincing. Ben managed to light up the red stones, the amber stones, both of the green ones, and one of the blue. He grinned over his shoulder at his sister, who glowered back at him.

"Thank you, Ben. Nicely done," Professor Delano congratulated him. He went back to stand next to his pouting sister with a smug expression.

Professor Delano turned to Lohan and me. "What you just observed was one of the differences between men and women sorcerers," she said in a lecturing tone. "In general, women have a higher internal resistance to the flow of vaetra than men. Most women light the meter from the first amber gem to the second green one. Most men light it from the second amber gem to the second blue one. The higher you can light the gems on the meter, the *lower* your resistance, so as we just saw, Ben has a lower resistance than Daisy."

"So what?" Lohan asked. "How does knowing this help us?"

Professor Delano frowned at his interruption, but answered his question with her next words. "The Resistance Test is part of understanding your limits as a sorcerer. Your resistance restricts the amount of vaetra you can release through your channel. Consequently, most men can cast a more powerful spell than most women." She looked over at Ben, who gave his sister a smug smile. Daisy stuck her tongue out at him.

Professor Delano suppressed a smile and went on. "But before you males get too self-congratulatory, you should be aware of another limitation that is different between men and women." Daisy nodded slowly in anticipation of where Professor Delano was going next. "Women have a higher capacity to generate and *store* vaetra. In a sense, men have more power and women have more stamina. A man may be able to cast a more powerful spell, but it will be over quickly."

"How typically male," Daisy said under her breath. Ben rolled his eyes at her.

Professor Delano failed to suppress a laugh this time and smiled fondly at the two youngsters. She turned to the resistance meter, moved the clip back to the right side, and gestured for Lohan to take his place in front of it.

"Remember," she instructed him, "don't use any of the control skills we've been teaching you for this particular test. You need to focus on channeling vaetra from the Well stone into the meter as quickly as possible. Open your channel all the way."

He nodded absently, his attention focused on the device. He placed his left hand on the Well stone and his right on the receptacle plate. A moment later, the gems lit up in sequence to the second green stone. I was able to mostly ignore the howl this time. Lohan stepped back after the light faded from the gems.

"Very good," Professor Delano remarked. "Your resistance is almost perfectly average, Lohan."

Lohan didn't seem particularly excited about being "perfectly average." He shrugged and moved back to his former position by my side.

"Jaylan, you're next," Professor Delano said to me as she moved the clip once again from one side of the meter to the other.

My stomach tingled as I moved into position. I knew this was one test that wasn't graded or assessed in any way, but since my resistance would affect how well I could channel vaetra, my score still had consequences. I placed my right hand on the Well stone and my left on the receptacle plate.

Drawing vaetra from a well stone was something I hadn't been able to do when I first arrived at the Archives. In addition to learning control, Lohan and I had been learning to draw vaetra from external sources instead of exhausting our internal well. According to Professor Delano, in time I would be able to tell how much vaetra was stored within the stone, but today, all I felt was a cold block of rock.

I concentrated on opening a channel between the well stone and the receptacle plate. As Professor Delano had instructed, I released all restraint on the channel, which felt wrong after doing all of those control exercises.

I watched the gems as the channel opened and a flood of vaetra poured through me into the meter. The gems flashed so quickly that I was certain I'd done something wrong. When the others had used it, the gems lit in quick sequence and then went out. This was a flash, and I could have sworn that all of the gems had lit briefly.

"Did I do something wrong?" I asked. "Did I break it?"

Professor Delano went over to the left well stone with a puzzled expression and placed her hand on the block. "I think you transferred all of the vaetra." She went to the right well stone and checked it as well. "Yes, this one is empty. How strange." She repositioned the connecting clip and stood next to me, staring closely at the meter. "Try that again," she said.

This time I placed my left hand on the full well stone and my right hand on the receptacle plate. I opened the channel and once again felt the flood of vaetra shoot through me into the meter. Just like the first time, all of the gems flashed briefly.

Professor Delano checked the well stones again and verified that all of the vaetra had moved from one stone to the other. She turned to me with a considering look. "Remarkable," she murmured. She cleared her throat. "You have the lowest resistance I've witnessed. It's fortunate that Wizard Ebnik is here at the Archives now. I'm sure he would like to see this for himself."

The twins whispered to one another while keeping an eye on me. Lohan looked from the meter to me, but said nothing. The look on his face was inscrutable.

I thought back over what Professor Delano had just told us about resistance. A lower resistance meant a more powerful spell. A lower resistance also meant quick depletion of vaetra. I wasn't sure if being "remarkable" in this way was a good thing or not.

Chapter 6
Collecting

Jaylan - Hidden Lakes Trail, The Archives

Lohan and I stopped our horses at the crest of Hidden Lakes Trail to let them rest for a moment. Patches, my brown and white gelding, puffed heavily, as did Lohan's big bay Striker. This was the first chance I'd had to take Patches out for a ride since I'd arrived at the Archives. I patted his neck and promised him I'd make time to give him more exercise. I'm not sure he shared my enthusiasm for the idea.

The view from the top of the ridge we'd just climbed was spectacular. Rocky peaks stretched into the distance like petrified, white-capped waves. Green swards carpeted the troughs between them. All of the deciduous trees were in full leaf now; the bright yellow-green hues of birch, aspen, and cottonwood dappled the hills between the darker blue-green stands of pine.

Half-turning in the saddle, I shaded my eyes from the morning sun and looked back down toward the Archives. We were at least two miles away, and I could only see the very top of the castle tower. We were on our own.

"I'm glad to have an excuse to explore the area," I commented to Lohan.

Professor Delano had asked us to go out and gather a few potion ingredients while they were still available. Summer on the mountain was brief and the life cycles of the tender plants was short. We would probably make several trips like this one before the first freezing temperatures of Autumn killed off the last of the summer perennials. She also said it would be good prep work for when we started our alchemy classes with Lissy.

Lohan looked up at the blue sky and took deep breath. "I'm just glad to be out of that hole in the ground they call a castle," he replied. "Speaking of exploring, I'd like to learn more about the layout of the castle interior. Are you up for some spelunking?"

I laughed at his characterization of the underground maze that represented the majority of the Archives structure. Calling it a cave was an unfair exaggeration. The sorcerers who had created the Archives put a lot of effort into making the walls and floors smooth and flat. The ceilings of the hallways were arched and reinforced with binding spells. The ceilings of the rooms were domed or vaulted. It was impressive, maybe even beautiful, in a solid and earthy way. "Sure. Sulana showed me around a little, but I'd like to get a better feel for the place myself."

Since my arrival, I'd visited only parts of the Archives' six levels. I'd never been to the council level at the top of the Archives, and it was unlikely I'd be allowed up there anytime soon. Most of my time was spent in the classrooms on the training level, the dining hall on ground level, and my chamber on resident level. I'd seen very little of the library level, except for the library itself, or the utility level, with the exception of my trip to see the convectors with Sulana.

Lohan interrupted my musings. "As much as I appreciate the opportunity to get some air, this assignment does make me feel like an errand boy. You'd think they'd hire some cheap labor to harvest potion ingredients."

"We *are* cheap labor," I replied. "I for one am glad for the chance to earn my keep around here. Besides, from what I understand, just about everyone participates in the summer harvest. Even the instructors."

"Yeah, well, I don't see anyone but us out here now," he said pointedly.

I shrugged. "It's early. We have horses and weapons skills, so we can go farther afield than the others. These mountains can be dangerous."

Lohan rolled his eyes. "Great. We're not only errand boys, but we're troll fodder too."

I laughed. "Don't worry too much about it. The trail crew patrols the area for trolls pretty frequently. We should keep our eyes open for bears and mountain lions though."

Lohan nodded absently and peered down the trail, which turned and disappeared into the trees below us. The larger predators rarely attacked people, but the dense forest that surrounded us increased the odds of a surprise encounter.

Lohan sighed and said, "Let's get on with this." He nudged his horse and started down the trail away from the ridge. Patches and I followed him.

The folds of the peaks surrounding the Archives cupped several small blue lakes, the "hidden" lakes that gave this trail its name. The trail would take us to the two nearest bodies of water, which were really not much more than large ponds. Most of the tender plants on the mountain grew along the shores of the lakes and the banks of the sparkling creeks that flowed between them.

Lissy had specifically tasked us with harvesting bear grass and a particular variety of lily, but she asked us to pick up anything else that looked interesting along the way. She warned us that we'd be lucky to find either of the desired plants at this elevation and with this much forest, but we might get lucky near the few open hillsides on the way down to the lakes.

Lohan called over his shoulder to me as we rode slowly down the steeply descending trail, letting the horses pick their way at their own pace. "So, you and Sulana, huh? What's it like to be the sweetheart of the Sword Sorceress?"

The personal nature of the question surprised me, but I was starting to learn that Lohan didn't have much sensitivity for interpersonal boundaries. "Sulana's a big part of why I'm here. She showed me that I could use sorcery and told me about the Archives."

"And it had nothing to do with the fact that you think she's hot."

"Okay. Sure I'm attracted to her. We've gone through a lot together and become good friends. Maybe a little more than friends."

He nodded his head. "That's what I thought. What about Lissy? Now that's a fine example of womanhood. She'd probably be a better choice for you than a woman who has sworn her life to the Archives and is constantly running off to protect mundane victims from the evils of sorcery."

Lohan's choice of words caught my attention. I got the impression that he didn't necessarily agree with the Archives mission regarding the Sorcery Accords. Or maybe he saw mundane people as inferior to sorcerers. I'd had enough of his line of inquiry regarding Lissy and Sulana, so I took advantage of the opportunity to change the subject.

"You don't think the mundane need protection from sorcery?"

He was silent for a moment. Not being able to see his face was frustrating because it was hard to tell how he was reacting to my questions. He finally answered, "I think the mundane have been *protected* from sorcery for long enough. The mundane paranoia regarding sorcery wouldn't exist if the Council didn't make such a fuss about allowing more sorcery into their lives."

Ah. So Lohan was an Integrationist at heart. I sighed, not wishing to get into a political discussion with him, but curious about what drove people like him to think the way they did.

"What would you change? Sorcerers are already spread throughout the empire, and their sorcery serves the people. Well, the people who can afford it anyway."

He barked out a derisive laugh. "We're spread throughout the empire, but we're cowering in the sanctuaries. We hide ourselves and our power from the mundane. Making it so only the rich and powerful can afford our assistance adds to the resentment of the less fortunate. We need to be more open about our abilities and share our skills in ways that benefit more people if we're ever going to come out of the shadow and be accepted back into mundane society."

Lohan was warming to the subject. He wagged his finger over his shoulder and kept turning in his saddle to emphasize certain phrases. He made sense, really. Perhaps the Integrationist agenda wasn't as bad as I'd been led to believe.

"What about the temptation of using sorcery to take control?" I asked. "If sorcerers end up in governing positions, all it would take is for one of them to use sorcery to resolve a dispute and it would escalate into the Wizard Wars all over again."

The path had flattened out for the moment. Lohan turned almost sideways in his saddle so he could glare directly at me. "That's a bunch of Isolationist propaganda. The ruling families have always had access to sorcery, but they know better than to use it against each other or the emperor. Do you remember what happened the last time someone stepped over that line?" He settled back into his saddle.

"The Grassgate Dispute," I answered. I felt proud of myself for knowing the answer. I had just learned about the Grassgate Dispute two days earlier during my history studies.

"Exactly. And that wasn't even a ruling family. That was two families who were vying to have one of their line selected as the Heir Designate for the Grassgate Province governorship. One family attacked the other with sorcery, and the second family defended itself with sorcery."

"The emperor resolved that conflict quickly enough," I said. "He stepped in and executed the patriarch of the family who first acted with sorcery, and he issued a Ruling Proscription against both families."

The emperor's proscription decreed that neither of the families involved in the conflict could ever become ruling families, nor could any member of those families hold any kind of government position. The proscription practically guaranteed the extinction of both lines because no other family would be willing to intermarry.

"That's precisely my point," Lohan insisted. "The Archives had *nothing* to do with preserving the Accords in that case. Everyone knows where the line is drawn and when it's been crossed. We don't need all this hysteria about keeping sorcerers isolated from the mundane to prevent another Wizard War."

I saw his point, but his example cut both ways. "The Isolationists would point to the Grassgate Dispute as proof of *their* arguments. Two potential ruling families used sorcery against each other while vying for power. They violated the Accords."

He shook his head, not accepting my argument. "And they were struck down. Isolationism has not prevented sorcery from being used in violation of the Accords, and sorcerers were not the ones to fix the problem when it happened."

I understood Lohan's point, but he was leaving out something important…deliberately, no doubt. "And then there was the Battle of Riverview."

Lohan made a humph noise and didn't say anything for a minute. When he spoke, his tone yielded the point. "That was a mistake. We'll never know what really happened, but the sorcerers of Riverview thought they were helping protect the town from a rogue band of Wintermen. The Archives and the emperor interfered because they claimed sorcerers had taken over the town, and they ignored any evidence to the contrary. Some of us think they overreacted."

Lohan's interpretation of the events at the Battle of Riverview was new to me. With a heavy sigh of impatience, I concluded that the Integrationists and the Isolationists had their own interpretations of events based on their own biases. They each believed firmly in their version of the truth. As Lohan had said, the *real* truth would probably never be known.

"So why are you here?" I asked him.

Lohan replied cautiously. "What do you mean?

"Here at the Archives. You obviously side with the Integrationists, so why aren't you at Thunderhead College? Your views would be far more popular there than here."

Lohan switched his tone to be lighter and more conversational. It rang false from the first word. "I considered going to Thunderhead College, but the Archives has better resources and has been around longer. I thought I'd get superior training here."

He did seem to be doing well in his classes, so maybe he had made the right choice. And maybe there was something else he wasn't telling me.

"Why did you wait so long to begin training? It sounds like you've known you were a sorcerer for a while."

He paused before answering. When he spoke, his voice was bitter. "Yeah, I've known I was a sorcerer for long time. So did my family and my entire village. They hated me for it. I tried to deny what I am and gain back their trust, but it was a waste of time. I had no choice but to accept my curse and leave."

"What did they do to you? Were they cruel?"

Lohan snorted and shook his head. "Cruel doesn't begin to cover it. After my family learned I could channel, my father started chaining me up at night. Like he thought I'd kill him in his sleep or something. I got the worst chores and lost my friends. The other kids ignored me when I spoke. I ran away a couple of times and no one came to look for me. They seemed disappointed when I came back and apologized for leaving. One day I left and never returned. I'm sure they're relieved I'm gone."

I was shocked into silence for a while. I'd never given much thought to how families might deal with the news when they discover their child is a sorcerer. From what I understood, sorcerers were usually born to sorcerers, but I knew first-hand that wasn't always the case. I was suddenly glad for my family's sake that I didn't discover my abilities until after I was on my own.

"That's harsh," I finally said. "How old were you when you left?"

Lohan slumped in his saddle. "This subject is depressing me. Let's talk about something else."

As it turned out, we had talked our way nearly to the first collection spot. I pointed out the glittering surface of the lake through the thinning trees at the end of the trail. We let the horses have a drink and then picketed them near the shore at a wide patch of grass. Patches set to eating the fresh and tender stalks with a gusto that I knew would keep him busy for a while.

Lohan and I separated and started searching around the lake for anything that bloomed. We stayed within sight of one another just in case one of us found a good cache to harvest or ran into trouble. We tried not to stray too far from the horses, but it was easy to get distracted by the search for collectibles.

I found a small group of the lilies we were hunting and pulled three of the six I'd discovered. Lissy asked us not to harvest more than half of whatever we found so more could grow back next year. The lilies had three wide, white petals with red and yellow stained centers. The roots included a bulb that was supposed to be edible. I wrapped them in a damp cloth and tucked them in the rope-handled collection sack I had looped across my shoulder.

I stood up to see where Lohan was and froze at the sound of a deep growl. Lohan was about fifty feet away, and he turned his head quickly in my direction with a questioning look. I nodded my head to let him know I'd heard the noise too. I slowly looked around for the source of the growl.

The first thing I saw was a pair of hungry yellow eyes that pinned me in place. The mountain lion was on the slope above the trail, crouched at the edge of a rock overhang. The overhang was about thirty feet up and the same distance farther down the trail. The big cat was between us and the horses. When our eyes met, it growled again, and long claws extended from its wide front paws to grip the edge of the rock. An adrenaline rush hit me so hard that my vision dimmed. My chest ached from the speed my heart was pumping.

Thinking that the animal was about to leap toward me, I unfroze and quickly drew my sword. The rasp of steel seemed to startle the creature. It turned and silently disappeared from the ledge. I frantically scanned the trees below its perch, thinking it might come around a different way.

"By the spirits, that was a big one," Lohan said with a tremble in his voice. I agreed, guessing that the feline was over two feet tall at the shoulders and had to weigh at least two hundred pounds. I decided that we were done collecting for the day.

"Let's get back to the horses," I said. "But move carefully and keep your eyes open. It may not have gone far."

Lohan nodded and drew his sword, his eyes round with alarm. He looked down at the weapon in his hand and pursed his lips. His look indicated that he felt insufficiently armed to fight such a beast. I concurred.

We stayed close together and started back toward the horses. I didn't have any experience with mountain lions. I wasn't sure if we should be silent or make a lot of noise. Had it been the sound of my sword being drawn that scared it away, or was it the fact that I had armed myself? I decided to alternate my approach. I walked quietly for a few paces, listening intently, and then I'd stop and ring my sword against a tree trunk or rustle some bushes with it. Other than my attempts to flush the animal, the forest was silent.

The ear-piercing scream of frightened horses galvanized my will and I broke into a sprint. Lohan crashed along the trail behind me. We both broke into the grassy area in time to see the big cat stalking Patches. Both horses were struggling to free themselves from their picket lines, and I cringed to see them pulling desperately at the rear leg hobble, worried they'd hurt themselves even if they survived the lion.

I yelled and waved my arms, trying to distract the enormous cat. It glanced at me, but kept its focus on Patches, crouched down and ready to spring. I knew I couldn't stop it in time. I almost threw my sword at it in frustration, but knew that could end badly. I choked out, "No!" around a big lump in my throat when it leaned back and coiled itself for a leap onto Patches back.

The lion sprang silently at Patches with it's mouth agape and long fangs bared to sink into the neck of its prey.

Then it crumpled in mid-air with a loud grunt and fell to the ground on its side. Not knowing what happened and not caring, I rushed toward the beast to take advantage of its vulnerable position. The lion sat up and rolled to its feet before I could get to it, and it turned toward me with an unnerving hiss. The malevolence in that hiss made me stumble, but I forced myself to keep my momentum. I was done being intimidated. This thing was going to taste the bite of my steel.

The lion took one last look toward the horses, before turning and leaping away. It vanished like smoke in the wind. It was already out of sight before I arrested my charge at the place where it had fallen.

"That was close," Lohan said. He was still breathing heavily from our run, as was I.

I stared into the forest, feeling the adrenaline drain from my system and my pulse slowing back to normal. Then I turned toward Lohan and stared at him with a serious gaze, my eyes squinting.

"That was a shield," I said accusingly.

Lohan looked at me and then shrugged. He took a small golden metal disk from his pocket and held it out toward me in his palm. "I have a shield stone. It's the one piece of sorcery I knew how to use before I came here for proper training." The disk had runes around the circumference and a half-sphere of some transparent stone in the center. The stone sparkled violet in the dappled sunlight that penetrated the forest canopy.

I felt like he had been holding out on me, but really, using the shield stone was probably no more difficult than what I had done with the seeker the first time I'd learned I could channel vaetra. Of all the things we were learning at the Archives, using an implement was probably the easiest.

Still, the revelation made me wonder what other surprises his past held. Where he got the shield stone might make for an interesting story. I looked forward to finding out more during our explorations of the Archives and other collection trips. I also hoped future journeys would be less eventful than this one.

The horses were still shifting around and straining to get free. It took several minutes for Lohan and me to calm them enough so we could get close and remove their hobbles. Both animals had scrapes above their hooves where the rope had been attached, but they didn't seem to be limping after we freed them. We decided to walk them back up the trail for a while to make sure they hadn't hurt themselves.

Lohan and I spent the entire journey back up the ridge jumping at every sound and peering cautiously around every bend in the trail. Patches and Striker were just as skittish as we were, but otherwise they seemed okay. When we reached the peak of the ridge where we'd stopped earlier in the day, we all rested.

"Next time we'd better go with more people. Or better weapons," I commented while we caught our breath. "A crossbow would have been useful back there."

Lohan looked at me like I was insane. "Next time? I don't think so. I've had enough wilderness adventuring."

I snorted. "If Lissy asks you to go out again, you'll do it. You won't want to look like a coward. Besides, we managed. It was close, but you saved the day. And we'll make sure we're better prepared before we go out again."

Lohan shook his head and chuckled. "You're a good man, Jaylan. A bit foolish maybe, but you're right. We make a good team. I'm glad to have you on my side."

I wasn't sure what he meant by "on his side," but I agreed that we worked well together. Lohan's Integrationist views would put him at odds with most of the sorcerers at the Archives. I didn't entirely share those views, but I didn't hold them against him either.

After a final check of the horses, we mounted up and walked them down the trail toward the Archives. We hadn't collected much on this trip, but at least we had a good story to tell.

CHAPTER 7

SKULKING

Sulana ~ Library Level, The Archives

Sulana closed the door to the Main Library and wandered down the hall, pondering the interview she'd just had with Senior Councilor Boris Underwood. Her distaste for the man's arrogance didn't stop her from probing for as much information as she could get about the days when Paeter Thoron still walked the corridors of the Archives. Councilor Underwood had known Thoron fairly well, partly because he was grooming the younger sorcerer for a position on the council. She shuddered as she considered the possibility of Thoron as a councilor.

Sulana suspected Councilor Underwood's insufferable attitude came from the fact that he was often the swing vote between the Isolationist agenda of Senior Councilor Rissik and the Integrationist agenda of Junior Councilors Asher and Shepherd. He had parlayed the power of his vote into an unofficial role as head councilman, and he saw himself as the unbiased voice of what was best for the Archives. To curry favor with Underwood, the other councilors were content to allow him his delusion.

Sulana now had a lot more information than when she started her investigation into Thoron's past. Too much, in fact. She believed that his past held clues to whatever plot he was developing, but she couldn't yet discern which pieces of information were significant and which were not.

She reached the main hallway on the library level and started toward the stairwell that would take her up. She came to a sudden stop when she felt a light breeze move across her face that carried the faint scent of human body odor. There were no breezes in an empty hall that was two levels below grade; at least, no natural breezes.

"Hello, is anyone there?" she asked. Her voice echoed in the hallway, but silence was the only answer she received. She stood still and looked around. She listened carefully, but all she heard was the sound of her own breathing.

Shrugging off the distraction, she continued toward the stairs, her mind going back to the problem of Paeter Thoron. But then she stopped again at the bottom of the stairs. Her curiosity about the breeze nagged at her, and her training as a Sword Sorceress had taught her to pay close attention to her instincts.

The stairs ascended at a right angle to the hallway. She went up the first flight to a landing that could not be seen from below. She intentionally stepped on the stair treads so her sandals made noise by flapping against her heels. She stopped at the next landing and quietly slipped her sandals off. The stone floor was cool and gritty against her bare soles.

Creeping silently back down the stairs on the balls of her feet, she stayed close to the wall and peered around the corner. She still saw nothing in the main hallway except blank walls and the half-circle pools of light created by the illuminators. Eventually the illuminators would go off, unless something was still moving within their range of sensitivity, so she watched and waited.

Illuminators varied in how long they would stay on and in how sensitive they were. Sulana thought back to several years ago, when one of the sorcerers had a pair of tame martens. The two animals would scamper and play through the halls of the Archives with abandon, much to the delight of most residents. But the illuminators had reacted inconsistently to the little ferret-like creatures. Their size put them at the limit of the illuminator's sensitivity, so they could usually sneak down the hallway in darkness when they were being stealthy.

Sulana missed the martens' antics. Their presence was tolerated by the Council only because they did an excellent job of keeping the rodent population under control. She had gotten in trouble more than once for feeding them and distracting them from their job. The day she learned that one of them had died, she cried. Although martens are normally solitary animals, the second became listless and expired soon after its sibling, leaving the halls of the Archives silent and somber.

Staring down the main hall from the stairwell, Sulana watched as the first illuminator turned off. It was the one in the side corridor to the library. Two others in the main hall remained on. Then the main hallway illuminator nearest her turned off, leaving only the further one on. When that one went off, the only light in the area would be from the illuminator behind her at the landing. She'd be back-lit, and any move she made would be obvious to an observer.

The second illuminator stayed on longer than Sulana expected, but it eventually went off too. There was always a little variation in how long the illuminators remained lit. She was about to turn around and go back up to the landing when she noticed a faint light farther down the main hall. It was coming from a side passage well beyond the library corridor. She watched for a moment more to see if someone would come out into the main hall, but no one did. The light in the far passage persisted.

Sulana debated going to investigate. The illuminators would come on again if she went down the main hall. Whoever was in the far corridor might notice that and realize someone was coming. But if she moved now, she might be able to trigger the illuminators back on before the person noticed that they had been off in the first place.

Putting her hand to the dagger at her waist, she decided to risk the illuminators giving her away. She crept out of the stairwell and slipped down the main hallway as silently as she could along the right-hand wall, smoothly drawing her dagger as she went. The first illuminator came on as expected, but the second one didn't come on until she was past the library corridor. That was telling. Apparently, *she* hadn't triggered that illuminator earlier; someone else had.

She silently approached the lit passage, staying back from the corner for a moment to listen. If the person in that passageway had noticed the illuminators coming back on, he or she might come back to the main hall to investigate.

Sulana thought about how it would look if someone who was on perfectly legitimate business came around the corner to find her sneaking up in her bare feet with her dagger ready. She'd look pretty foolish, and she'd have some explaining to do. But her intuition came to the fore and filled her with a caution that squashed her doubts. Something here felt *wrong*.

After a few seconds, she heard the rustle of cloth from around the corner and down the hallway. Holding her breath, she cautiously eased forward, crouched down, and put just enough of her head around the corner to see down the hall with her left eye.

The profile of a man in a dark cloak leaned forward to inspect the surface of the second door down the hall on the right. It was the door to the armory.

The man reached out to trace the dual symbols on the door with his finger. As he did, the hood of his cloak folded back away from his face enough for Sulana to see a distinctive pointed chin and thin nose. It was Lohan.

It was almost as if her recognition alerted him to her presence. He glanced over in her direction and she froze. Holding her breath to suppress a gasp, adrenaline flooded her system. She resisted the urge to pull back as the movement itself would make it more likely that he would notice her. Fortunately, she had crouched before peering around the corner to position herself lower than he would expect. That seemed to have been a good choice. Lohan returned to his inspection of the door.

Sulana slowly eased back and leaned against the wall once Lohan was engrossed in the door again. She let her breath out as quietly as she could and panted softly to calm her racing heart. What was Lohan doing skulking down here on the library level? There were few personal chambers on this level, and she knew that his chamber was on the level above her.

She stood and gathered herself. Lohan had no business down here, particularly near the armory. She clenched her jaw and allowed her indignity to cloak her like a mantle. She walked around the corner and stood with her hands on her hips.

"What are you doing here, Lohan?" she asked in a severe tone.

Lohan jumped and his hand went to the dagger at his waist. When he saw who it was, he straightened up to his full height and his mouth curved into a sardonic smile. "Hello Lana." He looked her up and down as he might assess a purchase, his eyes lingering on her bare feet.

Sulana's nostrils flared and her lips thinned to a line. "Sorry, only Lissy gets to call me that. It's Sulana to you."

Lohan tilted his head in condescending apology. "Whatever you say, mighty Sword Sorceress."

Sulana's face reddened at his disrespect, but she refused to be baited or distracted. "I asked a question. Why are you here?"

He walked slowly toward her as he answered. "Just exploring. This place is full of fascinating nooks and crannies. Jaylan and I have been learning the layout of the castle in our free time, when he isn't busy trying to catch Dru's eye."

He's lying. That's not true, Sulana thought, but the idea of Jaylan being interested in Lissy hurt anyway. Lohan was trying to distract her again.

"Don't let her hear you call her that. She'll poison your drink," she snapped as he came alongside her.

Sulana hated any abbreviated version of her name. She always corrected people who tried to call her "Sue" or "Lana." Lissy equally hated her given name of "Drusilla" or the diminutive "Dru." After commiserating at length one day, Sulana and Lissy had established a bond that was the start of a personal joke between them. Lissy began to call Sulana "Lana" and Sulana responded by calling Lissy "Dru." But no one else was allowed in on that joke, particularly not a miscreant like Lohan.

"And I'd appreciate it if you would restrict your exploration to less sensitive areas of the castle," she commented as she followed him back out to the main hallway.

He turned his raptor eyes back to her face and smiled again. "As you wish." His tone held nothing to suggest compliance. He looked around. "Castle? Huh. More like a dungeon."

This "dungeon" was her home. She bristled at his remark, but couldn't argue with its accuracy. And, of course, he was not the first to criticize the cave-like nature of the Archives. Some residents seemed uncomfortable having the weight of a mountain above their heads.

They walked together back to the stairwell and went up to the landing where Sulana stopped to retrieve her sandals. While she slipped them on, he watched her every motion. His steady gaze made her uncomfortable and she wished she had a cloak or something to cover herself. She did not fear him, but his intense scrutiny was unnerving and distasteful.

Sulana thought about Lissy and Jaylan again, wondering if there could be some truth to Lohan's remark. Lissy was a beautiful woman who routinely attracted male attention. Sulana had never shared the natural and playful ease Lissy had with members of the opposite sex. Sulana saw leering male attention as rude and intrusive, while Lissy treated it like a tool to be exploited. It would only be natural for Jaylan to be attracted to Lissy's smiling confidence.

As she climbed the stairs beside Lohan, Sulana broke her train of thought and came back to the moment. She didn't understand how Jaylan could like this man. Perhaps their friendship was just a matter of circumstance. They were both older students getting a late start in their training.

Sulana thought back on the incident that had just happened, and another question came to mind. With that question came the realization that she had allowed Lohan to distract her again.

They reached the next level and came to a halt. Lohan turned to go toward his chambers, but stopped short when Sulana spoke up. "How did you get past me? There was no one in the main hall when I came out of the library."

His eyes met hers and he chuckled. "I was in the side hall the whole time. I heard you come out of the library and head upstairs. Nice trick with the sandals, by the way. I had no idea you'd doubled back."

They stared at one another. He was lying. His mocking half-smile confirmed it. She guessed that he had passed by her under a Veil, a type of invisibility spell, which he had canceled once he reached the armory door. But he'd never admit that, and she was sick of his company.

She sighed and turned back toward the stairwell. "Just try to stay out of trouble." He snorted in response but otherwise remained silent. She felt his eyes on her and suppressed a shudder of disgust as she started up the next flight of stairs.

CHAPTER 8
IMPOSING GIFT

Dumont rose from his comfortable desk chair as Elerus Bogard, minister of the nearby town of Riverview, was escorted into his office at Thunderhead College. Paeter stood as well. The minister's small green eyes darted around the room, taking in the shelves of leather-bound books and the neatly arranged collection of arcane objects. Bogard licked his lips and flinched as the escort closed the door behind him with a loud thud.

Dumont smiled broadly in greeting, as he swept around his desk to meet the minister. He thrust his hand out aggressively, causing Minister Bogard to take an involuntary step back. The minister recovered his composure and hesitantly accepted the handshake as if he were reaching out to grip a snake's head.

Dumont towered over the minister, who was easily a half foot shorter. Minister Bogard had dark, curly hair that was graying to an even salt-and-pepper. The minister moved easily, in spite of being considerably overweight. His eyes watched Dumont's every move from underneath bushy eyebrows that nearly met in the center of his forehead. The minister wore a simple but carefully tailored dove-grey sleeveless robe over a maroon jerkin and long pants.

"It has been a while, Minister Bogard. I'm glad to see you're looking hale," Dumont said. He intentionally stood as close as politeness allowed, forcing the minister to tilt his head back.

Minister Bogard smoothed his hands over his robe and stood as tall as he could. "Greetings, Sorcerer Fortenz. It has indeed been a while. Your college is impressive."

Dumont nodded his head. "Thank you, Minister. Around here I'm known as Headmaster Fortenz, but you may call me Dumont. Our shared history puts us beyond the formality of titles, I would think." Dumont raised an eyebrow, turning his statement into a question.

Their "shared history" had ended abruptly about eight years ago during an event now known as the Battle of Riverview. The housemaster of the Riverview Sanctuary was accused of taking control of the town government and thereby violating the Sorcery Accords. Dumont, who was acting as an "advisor to the minister" at the time, was implicated, and if not for the reluctant support of Minister Bogard himself, would have been prosecuted as well.

After the Sanctuary was destroyed in a fight between the housemaster's supporters and suppression forces from the Archives and Imperial Guard, the people of Riverview forced Dumont to leave with the other surviving sorcerers who had been cleared of wrongdoing. To mollify his townspeople, the minister declared Riverview to be a sorcery-free town.

Banished to an abandoned and run-down manor miles from the town, Dumont turned the disaster into an opportunity by establishing Thunderhead College.

"I suppose you're right, Dumont. You may call me Elerus, of course," the minister replied. His tight voice belied his comfort with the familiarity Dumont was imposing. Although the minister had once helped Dumont avoid prosecution, he had never trusted the sorcerer.

Dumont introduced Paeter to the minister. The two men nodded to each other but did not shake hands.

Dumont's tone turned conversational. "So tell me Elerus, how are your lovely wife and children? Is your son studying to one day take his place as Minister of Riverview?"

The minister's jaw clenched and his eyes darkened. Dumont knew that the minister had no desire to discuss his family. The man who had banished sorcery from Riverview would probably perceive Dumont's question as an implied threat. And maybe it was.

Let him imagine whatever it takes to make him compliant, Dumont thought.

The minister spoke quickly, "My family is well, and my son is progressing nicely in his studies. In fact, I need to get back to Riverview as soon as possible so I can help him with his newest responsibility. Your message mentioned something about improving relations between Riverview and Thunderhead College?"

Dumont let his eyes go flat. "Straight to business then, Minister? That's fine. I wouldn't want to delay your return to Riverview unnecessarily." Dumont turned to Paeter and nodded once.

The minister's attention was so focused on Dumont that he didn't notice that Paeter had slipped a glass figurine from the edge of Dumont's desk. Paeter now held the figurine in his open palm. The minister's eyes widened in recognition of his peril at the moment Paeter said, "Freeze," and triggered the vaetric implement. The minister instantly relaxed, and his eyes took on a glassy stare.

Dumont snorted and walked around the minister. "You see, Elerus? Given the proper influence, even you can be cooperative. I sense relations improving between us by the moment." Dumont's path around the minister brought him back behind his desk. "Go ahead, Paeter."

Paeter put the figurine back onto Dumont's desk and stood in front of the minister. He pulled an amulet from his pocket and placed it around the minister's neck, settling it gently into place. Placing one hand on the device, he spoke the word, "Protector." The amulet was glowing when Paeter took his hand away. Paeter dropped the amulet behind the minister's shirt so only a bit of the chain was visible at his neck. He stepped back from the minister, picked up the figurine again, and canceled the restraint spell.

The minister's eyes regained focus and he glanced around in confusion. He started when he discovered Paeter standing directly in front of him.

Paeter looked into the minister's eyes and spoke with a serious tone. "You have been given a great honor, Minister. You are a Protector of the College. It is your duty to ensure that no one threatens the college, or the students, or the staff. It is important that you wear your new amulet at all times in devotion to your duty, but it would be best if you kept it hidden from others who might covet it. Do you understand?"

The minister's hand went to his chest to clutch the place where the amulet lay hidden. "Yes, Sorcerer Thoron, I understand."

Dumont squinted at the minister, and glanced over at Paeter, who looked back at him with a raised eyebrow. Dumont spoke slowly, "Well, Minister, I'm glad you are willing to work with us. I don't need anything specific for now, but I would appreciate it if you would let us know about any unusual activity in Riverview over the next several weeks."

"Unusual activity?"

"Yes. I'm afraid that the Archives Council and the emperor both have a rather unfortunate opinion of us these days, and they may take an interest in our activities again. If that should that happen, I would appreciate it if you'd let me know."

The minister gave Dumont a slight bow and said, "As you wish."

Dumont went to the minister and placed an arm around the shorter man's shoulders, turning and guiding him toward the office door. "Thank you for coming out to meet with us today, Minister. Our meeting was quite productive and I look forward to our improved relations with Riverview." They reached the door and Dumont opened it.

The minister stopped to shake hands with Dumont. He looked directly into Dumont's eyes, and his expression became concerned, as if he were trying hard to remember something. He shook his head and released Dumont's hand. "I need to be going. I have many things to attend to today, but I'll let you know if I see anything unusual in Riverview."

Dumont smiled down at the minister. "Thank you, minister. Your help is greatly appreciated."

The minister nodded once and followed his escort, who had waited outside the room during their meeting. The minister waddled swiftly away down the hall.

Dumont closed the door and turned to Paeter. "Not bad. He seemed a little dazed at first, but appeared to come back to himself before he left."

Paeter nodded knowingly. "Yes, the initial confusion fades over time as the Protector spell integrates itself with the subject's normal thought patterns. That aspect was what took me so much time to perfect. My initial efforts at the fishing village produced compliant but unmotivated slaves. It was far too obvious that their minds had been tampered with."

Dumont walked slowly back to his desk and Paeter returned to his seat. "Wasn't there a second spell built into the amulets?" Dumont asked.

"Yes. The Member enchantment was necessary to keep the villagers together and promote harmony. It is a relief to no longer need that effect, so I can focus all of my attention on the Protector enchantment."

As he passed the bookshelf near his desk, Dumont picked up a bottle of amber liquor and two crystal glasses from one of the shelves. Setting the glasses on his desk, he removed the stopper from the bottle and splashed liquor into each glass. He pushed one of the drinks over to Paeter.

Dumont lifted his glass in a toast. "Nice work, Paeter. Here's to your amulets working as well when we take one to Sunset Province." Paeter raised his glass to acknowledge the toast and they both took a sip of the smooth brandy.

Dumont turned introspective and spoke softly. "Eventually, we won't have to hide in the shadows and resort to such subtle trickery, but for now, I'm willing to be patient. The emperor won't see us coming until it is far too late." He held his glass in front of his face and turned it around. The light from the window behind him sparkled on the crystal and made the brandy within it glow. "And without the support of the emperor, the Archives won't stand a chance," he concluded, tossing back the remaining liquor.

CHAPTER 9
SWORD PRACTICE

Jaylan ~ Sparring Room, The Archives

My practice sword deflected Talon's attack with a clang and I swung the blade around for a slash that he parried easily in return. We had been practicing together since I arrived at the Archives, and I felt like I was starting to get a feel for his style. But then, every time I started to think that, he'd surprise me with a new move.

Talon had sought me out after Sulana told him I was looking for a sparring partner. I was surprised when he volunteered to train with me, assuming he had far more important things to do as the Archives weaponsmaster. I expected to be practicing with Barek or Daven. But he insisted that he always took the opportunity to work out against opponents with a different training background, and that I'd be doing him a favor.

It didn't feel like I was doing him any favors now. He had instantly adjusted to my attack forms and I was fairly certain that he was going easy on me. Having once been the captain of the Imperial Guard detachment in the city of Northshore, I fancied myself a fair hand with a sword, but Talon put me to shame. My only consolation was that I was getting the exercise I desired.

Frustrated, I pressed a carefully orchestrated attack designed to open his guard and score a hit on his torso. It was one of my trademark sparring moves that was difficult to defend against, although it wasn't much use in genuine battle against a well-armored opponent. Talon's guard never opened, of course. My strokes battered uselessly against the edge of his steel, which blocked or deflected my every move. Had I used that attack against him before? I didn't think so.

I stepped back from the practice circle and panted to catch my breath. "I feel like I'm wasting your time," I told him, unable to keep the exasperation out of my voice.

Talon inspected the edge of his practice blade. He seemed barely winded. "Not at all," he responded. "Aren't you enjoying the work out?"

"Sure I am, but I don't see how you could be. You seem to be able to predict every move I make."

He laughed. "I'm just good at reading my opponent. They didn't make me weaponsmaster for nothing, you know."

"So I'm learning," I said with a sigh.

"You said you needed exercise and wanted to keep your skills sharp. Do you want to do more than that? You *could* petition the Council to enter the Sword Sorcerer training program." His words were casual, but there was an insistence to them that caught my ear and made me wonder about his motivations for making the suggestion.

"Sword Sorcerer?" I scoffed. "I'm not even much of a sorcerer yet. I don't know how I'd split my time between learning sorcery and weapons training."

Talon shrugged. "I'll grant you that it's challenging to do both. But you already have a good start on the weapons training. Most candidates come to me with little experience or skill. You at least have a little of both."

A little? "Gee, thanks. I feel so much better now," I said, rolling my eyes.

He laughed again. "Sorry. I didn't mean to offend. You have a good foundation that I can build upon, if you are willing to put the time in."

I thought about what he was suggesting. Would becoming a Sword Sorcerer bring Sulana and me closer together or push us apart? Would we share missions or be sent out separately? Would she gain more respect for me or think I was encroaching?

Talon was waiting for my response, and I finally answered, "The Archives already has a Sword Sorceress. I'm not sure Sulana would appreciate me intruding into her responsibilities."

Talon nodded. "She's justifiably proud of her achievements, but she's also practical and dedicated. I think she'd welcome the help. The Council likes to have at least one Sword Sorcerer in training at all times. Daven would love to be next, but he isn't a sorcerer. Young Ben is enthusiastic, but he doesn't take weapons training seriously. I think he will lose interest in the idea before long."

"And that leaves me," I concluded. Talon just nodded his head slowly.

"The job of a Sword Sorcerer can be dangerous at times," he added. Once again, his voice had that casual but insistent tone. "If you go with Sulana on any of her missions, wouldn't you want to be as prepared as possible to help her out?"

There it was; the real reason he wanted me in training. He was concerned about Sulana's long-term safety and knew he could appeal to my emotions in that regard. And he was right. I *did* want to be as prepared as possible to help Sulana in any dangerous situation that might come up. But that wasn't reason enough to make such an important decision. And it certainly wasn't a reason that either of us would confess to Sulana.

I decided to steer the conversation back to practical concerns. My time with the Raven Company mercenary organization had taught me to keep my emotions at a distance when evaluating potential contracts, and that's basically what we were talking about here.

"I'll think about your suggestion. I need to know more about what I'd be committing myself to, and I need to talk to Sulana about it first."

Talon smiled and slapped me on the shoulder. "Great. Let me know what you decide, and the next time we meet, I'll show you some new tricks." He turned to put away his practice sword.

I followed him slowly and shook my head. It wasn't lost on me that he had just assumed my decision would be to begin the training program right away.

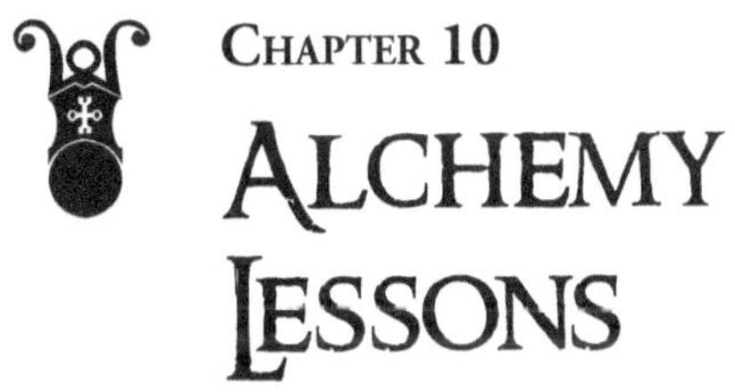

Chapter 10

ALCHEMY LESSONS

Jaylan ~ Alchemy Class, The Archives

A little over six weeks into my studies at the Archives, I started my first lesson in a subject I had been dreading: alchemy. Lissy was the instructor, so the class had that going for it. But every time I thought about potions, I saw the face of a young man who was stuck in a partially-changed state from wolf to human.

When Tam Overland had gone missing, his parents had hired me to find him. What I found was a young man who used a lycanthropy potion as a means of temporarily escaping a destiny he resisted. Tam had made the mistake of buying a particularly strong potion and drinking only part of it. When the potion finally wore off, he failed to revert completely back to human form.

In a tragic series of events, Tam ended up dying at the hands of his own father. It was during that horrible experience that I learned one of the only things I knew about potions; you must drink all of it.

Unfortunately, alchemy was a necessary course of study, even if I had no intention of becoming an alchemist. All sorcerers needed to understand the mechanics of potion-making, if for no other reason than to know how to use them properly. After the Tam disaster, I vowed I'd never experiment with potions myself, but I suspected that was a vow I'd have to break soon.

"Alchemy is the study of potion making," Lissy said, breaking into my dark musings. Her melodious voice caught my attention instantly. I focused my eyes to where she stood at the head of the long, high table where Lohan and I sat in the center of the room. "This is where you learn to take what would otherwise be a simple tonic, and turn it into a vaetra-infused liquid with incredible potential."

Now that Lohan and I were learning alchemy, part of our afternoons would be spent with the twins again. I looked over to where the two teens sat huddled together over a flattened scroll, whispering to one another about their potion assignment. They obviously didn't need the introduction speech that Lohan and I were getting.

The twins were sitting on a pair of tall stools at one of the darkly-stained, waist-high work benches that lined two walls of the room. At their feet was a bucket of sandy soil, ready to be tossed on any accidental fire that might start. Small oil burners sat on several of the benches, presumably to heat potions, so it seemed fire was a genuine hazard.

Lissy went on with her introduction. "The principles of alchemy are fairly easy to understand. What is difficult is learning which ingredients you should use for a particular effect and how they interact with one another. Also, to create a viable potion, you must be able to cast."

That was another reason why I didn't have much interest in being in this class. I didn't yet know if I could cast. I had to master my control over channeling before I would get the opportunity to try casting my first spell. In the meantime, learning to make potions that wouldn't work held little appeal.

I had shared the secret of what happened to Tam Overland with Sulana one evening, and she was supportive and sympathetic. Later, when I voiced my doubts about learning alchemy, she echoed my own words back at me.

"I thought you said knowing something about potions might have helped you save that young man from Delta," she asked me reasonably. "I can't cast, but I went through beginning alchemy training."

I couldn't really argue with her because I'd be arguing with myself. When faced with ignorance as an obstacle, my normal reaction is to attack the problem and learn what I needed to know. But in this case, my fear and guilt were battling with my desire to understand.

Lohan nudged me with his elbow, and I realized that Lissy had stopped talking and was looking at me with an annoyed expression. She had apparently noticed my distraction.

"Do you have something else you need to attend to Jaylan?" she asked curtly.

My face warmed, and I looked down at the table. "No, ma'am. I'm sorry for being distracted. Please continue." I sat straighter on my stool and gave her my full attention.

Lissy narrowed her eyes and watched me for a moment before going on. "I know you are probably wondering why we bother teaching potions to students who may be incapable of becoming alchemists." She stopped and looked at Lohan and me, giving us a chance to respond. I nodded and Lohan shrugged.

"There are several reasons, actually." As she continued, she ticked the points off on her slender, well-manicured fingers.

"First, potions are usually easier and faster to make than implements, so finding a potion that does what you need is more likely than finding the corresponding implement."

Lissy, like most sorcerers, referred to magical devices as "vaetric implements" or simply "implements." Each implement was enchanted to perform one or more specific functions. Unlike a potion, an implement could be used over and over again, as long as the sorcerer had the vaetra necessary to power it, but I knew from past conversations with Ebnik and Sulana that making most implements was time-consuming and difficult.

"Second, to use a potion effectively and safely, you need to know something about how they work."

Yes. Like, you have to drink all of it. An image of Tam's face floated to the foreground of my mind again, but I pushed it back and forced myself to keep my attention on Lissy.

"Third, anyone can use a potion, even a mundane person. That makes potions the most flexible of all vaetric creations, because the mundane can't use implements, and they certainly can't cast spells."

This was a piece of information I'd known for a long time. The use of potions was frowned upon in mundane society, but tonic shops often carried a secret supply of healing potions and other philters of magical origin. I'd never experimented with potions myself, mainly because I didn't trust the people who sold them.

"And fourth, all of us are expected to contribute to the store of ingredients here at the Archives. If you are traveling and you come across a rare ingredient, you need to recognize it as such and know how to properly harvest it so it can be used in potion making."

I hadn't thought about that angle before. The idea that I could help the alchemists even if I couldn't become one made me feel a little better about learning the discipline.

"Today, I want to give you an overview of the basic process by demonstrating how to make a simple potion. We'll get into the details of each step as you progress in your studies. You never know, you might discover that you have a hidden talent for alchemy," she added with a smile.

Sulana had told me that Lissy was a natural alchemist. Lissy had become so accomplished that Professor Delano let her run the alchemy class unsupervised.

Lissy instructed Lohan and me to move forward to her end of the table so we'd be able to see what she was doing. In the meantime, she bustled around the room collecting the ingredients and tools she would need for her demonstration. The light grey smock she wore to protect her clothing billowed around her as she moved.

A couple of minutes later, she stood at the head of the table again with several items arrayed in front of her on its dark, pitted surface. Lohan was seated on her left and I was on her right.

Noticing the marks from years of potion making scarring the tabletop, I looked around the room again and realized that all of the work benches looked similarly abused. The grey stone walls and ceiling of the chamber were darkened, and stain splatters marred the walls in a few places. I was briefly thankful for the six bright illuminators that lit the dingy room, in spite of the noise they generated. Now that I had been in the Archives for a while, I was almost able to ignore the constant background din of vaetric manifestation around the place, but six illuminators all in one room tested my ability to concentrate.

The room also had a smoky odor to it. It reminded me of what my clothes smelled like after I spent time near a campfire, although this was sharper and left a bitter taste on my tongue. Sulana had told me that the alchemy lab was one of the few rooms in the Archives that vented straight to the outside. Fortunately, the constant flow of air that came from the floor ventilation tubes kept the underlying smell to a minimum.

Lissy picked up a tattered tube of parchment from the table and unrolled it, pinning down the curled top and bottom with two flat bars of metal that appeared to be designed for that purpose. "This is a recipe for a simple wound-binding potion," she said. "It isn't particularly strong, but it's easy to make, and it will let me show you all of the essential elements of alchemy."

Lohan was watching Lissy as intently as I was, although is gaze seemed to be drawn more to her cleavage than to what she was doing with her hands. I wasn't exactly innocent in that regard myself, but since she was Sulana's close friend, I had to be more careful about getting caught at it. Lissy even wore a smock well.

Lissy looked over at Lohan and waited until his eyes rose to her face. Rather than being embarrassed, he gave her a sly grin and winked. She rolled her eyes and went on, ignoring him. "Pay attention, boys. This is the important part."

Lissy laid her hand on top of the unrolled parchment. "The first step is to find or create a recipe." She pointed at the bookshelves next to the door to the room. Each shelf was stuffed from top to bottom with a seemingly haphazard collection of scroll tubes. "We have a lot of recipes here in the laboratory, but more can be found in the library. The alchemy books are too valuable to keep in this room, so we copy the recipes we need onto a scroll and store the scrolls here."

"Do you blow things up often?" asked Lohan. "Are we in danger here?" he said, making a mock show of alarm and leaning back from the table.

Lissy chose to take his question seriously and answered, "Not with this potion. Fire is the biggest danger, but mostly when we are working on a potion that has an oil base. Potions almost never 'blow up.' However, thanks for the segue; the next step is to start heating the base liquid."

Lissy picked up a thin metal rod from the table. At the end of the rod was a tiny crystal. She held the crystal next to the wick of the burner that sat in front of her and said, "Spark." The crystal emitted a tiny flash and a flame crawled across the wick of the burner. She adjusted the height of the wick until it burned relatively smoke-free. She held up the metal rod and looked first at Lohan and then at me. "We have three spark sticks to light the burners. Please don't take them out of the lab." We both nodded.

She slid a thick, metal crucible with a worn wooden handle into the open space in front of her. "This recipe calls for a water base." Lissy removed the stopper from a clear glass carafe and poured some of the liquid into the crucible. When the crucible was about two-thirds full, she stopped pouring and re-stoppered the carafe. She then placed the crucible on top of a three-legged metal stand that surrounded the burner. The flame from the burner spread out across the bottom of the crucible, licking up the sides here and there. Lissy adjusted the burner until the flame evenly heated just the bottom.

"While the base is heating, we can move on to the next step, which is to enchant the ingredients." Lissy reached over and picked up a small metal bowl with an odd lid and set it down in front of her. "This is an enchanting press; a rather nice one, actually. Some are just a pair of flat metal plates. This one is better because it cups the ingredients, keeping them all in the press and making it easier to pour them into the crucible. It can also double as a mortar." She lifted the lid out of the bowl, and I could see that it was curved to match the interior surface. It wasn't really a lid at all, but the top half of a concave press.

She set the lid aside and went on with her explanation. "We'll get into the purpose of all these ingredients during your studies, but for now, all you need to know is that each ingredient matches a specific phrase of the incantation to be used, and some ingredients are better than others for specific uses. For example, this is a healing potion, so the recipe specifies the herb yarrow for the wound-binding phrase of the incantation." Lissy pointed at one of the sealed ingredient jars she had arrayed on the table. "Yarrow has a natural affinity for healing enchantments. Even mundane tonic brewers use the herb as a wound balm."

Lohan interrupted. "Good thing the ingredients are labeled. They all look like a bunch of dried weeds to me." I had to agree with him. The contents of the ingredient jars all looked pretty much the same. The yarrow that she had pointed out had a bit more of a grayish cast to it and there were other subtle differences, but overall, Lohan's description was accurate.

Lissy frowned at him and looked like she might disagree, but shrugged instead and said, "Don't worry. You'll be able to recognize ingredients quickly by smell, appearance, and texture with a little experience. I hardly need the labels any more to know what's in the jar."

"Yeah, but you're special, Dru," he said with a snort. From across the room, Daisy gasped and glared over her shoulder at Lohan's back. Lohan ignored Daisy and just arched his eyebrows at Lissy, waiting for her reaction.

She leaned over and put her face right in front of his, her hands closing into fists. "I've asked you not to call me that," she hissed between her teeth. "I can throw you out of this class, you know."

Lohan narrowed his eyes at her and said nothing for a moment. He looked over at me and I shook my head slowly, advising caution. He eased back from her and folded his arms over his chest. "Fine, Lissy it is."

Lissy continued to stand over him for a moment. Finally, she took a deep breath and looked down at the table, taking a moment to calm herself. Lohan sure had a way of getting under people's skin, particularly women. I didn't know what his problem was, but his attitude certainly hadn't endeared him to Lissy or Sulana.

Lissy collected herself and went on with the lesson. She peered into the crucible and looked satisfied to see steam rising from the surface of the water.

"We'll give the water a moment to get a little hotter. You could use vaetra to heat it more quickly, but you'll want to get in the habit of conserving your internal well of vaetra for enchanting the ingredients. A complex potion can really test your capacity. Once you start the incantation, it's important to maintain a consistent cadence without interruption. If you run out of vaetra before you finish, you pretty much have to rest and start over."

Lissy busied herself with double-checking the recipe against the items she had on the table in front of her. Her studious focus and sharp movements told me she was still upset by her confrontation with Lohan. Maybe a question or two would help her relax again.

"Can you use an external source of vaetra?" I asked. I was thinking back to the stone blocks that were part of the resistance test. If we could draw vaetra from a well like that, we wouldn't be dependent upon how much vaetra we had in our internal well.

She looked over at me and gave me a tight, brief smile. I think she knew what I was trying to do. "Yes, but that's an advanced technique," she answered. "It's difficult to draw vaetra from external source and use it to enchant potion ingredients at the same time. For one thing, all the recipes assume you are channeling from your internal well, so you'd have to rewrite that part of any recipe you wanted to use. Realistically, it's not worth the bother. I've never seen a potion recipe that couldn't be completed by a fully-rested sorcerer."

The steam rising from the crucible prompted another question. "Does the water have to be boiling before you add ingredients?" I asked.

"No. Ideally you add the ingredients while the water is heating so they have time to steep before the mix reaches a boil. In a perfectly timed incantation, you fuse the potion right as it reaches a roiling boil."

"Fuse?" I asked.

She shook her head. "Sorry, I'm jumping ahead a little. The last phrase of the incantation fuses the potion by binding the enchanted ingredients to each other and to the liquid base. Fusion also preserves the order of the incantations' phrases."

Lissy loosened the draw strings on a small black velvet sack and removed a tiny glass bead that was only a little bigger than a mustard seed. She held it up, gingerly pinching it between the tips of her thumb and forefinger. "When we bottle the potion, we add a combit like this one. A combit is essential for manifesting the potion's incantation later." She set the glass bead into one of the many dings in the surface of the table so it wouldn't roll, and then she closed up the sack.

I couldn't resist picking up the combit to take a closer look. As far as I could tell, it was just a tiny sphere of glass. "Is there something special about the combit, or is it just glass? How does it activate the potion?"

She shook her head again and answered my last question first. "It doesn't activate the potion. The combit doesn't do anything until someone drinks the potion. Consuming the potion is what triggers the incantation, and the combit is the focusing device that allows the incantation to manifest. And you're right; it's just plain glass."

So potions followed the same basic rules of all sorcery. You needed a *well* of vaetra as a power source, a *link* of some kind to channel the vaetra, an *incantation* to direct and shape the vaetra, and a *focus* to manifest the spell in the physical world.

I reached over to set the combit back on the table, but I pinched my fingers a little too tightly and it squirted out to bounce twice on the tabletop before disappearing onto the floor somewhere. Lohan made a grab at it on the first bounce, but it deflected off an irregularity on the table surface and shot past his hand. "Bye, bye," he said, looking in the direction the tiny bead had gone.

I looked sheepishly at Lissy, and she laughed. "Don't worry about it. That happens all the time. There are probably thousands of combits in the nooks and crannies of this room. We have plenty more." She opened the black bag and retrieved another one.

Placing a new combit on the table, Lissy continued. "Now that I have everything ready, I can start the enchanting process. Please don't interrupt or distract me until after I fuse the potion. Any more questions before I begin?" Lohan and I both shook our heads. "Okay, here I go."

Lissy took one last look at the recipe and her face became a mask of concentration. She sprinkled a thin layer of leaves from one of the jars into the enchanting press and spread them around with a stone pestle. She set the lid back into the press and pushed down on it while voicing part of the potion's incantation. She then lifted the lid off the press, picked up the bottom half, and poured the newly-enchanted herbs into the heating crucible.

She went through the same process with three more ingredients. By then, the water in the crucible was just starting to bubble. For the final ingredient, Lissy held on to the wooden handle of the crucible. She placed her thumb on a metal tab that came up through the handle. With a flourish, she dropped in the final ingredient and spoke the last phrase of the incantation.

With her final word, the crucible emitted a subtle "ting" that sounded like a single toll of a tiny bell. At that moment, I realized how silent the enchanting process had been. I hadn't detected any manifestation noise from the individual steps of the incantation, only from the final "fusion" phrase. I might actually learn to like alchemy. It would be nice to do something with sorcery that was relatively quiet for a change.

Lissy let the potion reach a full boil for a moment, and then took the crucible off the burner. She set it on a metal trivet. "The potion is done at this point, and it's ready to consume as soon as it cools down. However, it would be a little chewy if you tried to drink it as it stands," she said.

Lissy picked up a funnel and poked a square of cheese cloth into it. She took the stopper out of a small, empty glass bottle and set the funnel into it. She said, "Now that the potion has been fused, we can filter out the steeped ingredients. We usually bottle the potion while it's still hot and then seal it."

She poured the potion from the crucible into the funnel, where it quickly drained through the cheesecloth. We watched the liquid rise in the bottle; although the glass was such a dark brown that we could barely see through it. Once the crucible was empty, Lissy removed the funnel, dropped the combit into the bottle and pushed a cork stopper into the top. She set the newly bottled potion aside.

"That's it," she said with satisfaction. "You've now seen all of the basic steps necessary to create any potion. Any questions?"

Lohan and I asked her questions about the ingredients and the incantation. She explained how each ingredient contributed to the incantation and about how most of the ingredients in this simple potion were actually common to all potions. Every potion needed a "binder," which was what she added during the fusion step, and a "catalyst," which was what triggered the incantation upon drinking. Most also included a natural preservative of some kind, unless the potion was going to be consumed immediately. She also explained how some of the other equipment in the room was used to distill or refine more complex potions.

When we had exhausted our questions, Lissy reached over and put her hand around the bottle, tapping it lightly with her fingers before settling them gingerly on the glass.

"It's still warm, but cool enough to drink now. Later in your lessons, we'll make some fun potions that you can go ahead and try out."

Lohan shrugged and pulled a knife from his belt. "Why wait?" He sliced into the fleshy part of his palm and blood welled in the shallow cut. It started to pool in the center of his hand as he placed the bloodied knife on the table.

Lissy gasped and stared at him with her mouth open. I had started to get up from my seat when he pulled out his knife, but after he cut himself, I settled slowly back down in disbelief. The twins overheard and came over to see what was going on, but they stayed back a step or two from Lohan when they saw the blood on his hand.

Lohan gazed at Lissy with a twisted grin. "Well? May I try your potion now?"

Lissy narrowed her eyes at him, her lips pressed into a thin line. Keeping her eyes on Lohan, she popped the cork of the potion and slid the bottle toward him. She leaned slightly away as she extended her arm in his direction.

"Thanks," he said. He swirled the bottle and wiggled his eyebrows before tipping it up to his mouth and draining the contents with a few quick swallows. He thumped the bottle back down to the table, making everyone jump, and then he smacked his lips. "Not bad."

The rest of the group and I watched in morbid fascination as Lohan placed his hand down on the table and stared at the blood pulsing sluggishly from the cut. Within a few seconds, a steady hum came from his direction as the healing incantation manifested inside him. Slowly, the bleeding stopped. After a few more seconds, the cut began to close as the flesh on either side of the slice knitted back together. Soon, the wound was fully closed, leaving behind a bright pink welt where the flesh had been sundered.

Lohan picked up a cloth from the table and wiped the remaining blood from his hand and his knife. "Nice work, D...Lissy. You really *are* good at making potions." He slipped his knife back into its sheath.

Ben shook his head in disgust and walked back to his workbench. Daisy glared at Lohan for a moment more before declaring, "You're weird." She turned on her heel and returned to the bench with her brother.

I was so used to fighting on Lohan's side against the twins that I almost spoke up to defend him, but in this case, I was inclined to agree with Daisy. Lohan had a dark side that was decidedly creepy.

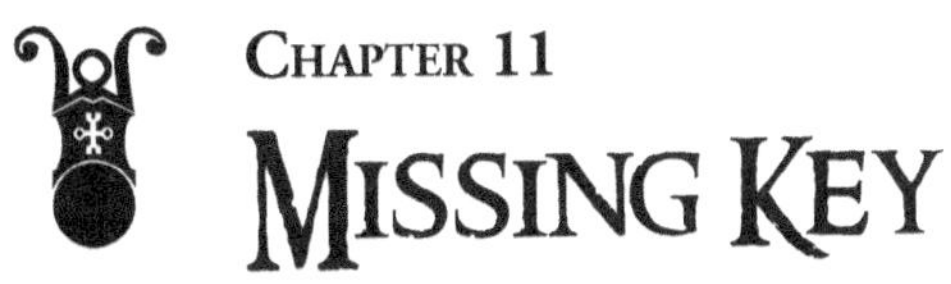

CHAPTER 11
MISSING KEY

Sulana looked around the dark and musty chamber. The two illuminators on the near and far walls waged a losing battle against the shadows cast by looming storage shelves that lined the walls and segmented the room. A maze of narrow, dusty walkways wove between the tall, wooden shelf units. The shelves were laden with hundreds of objects of various sizes and shapes. Some of the items were heavy enough to bow the wood they sat upon, and most were loosely wrapped in cloth. Some were labeled, some not. A thin coat of dust muted the colors of everything in sight, adding to the weighty ambiance of the room.

Sulana was certain that no place in Mundia held a larger collection of vaetric artifacts than the Archives armory. The purpose of some of the items in this room had been lost to time. Others had been placed here not so much to safeguard the artifacts themselves, but to protect the world from their use.

Senior Councilor Gregor Rissik emerged from a walkway between the shelves shaking his head. "It doesn't look like anything else has been taken, but by the spirits Ebnik, how could you let this happen?" His voice was tense and sharp.

With a concerned frown etched into his features, Ebnik bowed his head. "I'm sorry, Gregor, but I'm sure the door was secure."

"How can you tell nothing else is missing?" Sulana asked the councilor.

"Most of these artifacts haven't been moved in decades," he answered. One of the items on a shelf next to him was covered with a black cloth that was grey with dust. He demonstrated his point by gingerly lifting the cloth with his thumb and index finger, revealing a dust-free spot underneath. After lowering the cloth back into place, he wiped his fingers on his robe and walked back to the armory door. He waved toward a few relatively dust-free shelves on the other side of the room and added, "I'm familiar with the latest acquisitions, and they're still where they belong."

The armory was Councilor Rissik's domain. Of all the sorcerers at the Archives, no one knew more about the ancient secrets locked in this room. Author of several compendiums on artifact lore, Rissik spent virtually all of his spare time researching artifacts and documenting what he learned.

"I still don't understand how the thief got in," Sulana mused.

Although she trusted the councilor's assessment, she walked deeper into the room looking carefully for evidence of disturbance. She couldn't see onto the upper shelves, but getting at those shelves would leave marks on the lower ones. A levitation spell would have left behind force rings in the grit on the floor. A step ladder stood against a shelf at the back of the room, but Sulana could see the untouched dust on it's rungs from where she stood.

"That's at least partly my fault." Ebnik said under his breath.

The armory door was sealed by both a physical lock and a vaetric one. The physical lock consisted of a levered pair of bars that slid into slots in the stone wall of the doorway. The armory key that operated the lock was large and heavy; it was really more of a pry bar than a key. The vaetric lock that restricted the movement of the bars was a "sigil lock," so named because of the symbols that were etched into its glass surface. To disable or enable the sigil lock, a sorcerer needed to know the correct incantations, and few sorcerers were privy to that information.

Ebnik explained to Sulana and Councilor Rissik that he had come down to the armory earlier to store a Portal Key when he saw two of Paeter Thoron's amulets, which shared the same shelf. The sight reminded him that he had a couple more of the amulets to put into the room, so he left to retrieve them. Ebnik said he distinctly remembered closing the armory door and locking it before leaving. However, he had left the heavy lever-key outside the door rather than haul it up to his quarters and back. With the sigil lock engaged, the key was of little use anyway.

When Ebnik returned to the armory a few minutes later, something felt off to him. The armory key wasn't exactly where he'd left it. Then, when he went to disable the sigil lock, he didn't feel the corresponding thump within the door that indicated a freeing of the bar lock. The thief had apparently not known or had not bothered to use the separate incantation that re-engaged the sigil lock. Upon entering the armory, Ebnik saw that the Portal Key he had just placed there was gone.

Ebnik immediately reported the incident to Sulana. On their way back down to the armory, they had collected Councilor Rissik as well. The Councilor was the person most likely to notice if anything else was missing, and he had been working with Ebnik on evaluating the amulets.

Now, Councilor Rissik's tall, thin and loosely-robed frame stood at the doorway to the armory. The illuminator above him put his grey eyes into deep shadow below his brow, contrasting with the light reflecting off his prominent hawk nose and pointed chin. Sulana had rarely seen him overtly angry or jubilant; his demeanor was almost always one of calm confidence. His current agitation indicated how disturbed he was about the break in.

The councilor folded his arms and tapped one finger rapidly in annoyance. "Are you absolutely certain you engaged the sigil lock when you left?" he asked Ebnik.

Ebnik sighed and returned the councilor's direct gaze. "Yes. I distinctly remember hearing the thump of the lock before I walked away."

The councilor's eyes roamed the room. "You have to use the lever key to open the armory door, but it's not enough by itself. The thief had to know the incantation that controls the sigil lock." He looked at Ebnik and his tapping finger stopped. "Realistically, I doubt they got that from your lips, old friend."

Councilor Rissik's comment referred to the fact that Ebnik was a wizard: a sorcerer capable of casting incantations without speaking them aloud. It was a rare gift, and one that Ebnik used effortlessly and unconsciously. The thief had undoubtedly learned the unlocking incantation from someone else.

Sulana made her way back between the shelves to stand with the two men. "So, as far as we know, the only thing missing is a Portal Key?" She looked at the shelf where the portal key should have been.

Ebnik shook his head. "No, there's more. The two amulets that were on that shelf were taken as well. "

Sulana froze, staring at the empty shelf. Paeter Thoron had been making amulets in the village of Buckwoods while he waited for the delivery of a stolen Portal Key. Now a Portal Key was missing and so were some of the amulets that she and Ebnik had confiscated when they interrupted Paeter's plans. Someone at the Archives was involved with whatever Paeter was doing.

Sulana asked Ebnik, "You don't think Paeter could have gotten in here somehow, do you?"

Ebnik thought for a moment. "I don't see how. Even if he came in under a Veil, there are just too many ways he might be discovered. His timing would have had to be perfect, because there's no way he could know that I would temporarily leave the key outside the door. I think the thief knew exactly what he or she was after, and has been lying in wait for this opportunity."

The words "Veil" and "lying in wait" tickled at Sulana's mind, but Councilor Rissik spoke and interrupted her train of thought.

"Paeter was a dedicated Integrationist, and the Archives has plenty of sympathizers. Do you think one of them might be helping him?" The way the councilor stressed the words "Integrationists" and "sympathizers" made his negative opinion of them perfectly clear.

Sulana considered his question. Integrationists were sorcerers who believed that the way to heal the rift between sorcerers and the mundane was to integrate sorcery back into mundane life. But integration was a risky proposition. It would be easy for a sorcerer to go from being an advisor to being a manipulator and step over the line drawn by the Sorcery Accords.

Councilor Rissik was an Isolationist, the political opponents of the Integrationists. Isolationists believed that the only way to preserve the Sorcery Accords was to keep sorcerers away from mundane society as much as possible. They argued that sorcery should only be made available to the mundane under specific circumstances, and only at the request of a mundane person with a legitimate need.

The debate between the Integrationists and Isolationists had raged over the centuries since the Sorcery Accords were drafted. At various times, the Archives had been under the control of both factions. The Isolationists were in control at the moment, partly because of a small but significant incident known as the Battle of Riverview. About eight years ago, an unscrupulous Integrationist sorcerer had taken over the town of Riverview, and the Archives had sent a Sword Sorcerer to correct the situation. That Sword Sorcerer had been Sulana's father, and though he had won the battle, he had sacrificed his life to do so.

Not surprisingly, Sulana grew up hating the Integrationist agenda. Her feelings played no small part in her commitment to becoming a Sword Sorceress and dedicating her life to protecting the Sorcery Accords.

This theft was definitely not random. Sulana knew that Paeter Thoron wanted a Portal Key for some reason because she had already foiled one of his attempts to steal one. The mind-control amulets would have little value to most sorcerers when compared to the other treasures in this room. However, those amulets were evidence relating to whatever plans Paeter might have.

Someone who knew the unlocking incantation had been hiding nearby, possibly under a Veil, waiting for an opportunity to slip into the armory and steal those particular items. The image of a man inspecting the sigil lock on the armory door surfaced in her memory. "Lohan," she exclaimed.

Councilor Rissik gave her a penetrating look. "Who is Lohan?"

"He's a new student here. I caught him skulking near the armory door." Everything fell into place in Sulana's mind. Lohan had arrived at the Archives just before she and Jaylan did. Lohan claimed to be new to sorcery, but he picked things up much more rapidly than most students. That's because he wasn't a student; he was a spy. He had grabbed the amulets because he knew what they were. She was willing to bet that he was working with Paeter Thoron. It was even possible that he was the mysterious "second man" who had hired the Portal Key thieves she intercepted on her first mission. The timing of everything was too perfect to be coincidental.

"I've been a fool," she concluded, spitting out the last word with vehemence.

Ebnik raised his eyebrows. "You believe Lohan is responsible for the theft?"

Sulana nodded, still thinking through her theory. "The more I think about it, the more certain I am. We need to find him and question him immediately." Her hand went to the pommel of her sword, and she moved toward the armory door.

Councilor Rissik stepped back out of her way and Ebnik followed her out of the room. Ebnik pushed the massive door shut and slid the blade of the enormous key into the keyhole. He turned the T-shaped handles of the bow to engage the locking mechanism with a deep, metallic clang.

With the bar lock in place, Ebnik placed his hand over the sigil lock, and a dull thud confirmed its engagement. However, the sense of security that normally accompanied that sound was lost. They'd have to replace the sigil lock right away.

Sulana turned and strode down the hallway. Burning anger added speed to her stride and her jaw clenched with determination.

Chapter 12
Truant

Jaylan ~ Alchemy Class, The Archives

Lissy and I sat side-by-side at a work bench in the alchemy lab. Lohan was late for class and the twins were out, so I took advantage of the opportunity to ask Lissy about lycanthropy potions. Without telling her the entire story of the Tam Overland tragedy, I explained that I knew of someone who had experimented with lycanthropy, and I wanted to know more about how it worked.

She rummaged through the scrolls in the lab until she finally found one that was amber with age. It was brittle but otherwise undamaged, indicating that it had been there a long time but had not seen much use. She brought the scroll over to the work bench and carefully unrolled it. Our heads nearly touched as we looked at the potion recipe.

"I'm honestly surprised that we had this recipe here in the lab," Lissy said, as she carefully smoothed the scroll with the flat of her hand. The curl of the parchment was so strong that the metal bars were barely able to hold down the ends. "I've never known anyone who made a lycanthropy potion. I thought for sure we'd have to go down to the library. If you want more background information on this recipe, we may have to go down there to do more research."

We were sitting so close together that I could feel her body heat. The subtle flowery fragrance she always wore was much sweeter when warm. Sulana usually smelled of musky leather tinged with the sour tang of rusting metal, which was more familiar to me because I carried the same scent around.

Lissy was much more feminine than Sulana in many ways, and being this close to her made me a little nervous.

I cleared my throat and said, "Let's start with what we have here and see what we can learn."

"Sure. Let's see…well, the setup is definitely unusual," she observed.

"How so?"

"Most potions can be brewed anywhere. With this one, you have to be outside under a moon. It says that for the strongest potion, the moon should be high in the sky, unobscured by clouds, and as full as possible. I don't think I've ever seen a recipe that depends upon environmental factors like this. No wonder nobody makes this stuff."

"Someone is making it somewhere," I asserted. "It's expensive, but not difficult to acquire if you know the right people." I tried to interpret the words on the scroll, but they weren't in the Tanesian language I knew. "Does it say anything about brewing during an eclipse? What language is this, anyway?"

The label on the lycanthropy potion Tam had partially consumed identified it as a variety named "Eclipse." Tam's young friend Alain had claimed it was the strongest variety available. I wondered if the name tied into the recipe somehow.

Lissy answered, "No, there's nothing here about an eclipse, but given the other factors mentioned, I'm sure an eclipse would have a significant influence on the potion's strength one way or the other. The scroll is written in Old Empiric, which you should probably learn if you want to do any serious research. Half the books in the library are written in it."

"Great. More studying," I said with a sigh.

Lissy giggled and placed her hand on my arm. "Don't worry. Most of the words are similar to modern Tanesian. It's just the Old Empiric alphabet that's different. It's not like learning an entirely new language. Mostly, you just need to learn how to read it, and I can help you with that."

"Thanks, that's nice of you," I said. I mentally added yet another block to the wall that stood between me and my goal of becoming a sorcerer. At this point, it seemed like more blocks were being added than taken away. I was still learning what I *didn't* know.

I was here at the Archives to learn sorcery, and Talon was urging me to become a Sword Sorcerer. But trouble was brewing, and my main concern was being able to help Sulana when it boiled over. Paeter Thoron would eventually resurface, and I wanted to be ready when he did. Everything that prevented me from being ready was an unwelcome obstacle.

Lissy squeezed my arm and asked, "What's on your mind. You look like something's bothering you."

I realized that I had been staring at the scroll and frowning. Lissy was perceptive, but I wasn't sure how many of my concerns I should share with her. I wondered how the coming difficulties would affect the people here at the Archives. Would Lissy be in danger? She seemed to be a capable sorceress, so I was sure she could take care of herself, but I hoped she wouldn't have to face that challenge. Did she have anyone she could turn to for help?

I looked into her dark blue eyes and put my hand over hers where it still held my arm. "Do you have a suitor or someone you can turn to for support, Lissy?"

A corner of her full-lipped mouth raised in a half-smile. "Why? Are you interested?" she asked, adding a playful eyebrow wiggle.

I blushed and looked down at the scroll again. "It's just that I think we may be in for dangerous times, and I'm concerned for your safety," I said.

"Good answer," said Sulana from behind us.

Lissy slipped her hand from under mine and we both turned in our seats. Sulana stood in the doorway to the lab with her hands on her hips, looking at me with a dangerous glint in her eyes. Ebnik and Senior Councilor Rissik stood behind her. Ebnik was unsuccessfully trying to hide a smirking grin, obviously enjoying my predicament. Councilor Rissik looked slowly back and forth between Lissy and me, his expression neutral.

"What's going on?" Lissy asked.

Sulana moved forward so the two men following her could enter the room behind her. She folded her arms across her chest and said, "I was about to ask you the same thing."

Lissy smiled and said, "Don't worry, Lana. I'm not trying to steal Jaylan away from you." She patted me on the shoulder as she spoke, and I winced, thinking that any more contact between us in front of Sulana was a bad idea. "We're just going over a potion recipe," she added.

Sulana dropped her arms and eased forward, looking between Lissy and me at the potion recipe on the work bench. She then looked up sharply at me and said, "Lycanthropy?" in a low voice. She understood the significance of my interest in this particular potion. I nodded in response.

Ebnik cleared his throat from his position by the doorway. "I don't see Lohan here, Sulana."

His comment reminded Sulana of why they were there and her expression turned serious again. She glanced around the room and settled her gaze on Lissy. "Lohan didn't show for class today?"

Lissy slowly shook her head and looked from Sulana to the two men at the doorway. Like me, she could tell that this visit wasn't casual. "No, he hasn't shown up yet. The twins are out collecting potion ingredients, so Jaylan and I decided to work on a...personal project. What's going on?"

Sulana ignored the question and looked directly at me. "Remember when I asked you about the exploring you and Lohan were doing around the Archives? And how I caught him skulking around the armory?" I nodded, and she continued. "Well, now someone has managed to get into the armory and steal a Portal Key."

I bristled at her implied accusation. Lohan was one of the few friends I'd made since coming to the Archives. "Just because you don't like Lohan doesn't mean he's a thief. I agree that he's a bit strange, but he could be absent from class for any number of reasons."

Sulana glared at me. "Okay. You're the investigator. Let's look at the facts. Lohan arrived at the Archives barely a week before we did. Lohan has been doing better in his classes than he should be; almost as if he already knows most of what we are teaching him. He has been casing the Archives, and I caught him sneaking around the armory. Now something has been stolen from the armory and Lohan is missing. You tell me; is all of that just a coincidence?"

I thought about what she said. Her feelings about Lohan put a definite bias into her choice of words, but her presentation of the facts was more or less accurate. I had to agree that Lohan deserved investigation. "I don't believe in coincidences," I finally said, and Sulana's gaze softened.

What we were missing was a motive, and as I considered that, my mind was drawn back to the first thing Sulana mentioned. Lohan had arrived here a week before she and I did. If Lohan did steal the Portal Key, he had to be connected with Paeter Thoron somehow. So, what was he doing before he arrived at the Archives? "Lohan was the second man," I blurted out as I realized that he could have been the unknown second man that had helped Paeter take over Buckwoods Village.

Sulana gave me a satisfied smile. "Exactly."

If what we were thinking was true, Lohan was just pretending to be a student. He was really here to spy for Paeter Thoron. As disappointed as I was to discover that our friendship may have been a sham, I had to admit that my pride was salved by the possibility that Lohan's apparent superiority in learning sorcery might actually be because he had previous experience. I was going to have to reassess everything that had happened with him.

But first we needed to prove that all of this conjecture was true. "We need to find Lohan and confront him."

Sulana tensed. "No, *I* need to find Lohan and confront him. You are a student here. There's no *we* about it."

Attempting to apply my most reasonable tone, I said, "I'm not exactly helpless, Sulana. Besides, we're just guessing about all of this. It's still possible he had nothing to do with the missing Portal Key, and I think he'll be more willing to talk with you if I'm there."

She paused for a moment, tapping a foot. "Fine. But let me do the talking."

I got up to accompany Sulana and Ebnik in the search for Lohan. Councilor Rissik chose to remain behind, pointing out that Sulana had the search well in hand and that he would just be in the way.

The first place we checked was Lohan's room. It was empty. Lohan wasn't there, and neither were his belongings. I started to get a sinking feeling in my stomach. The three of us continued to search inside and outside the Archives to no avail.

Lohan was gone, and he'd taken a Portal Key with him.

CHAPTER 13
LISSY'S ORDERS

Gregor ~ Alchemy Class, The Archives

Councilor Rissik stood inside the door to the potions lab and waited for the footsteps and voices of the search party to fade down the hallway. He saw no reason to accompany them when they already had two people skilled with arms and two sorcerers in their group. Besides, he wanted to take this opportunity to speak privately with Lissy.

He quietly closed the door, and Lissy gave him a questioning look. Lissy had her mother's dark hair and her father's round face, but those dark blue eyes were uniquely hers. Not many people would recognize the family resemblance in her features; Gregor was one of the few people who knew who her real parents were.

To the rest of the Archives, she was Lissy Aragon, one of many daughters from a large, rich family in Cassandria. The Aragon name was a good cover for the child of an emperor who wanted her to develop her sorcery skills. Her father hoped that, one day, she would replace Gregor as his eyes and ears at the Archives.

In his time as Lissy's mentor, Gregor had become quite fond of the young woman. He never had much interest in starting a family of his own, but there were times when he wondered if that might have been a mistake. Helping Lissy develop into a politically astute young sorceress had been one of the most rewarding things he had done in his life.

As Gregor walked over to stand next to Lissy, he commented, "I believe they are wasting their time, but I suppose we should verify that the spy has really escaped."

"I never liked Lohan," Lissy said with a frown. "He gave me the creeps from the moment he arrived, and he seemed to go out of his way to antagonize people."

"Everyone but Jaylan, it seems."

She shrugged. "He wasn't much better with Jaylan, but Jaylan seems to have more patience with obnoxious people than the rest of us."

"It could be more than that. They did both arrive within a week of each other, and they explored the Archives together."

Lissy waved her hand dismissively. "Jaylan's no spy. He came here with Sulana after helping her *fight* Paeter Thoron. He's just new to all of this sorcery business and needed someone to commiserate with."

Gregor pursed his lips. "Perhaps. But I wouldn't place too much trust in him. He is a mercenary with no strong ties to either the Archives or the Empire. Don't let your feelings for him take your guard down as Sulana obviously has done."

Lissy's posture stiffened. "My feelings for Jaylan are not an issue. Yes, we're becoming friends, but I have no interest in competing with Sulana for him. And I will not let my friendship with him interfere with my mission."

Gregor inclined his head and settled onto the stool next to hers where Jaylan had been just moments before. "That's good to hear. The Empire needs your undivided attention on what's happening here. The Integrationists are on the move again, and I'm certain that trouble is coming."

Lissy's posture relaxed as she shifted to face him. "You think Lohan is working with the Integrationists? I guess that makes sense."

"I'm sure of it," Gregor replied. "I want you to put together a report on everything you remember about Lohan and his activities since he arrived. And start a report on Jaylan as well. I don't want to be caught unaware if his actions develop a questionable pattern."

Lissy pursed her lips and squinted at him. It looked like she might argue, but then she sighed in acceptance of her orders. "Yes, Councilor. I'll do my best."

"I know you will," he said with a smile, giving her knee a single pat. "You always do. Well, I need to get back to my office and work on my own report to the emperor about today's revelations."

Gregor trusted that Lissy would do as she was told. She was a smart woman and her loyalty to both the Archives and the Empire was unquestionable. Her report on Lohan would undoubtedly shed some light on the events leading up to the theft of the Portal Key. And having to write a report about Jaylan would help her maintain an emotional distance from the man.

The emperor would not be pleased when he got the news about the stolen Portal Key. The last attempt by the Integrationists to side-step the Sorcery Accords in Riverview had been bold and clumsy. They seemed to have learned subtlety since then, and that made them far more dangerous.

Now this man Jaylan was distracting both Lissy and Sulana from their duties. Jaylan was a wildcard who needed to be watched carefully. The loyalties of a mercenary were often unpredictable and untrustworthy. However, by all accounts, he had the potential to become a Sword Sorcerer. If he could be enlisted into the service of the Empire, he could also become a valuable asset.

As Gregor opened the door to the potion lab and walked down the hall, he decided that Jaylan's loyalties would have to be proven. Otherwise, the distraction he caused would have to be eliminated somehow.

CHAPTER 14
DELA'S NUPTIALS

I watched Sulana while she enthusiastically worked her way through her dinner. It made me happy to see her enjoying herself. Her every movement was visual poetry for me.

We were at a large table along one wall of the dining hall, sitting across from one another at the ends of the long bench seats. The kitchen had served spicy roasted chicken and potatoes, and both of us preferred to save conversation for after the delicious meal. The dining hall cooks didn't produce the variety or quality of food that I was used to getting at the Snow Creek Inn back in Northshore, but once in a while they surprised me with a savory dish.

Sulana caught me watching her and stopped chewing. After swallowing her food, she looked down at her shirt and said, "What? Did I drop food on myself?" She wiped her mouth with the cloth napkin from her lap and looked at me with wide eyes. "Do I have something on my face? You'd tell me, right?"

I chuckled at her reaction. "No. I mean, yes, I'd tell you, but everything's fine. I was just thinking about how cute you are, that's all."

She gave me a shy smile and reached across the table to pat my hand. "That's sweet. I think you're cute too." Potential embarrassment averted, she wasted no time getting back to her meal.

I peripherally caught some movement near the entrance to the dining hall and turned to see Cyrus, an Archives courier, wander in with a shallow wooden box in his hands. He spotted us and weaved through the tables and benches. He put his message box on the table, threw a leg over the bench I was on, and sat facing me.

Cyrus rummaged around in his box as soon as he sat down. "Hi Sulana. Hey, Jaylan. I have a message in here from the Northshore Sanctuary for you." He plucked a tightly rolled and sealed parchment from the box and handed it to me.

I hesitantly took the tube from his hand. "Who at the Northshore Sanctuary would send *me* a message?"

The Archives operated sorcerer sanctuaries in cities and towns all over the empire; the sanctuary at Northshore was just one of them. Northshore was my home town, and like most of the other residents, I'd been careful to avoid the sanctuary that was located there. We were taught that sorcerers were dangerous and untrustworthy, so we kept our distance from them. But then I learned I had sorcery abilities of my own, and now I sat in the dining hall of the Archives surrounded by some of the most powerful sorcerers in the empire.

Cyrus shrugged. "Hey, I just deliver them. You'll have to open it to find out who it's from." He looked down at my plate. "Is that as good as it looks?"

Sulana swallowed a gulp of watered wine and replied for me, "It's excellent. You should get some while it lasts."

Cyrus winked and hopped up from the bench. "You bet. I'll be right back after I deliver a few more messages." He grabbed his delivery box and hurried off on his mission before either of us could comment further.

The message tube did not say who sent the note, but the spidery text that spelled out my name was all too familiar. The note was from Dela, a young woman from the Snow

Creek Inn who, until recently, had been trying to talk me into settling down and running the inn with her. Technically, I was still a partner in the inn, but I had always meant my involvement to be mostly financial. Settling down with Dela and becoming an innkeeper had never been in my plans, and that was even before I met Sulana and learned of my potential to become a sorcerer.

A harrowing adventure to the fishing village of Buckwoods taught me that I could not continue to ignore my abilities with sorcery. When I returned to the inn, I told Dela that I had decided to go to the Archives and learn sorcery.

She didn't take the news well. She slapped me hard and yelled at me before storming off to her room. Nothing I said would get her to speak with me again. I doubted that any explanation would have been satisfactory, but still I wanted to try. Dela was convinced that my decision was more about being with Sulana than learning sorcery, and she didn't understand how I could involve myself with "those magicians" in the first place.

Dela must have found out that she could get a note to me through the Northshore Sanctuary.

With some amusement, I imagined her pounding on the front door of the building, thrusting the note into the hands of the surprised sorcerer who answered her knock, and stomping back to the inn. More likely, she had sent someone else to deliver the note.

"Are you going to open it?" Sulana asked me. She had been watching me while I stared at the note in my hand. "What's wrong?"

"The message is from Dela," I replied.

We looked at each other in silence for a moment. Sulana knew that I loved Dela, and she took my word that my love was more familial than romantic. She also knew how unhappy I had been when Dela had rejected my attempts at explaining why I had to go to the Archives.

"Do you want me to leave?" she asked.

I shook my head. "No, go ahead and finish your dinner. I don't even know what this is about."

Sulana went back to eating, but watched me closely as I peeled off the wax seal on the outside of the tube. I unrolled the message, revealing more of Dela's handwriting.

Dela wasted no time with niceties and got straight to the point. She and Meldon were getting married. They were moving my things out of my apartment and taking it over. When I returned, we would negotiate how we would deal with my share of the business and the apartment.

As I reread the few words of the note, I felt the last vestiges of my former life floating away like dandelion fluff.

Some part of me had always thought that my old life would be waiting for me when I completed my training at the Archives. But I now understood how unrealistic and irrational that expectation had been.

The meal that had been so delicious just a moment before no longer held appeal. I crushed the note in one hand and grimaced as I put the other hand over my cramping stomach.

Sulana looked at me in alarm. "Bad news?"

I moved my mouth a couple of times, but nothing came out. I wasn't sure what to say. I finally stammered, "Yes… No…I need to go to my room." I started to get up, but Sulana reached out and put her hand on mine.

"Do you want to be alone?" she asked.

"No, I just can't stay here."

She walked with me as I went back to my room in a daze.

I felt cut off from my past. My selfish decision to follow Sulana and learn sorcery had hurt Dela and cost me the chance to ever return to Northshore as a normal person. I was forever accepting the designation of "sorcerer" and all of the prejudice that came with it. I was becoming the very thing I once feared and avoided. In the meantime, the people I cared about were moving on with their lives without me.

"What did she say?" Sulana asked me as she caught up to me in the hall.

I cut to the news that would most interest Sulana. "Dela is marrying Meldon."

She was silent for a moment as we moved together toward the stairwell that would take us down to the next level and to my room. Movement felt good to me. I had a yearning to escape, but I had nowhere to go except my chamber, the one refuge that remained to me.

Sulana finally responded, "That was fast."

"No kidding," I said. When I left Northshore a little less than two months ago, Meldon had been showing increasing interest in Dela. At the time, she seemed unaware of his affections. I knew Dela was anxious to start a family and get help with the inn, but I was surprised she would marry so quickly.

Then again, she was a woman of high passions, and it really wasn't out of character for her to fall completely in love with someone who adored her in a short period of time. I felt a stab of disappointment that her affection for me could be so easily replaced, but then what right did I have to expect her to hold on to feelings that I didn't return?

We came to my room and went inside. I tossed the crushed note onto the lamp table and sat on the bed.

Sulana stood in front of me with concern in her eyes. "Do you want to talk about it?"

I shrugged. I wasn't sure how to explain what I was feeling. "I guess. Dela and Meldon are taking over the apartment and want to negotiate a settlement with me regarding ownership of the inn. I think they want me out of their lives."

"That seems harsh. But you know how Dela feels about sorcerers, and weren't you the one who encouraged Meldon to pursue his feelings for Dela and help out at the inn?"

I took a deep breath and let it out. "That's true, but I didn't expect to be cut off from my old life so quickly. I always thought I had the option to go back."

"I thought you were enjoying it here," Sulana said.

"I am…most of the time…it's hard to explain. I've been cut off from my place of retreat, and I have no idea what lies ahead for me here."

Sulana's voice grew stronger. "You know what mundane society thinks about sorcerers. You can't have it both ways. You either abandon your studies and go back to a mundane life, or finish what you've started and become a sorcerer."

In our time together, I'd noticed that she had a low tolerance for whining. She was telling me what I already knew, and I found it irritating. "Thanks. You're a big help."

Sulana's face softened and she sat next to me on the bed. She put her arm around me and laid her head on my shoulder. "I'm sorry. I know you are hurting. But maybe you should look at this as a beginning instead of an ending."

I didn't respond at first. She was right. I hadn't been happy in my mundane life, and I had never intended to marry Dela anyway. I was pouting about something I had brought upon myself and could no longer change. Meanwhile, this lovely woman cared for me and was helping me learn to be the man I had chosen to become. Dela represented the past and Sulana the future. That future was still a bit scary, but it was a new and exciting path as well.

I put my arm around Sulana's waist and turned my head toward hers. She looked up into my eyes, waiting for me to say something. I realized then that she was feeling vulnerable. Here I was, pining over my prior life. A life that didn't include her. In that moment, I knew for certain that having a life that didn't include Sulana was unacceptable.

"You're right." I said quietly. "I choose you."

"Smart man," she whispered just before our lips met in a soft kiss. The warmth that flooded me washed away all lingering doubts about my decision to move forward. The past was in the past. As our kiss deepened, I eased Sulana down to the bed and caressed her face. She put her hand behind my neck and pulled my lips tight to hers. By unspoken agreement, we started to undress one another.

That late afternoon, in the depths of the Archives, we took our relationship to a new level. I would start the next day with a renewed sense of purpose and a stronger commitment to Sulana and this musty castle that we called home.

Chapter 15
EBNIK'S SECRET

Sulana ~ Council Chamber, The Archives

Sulana climbed the stairway to the top level of the Archives, also known as the council level. Two guards, alerted by the sound of her footsteps, stood ready at the opening of the stairwell, blocking her access to the hallway beyond. When they saw who it was, they stepped back and nodded as she passed. She nodded back and smiled her thanks. As Sword Sorceress, Sulana was one of the few people other than the councilors themselves who had unchallenged access to the council level.

Sulana strode down the main hallway toward Council Hall, her cloak softly fluttering behind her. She wore her official uniform, which consisted of a long-sleeved jacket with brass buttons and leggings made from a heavy, dark blue felt trimmed in council maroon. The symbol of sorcery was embroidered onto the left breast of the jacket. In place of her sword, she was armed with a long, jeweled dagger that had been given to her at her confirmation ceremony when she was officially sworn in as a Sword Sorceress. Although she didn't take the fancy symbol of office on the road, she always wore it to official council functions.

Why she had been summoned to the private council meeting room was a mystery. She had no idea who issued the summons or who might be attending the meeting. Given the circumstances, she thought it best to dress up for the occasion.

As Sulana passed through the Council Hall antechamber, she reflected on the many hours she had already spent there in her short career, waiting on those hard wooden benches for a council decision. Pushing the Council Hall door open, she gave the massive wooden portal just enough of a shove to slip in. She had witnessed more than one person push too hard on that door, forcing them to perform an embarrassing, stumbling dance to stop its wide swing before the well-oiled hinges allowed it to crash noisily against the interior wall.

The expansive Council Hall was empty. Backless benches were stacked along the walls, leaving the majority of the floor bare, as if it had been cleared for a dance. The doorway she had just entered opened about mid-way along the east wall, across from windows that let natural light flood into the room. Council Hall was rectangular, with the longest walls on the east and west sides.

Three square tables were arranged near the windows where you often could find one or more of the councilors bent over a book or a meal. During the summer, dust motes danced in the late afternoon sun that streamed through the windows and heated the stone floor, sometimes raising the temperature in the room to an uncomfortable level. This morning however, the clatter of Sulana's boots echoed in the otherwise silent room that still held the characteristic chill of the Archives interior.

Sulana turned toward the Council Seat, which was an elevated platform along the south wall. The platform supported a long, dark wooden table with five chairs behind it, one chair for each member of the Archives Council. When the entire council of senior sorcerers assembled in those chairs to conduct official Archives business and hear proposals, their vantage point gave them a clear view of the entire hall and simultaneously made them appear larger and more powerful. Having pled causes before the Council Seat in the past, Sulana appreciated how intimidating the arrangement could be.

She slowed and softened her steps as she approached a door to the left of the platform. Sulana had rarely been invited to visit the private Council Chamber. By the time the councilors sequestered themselves in that room, they usually had all the information they needed to reach a decision.

Sulana squared her shoulders to present an air of confidence as she opened the door and stepped into the Council Chamber. Stopping just inside the doorway, she was surprised to see that the room held only two occupants: Ebnik and Councilor Rissik. Both men stood when she entered.

The tapestries lining the walls muffled sounds in the large room, making it seem smaller and more intimate than it was. The two men had been seated at a large, round table with five high-backed chairs positioned around it. As Sulana closed the door, she was distracted by something on the table in front of Ebnik that glittered in the cold light of the illuminators.

Councilor Rissik held out his hand and indicated the chair on his left. Ebnik sat on his right. "Thanks for joining us Sulana. Please have a seat."

Sulana took the proffered chair. Once seated, she looked more closely at the object in front of Ebnik.

"Look familiar?" Ebnik asked with a smile. He picked up a ring that was attached to a chain. As he lifted it from the table, she saw that the other end of the chain was attached to a glass rod.

Sulana had little doubt about what it was. "A Seeker."

Ebnik nodded and put the ring back down on the table.

Councilor Rissik cleared his throat. "Now that the Sword Sorceress is here, will you tell me what this is about?"

Ebnik toyed with the Seeker's chain. "Yes, sorry. I don't mean to be mysterious, but I think secrecy is important in this matter."

"What matter?" Councilor Rissik asked. "Get to the point, Sorcerer Vlastorus."

Ebnik raised an eyebrow at the councilor's impatience. "I think I have a way we can get our Portal Key back."

Councilor Rissik leaned back in his seat. "We already sent out riders, and they lost the man's trail. We know he went south toward Northshore, but that's about it."

Guessing at the implications of the Seeker sitting in front of Ebnik, Sulana said, "I thought your Portal Key is the only one that has a Seeker attuned to it. The one Lohan stole wasn't yours, was it?"

Ebnik gave Sulana a sly smile. "No. Lohan took the key we stored in the armory. But mine is no longer the only one that has a Seeker attuned to it. While I was working on the amulets, I noticed the other Portal Key sitting in the armory, and decided that it needed a Seeker too."

A thrill shot down Sulana's spine, and she leaned forward, placing both hands flat on the table as if to propel herself out of her seat. "So I can track down Lohan just as I did the last pair of thieves." She turned toward Councilor Rissik and added, "I can get my team together and we can ride out today. The sooner we go after Lohan, the better."

Councilor Rissik held up his hand. "Hold on a moment, Sorceress Delano. I agree with you, but I am not the only councilor you must convince. Ever since the incident at Buckwoods, I've been getting increasing resistance from two of the junior council members, and they have become more effective at influencing the votes of the others."

Sulana knew exactly who Councilor Rissik was talking about.

The council was made up of five seats: two senior councilors and three junior councilors. The three junior councilors voted among themselves; their collective vote had the weight of one senior vote. Their single vote was tallied with the votes of the two senior councilors to decide the matter at hand.

Two of the junior councilors were strongly Integrationist and almost always voted together. Their collusion made the third junior councilor's vote irrelevant. Boris Underwood was the senior councilor Sulana had interviewed about Paeter Thoron's time at the Archives. He was the councilor who thought himself above politics and believed that his decisions always reflected what was best for the Archives. That pride and confidence made him susceptible to manipulation by a cunning opponent. Velna Asher, the strongest of the junior councilors was that cunning opponent.

Sulana sat back and folded her hands together, clenching them tightly. "Any delay is only going to give Lohan more time to reach his destination. If I can catch him on the road, I won't have to face whatever opposition may be waiting there. I'm sure Paeter Thoron will be part of the welcoming party."

"Be that as it may, I cannot authorize your trip on my own," Councilor Rissik said. "I will put the issue before the council when we meet tomorrow afternoon. I'm confident that Councilor Underwood will understand the urgency of recovering the Portal Key and vote as he did before, so you will be on your way soon. Go ahead and prepare your team, but don't be obvious about it."

Sulana twisted her mouth in a half frown, but didn't try to argue the point further. She knew that Councilor Rissik was on her side, which was why Ebnik had selected him for this meeting. Still, it was frustrating to have to wait another day.

On the other hand, the delay gave her more time to prepare for her mission, and she'd get a chance to say a proper goodbye to Jaylan.

Before they adjourned, Ebnik suggested that they keep the information about the Seeker to themselves for the moment. "We don't know for sure that Lohan was working alone, and I'd rather not let potential conspirators know that we have the means to track him." Councilor Rissik and Sulana agreed.

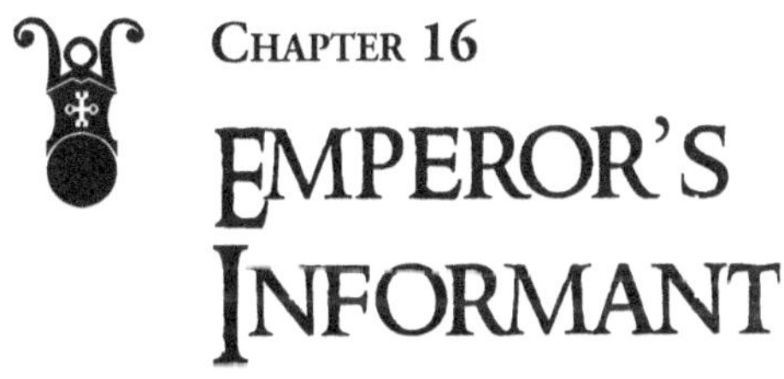

CHAPTER 16
EMPEROR'S INFORMANT

Gregor ~ Journey Room, The Archives

About an hour later, Senior Councilor Gregor Rissik came to a stop in front of the journey room guard and nodded toward the stout wooden door the man protected.

"If you would be so kind, Amil," he said.

"Certainly, Councilor," the guard responded. The guard first removed a thick board that barred the door and set it aside. He then extracted a key from a pocket behind the breastplate of his padded armor and turned the key in the lock. Holding the key in place, Amil pulled the heavy door open to allow the councilor ingress to the room beyond. A metallic tang wafted out into the hall making the councilor wrinkle his nose.

The councilor walked through the door and into the dark room, triggering two illuminators. The chamber they revealed was cramped and poorly ventilated, which allowed the natural moisture of the underground walls to permeate the room. The metallic odor came from two circular metal grates set into the floor on the right side of the room. A thin steel pedestal rose from the center of each grate. Both pedestals were etched with runes and curving lines. One of the floor grates was noticeably more worn, with rust showing through in the places where countless feet had worn away the protective paint coating. A thin yellow line circumscribed each grate.

"Will you be returning today, Councilor?" the guard asked from behind him.

"Yes," Gregor answered, looking over his shoulder. "Thank you, Amil," he added, dismissing the guard.

Being an Archives Councilor had its privileges, and one of those privileges was unlimited access to this "journey room" with no questions asked. Gregor appreciated both the access and the lack of scrutiny.

The councilor turned his attention to a honeycomb of square cupboard doors on a floor-to-ceiling cabinet across the room from the pedestals. Most of the doors were labeled with the name of a sorcerer sanctuary. A few of the cupboards remained unassigned and had no label. Without hesitation, he opened the cabinet door labeled "Cassandria."

Inside the cubby hole, a translocation orb rested in a shallow bowl that was carved into the wood of the shelf. Made of crystal, the orb was about the size of a medium apple. Silver tracings delicately webbed the sphere, giving it the appearance of a tiny, stylized, sparkling pumpkin.

Gregor gingerly picked up the translocation orb, or T-orb as it was more commonly called, and closed the cabinet door. Cupping the device protectively in his hands, he turned around and walked slowly over to one of the pedestals. The metal grate that encircled its base rang hollowly as he stepped onto it.

The metal tracings on the orb came together at the top and bottom. On the bottom, the tracings flowed into a circular base with a raised edge. The edge exactly matched a slot in the cupped surface at the top of the pedestal. Gregor placed the orb onto the pedestal and pressed the mated connectors together.

Verifying that he was completely within the area defined by the circular grate, the councilor placed his right hand over the T-orb and steeled himself for the sorcery he was about to perform.

Gregor opened a channel to the orb and felt it accept his flow of vaetra. He spoke the word that invoked the orb, and it began to glow a bright yellow as it manifested its power. Unlike most implements, the orb automatically dropped the channel he had opened and shifted its draw of vaetra to the surrounding chamber. The illuminators in the room immediately dimmed and flickered as the shift occurred. Gregor shook his head in awe of the tremendous amount of vaetra the orbs consumed, thankful that he did not have to supply it personally. In fact, he doubted that three sorcerers working together would be able to provide all of the necessary power.

Although he had used the journey room to translocate on many occasions, the next part of the ride always made him anxious. A golden sphere of visual distortion, like heat waves rising from the road in summer, appeared around him. The sphere was centered on the T-orb and exactly encompassed the platform. The purpose of the yellow line painted on the floor would be obvious to an observer at this point; it was a "clearance line" that demarcated the widest point of the translocation sphere around the orb.

The distortion grew in intensity, and the room around him faded to grey, finally blinking to black. With a pop reminiscent of a cork coming free from the neck of a bottle, the encircling sphere disappeared, the T-orb went dark, and the room around him reappeared. Except it wasn't the same room.

Gregor stood in the corner of a much smaller room that smelled faintly of mildew. A single illuminator came on the moment he appeared. The wall opposite him had a cabinet that was similar to the one in the Archives journey room, but with fewer doors.

He left the translocation platform and walked over to a chest of drawers that stood against the wall to his left. Opening the drawer that was his, he extracted a plain tradesman's outfit. Gregor stripped out of the fancy robe that identified him as being a Senior Councilor of the Archives and changed into the simpler garb. He transferred his small casting orb into a pocket of his leather vest, but left everything else behind.

Gregor listened at the single door of the room. Satisfied that no one was wandering around on the other side, he quietly slipped out. When he pushed the door closed behind him, it clicked shut and blended into the wall so well that he would never recognize it as a door if he didn't already know it was there.

He moved swiftly down the hallway and ascended a set of stairs. Opening the door at the top of the stairwell, he stepped into the large reception room of the Sorcerer Sanctuary at Cassandria, the capital city of the Tanes Empire. The room smelled strongly of incense and Gregor suppressed a sneeze. The sanctuary was not in the best neighborhood of Cassandria, and the incense helped mask the less pleasant odors that wafted in whenever someone opened the front door.

At the reception desk, a young man in a plain grey robe looked up from a book and scurried over. He came to an abrupt stop in front of Gregor and bowed deeply. "Councilor Rissik, it is an honor to have you here. My name is Tolby, at your service. May I be of assistance in any way? Should I get the Housemaster?"

Gregor smiled at the boy's enthusiasm. He didn't see such subservience at the Archives very often, thank the spirits. "Thank you, but no. I won't be here long. Unless you have any recent news about the state of affairs here in Cassandria?"

Happy to serve, the young sorcerer launched into a breathless report on the sanctuary's gardens, the surliness of the emperor's guards, and the financial well-being of the sanctuary. He related nothing of particular use to the councilor, who endured the recitation with polite attention.

When the young man began to speak more quietly of the political maneuverings within the sanctuary, Gregor held up his hand to stop the monologue. "I appreciate the information, but I have to leave soon for an appointment."

The younger man blushed and looked down. "Sorry sir, I didn't mean to blather on like that. We don't get visitors like yourself very often, sir, and I didn't want to let you down."

Gregor snorted. "Don't worry about it, Tolby. You did fine. I don't mean to be rude, but I really do need to get going."

The young sorcerer smiled shyly at the compliment and squared his shoulders. "Yes, sir. I understand, sir. Do you need a guide or a porter?"

Gregor shook his head. "No, thank you. I know my way."

"Of course, sir. Just let me know if I can do anything for you during your visit with us."

Gregor thought for a moment and concluded that it would be rude to pass through without at least exchanging pleasantries with Housemaster Nedminer. "There is one thing you can do for me. Let the Housemaster know that I would like a bit of his time this afternoon to speak with him, if his schedule allows."

Tolby grinned and replied, "Absolutely, Councilor! I'll set it up. I manage the headmaster's schedule, so I know he can see you this afternoon."

"Very good, Tolby. I'll be on my way, then. I should return in a couple of hours."

Stepping out into the brightness of the full morning sun, Councilor Rissik turned his head and blinked to clear his watering eyes. His nostrils were assaulted by the odors of a city crowded with humanity. A strong scent of juniper overrode the city odors to some degree, but it could not mask them entirely.

A large front yard stretched away from the entryway, enclosed by a rock wall that was topped by wrought-iron fencing. Gregor saw only hints of the fence through the tall, blue-green juniper trees which grew so close together that they formed a second, living fence within the wall.

Raised garden beds lined either side of the wide path to the main gate. Three gardeners moved slowly and deliberately along the narrow pathways between the beds, removing weeds, harvesting leafy vegetables, and generally checking the state of the many growing green plants.

Gregor went down the front steps and strode down the path. The gardeners glanced up from their work but otherwise ignored him. At the end of the path, a massive iron gate blocked the only gap in the surrounding sanctuary wall. Two Imperial guards stood on the other side of the gate, observing the many people passing by on the facing street.

One of the guards heard the councilor's steps and opened one side of the gate for him. The guard nodded to him and smirked in amusement as he took in the councilor's simple attire. Gregor nodded back, but said nothing as he swiftly moved into the crowd.

There was no point in speaking to the guard. The man would only make a snide comment about Gregor's disguise. The guards were "on loan" to the sanctuary, although the housemaster had made no request for protection. The guards were there to act more as the emperor's eyes than to protect the sorcerers from the mundane citizenry.

Gregor clenched his jaw and kept his head down as he merged into the flow of pedestrians. He crossed to the opposite side of the street and matched his pace to the others. A man in dirty workman's clothes looked at the guard closing the sanctuary gate and then at Gregor with a suspicious narrowing of his eyes. Gregor rolled his eyes and shook his head while muttering the word "sorcerers" under his breath. The man returned a grim nod.

The disguised councilor walked along Southwest Merchant Avenue past small shops and residences that were built so close together that they often touched. The poorly-maintained buildings sagged and leaned upon each other for support, with loose planks and posts that were dark grey and cracked with age. The poor laborers of this district had neither time nor money to invest in repairs. In most cases, they didn't own the buildings they inhabited anyway.

Like most of the foot traffic, Gregor stayed away from the middle of the roadway, which was littered here and there with dung from the ponies that pulled delivery carts through the city. Horses were not allowed within the walls of Cassandria. The only conveyances permitted inside the city were narrow carts pulled by short, round ponies. The ponies were shod with leather booties, which gave them a better grip on the flagstone that paved the city's streets and quieted their clopping at the same time. Each pony wore four small bells on their harness to warn pedestrians of their approach.

All deliveries that arrived at the gates had to be transferred to one or more of the pony carts. This requirement gave the Imperial Guard a convenient opportunity to check for contraband and to levy a transportation fee "to cover the cost of operating and maintaining the carts." The Guard's monopoly over transportation within the city was the source of much grumbling among the merchants, although those same merchants had no qualms about passing the additional expense on to their customers.

Gregor reached West Road and glanced toward the city's west gate. Men were busily transferring large sacks from a wagon parked outside the city to a pair of pony carts parked just inside the gate. People entering and leaving the city streamed through the gateway, dodging the sweating laborers.

Upon entering through one of the city gates, visitors to Cassandria were presented with a long, straight "compass road" that led directly to the Imperial Palace. The high-walled palace was positioned in the very center of the city, its peaked upper level towering over all of the other buildings. North Road ran from the north gate to the palace gates. The other roads ended at Central Avenue, which was a circular street that circumnavigated the outside of the palace walls.

The compass roads divided the city into quarters. The northeast quarter, known as Nobility Quarter, was the finest. Wizard Quarter, the southwest quarter where the sanctuary was located, was the poorest. The quality of the buildings in the Merchant Quarter to the southeast and Spirit Quarter to the northwest were a sharp step down from the affluence of the Nobility Quarter, but they were also far more pleasant than the squalor of the Wizard Quarter.

Gregor slipped into the thicker foot traffic that moved along West Road and focused his attention on the distant palace walls. The ambient noise of the city increased along the wide compass roads. The jingle of pony harnesses mixed with the constant, incomprehensible din of many people talking and shouting out greetings, offers, or warnings. Street vendors hawked food and other wares from small tables and carts along the roadside. The foot traffic variably flowed toward the center of the road around the vendors or away from the center when pony carts, led by stern-faced guardsman and followed by anxious merchants, jingled down the roadway.

No one paid attention to the tall, thin tradesman who moved among them toward the palace. Gregor's disguise rendered him virtually invisible. If he had remained in his fine sorcerer robes, the crowd would have parted around him even more readily than it did for the ponies. For this mission, he needed to avoid that kind of attention.

Traffic thickened and slowed noticeably after he passed Nobility Avenue and approached Central Avenue. As the crowd around him intensified, the councilor paid close attention to the street urchins who darted through the narrow gaps. He took careful note of those among his fellow pedestrians who seemed to move with more stealth than purpose. The vest pocket that held his casting orb was safe compared to a dangling purse, but when it came to a skilled pickpocket, safety was relative.

Gregor had no more than finished that thought when he was bumped from behind and pushed into a young couple ahead of him. As he apologized to them, he felt the weight of his vest pocket lighten and he reached behind to grasp a retreating arm.

The dirty-faced urchin Gregor had caught stared in surprise at the orb that filled his little hand. The child's brown eyes widened in terror and he abruptly looked up at Gregor's stern face. Panic lent strength to his skinny arm as he twisted it expertly to break Gregor's grip, and he dropped the orb as if it had burst aflame. Gregor caught the orb as it fell from the child's hand, slipping it back into his pocket while the young thief melted into the crowd.

The whole exchange had taken only a few seconds. None of the people streaming around him seemed to have noticed the orb. The child would undoubtedly tell his friends that a sorcerer was in the crowd, but Gregor would be long gone by then. He fell back into the flow of traffic and decided he would take a different route on the return trip to the sanctuary.

Few people knew the streets of Cassandria better than Gregor. The Rissik family had helped build the city, and he visited his ancestral home whenever his duties at the Archives allowed. His visits weren't just for the pleasure of visiting family, however. His family had served the Imperial line since the first Emperor Tanes received his crown more than three centuries ago. That family history imparted additional duties upon Gregor that the other Archives councilors knew nothing about.

After circling the palace wall on Central Avenue, Gregor was relieved to finally step out of the milling crowd and walk through the palace gates. The four gate guards looked him over when he entered the courtyard, but made no move to stop him.

The palace rose three full stories in height and had a large cupola at the peak of the third story. It was the tallest building in Cassandria, since the emperor had decreed that no other construction in the city could exceed two floors. The lowest floor was made entirely of stone, while the second and third levels were a combination of stone framework and log walls. Gregor had always thought it resembled a giant hunting lodge.

The palace was not as large as one might expect. The structure left plenty of room in the courtyard that surrounded it for gardens, livestock pens, and outbuildings. If necessary, the palace could survive a siege for quite some time, although the walls and the building itself would not resist heavy bombardment for long.

Gregor walked up the path toward the short steps that fanned out from the palace entrance. To his right, two large pigs were lying flat in livestock pens, absorbing the sun that had just risen above the eastern wall. The sheep were gathered at a pile of feed that had been tossed into their enclosure.

The doors to the palace stood open, and Gregor stepped out of the warm sun into the cool, dark antechamber of the Great Hall. As soon as he entered, a lieutenant of the guard approached him and asked him his business. As his eyes adjusted to the darker space, he noticed two more guards at the closed doors to the Great Hall.

When he drew closer, the guard recognized Gregor and snorted in amusement at his clothing.

"You know the routine, Councilor," he said, holding out his hand.

Gregor removed the dagger from his waist and handed it to the guard. He also removed his focusing orb and handed it to the man. The guard frowned at the orb, and closed his hand around it. He went back to his desk and placed both items in one of the drawers. The guard returned to Gregor who obligingly raised his arms so the guard could check him for additional weapons and implements of sorcery. Satisfied that Gregor was disarmed, the guard nodded to the two other men, and they opened the doors to the Great Hall for him.

The councilor left the low-ceilinged antechamber and stepped down a few steps into the expansive space of the Great Hall. A wide maroon and gold carpet ran from the hall doors to the base of the throne dais at the far end of the room. Giant log columns, each fully three feet in diameter and dark with age, were evenly spaced on either side of the carpeted walkway. Four guards stood along the walls, two on each side of the room. Their relaxed stance was a sure sign that the emperor was not in attendance.

Other than the guards, the only person present was Seneschal Sorman Tanes. The emperor's steward was hunched over a document at his seat on the dais, the scratch of his quill audible across the length of the hall.

Visitors from foreign lands were often surprised and confused by the emperor's throne, such as it was. At the time of his coronation, Meritus Tanes had received his first oaths of fealty from the encompassing seat of a huge and ornately carved throne, as one might expect. But two years into his reign, he had the massive throne pushed to the back wall of the dais where it still loomed. He replaced the throne with a comfortable, high-backed chair and put it behind a long and heavy table. His seneschal sat to his right, and the rarely-occupied chair to his left was reserved for his empress.

Initially, the seneschal had been apoplectic that the emperor would break with tradition in such a way. But the emperor had insisted that the throne was impractical and unsafe. He felt small and exposed sitting on the old throne in front of the entire hall. His table gave him a convenient surface on which to place documents and refreshments.

The table also gave him protection. A thick panel with the Imperial rampant eagle carved into it ran across the front. The top was hinged so it could be raised as a shield in the unlikely event of an assassination attempt.

The scandalized seneschal had eventually relented when he learned that palace visitors were intimidated by the massive table. Although the unorthodox arrangement diluted the impression of royalty, it heightened the impression of judgment, which was arguably more discomforting to supplicants. In time, the seneschal also grew to appreciate the convenience of a seated workspace and became proud of his privileged seat next to the emperor.

As Gregor approached the dais, Sorman looked up from his work and set down his quill with a slow and deliberate motion. He sat back in his seat and looked down his nose at Gregor. In a challenging tone, he asked, "Do you have something to report, Councilor?" The elderly man bitterly resented the fact that he was rarely included in the discussions between Gregor and the emperor. He didn't seem to realize that his open contempt for sorcerers was exactly what kept him out of those meetings.

The seneschal was one of the emperor's many cousins. He was the child of a great uncle whose line, while royal, was not in direct contention for the throne. Had he wished it, Sorman could have asked for an appointment as a town minister, or even a province governor, but his fussy attention to detail and lack of desire for leadership made him perfect for the administrative role he now held and had served in for several decades. He was the emperor's gatekeeper, and he relished that responsibility. The fact that some sorcerer could show up unannounced and get instant access to the emperor, effectively side-stepping his control over the emperor's schedule, was an affront.

"I do have something to report, Seneschal Tanes," replied Gregor with a slight bow. The terseness of his answer supplied the rebuke he couldn't utter.

The seneschal glared at Gregor for a moment and grumbled in frustration. He finally sighed and rose stiffly from his seat, knowing he'd get nothing more out of the councilor. They'd danced to this tune on many occasions before. Pursuing the matter would only end with the emperor telling Sorman to mind his own business.

Sorman took his time shuffling around the table and down the dais steps. Gregor followed him to a large tapestry that hung from the west wall. The seneschal pulled aside the tapestry to reveal a door. He opened the door and stood aside, holding the tapestry so the councilor could enter the room. "I'll let His Majesty know you're here," Sorman muttered as he closed the door, leaving Gregor alone in the room.

Knowing that Emperor Tanes was a busy man and that he might have to wait a while, Gregor went over to the long, heavy table that practically filled the room. He took a seat at one of the two dozen chairs arrayed along the sides.

Although the room was officially called the Map Room, the more military minded often referred to it as the War Room. Almost every inch of wall was covered with modern maps inked on animal hide and ancient tapestries depicting famous battle scenes. One set of antique maps showed countries and borders that no longer existed. The room was both a modern chamber for devising strategy and a museum of imperial history. The thick stone exterior wall and the hangings muffled all sound. In the soothing heavy silence, the councilor's neck and back muscles started to release some of the tension from his walk through the streets of Cassandria.

Gregor sat back in his chair and tried to compose his thoughts. He needed to present his news to the emperor honestly, but in a way that would not cause too much alarm. He had to convince the emperor that the situation was best left in the hands of the sorcerers, at least for the moment. Any action on the emperor's part would be premature and make the Integrationist opposition leaders move even more secretively than they already were.

His musings were interrupted by the sound of heavy booted steps and the jingle of mail outside a second door to the room. A deep voice murmured instructions and one set of booted steps faded away. Gregor had no doubt that the second man was sent to guard the door through which he had entered from the Great Hall.

Gregor got up from his seat as soon as he heard the noises outside the room. By the time Emperor Meritus Tanes entered, Gregor had dropped to one knee and bowed his head. "Greetings, Your Majesty. I hope things are well with you," he said to the floor.

"You may rise, Councilor Rissik, and please sit down. I trust your journey was uneventful?"

Gregor rose to his feet to find that the emperor was looking him over with the same bemused expression that the guard in the antechamber had worn. Although Gregor frequently disguised his vocation on these occasional visits to the palace, everyone seemed to find his trader's garb the most amusing.

The emperor was dressed in a maroon doublet trimmed in gold thread and silk pantaloons with white hose up to his knee. Over the doublet, he wore a light silk jacket with loose, flowing sleeves. He stood a good head shorter than Gregor and had a more stocky build. The man's dimpled smile seemed genuine as it was echoed in his grey-green eyes.

Gregor settled back into his seat at the same time the emperor took his place at the head of the table. "Yes, Your Majesty, my journey went well."

Emperor Tanes gestured at the pitcher of watered wine that sat on the table. "Pour us a drink, councilor, and tell me how things are going at the Archives."

Gregor poured each of them a cup of wine and set one in front of the emperor. As protocol dictated, Gregor drank first. The emperor would wait for a few minutes before taking a sip from his cup.

"I do have a bit of news to report, Your Majesty."

The emperor nodded for him to continue.

"A Portal Key was recently stolen from the residence of former councilor Ebnik Vlastorus. Our newly-appointed Sword Sorceress was dispatched to find the thieves and recover the device. She was successful, but in the process she discovered that a sorcerer was behind the theft and that this sorcerer had set up shop in a fishing village on Teardrop Lake."

The emperor chuckled and said, "I'm surprised the villagers put up with that. It hardly seems worthwhile to establish a sanctuary in a fishing village."

Gregor shook his head. "He wasn't setting up a sanctuary, Your Majesty. He was fabricating mind control amulets and testing them on the villagers."

The emperor sat forward and narrowed his eyes at Gregor. "I trust the situation has been dealt with?"

"Yes, Your Majesty. The sorcerer was driven out and the village is safe now, but the perpetrator escaped."

Emperor Tanes relaxed back into his seat and took a sip from his wine cup. He pondered Gregor's news for a moment and then looked sharply at the councilor. More as a statement than a question, he said, "There's more to tell, isn't there?"

Gregor looked down at the table and absently rotated his cup a couple of times. "Yes, Your Majesty. The rogue sorcerer was a man named Paeter Thoron, a known Integrationist sympathizer. We believe he had an accomplice who posed as a student at the Archives. While we were distracted by searching for Paeter and researching his amulets, the accomplice successfully acquired a second Portal Key from the Archives itself and escaped with it."

The emperor was taken aback. "How is that possible? I thought such devices were kept in the Archives armory and that the armory was secure." Many powerful and dangerous devices were stored in the Archives armory. The emperor was clearly alarmed by the idea that it could be breached.

Gregor spoke quickly to calm the emperor. "I assure you that the armory is still secure, Your Majesty. The thief managed to get in through a clever combination of observation, timing, and stealth. Also, we have verified that nothing but the Portal Key and some of the amulets we confiscated from the village were taken."

The emperor was silent for a moment. He didn't seem entirely convinced by Gregor's assurances, but then he waved his hand, prompting Gregor to continue.

Gregor obliged him. "What the thief apparently does not know is that the Portal Key he stole has a Seeker attuned to it, thanks to the foresight of Wizard Vlastorus. Sword Sorceress Delano should be able to track the thief and recover the Portal Key just as she did before."

The emperor gave Gregor a satisfied nod. "Good. It sounds like you have the situation well in hand. Make sure it stays that way. I want a progress report every week until you catch the Portal Key thief and bring this Paeter Thoron to justice."

Gregor bowed his head in acquiescence. "Yes, of course, Your Majesty."

The emperor sighed deeply and took another sip of his wine. "Now, tell me about my daughter. How is she doing?"

Gregor's mouth twisted into a half smile. "Lissy is making all of us proud, Your Majesty. She is the most accomplished alchemist we've seen in a generation. She has virtually taken over as alchemy professor and is growing into a confident and beautiful woman."

The emperor smiled as well. "I'm glad she's doing well. Is she still all about study and work, or has she finally put a young man under her spell."

Gregor chuckled politely at the emperor's joke and answered, "She's as dedicated as ever, but she does seem to have taken an interest in a new apprentice."

The emperor's forehead wrinkled in puzzlement. "A new apprentice. Wouldn't he be a little young for her?"

"Not this one," Gregor said. "Sword Sorceress Delano discovered this man during her mission to deal with sorcerer Thoron, and as I understand it, he was quite a help to her.

When she learned he had the ability to channel, she convinced him to attend the College of Sorcery at the Archives."

The emperor raised an eyebrow. "I'm guessing there's more to that story as well."

Gregor snorted. "Yes, Your Majesty. You'd be guessing correctly. If your daughter develops a genuine interest in this man Jaylan, I suspect she'll have to compete with our Sword Sorceress for him."

Emperor Tanes nodded once and pushed his wine cup away. "A little competition will be good for her. Is there anything else, Councilor?"

"Not at the moment, Your Majesty," Gregor answered.

The emperor moved his chair back and stood, and Gregor followed his lead. The emperor's face tightened and he looked straight into Gregor's eyes. "The Archives must get this situation with Sorcerer Thoron under control immediately, particularly if it is part of some kind of Integrationist plot. I will not have citizens of the empire being abused by rogue sorcerers. I can assure you that you don't want me to get involved in this matter, Councilor Rissik."

Gregor had expected the warning, but he paled anyway under the intense stare of the emperor. He bowed deeply and managed to respond without a quaver in his voice, "I understand completely, Your Majesty. We shall move with all haste."

"See that you do," the emperor said as he turned on his heel and exited the room.

After the emperor had departed and the door was closed behind him, Gregor stared pensively up at the wall and the map of the empire that hung there. He mumbled aloud to himself, "Where are you Paeter, and what are you up to?"

His eyes rested on the tiny dot that marked the small waterside town of Delta, Paeter's last known location. His eyes rose up the map, north past the Archives and on to another dot labeled Riverview. Thunderhead College, a haven for sorcerers with Integrationist convictions was nearby, and Gregor would not be surprised in the least to learn that the college's snake of a headmaster, Dumont Fortenz was somehow involved in this mess.

The door to the Great Hall opened and the seneschal held the tapestry back for Gregor so he could leave the room. Sorman must have noticed Gregor's consternation because the seneschal's expression relaxed into a smug, self-satisfied smirk, rather than the air of bored, longsuffering patience he normally affected. Neither man spoke as Sorman escorted Gregor back to the antechamber.

The lieutenant must have taken heed of the councilor's preoccupation as well, for he said nothing when he returned Gregor's belongings. The man's parting wish for the councilor to have a good day was nearly inaudible.

On his way back to the Cassandria sanctuary, Gregor considered the difficult task that lay ahead. He had to convince the rest of the Archives Council that the situation with the stolen Portal Key was critical. It might even be necessary to hint that failure to take action could invite Imperial intervention, although he'd have to be careful how he presented that information. It wouldn't do for the other council members to know exactly how well-informed the emperor was. Or who did the informing.

CHAPTER 17
KEY DELIVERY

Dumont - Headmaster's Office, Thunderhead College

Dumont Fortenz, Headmaster of Thunderhead College, was deep in conversation with his Head Prefect, Paeter Thoron, when someone knocked at the door to his study. They both stopped talking and looked up at the suntracker on the wall. It was early evening, which was an unusual time for them to be interrupted.

Paeter got up and went to the door. He opened it just enough to see who waited on the other side, and then stepped back pulling the door wide. Lohan Fletcher walked into the room, his wet clothes hanging heavily from his thin form. Water dripped from the rim of his wide-brimmed hat as he reached up and removed it.

Dumont stood, holding up the flat of his hand to stop Lohan from stepping any further into the room. "Lohan. I'm glad you made it. I see the rain we've been expecting has arrived as well."

Lohan ran a hand through his damp, stringy hair. "Yes, Master. The rain caught up to me a few miles out." He looked at the floor where a small puddle of water was pooling at his feet. "Sorry for the mess, but I thought I should come and see you right away."

Paeter gave Lohan's appearance a disapproving look and said, "What took you so long?"

Lohan looked blankly at Paeter and replied, "There were complications. It took time to arrange access to the Portal Key, and I had to detour toward Northshore to throw the pursuing riders off my trail." He narrowed his eyes and added, "At least I completed my task and got the key."

Paeter inhaled sharply and drew himself up. "No one expected the Archives to react so quickly when the first key was taken. Besides, I accomplished an important part of our mission during my stay in that spirit-forsaken village."

Dumont raised his voice and interrupted them. "No need to argue. We've had some setbacks, but everything is moving forward as planned. Where's the key?"

Lohan reached into his cloak and took out a soft leather pouch. A long object within the pouch poked at the top and bottom, and a couple of other items rattled inside as he hesitantly handed it to Paeter. Snatching the pouch, Paeter walked it over to the headmaster. Dumont untied the strings and carefully poured its contents onto his desk. The first item to emerge was a short wooden wand with a ruby set in one end. Two familiar-looking amulets slid out next.

Upon seeing the amulets, Paeter turned back to Lohan and hissed, "You fool! You took my amulets from them as well? Why didn't you just stand in Council Hall and announce that we are all working together?"

Lohan pointed his hat at Paeter and shouted back, "You weren't there. I was. They were investigating the amulets, and I thought the less they knew about them, the better."

Dumont broke in smoothly, keeping his tone even. "It doesn't matter, Paeter. I'm sure they would have made the connection between you and Lohan by now anyway. Taking the amulets wasn't necessary, but it might prove to be an inconvenience for them. The important thing is that we have the Portal Key." Dumont held up the small wand and twisted his mouth into a half-smile.

Lohan crossed his arms, calmed by Dumont's support. Paeter clenched his jaw and continued to glare at Lohan, but said nothing more.

Dumont waved Lohan toward the door. "Go change into some dry clothes and get yourself something to eat. We can talk more tomorrow after you've rested."

Lohan gave Dumont a slight bow and said, "Yes, Master. Thank you."

As Lohan turned to leave the room, Dumont said, "And tell the house staff to have someone come clean up this mess."

Lohan looked back down at the puddle on the floor behind him and nodded, "Yes, Master, I'll do that."

Dumont turned his attention to Paeter. "Close the door for a moment."

Paeter closed the door and returned to Dumont's desk, careful to avoid Lohan's puddle.

Dumont held up the Portal Key in the palm of his hand. He was a little surprised that the smith had created it in the form of a wand. Wands were not as convenient to carry nor as durable as many of the other forms an implement could take. Nevertheless, some sorcerers had an inexplicable preference for wand-shaped implements. "Do you think this is the same key that was taken from Wizard Vlastorus?"

Paeter shook his head once. "No. The other key was in the form of a ring."

Dumont let out his breath and set the wand down on his desk. "Good. The Archives agents were able to find and intercept the thieves you hired a little too easily. I believe that was because Wizard Vlastorus had made a Seeker for his key."

Paeter nodded. "I agree. That was the same conclusion I reached. But the odds of anyone else doing that, particularly for a key that was stored in the armory, are fairly low, don't you think?"

Dumont considered for a moment, and then said, "Yes, but we should keep the possibility in mind. We should expect a visit from an Archives team eventually. Even if they don't have a Seeker, Lohan may not have successfully misdirected them toward Northshore."

Dumont picked up the amulets and handed them to Paeter. He put the Portal Key wand back into the leather pouch and tucked it into a desk drawer. He'd find a more secure place for it shortly when no one else was around.

Looking at Paeter, he said in a serious tone, "We need to move quickly now. We have the key, so there's no more time to fuss with the amulets."

Paeter smiled and inclined his head slightly. "I understand, Master. After our successful test with Minister Bogard and my adjustments since then, I'm confident the amulets are ready now."

Someone knocked tentatively on the door and a muffled voice asked if the headmaster had called for housekeeping.

Dumont lowered his voice. "I'm glad to hear that. We'll finalize our plans tomorrow morning and move forward with the next step of the operation within the next couple of days."

Paeter bowed in acknowledgement of the dismissal. On his way out, he let the maid in to clean up the watery mess on the floor.

While the servant girl worked, Dumont stared out a window into the deepening darkness outside and watched drops of rain slide down the glass panels. Smiling at his reflection, he felt a thrill shoot down his spine. The past few years of preparation and planning were finally leading to something tangible. Thanks to Paeter, he could be in control of his first province within the week.

CHAPTER 18

SPIRIT FISH

Jaylan ~ Castle Tarn, The Archives

Sulana and I sat together at the end of the short pier that extended out onto Castle Tarn. The Archives bailey wall was at our backs, just a short walk away. The morning sun had risen above the eastern peak of the granite amphitheatre that embraced the small lake on three sides, and a light mist from evaporating dew floated from the shrubs along the shore over the water. The mirrored surface was marred only by the splash of an occasional jumping fish.

"I can't believe you won't let me go with you," I complained.

Sulana sighed and said, "My team was created for missions like this, and you aren't part of that yet. You are still in training, and this mission requires skilled sorcerers."

"Three members of your team aren't sorcerers at all!" I exclaimed, louder than I intended. My voice echoed back at me from across the lake, and I felt embarrassed for disturbing the peaceful morning.

Sulana's voice grew stern. "Don't yell at me. You know I'm right."

"Sorry," I said, and I meant it.

Sulana put her hand in mine. "We've been over this already. Let's not ruin our time here arguing about something that isn't going to change."

I looked over at her and her smile convinced me that she was right. I had no idea how long she'd be gone on her mission, and I really did want to make the best of this short time together before she left. I smiled back, and then leaned over and kissed her. "You're right. I'm just worried about what might happen and frustrated that I can't go with you."

She leaned over and rested her head on my shoulder. "I understand. I'm sure you'll be able to go with us before too long."

I snorted. "Yeah, the mighty Sword Sorceress and Sword Sorcerer riding forth to tame those who would defy the Sorcery Accords."

She sat up and looked squarely at me. "What are you talking about?"

Oops. This is not how I intended to break the news to her.

I tried to think of a good way to explain away my slip, but concluded that I should just forge ahead with the truth. "Talon asked me to consider Sword Sorcerer training. I told him I'd have to talk to you about it."

Sulana slipped her hand from mine and frowned at the water. "You just got here, and you're still having misgivings about becoming a sorcerer. Why would you want to make a commitment to an organization you know almost nothing about that is populated by people you don't know?"

"You doubt my sincerity?"

"No. I just don't understand where this is coming from. Are you considering the training just to be closer to me? If so, that's not a good enough reason. Becoming a Sword Sorcerer is a serious matter."

I took a deep breath. Was this all about being closer to her? Maybe partly, but not entirely.

"You're right. It is serious, and I've been thinking about it a lot. I know how hard you worked to become a Sword Sorceress, and I don't mean to trivialize what you've achieved. I just want to prepare myself as best I can so I can hold my own and be more of a help than a hindrance. Sword Sorcerer training would be the best way to do that."

I couldn't tell if she was objecting because she didn't want me to try, or if she was just cautioning me on making a hasty decision. Either way, her reaction was depressing. "Don't worry about it. I'll probably wash out anyway."

She turned her head quickly and squinted at me. "You don't believe that. I don't believe it either. And if you *do* believe it, you shouldn't even begin the training."

"So you think I shouldn't petition the Council?"

"I didn't say that. I just think you should wait until you're sure that's what you want to do. The Archives can always use another Sword Sorcerer. This job has its…hazards."

I reached for her hand, and she hesitantly allowed me to take it. I said gently, "I want to face those hazards with you. If becoming a Sword Sorcerer is the best way to prepare myself, then that's what I want to do."

She nodded slowly. "It is a good fit for your abilities. Just be sure it's what you want. You'd have to complete the training and commit to the position for five years."

She scooted closer to me and I put my arm around her shoulders. We looked down into the water for a few moments, allowing ourselves to relax. The warmth of her body against mine helped the tension drain from my back, and I could tell our embrace had a similar relaxing effect on her.

Wanting to change the subject, I asked her, "Now, why do you suppose that fish is watching us? It has been going back and forth and stopping here as if it's listening to our conversation." The fish in question was a long, dark trout of some kind. If I had a spear handy, it might have become dinner.

Sulana answered dreamily, "Maybe it's a spirit fish."

I chuckled and mumbled, "That's a good one. I wonder if spirit fish are tastier than regular fish."

"You don't believe in the spirits?" she asked.

That brought me up short. We had never discussed religion or spirituality, and I didn't think it would be a good idea to get into the subject when she was about to leave, but I couldn't leave her question unanswered.

"I've never had much exposure to religion. Our family respected the traditions of the druids, but we never attended the temple rituals," I said.

Sulana sat up straighter, but stayed at my side. "I'm not talking about religion. I'm talking about the spirits." She took off one of her shoes and slipped her bare foot down into the water, swirling it around. I expected the fish to dart away, but it just changed direction and continued to watch us.

I wasn't sure what she was getting at. To me, religion and spirits were one and the same. Druids worshipped the spirits, and you either believed in them or you didn't.

"Do you mean the myths like sprites and nymphs? I never gave them much thought. I always figured they were just another invention of the druids to feed overactive imaginations."

Sulana laughed. "The fish says you are foolish not to believe what you see with your own eyes."

I looked at the fish. It floated in position, barely moving its fins while it watched us. I shuddered and the back of my neck tingled.

Sulana pulled her foot from the water. It had turned red from the cold, and when she folded her leg into her lap, I reached out to massage some warmth back into her frigid toes.

"Put your foot into the water," she told me.

"What? Are you nuts? That water is freezing!" I exclaimed, opening the hand that massaged her cold, wet foot in emphasis.

"Just trust me for a minute," she said.

I was willing to do just about anything to maintain the relatively peaceful conversation we were having, so I took off my shoe and put my foot into the water. The shock of the cold was everything I expected and more. I nearly yanked my foot back out of the water, but Sulana placed her hand on my knee to encourage me to keep it in.

"Now, open a channel through the water to the fish. Keep the flow of vaetra to a small trickle at first."

Her request confused me. I knew that sorcerers could open channels to one another, but to animals? What would I be trying to accomplish? Frowning in concentration, I tried what she suggested. I had never channeled through water before, so it was a strange sensation to feel the channel open through my foot and then diffuse into the water. I concentrated on linking with the fish and felt the channel focus more narrowly in the fish's direction. The fish obligingly came closer to complete the connection, nearly breaking my concentration with its unexpected cooperation.

I felt the channel snap into place and I let vaetra flow through the link to the fish. I experimentally allowed a stronger flow, but the fish only accepted a portion of it, not unlike an implement. The fish took only what it needed. While I marveled at this bizarre experience, my foot began to tingle from more than the icy water. I felt a strange pressure on my mind, and then a message flashed through my conscious. It wasn't a voice exactly, more like an impression of a meaning. The message was simply, "Thank you for the gift." Message delivered, the fish disconnected from the link and slowly swam away.

Sulana was looking up at me with a tender smile, watching my face closely. "Pretty neat, huh?"

As soon as the fish closed the link, I pulled my foot back out of the water and used my sleeve to dry it off. My heart was pounding and my mind reeled with trying to understand how a fish could talk to me. "What just happened? Are we able to talk to all animals like that?"

Sulana laughed. "Nope. Just spirit animals."

I looked at her closely to see if she was joking or making fun of me. She just continued to smile back at me.

"You're kidding, right? Spirit animals are real?" I'd heard stories all my life about how spirit animals were like regular animals, but they behaved with intelligence and could even communicate with people. I'd never truly believed the stories before, but it was hard to argue with personal experience. I looked around the lake to make sure we were still alone and that Sulana wasn't playing some joke on me, but I saw no one.

"As real as the spirits," she answered with a matter-of-fact tone.

Her answer only increased my confusion, so I decided to come clean. "To tell the truth, I've never really believed in the spirits. The druids teach that the spirits surround us and make things grow; that they protect us when we respect the land and punish us when we don't. Are you saying that's all true?"

Sulana shook her head. "Not exactly. The druids teach a simple message for simple understanding. The truth is a lot more complicated, as it often is."

"So, what's the truth?" I asked. She had my attention now. I'm just not the kind of person who can blindly believe in spirits I couldn't see. The possibility of there being a real explanation for spirits was something that interested me. At the same time, I was a little uncomfortable with the religious implications.

Sulana seemed to sense my hesitance, so she spoke slowly and calmly. "The spirits are pure vaetric beings. They have no physical body, but they can temporarily inhabit lesser animals like the fish we just met. That 'spirit fish' was really a sprite who protects these waters and decided to observe us. The sprite is what spoke to you. It takes a lot of energy for them to communicate with us, so out of courtesy, we replenish them with some of our own vaetra."

I took a moment to fit what Sulana was telling me into my understanding of the myths. The druids taught that spirit animals and plants served the spirits that protected them. The druids also taught that sprites inhabited the waters and dryads the trees. The drawings and sculptures of the spirits always showed some tiny human form.

But spirit animals weren't special, they were just ordinary animals that were temporarily possessed by a spirit. And the spirits themselves didn't have a physical form, much less the appearance of a tiny human. Spirits were certainly extraordinary creatures, but in the end they were just another life form trying to protect their habitat, not the all-knowing beings the druids convinced people to worship.

"It's all a lie," I mumbled in conclusion to myself. I had always suspected as much, but surprisingly, I was a little disappointed to have it confirmed.

"Not at all," Sulana said quickly. "The mundane can't sense the spirits or communicate with them as easily as we sorcerers can, so they must take the existence of the spirits on faith. The druids have taken some liberties by explaining the spirits in terms everyone can understand, but their message is based in the truth."

I rolled my eyes. "Yes, but the message itself is a lie. Their religion is a lie. Spirituality is a lie."

Sulana looked down into the water for a moment before saying more. "I once had the same misgivings that you are having now. Ebnik told me something that his mentor had imparted to him. He said that spirituality isn't about religion or gods. Spirituality is about acceptance; acceptance of yourself, of others, and of the world around you."

I felt something ring inside my head. I felt the truth of what she said, and I knew I'd never forget it. I gathered her into a hug and kissed the top of her head. I spoke into her hair, "You never cease to amaze me. I don't know how or why our lives came together, but I'll be forever grateful to whatever fate or spirit made it happen."

"I'm thankful as well," she said quietly. "But I worry about what might happen to you too, you know. I have no idea what I'm going to find on this mission. We might catch up to Lohan and discover he has friends. I wouldn't want you to get hurt."

"Hey, I did okay when we took on Paeter Thoron," I said.

"Yes, but you were already in the middle of that situation and we knew we were dealing with a single sorcerer. Ebnik was with us, so you weren't expected to hold your own in a battle of sorcery."

She was trying to make me feel better about staying behind, but her mention of sorcery battles just made me more anxious about her leaving. "Are you expecting to get into a battle of sorcery?"

She shuddered in my arms. "I hope not," she answered. "I'll be prepared with several offensive and defensive implements, and even though using an implement is faster than casting a spell, I'll have limited options compared to a sorcerer who can cast any spell he knows. My lack of casting ability almost cost me the Confirmation, but the Council was desperate for a Sword Sorcerer."

I knew I was returning to dangerous waters, but I wanted her to start thinking positive thoughts about us working side-by-side in the future. "Well, there you go. Between the two of us, we can be prepared for twice as many contingencies."

She looked up at me and gave me a wry smile. "Yes, and then again, you might be able to cast."

I snorted. "What are the odds?"

She shrugged. "About even, actually."

"About even? I had no idea the odds were that good. We really would make a great team. You'd have speed and I'd have diversity. Wouldn't that be excellent?"

I waited for her answer as Sulana disengaged from my arms and slipped her shoe back on. She stood up and held her hand out to help me up. As I rose, she finally spoke. "The Council would be very pleased."

Sulana still seemed unconvinced that I was making the right decision, but I hoped she'd get used to the idea over time. In spite of her misgivings, my conviction was growing stronger by the moment. I still needed time to think it through, but deep inside, I was beginning to feel that becoming a Sword Sorcerer was just the kind of opportunity I had been seeking since I lost my position with the Imperial Guard.

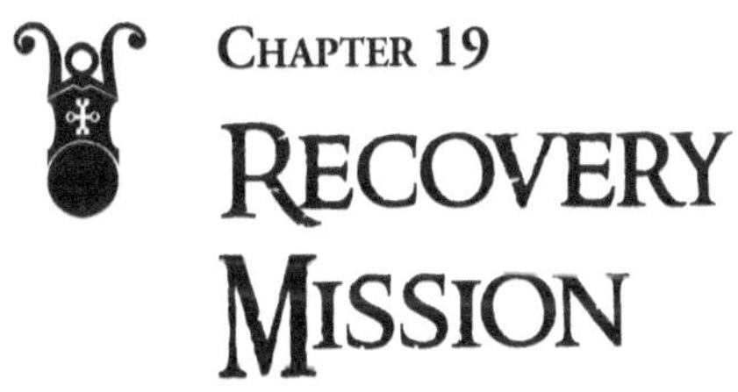

CHAPTER 19

RECOVERY MISSION

Jaylan ~ Dining Hall, The Archives

I sat near a window in the Dining Hall, picking absently at a pastry and looking up every few seconds to see if the Council messenger had arrived yet. Councilor Rissik had promised to put Sulana's mission first on the afternoon's agenda. Through the window, I could see Sulana assembling her team at the stables on the assumption that Councilor Underwood would support the mission. I tried to convince myself that I was just staying out of the way, but the truth was that I was sulking about having to stay behind.

When the messenger flashed past the dining room doors, I watched intently as he ran out to the stables and spoke briefly with Sulana. I was up from my seat and on my way out the moment I saw him jog back toward the castle entrance. I intercepted him as he came in, and he confirmed that the Council had voted in favor of the journey.

The cold wind tugged at my cloak as I stepped outside, working its way into every loose fold. Although it was nearly June, the high mountains still turned wintry when a storm blew in from the north. The courtyard was tinted white from the icy beads of snow that the clouds had sprinkled around. More of the tiny snowballs bounced to the ground as I walked swiftly over to the stable, clutching my cloak closed across my chest.

Sulana and her team had saddled their horses and were making final preparations for their journey. I briefly considered saddling Patches so I could at least ride out part of the way with them. But joining them would only cause confusion and agitation if anyone from the Council observed my departure. I needed to get back inside before too long for my next alchemy lesson anyway.

Talon spotted me walking over and nodded in my direction. I nodded back. I was glad to see that he was going on this trip for a couple of reasons. He would do everything he could to protect Sulana, and I'd be off the hook from his intense style of sword training for a while. I'd promised to keep up my practice while he was gone, but sparring with Benjamin and the other trainees would be more like exercise than training.

Barek and his horse made the others look like children with their ponies. His northern war horse was 18 hands tall, which suited Barek's oversized frame. Standing more than six-and-a-half feet tall himself, he was easily able to reach over the animal to adjust the straps of his saddle bags. What Barek lacked in Talon's finesse and style with a blade, he made up for in sheer power. After sparring sessions with him, I had walked away more than once with an arm numbed from stopping even his casual blows.

Daven actually smiled at me as I approached, which surprised me. Relations between us had gotten steadily worse as my relationship with Sulana grew more intimate. But now he seemed to accept that Sulana had made her choice, and alienating me would not help his friendship with her. Either that, or he had decided to bide his time. Whatever his motivations, I was thankful for having one less thing to worry about, and I smiled back.

Sulana was involved in a conversation with Ebnik and Lissy, so I approached Talon first, noting that Sulana's mother was absent. "Good morning, Weaponsmaster. I'm surprised Professor Delano isn't here to see you off."

Talon winked at my teasing remark and said, "We said our farewells earlier, and I convinced her that there was no point standing out here in the cold while I saddled my horse. What about you, Jaylan. What brings you outside on this blustery morning?"

"Oh, I just thought I'd get some fresh air," I answered. At the edge of my vision, I saw Daven roll his eyes and Barek shake his head.

Talon glanced over at Sulana and leaned in closer to me, lowering his voice. "This could be you, you know. The sooner you complete your training, the sooner you'll be able to ride out on missions. Besides, I'm getting too old for this sort of thing."

I chuckled and kept my voice low as well. "I don't believe that for a minute. You're still the weaponsmaster for a reason. But I know what you are getting at, and I've talked with Sulana about the possibility. She's not convinced it's the right choice for me yet, but I think the idea will grow on her after she's had time to think through the implications. If I decide to petition the Council and they accept it, perhaps we can start Sword Sorcerer training after you get back."

Talon grinned and stopped his preparations to shake my hand. "Glad to hear it! And don't worry about Sulana; she'll come around. Her mother and I will make sure of it."

Sulana glanced over in our direction at the mention of her name, and we both smiled at her. She narrowed her eyes at us but went back to her conversation with Ebnik.

"Safe journey, gentlemen," I said to the three men. "And good luck on your hunt." Barek lifted a hand in farewell.

Lissy moved aside to accommodate me in their conversational circle as I approached. Her welcoming smile was tinged with uncertainty, which did nothing to ease my own concerns for Sulana. Ebnik's expression was serious, and he spoke in low tones with none if his usual jocularity. His posture eased and his voice took on a more casual tone as I joined them.

Sulana responded to whatever Ebnik had been saying before I arrived. Her tone was as serious as his had been, but it was tinged with exasperation. "Stop worrying, Ebnik. I understand the danger, and I'm as prepared as I can be. I'll only confront Lohan if he's still alone."

"You may not even find him," Lissy said. "He has a two-day head start, and you only know that he initially went south on Trench Highway. He could have doubled back or gone in any direction once he reached Northshore."

Sulana looked questioningly at Ebnik and he gave her a subtle head shake. She looked down at the ground and said, "You're probably right, but Barek is a good tracker, so I have reason to believe we'll find him regardless of where he went."

Lissy looked back and forth between Ebnik and Sulana. "What are you not telling me?"

"Nothing," Sulana answered quickly. "I just refuse to believe we won't find Lohan after that little snake wormed his way in here and stole from us."

Lissy stared at Sulana for a moment with a calculating look. She obviously didn't believe that there was "nothing" more to be told any more than I did, but she didn't press the issue.

I wasn't sure what Sulana was hiding either, but I trusted her judgment regarding information that needed to remain secret. I interrupted to move the conversation along. "However you do it, I hope you manage to find Lohan and get back soon. Maybe next time I'll be able to go with you."

Sulana looked at me and then over at Talon. I glanced at him too. He pretended not to be listening and did not look back at us, but the bemused expression on his face as he readied his horse told me he had heard my comment.

"We'll see," she said. "If we catch Lohan and recover the Portal Key, maybe that will be the end of whatever plans he and Paeter had for them."

Lissy squinted at Sulana. "Do you believe that?"

Sulana looked down and shook her head. "No, not really. The Portal Keys are a means to an end. I don't think they'll abandon their plans just because they can't access the Portal Keep. But if we can get the key back, it may slow them down long enough for us to figure out what they are up to."

Ebnik nodded in agreement. "If you are able to capture Lohan, we may be able to question him and find out who else is involved. Perhaps Lissy can work up a fresh Elixir of Veracity," he said with a chuckle.

Lissy responded seriously to Ebnik's joke, "That's exactly what I plan to do." She looked at Sulana and said, "Bring Lohan back with you, and we'll get to the bottom of this once and for all."

I shrugged and said, "You're assuming Lohan knows the plan. He might just be an errand boy."

Lissy said, "That's fine. We can at least find out what he *does* know and who is sending him on these errands."

Sulana looked over her shoulder at her horse and said, "Well, I'd better finish getting ready. We've been delayed long enough and we need to get moving if we have any hope of catching up to Lohan."

Ebnik and Lissy took the hint and both of them gave Sulana a brief hug before walking off toward the castle. The wind blew their hair around and pressed their clothes tight to their bodies. Lissy glanced back at us with a smirk and a mischievous glint in her eye. I watched them walk away, glad to have a brief moment with Sulana before she left.

"Don't go getting too friendly with your alchemy teacher while I'm gone," Sulana said when I turned back to her. She said it lightly in a teasing voice, but her tone had an undercurrent of genuine concern.

"Don't worry about that," I said, and I hugged her close to me. While she was still in my arms, I looked down into her eyes and said, "You're the one I want." I kissed her deeply, and she responded hungrily, until Talon cleared his throat.

We released one another and I took a step back, still reveling in the flood of warmth I always got whenever I held her close. The cold wind just couldn't compete with that feeling. "Please be careful," I said.

"I will," she replied in a husky voice.

Sulana cleared her throat and gave her gear a final check before climbing up into her saddle. Everyone else was already mounted and ready to leave. Sulana reined her little appaloosa around and everyone started to head out.

"Good hunting," I called to them as they rode away. They all waved goodbye and Sulana gave me a farewell smile.

I watched them ride away until they exited the castle gates and my view was blocked by the bailey wall. I took a deep breath and let it out, hoping that Sulana would come back quickly and safely with Lohan in custody.

In the meantime, I had to get back inside and find out what Lissy had in store for me in alchemy class today.

CHAPTER 20
WHERE FAITH ENDS

Sulana ~ Alpine Lakes Trailhead, The Archives

Sulana looked back over her shoulder toward the Archives main gate, but she could no longer see Jaylan. He probably had the good sense to go back inside and get out of the cold.

She really did wish he was going with her, but it would have been selfish to invite him. He needed to focus on his training, and she couldn't let this simple recovery mission interfere with that. Taking him into the field untrained would only increase the danger to his safety and distract her from her duties.

Where did this idea of becoming a Sword Sorcerer come from, anyway? She suspected her mother's influence, probably working through Talon. She understood their concern for her safety, as long as they weren't thinking she could not take care of herself.

A brief thrill sparked in Sulana's chest when she thought about going on missions with Jaylan as Sword Sorcerer and Sorceress. To her knowledge, a couple had never sworn the Commitment together. But their relationship was at a delicate stage. Being lovers would complicate a working partnership. If things didn't work out between them, the situation would be even worse. She was trying to slow things down with Jaylan, but it was difficult. She was realistic enough to understand that her heart had no intention of letting things slow down.

She noticed that Talon had fallen back and was watching her while she silently deliberated.

When he saw he had her attention, he said, "Have faith in yourself and have faith in him. The rest will work itself out."

Sulana looked down at the neck of her horse and added in a low voice, "Or it won't."

She thought he might argue with her or chastise her for being negative, but he surprised her by saying, "Exactly. Where faith ends, hope and determination begins."

She smiled and looked over at him. "Is that your way of saying I have to work at it if I want the relationship to succeed?"

Talon shrugged, "You don't have to do anything you don't want to do. But if you have a desire to see things turn out a certain way, you have to take action to make that happen."

Sulana rolled her eyes. "Thanks for that cryptic advice. If only my desires were that clear."

Talon chuckled and urged his horse to move faster. As he pulled away from her, he said, "You're a smart woman. You'll figure it out."

A gust of wind flew into their group, bringing with it a fresh pelting of miniature snowballs. Sulana cringed and flipped up her hood after a few beads of the icy precipitation slid down her cloak and melted on the back of her neck.

Behind her, Daven cursed. He moved up alongside Sulana and said, "I'll be glad to get off this spirit-forsaken mountain. It's probably sunny and warm down in the valley. I don't know why they built the Archives castle up here on top of this rock. We get maybe two months of summer, and half the time it does something like this."

Barek's deep voice responded to Daven's whining. "What keeps you here? You have skills. You could live anywhere you choose."

Daven glanced over at Sulana and set his jaw. He stared forward down the tree-lined, rocky trail and answered in clipped words, "I guess you're right. There's nothing keeping me here now."

A jolt of surprise and hurt went through Sulana. "Are you really thinking about leaving? I thought you liked being part of the team."

Daven gave her a frustrated look that melted into one of sadness. "I did. I mean I do. But things have changed. When Jaylan finishes his training, he'll probably join you and you won't need me any more."

Sulana realized that here was another casualty of her growing relationship with Jaylan. She had ignored Daven's crush on her for some time, hoping he would realize that she didn't reciprocate his romantic intentions. Ignoring it was turning out to be a poor strategy. Daven was known for his impatience, but when it came to his feelings for her, he seemed willing to wait indefinitely for her to come around to his way of thinking. Her relationship with Jaylan had probably forced him to accept that he might be waiting for something that would never happen.

She owed Daven an honest response. "I'll always need you. We grew up together and share a friendship like nothing I have with anyone else. My being with Jaylan doesn't change that. If you feel you need to move on and start a new life, I'll support you in whatever you decide. But right now, I really need you here and focused on the mission."

Daven's face flushed red. "I don't need a lecture Sulana," he retorted. "Don't worry about it. I'll do my job." He pulled back sharply on his reins to slow his horse back behind Sulana, putting an end to their conversation.

She cursed herself for being insensitive when she thought about how her last words must have come across. "Daven, that's not how I meant it," she said, but he ignored her. She hadn't intended to lecture or offend him, but could think of nothing to say now that would repair the situation. She really did hope that Daven could get over this distraction because they were all traveling into a potentially dangerous situation, and they needed to remain alert.

She needed to take her own lecture to heart. Being distracted with thoughts of Jaylan and concerns about the future wouldn't help her solve the problem that was in front of her today. She gripped her hood tightly at her neck as another gust threatened to flip it off her head, and she tried to clear her mind of distractions. The mission was to find Lohan and return the Portal Key. All other considerations were secondary for now.

CHAPTER 21
FORK IN THE ROAD

Sulana and her team traveled Alpine Lakes Trail, which was the primary route between the Archives and the valley below. They rode for a few miles through dense conifer forest that occasionally opened up near rocky overlooks.

After Lohan had disappeared, the riders who were sent after him followed his tracks along this trail. But when they reached the valley, evidence of his passage disappeared into a multitude of hoof prints and wagon tracings along the popular Trench Road.

Still high on the mountain, Sulana called for Talon to stop when they reached a fork in the trail. She waited for everyone to gather at the intersection. The wind whistling through the waving tree branches made conversation difficult, so she needed everyone to be close before she could explain what she was planning to do.

Alpine Lakes Trail continued straight through the intersection, and Eagle River Trail forked off to the left. Eagle River Trail also dropped into the valley from here, but it went east toward Riverview.

Sulana raised her voice so everyone could hear her clearly. "Before we left, Councilor Rissik suggested that I stop at this intersection and see if Lohan might have doubled back when he reached the valley. It's possible he went north toward Riverview instead of south toward Northshore."

Daven squinted at her and half-shouted back, "That doesn't make any sense. How would we be able to tell from here whether or not he doubled back in the valley?"

For an answer, Sulana took out a Seeker and held it up by the ring attached to its chain. The short glass rod at the other end of the chain spun lazily in the wind that washed around her. "Before the Portal Key was stolen from the armory, Ebnik created a Seeker for it. He kept it a secret because he was worried that Paeter might have sympathizers at the Archives."

Daven's mouth split into a big grin. "That crafty old wizard! He probably saved us days of trying to track down Lohan."

Talon smiled too and he nodded in appreciation of the wizard's foresight. Even Barek twisted his lips into a satisfied half-smile.

"We'll see. Lohan could still be anywhere," she said as she dismounted from her horse. Walking a few steps away from the others, she slipped the Seeker's ring onto her middle finger and let the rod dangle. She tried to block the wind with her back, but finally had to step closer to the trees and find a calmer spot. Daven dismounted as well and stood next to her, peering into the trees with his hand on his sword hilt.

Sulana channeled vaetra into the Seeker and saw it begin to glow and spin. When the green colored tip of the rod was pointing almost due east, the Seeker stopped turning and the brightness of its glow increased. Sulana cut the flow of vaetra and the Seeker stopped glowing. The rod dangled aimlessly once again.

Councilor Rissik's instincts were apparently correct. From where they stood now, Riverview was nearly due east. And so was Thunderhead College. The councilor had warned her that Paeter Thoron might be operating out of the college because it was a haven for Integrationist sorcerers. He'd have no shortage of supporters there. Sulana hoped that wasn't the case. Relations between the college and the Archives were strained enough as it was.

If Ebnik hadn't given her the Seeker, her team would have continued on to Northshore and probably spent days searching for Lohan, only to discover that he had gone north instead of south when he reached the valley.

Not for the first time, Sulana wondered about Councilor Rissik's "instincts." She trusted the man, but he was secretive and aloof. He always seemed to know far more about what was going on elsewhere in the empire than anyone else, and his insights were uncanny at times. He did come from a prominent family in Cassandria who he visited fairly often, so maybe that was where he got his information.

Daven interrupted her thoughts. "So, off to Riverview then?"

Sulana put the Seeker away and started back to her horse. "It looks like Lohan went to Riverview after all," she said loudly, answering Daven's question so everyone could hear.

"Good," Barek said. His deep voice was curiously unaffected by the wind, even though he made no attempt to raise it. "We'll catch our rat faster."

Barek had little tolerance for traitors. His people lived in a loose confederation of insular tribes that spent more time warring with each other than with other nations. Tribal loyalty was paramount to the Wintermen, and traitors were punished without mercy. In a sense, the Archives was Barek's adopted tribe, and his feelings about treachery held true.

"I hope you're right," Sulana said as she mounted up again. "Let's try to get off the mountain before nightfall and make camp in the valley. We'll pick up Lohan's trail again tomorrow morning."

At least, Sulana hoped they would be following Lohan. The Seeker was pointing the way toward the Portal Key, but there was no guarantee that the key was still in Lohan's possession. If Lohan had the key with him in Riverview, they should be able to get it back without too much difficulty. However, if Lohan was at Thunderhead College, recovering the key could be far more complicated.

CHAPTER 22

RAISE FOG

Jaylan ~ Incantations Class, The Archives

That morning, Professor Marlene Delano had finally declared that I could control my channeling well enough to move on to the next phase of incantations study. I was able to operate all three of the Levitators without incident, although the professor suggested I keep working with them to refine my control. She said my control was still a bit coarse because my low channeling resistance meant I had a wider range of vaetric flow to master than most students. It remained to be seen whether having such low resistance was a good thing or a bad thing.

A spell book was open on the table in front of me. The scribe who had penned it had an erratic hand, making the spidery text difficult to read. Professor Delano encouraged me to create my own spell book with a collection of my favorite spells, if we discovered that I was able to cast. Then I wouldn't have to struggle with someone else's penmanship every time I needed to refresh my memory. I was starting to think her suggestion was a good idea.

To be fair, my concentration was not at its best. I'd been thoroughly distracted since Sulana had left the prior afternoon. I'd slept poorly the previous night, and I kept wondering where she might be and how her mission was going.

"That's the incantation we're going to try today," Professor Delano said from behind me where she stood looking over my shoulder. "Let me hear you chant it."

The aged and brittle page was laid out in three parts, which I had learned was typical. The first part explained the purpose of the incantation and described its effects. The second part was the incantation itself, which was usually arranged like a poem so the sorcerer would know where to pause. The third part gave additional hints on how to successfully complete the spell.

Many of the spell books were written in Old Empiric as Lissy had warned me, so my studies included learning the ancient language. As she had promised though, the Old Empiric words were similar to their modern counterparts, so learning to read the spell descriptions and instructions wasn't too difficult.

I read through the instructions once more. It was a fog spell. The purpose was to generate fog from a body of water. Over on a nearby table, the professor had placed a large clay bowl and filled it nearly to the brim. It was a small body of water, but it would do for the task at hand.

I read through the incantation twice, mouthing the words silently to myself. The key to an incantation was in how it was verbalized. The syllables required precise pronunciation and cadence. At times, these vocalizations stretched the phonetic limits of the written language in which they were recorded, and the sorcerer had to learn to recognize the letter combinations the scribes had selected to express specific sounds. Professor Delano had told me that sometimes it helped to look at two different translations of the same spell to get a better feel for how to properly deliver the chant.

Feeling ready, I started the chant. As previously instructed, I cleared my mind of other distractions and concentrated on getting the vocalizations right. When I finished the chant, I looked up at Professor Delano.

"Not bad," she said. She pointed to one of the words of the incantation. "But remember that this vowel combination should be vocalized with more of a rounded tone. Try it again."

I went through the chant a couple more times until she was satisfied with my cadence and vocalizations. A tingle of excitement went down my spine when I got it right. Although I had practiced chanting in previous sessions, this was the first time I would be allowed to try manifesting the spell.

"Good!" the professor exclaimed after my last recitation. "The next step is visualization. You need to visualize what you are trying to do while you are chanting. It's much easier to do that if you have actually seen the effect you are trying to create. Come over here for a moment and I'll show you what I mean."

I got up and stood next to Professor Delano at the table with the clay bowl. The ceramic was thick and had decorative runes etched into the sides. I placed a hand on the table, and the vibration of my touch sent tiny ripples moving across the surface of the water in the bowl.

Next to the bowl of water was a glass globe with a circular, metal base. The base was decorated with swirls that extended down to form three short, silvery legs. The globe was about the size of an apple, and it was filled with water or some other clear liquid. When the professor picked it up, tiny reflective flakes, possibly mica, stirred around on the bottom. She tipped the globe upside down and righted it again, making the flakes swirl around inside the globe.

Professor Delano smiled and shook her head. "Some smiths can be creative with their implements, don't you think? I find this one a bit overdone, and certainly not practical for travel, but it is lovely."

I imagined trying to keep the globe safe while traveling on horseback. "I see what you mean. Is that the fog implement?" I asked.

"Yes it is," she answered, handing the implement to me. "The trigger word is 'mist,' which is why we call it the Mist Globe."

I looked at her to see if she was making a joke, but she shrugged. "I'm serious," she said. "This particular smith had a whimsical streak," she added almost apologetically.

I chuckled and held the globe upright in the palm of my hand with my fingers curled around the base. The flakes had started to settle again, so I gave it a quick tip to set them swirling. They reflected light in a rainbow of colors, like tiny stars shooting around in their own private universe.

I opened a channel to the base of the globe and established a connection with it. I then focused my attention on the bowl of water and spoke the trigger word. The globe emitted a low throbbing sound and I allowed it to pull a trickle of vaetra through the channel. The flakes within the globe darted around more energetically, as if I had tipped it again. Within seconds, mist started to rise from the surface of the bowl. Perhaps the trigger word wasn't so whimsical after all.

The professor held her hand out to toward the bowl. "That's what we're after," she said. The water vapor conjured from the bowl started to float over the table. "You can stop now."

I cut the flow of vaetra to the implement and dropped my channel to it. The flakes started to settle once again and I put the globe back down on the table with a smile. Whimsical or not, the Mist Globe was fun to use.

I looked at Professor Delano to find her considering me silently. I recognized the expression I saw on her face. Sulana had narrowed a similar pair of blue eyes at me on many occasions. "Something on your mind?" I asked.

"My daughter seems quite taken with you," she answered.

The non sequitur caught me off guard. I stared blankly at her for a moment, but could read nothing more from her expression. "And I with her," I finally responded.

She smiled and gave me a short nod of encouragement. "Talon tells me you are considering becoming a Sword Sorcerer," she said.

I answered her guardedly, still not sure where this conversation was coming from or where it was going. "Yes, I've considered the possibility, and I've talked with Sulana about it."

"I think it's a good idea," she said. "Talon says you are talented with a sword, and from what I've seen, you'll make a fine sorcerer."

Still off-balance, I stammered, "Thank you."

"Do the two of you plan to have children?"

My breath caught in my chest. This conversation was like some kind of test I wasn't remotely prepared to take. I wasn't sure how Sulana felt about having children. I wasn't even sure how *I* felt about having children. "We haven't really gotten that far in our discussions about the future."

Marlene gave me a serious look. "You should. You do plan to marry her don't you?"

I froze again, my mind swirling with the implications of any answer I might give. Her question was so direct that my first reaction was a strong desire to end the conversation immediately. And run.

I shook my head and took a deep breath to calm myself. Marlene waited patiently for my answer. "I love Sulana, but I think that she should be the first to know about any marriage plans I may or may not have."

She raised an eyebrow and said, "May not?"

Did she know that Sulana and I had taken our relationship to a physical level? Could that be what this was about? She wanted me to do the honorable thing? The truth was that I couldn't imagine life without Sulana, but the two of us were still getting to know each other. We hadn't discussed marriage, or children, or where we might make our home together. Marlene wanted answers I couldn't give.

I finally looked her in the eye and said, "Can we have this conversation at another time? Like after Sulana and I have a chance to figure these things out together? I honestly don't know what to tell you right now."

Marlene crossed her arms and was silent for a moment. "All right. But you shouldn't put it off. I'm sure you share my concerns for Sulana's safety. If she were to become pregnant, I'm sure the Council would release her from her Commitment, especially if another Sword Sorcerer were available."

Everything clicked into place. So that's what this was about. Marlene was hoping I would take Sulana's place as Sword Sorcerer and keep her daughter at home raising children. I could just imagine Sulana's reaction if she found out about *that* plan.

Professor Delano seemed to realize how transparent she was being and had the grace to blush. "I'm sorry, Jaylan. I shouldn't pry. Please don't tell Sulana I said that, and please forgive me for being so pushy."

I looked her in the eyes and said. "I understand, but we're just going to have to see how things turn out. I promise I'll do my best to see that they turn out well."

She closed her eyes for a moment and then looked down at the floor. "Let's continue with your lesson," she said finally.

"Thank you," I said with relief.

Professor Delano straightened her posture and ran her hands down her sides to smooth out her dark green dress. "Now that I've thoroughly distracted you, do you think you can still recite the incantation?"

"From memory?" I asked, startled.

She shrugged and answered, "That isn't necessary for this exercise, but yes, eventually you'll have to memorize the incantation in order to cast it. You can't concentrate on controlling your flow of vaetra, getting the vocalizations right, and visualizing the desired result while reading the incantation. You have to know it and feel it to cast it."

She went over to the table I had been sitting at earlier to retrieve the spell book, and she set it down in front of me on the table with the water bowl.

"Go ahead and read the incantation from the book, but I want you to also visualize the fog rising from the water bowl as you do so."

I did as she instructed. About half way through the chant, a strange feeling came from within me. It was a stirring not unlike opening a channel to an implement, and a sensation of pressure started to build. The pressure eased off quickly after I completed the chant. Uncertain if something was wrong, I described what had happened to the professor.

"That's good!" she exclaimed. "Your mind and body are resonating with the chant. Try it again, but try to recite from memory rather than reading it as much as possible."

So I tried again. And again. Each time, the vocalizations became easier and I was able to remember more of the incantation without reading it. I started to anticipate the pressure sensation. By the fourth recitation, I was becoming much more relaxed. The cadence of the chant lulled me nearly into a trance, and that's when something new happened.

As I started the incantation over from the beginning, I got distracted by a memory of a rune. The rune had a similar meaning to the vocalizations I was using at the start of the incantation. Both invited the opening of a channel from the spell caster to the focus crystal. I lost the cadence of the chant, and my voice faltered to a stop.

"What happened there?" the professor asked. "You were doing so well."

"I was starting to relax into the chant, but then I started thinking about a rune from my studies."

The professor put a hand on my shoulder and scanned my face with her eyes. "You do look tired, Jaylan. You've been studying hard, and that's probably affecting your concentration. Try not to get quite so relaxed by the chant and focus your mind on the task. Your rune studies can wait their turn." She gave my shoulder a quick squeeze and then let go.

She had me go through the chant a few more times. I was careful not to let myself get quite so relaxed, and I kept my mind on visualizing the mist rising from the bowl. She stopped me when I was able to complete the chant while staring at the bowl of water and without glancing at the spell book in front of me.

"Very good! I think you're ready to do this for real," she said.

"For real? You mean actually try to cast the spell?"

She reached into a pocket in the side of her dress and pulled out a small crystal sphere. As she handed it to me, she said, "Yes, but don't think of it that way. You don't *try* to cast a spell. You either do or you don't. Vaetra gives you the power, but it only works through an implement with all four aspects of sorcery. The sphere you have in your hand is the focus, your body is both the link and the well, and your mind holds the incantation. When everything is in place, that pressure you feel building as you chant will release through the focus as a manifestation. The one thing that pulls all of it together is the *belief* that it will work."

Professor Delano had said most of this before, of course. When I first started studying incantations, I learned that my body would effectively become a vaetric implement that could be used to manifest a spell. But her words had been an abstract concept until today when that disconcerting sense of pressure had built within me.

The Seeker I had once seen Sulana use consisted of a link in the form of its finger ring and metal chain, a glass rod for the focus, and runes within the glass rod that held the incantation. The well of vaetra that powered the implement came from within Sulana herself. All she had to do was open a channel to the Seeker and trigger the embedded incantation.

Casting involved the same elements of sorcery as using an implement like a Seeker, except my chant would be the incantation, and vaetra would flow through the link of my hand into the sphere. That was the theory, anyway. Many sorcerers got this far in their studies, but weren't able to complete the transition from channeler to caster.

I held the sphere with the tips of my fingers and looked it over. It was about the size of an apricot and mostly clear. The clarity was marred by cloudy veins and striations throughout the crystal. A transparent mineral was an essential element of sorcery because it was the catalyst that transformed the power of vaetra and the intent of the incantation into a physical manifestation.

"What should I do now?" I asked.

"For now, just relax," she said. She came over and stood next to me, facing the table and bowl by my side. "Listen to all of my instructions before you do anything. First, you'll open a channel to the casting sphere. Begin your chant and let vaetra flow into the casting sphere, but only a little bit at a time. Look at the bowl of water and visualize the mist rising from it as it did when you used the Mist Globe. Okay, now you may begin."

That all sounded easy enough.

I concentrated on the casting sphere and opened a channel to it. The sensation was different from what I was used to. When I opened a channel to an implement, it usually snapped into place like a dagger sliding into a sheath. With the casting orb, the channel skidded around the surface of the sphere as if it were trying to find a point of entry and failing. I described the sensation to the professor.

She responded in a soothing voice, "That's okay. Just keep going. You have an unusually keen awareness of your channeling if you can feel the resistance of the casting sphere that readily. Let the incantation complete your connection to the sphere and shape the manifestation."Taking her at her word, I started the chant. Trying to get the vocalizations right, control my flow of vaetra into the casting orb, and visualize the mist rising from the bowl all at the same time was almost impossible. My channel to the casting sphere started to feel more solid, but by the end of the chant, nothing had happened. The bowl of water looked just as it had when I started. I dropped the channel to the casting sphere with a sigh.

Professor Delano gently patted my arm. "Don't worry. I don't know of anyone who managed to cast on their first attempt. I certainly didn't."

"And some never do," I said with a shrug, thinking of Sulana.

"We don't know why some sorcerers can cast and some can't." More quietly, she added, "And I'll admit I may not have been the best teacher for Sulana."

"Why is that?" I asked.

Marlene looked down at the floor and wouldn't meet my eyes. Her face grew a little red as she answered, "Because I didn't want her to succeed, and she knew it."

"I don't understand. Why would you want your own daughter to fail?" I didn't mean to sound accusing, but my words came out that way.

She looked up at me, with both pain and anger in her eyes. "Sulana was intent on becoming a Sword Sorceress no matter how hard I tried to talk her out of it. I had hoped her inability to cast would dissuade her. But it didn't. It only made her more determined."

"Maybe she had something to prove to herself," I said.

Marlene shook her head. "To her father."

"What do you mean?" I said automatically, but a glimmer of understanding had begun.

"She had something to prove to her father," she repeated.

"But her father is gone," I pointed out.

She frowned and her voice became husky and bitter as she corrected me. "No, her father is dead. He got himself killed being the great Sword Sorcerer, Defender of the Accords. And now Sulana has picked up his mantle."

I wasn't sure what to say. "She must have loved him very much."

Marlene sniffed and wiped moisture from under her eyes. "She idolized him. Since his death, her image of him has only grown more fanciful. She doesn't remember how hard-headed he could be. If she did, she might be able to temper that same quality in herself."

I laughed in spite of the seriousness of our conversation. "She can be single-minded at times."

Marlene seemed to relax a little and sighed. "Yes, I tell myself that's one of the qualities that stopped her from being able to cast." The bitterness returned to her voice. "The alternative is accepting that I may have sabotaged her and weakened her ability to defend herself, putting her life at even greater risk."

I narrowed my eyes. If what she said was true, I didn't want to make her feel better about it. Sulana had worked hard and deserved every advantage. If her mother had compromised her abilities, she deserved to feel guilty about it. But perhaps redemption was still possible.

"Maybe it's not too late." I said.

She tilted her head to the side and looked up at me. "For Sulana to learn to cast? No. It's never too late if you have the ability. But she refuses to 'waste' any more time on it. She has decided that she can't do it, so she focuses on other things."

"We'll see about that," I said.

Marlene snorted, "Good luck." Then her voice grew serious. "Let me know if you can get her to try again, and I'll do everything I can to help."

I tried to hand the casting orb back to her, but she waved my hand away. "We aren't done here, Mr. Forester. I want you to do the exercise at least twice more."

I shrugged and went through the exercise a second time. This time I was able to maintain the channel and get through the incantation without making a mistake, but I couldn't focus my mind on the image of mist rising from the bowl. Once again, I was distracted by a feeling of separation and images of runes. When I finished, the water bowl sat in mute testimony to my failure. I explained what happened to the professor.

Her voice grew stern. "I know you're tired, and being relaxed is good, but you need to put your full attention on casting in order to succeed. Put your rune studies out of your mind and do it again."

Squaring my shoulders, I started once more. This time I was able to keep the lassitude at bay and my mind focused on the image of mist rising from the bowl. About half-way through the incantation, my channel to the orb started to… twist, for lack of a better description, and vaetra began to flow into the orb. As I neared the end of the chant, a pulsing hum began. The sound was similar to what I'd heard come from the Mist Globe. A tenuous tendril of water vapor started to rise from the water bowl, and I no longer had to imagine it happening. In that instant, all doubt dropped away: I *knew* I could cast.

A thrill ran through me, and I experimented with the flow of vaetra to the orb. Adding more vaetra to the flow increased the amount of vapor that rose from the bowl. The floating mist started to form clouds and drift around the top of the table.

Marlene clapped her hands together and said, "Excellent! The third time's a charm. You can go ahead and drop the channel now. No need to fill the room with fog."

I dropped the channel to the casting orb, ending the spell and silencing the manifestation noise. For the first time, I truly didn't mind that I could hear manifestations. This time it was the sound of success. I looked at Professor Delano with a big grin on my face that I couldn't have suppressed if I'd wanted to.

She smiled and nodded, accepting the casting orb back from me this time. "Remember this moment, Mr. Forester. Being able to cast opens up the world of sorcery to you. Your potions will fuse and your implements will seal. How you choose to develop your skills is up to you, but from this moment on, you are a full sorcerer."

"Thank you, Professor. I will remember," I said in the same formal tone she had used.

I took a deep breath and held it for a moment. My limbs ached and I had a strong desire to go lie down somewhere for a nap. But my nerves were buzzing from the excitement of my first casting experience.

My resolve to develop my abilities with sorcery strengthened when I thought about the fog bank Paeter Thoron had raised in Buckwoods to conceal his escape. I had just done the same thing, albeit on a much smaller scale. But now I was confident that I would one day be able to face Paeter Thoron sorcerer to sorcerer.

CHAPTER 23
BREAKFAST IN CAMP

Sulana woke to a clear and chilly morning. The storm had eased off to a misty drizzle as they came down the mountain trail the prior afternoon. It was nothing but a light breeze by the time they reached their camp site on the valley floor.

She crawled out from under her blanket and emerged from the simple canvas tent she had erected in case the clouds descended from the mountain during the night. She yawned, stretched, and combed the tangles out of her hair with her fingers. Smoke from the camp fire drifted her way, making her cough and forcing her to move out of the plume.

Talon and Barek were already up. Talon was tending the camp fire and Barek was keeping an eye on the surrounding forest, stopping to pick up dry pieces of wood for the fire when he ran across them on his circuit around the camp.

Talon called over to her, "Good morning. Sleep well?"

"Not bad, once I found and dealt with the rock that was trying to dig a hole in my shoulder," she replied. She looked around the camp site at the empty bed rolls. She was the last person up. "Where's Daven?"

"Right here," he answered, walking into the camp site with a short string of fish. He handed the string to Talon and said, "They're small, and I didn't get very many, but I think there's enough for breakfast. I know you said you'd clean them, but I was right there at the water, so I went ahead and took care of it."

Talon nodded and looked over the fish as he took the string from Daven. "Thanks. They'll do just fine." Talon tied the string to the branch of a nearby tree and retrieved a frying pan from a pack that was lying over by where the horses and pack mule were tethered.

While Talon began to prepare breakfast, Sulana went to her own pack and returned to stand near the fire with the Seeker in hand. The fire's warmth felt good in the chill, moist, morning air, but she'd be sweating later when the high summer sun reached down through the trees and added its warmth to the humidity.

Sulana slipped the Seeker's ring onto her finger and let the rod dangle. She activated it and it began to glow and rotate slowly. From their camp site, Riverview was still mostly east of them, but Thunderhead College was almost due north. The tip of the Seeker rotated counter-clockwise from the south and Sulana watched it carefully. She grew tense as the tip swung toward the east without stopping and continued around toward the north. Her tension changed to puzzlement as the tip continued around and started its sweep for a second time.

Talon must have seen her confusion, because he looked up from his sizzling fish to ask her what was wrong.

"I'm not getting a read on the direction of the Portal Key," she answered. She allowed the Seeker to make one more full sweep before shutting it down. She gathered the device into her palm and stared at it. It seemed to be functioning normally; it just wasn't finding the key.

"What could cause that?" Daven asked. He kneeled next to her, holding his hands out toward the fire.

It was a good question. What had changed since yesterday afternoon? "The only things I know of that defeat a seeker are keeping the target object underground or far away." She glanced at Daven and added, "Or putting it in a stone box." He smiled and nodded at the shared memory.

The last time Sulana's team went in search of a Portal Key, the Seeker they were using had stopped working as well. It turned out that an old healer had placed the key they were tracking inside a stone box, unwittingly blocking the Seeker's connection to the key. However, not many people knew about that little trick, and stone boxes were uncommon.

"So, what do we do now?" Daven asked. He licked his lips while he watched Talon lay a couple of the small fish into the frying pan where they immediately began to sizzle.

Sulana shrugged and closed her hand tight around the Seeker. "We continue the search and keep checking the Seeker once in a while. If the key is underground, it's probably in storage, so at least Lohan isn't using it. But if he did use it, he could easily have traveled out of the Seeker's range."

Talon flipped the fish over and looked up at her from his cooking task. "Do you know what that range is?" he asked.

She knelt next to Talon and watched him prepare the fish. "Ebnik told me that Seekers have a range of thirty to fifty miles. If Lohan went through a portal, he could easily have gone farther than that. He could be anywhere in the empire."

Talon added some water to the frying pan. It hissed and steamed, slowing down the cooking and poaching the fish at the same time. He shook his head and frowned. "Does the Council have any idea of what's really going on? We're always going to be one step behind if we don't come up with a better strategy than chasing them down *after* they make a move. We at least need to know who else is involved."

Sulana nodded, her lips forming a thin line. "We're still guessing at this point. Our contacts in Riverview have always been tenuous, and lately we've heard almost nothing. And we've never managed to get a spy into Thunderhead College." She thought about how Lohan had fooled them all, and added, "Headmaster Fortenz seems to be much better at identifying spies than we are."

Talon slipped two of the fish into a shallow wooden bowl and handed it to Daven. Daven took the bowl eagerly and sat cross-legged next to the fire. He made noises of appreciation as he tasted the first few bites. Talon handed a second bowl to Sulana, and she slowly picked at the fish while Talon started frying more for Barek and himself.

Once the second round of fish was sizzling, he turned his attention back to Sulana. "Headmaster Fortenz has an advantage. When he established Thunderhead College, he made it clear that it was a refuge for Integrationist thinkers and that no one else was welcome. The Archives has always accepted anyone interested in learning sorcery, regardless of their feelings about the Accords. The Council is under mandate from the emperor to protect the Accords, so the leadership is generally Isolationist, but the place is crawling with Integrationists as well."

Sulana looked up from her breakfast in surprise. "I had no idea you were so well-versed in Archives politics," she said.

Talon shrugged and fussed with his fish as a blush rose into his cheeks. "Spending time with your mother has had something to do with that," he said softly.

Sulana snorted. Before raising a fork of fish to her mouth, she asked with a teasing tone, "So are you going to make an honest woman of her?"

Talon glanced over at Sulana and then at Daven, who was waiting for his response with a smirk. "If she'll let me," he answered.

Chapter 24
Paeter's Legacy

Dumont ~ Dusk, Sunset Province

Dumont stepped through the portal onto a hill overlooking the confluence of the Merciless and Teardrop Rivers. One flowing ribbon of blue merged with the other. They came together at the southern end of the Merciless Valley, which lay between steep-walled mountain ridges that formed its east and west boundaries. Behind him, Paeter closed the door to the Portal Keep and then came over to stand at his side.

Dumont glanced at Paeter, who gazed over the valley with a relaxed, half-smile on his face. For Paeter, this was a homecoming.

From the top of the overgrown trail that dropped to the valley floor, they could see the cultivated fields that stretched across the short plain from one rocky foothill to the other. Tiny distant shapes moved against the backdrop of growing grains. The farmers from the town of Dusk were tending their fields.

Agriculture in the Merciless Valley was a frantic affair. The spring snowmelt and rains conspired to flood the valley every spring, and the moment the waters subsided, the farmers had to get busy sowing so the plants would mature in time for a fall harvest. The bounty of silt and nutrients brought into the valley by the floods was welcome, even if the risk of a late melt and the resulting loss of crops was not. Then, after a hot summer of explosive growth, the harvest would have to be processed and stored before the first frost and the snows of the area's too-early winter.

Across the valley, a road zigzagged in switch-backs up the eastern ridge, curving in places to dodge granite outcroppings. Sturdy houses fronted the roadway most of the way up the mountain. All of the buildings were constructed in the style common to the Northern provinces, with high stonework foundations topped by timber framing or log walls. The roofs were slate or wooden shingles, and moss grew like dark green fur on top of the most shaded homes. Perched on the hillside, the homes were safe from the spring floodwaters and had a commanding view of the valley below.

"I once dreamed that all this would be mine one day," Paeter mused aloud. "Discovering I could channel destroyed that dream until Astin was born. Then the dream was destroyed again when my father died and Frederick Brachus successfully petitioned the emperor for the governorship. I'm afraid to reawaken the dream only to be disappointed yet again."

Dumont gauged Paeter's mood and decided careful encouragement was needed. "You have a real opportunity now to restore what was taken from you. The planning is done, and the preparations have been made. All you need to do is carry it through and Astin will be the next Governor of Sunset Province with you by his side." *And with me whispering into your ear from the shadows.*

Paeter glanced at him and gave him a sardonic smile, showing that he appreciated the effort to bolster his courage. "Thank you, Master. I appreciate all you have done to help me recover my son's birthright."

Dumont motioned for Paeter to take the lead down the trail that would take them into the valley. "I'm happy to help you correct the emperor's mistake, Paeter. And I think you should avoid calling me 'Master' for this visit. For now, it's just 'Dumont' or 'Headmaster Fortenz.'"

Dumont followed Paeter off of the portal's rocky shelf and descended through trees that thinned as they approached the valley. Near the bottom of the trail, they passed through the ruins of the original Dusk town site. Paeter explained that most of the ruins had been swept away by floods over the intervening century since the location had been abandoned. A few moss-covered outlines of rocky base walls jutted up from the tall grass, and rotting poles angled high above the ground where homes on stilts had once stood. The founders of Dusk had been unable to devise a building technique that proved effective against the floodwaters, so they had left the original town site for the relative safety of the far mountainside.

As Paeter and Dumont reached the valley floor, the air grew thick with humidity and flying insects. The sun beat down upon their backs when they emerged from the last trees, prompting both sorcerers to remove their vest jackets. The trail ended at a rutted and dusty road that would take them across the valley. Folding their jackets over their arms, they started down the road, swatting at mosquitoes and veering around milling clouds of gnats.

They crossed the "summer bridge," so called because every year it was erected in late spring after the Merciless River had receded back within its banks. The bridge was then disassembled after the fall harvest. Summer-tamed river waters flowed calmly under the bridge after winding out of the rocky peaks that sealed the north end of the valley. Dumont relaxed and enjoyed Paeter's confident recitation of area lore as they walked. Dumont mostly kept silent and let the man rebuild his bond with his birthplace. That bond would be a valuable anchor to keep the man focused on their goals here.

Only once did they get close enough to the field workers to elicit a few curious stares and hesitant waves. It was unusual for the workers to see two well-dressed men walking down the road, as opposed to riding on a horse or in a carriage. The workers didn't know about the portal, and if they did, they might have been less welcoming. Dumont wondered what their reaction would be if they recognized Paeter as the one-time heir of their prior governor.

Leaving the fields behind, their path joined with Dusk Road, the main road that brought most of the wheeled traffic into the valley. They waited for a northbound wagon loaded with crates to go by and then followed after the dust that swirled in its wake had settled.

A wide climbing curve to the right brought them between two enormous rock pillars which formed the only break in the Dusk defensive wall. Two guard towers rose above the wall, one on each side of the gateway. The pillars were vertically slotted for nearly their full height, and they were heavily buttressed on the inside.

After passing between the pillars, Dumont looked back in curiosity and saw a complicated array of pulleys and ropes attached to a massive gate which had several large wheels along the bottom. Paeter noticed his interest and launched into an enthusiastic explanation of how the gate system worked.

Paeter's father, Darius Thoron, had devised the wheeled gate system to replace a dilapidated pair of swinging gates nearly two decades ago. If danger appeared, a couple of guards could use the pulley system to roll the gate through the pillar slots and into place quickly. The newer gate was stronger because it had no break in the middle, and it was easier to keep it operational in the winter. Swinging gates tended to get stuck on the snow and ice that built up on the roadway. Although it was tested regularly, Darius' Gate had never been closed in response to a genuine threat.

Dumont began to have a more personal understanding of why Paeter was so intent on regaining control over Sunset Province. Paeter's family had done more than just govern Dusk; they had helped build it. Some ruling families behaved as if their governorship were ceremonial, delegating administration of the town to local functionaries. This hands-off approach was especially true when ruling families emigrated to their holdings from other areas of the empire, which was rare, but not unknown.

Beyond the gates, Dusk Road started to climb. The first segment of road was carved into the mountain and only wide enough for a single wagon. Fortunately, the full stretch of road could be seen from the top and bottom, so drivers could wait until the way was clear before proceeding.

The road ascended quickly from the valley floor in a series of shallow steps. Although the incline was not terribly steep, the sorcerers were sweaty and winded by the time they reached the top of the first segment. At the switchback, the lane spread out onto a wide bench where drivers could rest their teams or wait for their turn on the roadway. The sorcerers took a moment to catch their breath and enjoy the view overlooking the valley below.

The breeze coming down the mountainside flowed around Dumont, ruffling his shirt and cooling the sweat on his neck and face. His breathing quickly returned to normal. "Shall we continue up?" he asked Paeter.

"We could wait here if you want and take the next passenger cart. I'm not sure how long it will be though." Paeter looked down the path they had just ascended and then up at the next segment. A donkey cart led by a man on foot was coming down from the higher level, and a rider on horseback was coming up from the valley floor. "With this little traffic, there's probably only one cart running, so it could be a while."

Dumont shook his head and started walking. "I don't want to waste time waiting. If we encounter the passenger cart along the way, we can take it then."

The second switchback was longer and less steep. The first houses appeared alongside this stretch of road. They were backed up almost against the slope behind them, with just a small gap to allow for the runoff of rain and snowmelt. Rock-lined ditches merged into a common trench alongside the road, draining water away from the homes as well as the roadbed. Small footbridges of various makes spanned the trench in front of the residences.

The third switchback was like the second, but the terrace at this level was wider, and they encountered the first shops. They passed by a stable with two boys working out front. The older boy stopped grooming the mane of the horse he was tending and watched them walk by. Dumont nodded briefly in his direction and the boy waved with the stiff brush in his hand.

The fourth and final switchback was similar to the third. The terrace was even wider and included a second, narrow road that looped away from the main road through the homes and shops.

Dusk Road finally spilled into a large town square on Dusk's topmost and widest terrace. Narrow lanes branched away from the square and disappeared between the buildings. A stone monument stood in the center of the square. It was a statue of a well-dressed man gripping the lapels of his vest with both hands. The man bore a passing resemblance to Paeter, so Dumont stepped closer to read the inscription on the monument's base. It read: "Bascom Thoron, Dusk Architect and Founder."

"My great-grandfather," Paeter explained. "He was the visionary who came up with the idea of moving Dusk to this side of the valley."

Paeter's face darkened as he looked toward the governor's complex, and Dumont's eyes followed the direction of his gaze. A narrow road ran straight from the town square to the open gates of the complex. The squat governor's residence rose up from behind the wall in multiple stories of wide terraces that mimicked the terraces of Dusk itself. The construction of the wall was similar to the houses, having a stone base and timber ramparts.

Dumont waved his hand toward the complex and said, "Dusk belongs in your family, Paeter. Let's get it back."

Paeter narrowed his eyes and pressed his lips together. His hand went to the pouch at his waist that contained a special amulet. Without another word, he started up the road toward the governor's complex with purposeful strides. Dumont smiled to himself and followed.

CHAPTER 25
FINDING LOHAN

Sulana ~ Pinewoods Road

After breaking camp, Sulana and the rest of her team continued down Eagle River Trail until it met with Pinewoods Road. When he reached the trailhead, Talon stopped his horse and waited for her to catch up.

Sulana pulled a map out of her saddlebag and consulted it. It showed that Pinewoods Road ran north and south along the base of the mountains. The road devolved into a game trail a couple of miles to the south, but to the north it turned east at Eagle River and followed along the river to the town of Riverview.

After the rest of the team gathered, Sulana pointed toward the north and said, "The road to Thunderhead College meets this road about a mile from here. Stay vigilant. The college probably patrols the area around the facility."

"That we do," said a voice from the trees. Lohan stepped out of concealment with a wand leveled at Sulana's chest. A moment later, her team was surrounded by a combination of sorcerers and armsmen, all wearing the black and blue colors of Thunderhead College. Several of the outfits were embroidered with the college symbol of a lightning bolt inscribed within a circle. "Were you looking for me by any chance?" Lohan asked with a mocking smile.

Sulana looked around at her team and motioned for them to hold. Talon gave her a subtle nod.

Turning back to Lohan, she sat up straight and said, "Yes, I am looking for you. You have something that belongs to the Archives, and I'm here to get it back."

Lohan nodded slowly. "I see. Well, I would say your mission just hit a snag."

Sulana looked around at the men who surrounded her team and clenched her jaw. The original plan of capturing Lohan was definitely out. She decided that getting back the Portal Key was the most important goal, so she tried to bluff her way through the encounter. "The Portal Key doesn't belong to you, Lohan. If you give it to me now, we'll leave and that will be the end of it. Otherwise, the Archives will hunt you down and hold you accountable for the theft."

Lohan widened his eyes and said in a dramatic tone, "Hunt me down? Spirits save me!" Keeping his wand pointed at Sulana, he rapidly patted his pockets with his free hand. "Here, let me hand it right over." The patting slowed. "Oh, wait. I seem to have misplaced it." The rest of his group chuckled at his antics.

Despite being surrounded by a superior force, Sulana was tempted to reach for a weapon and force the smirk off of Lohan's face. But the bastard had the drop on her. She had no idea what spell had been enchanted into his wand, and she didn't want to find out the hard way.

Lohan wasn't done needling her. He laughed once and said, "It seems to me that the Archives has already hunted me down, and they are having trouble holding me accountable for anything. More proof that the Archives is no longer competent at managing sorcerer affairs. Maybe it's time for someone else to take over."

Sulana's breath caught. This was a new angle. She looked at him incredulously and said, "You?" She laughed at him and shook her head. "Do you actually believe you could do a better job?"

Lohan narrowed his eyes at her and answered evasively, "Me, among others."

Surprised, Sulana sat back in her saddle. What Lohan was suggesting made no sense. The Archives was under Imperial mandate to uphold the Sorcery Accords, which by extension made them responsible for all sorcerer activities. The only way to "take over" was by convincing the emperor to transfer that responsibility to another organization or by taking control of the Archives Council. Neither of those events seemed likely, and the idea of Lohan becoming a council member was ludicrous.

Somehow, the Portal Key had a role in all of this. Sulana believed Lohan when he said he didn't have it. If he did, he would have taken it out and waved it in front of her face, daring her to take action. She was willing to bet that one of his co-conspirators had the key, and judging from the clothing of the people surrounding her, it was someone from Thunderhead College. Her heart sank as she realized who that someone must be.

"Dumont Fortenz," she concluded under her breath.

Lohan nodded. "That's Headmaster Fortenz to you. And I'm here to cordially invite you to visit the college and see how a *real* learning facility operates...although it may be challenging to observe much from your guest room in the dungeon."

Sulana was speechless with outrage. Daven shifted in his saddle, and Lohan pointed his wand briefly at Daven before returning it to Sulana. "Don't try anything, soldier boy. I have no intention of hurting you or your Sword Sorceress, but if you refuse my invitation, I'll be forced to avenge my hurt feelings somehow."

Having little choice, Sulana and her team dismounted and relinquished their weapons to their captors. Daven's face was red with anger and frustration, and Sulana admonished him to settle down. So far, no one had been treated roughly, but she didn't want to test Lohan's patience.

Their hands were tied in front of them and looped together on a common rope. Lohan got onto Sulana's horse and tied one end of the rope to the pommel. As the captives trudged dispiritedly down the road toward Thunderhead College, Daven commented from his position in line behind Sulana, "Lohan sure has a strange notion of what cordial means." She had to agree.

CHAPTER 26

MISTRESS OF THE HOUSE

Dumont - The Governor's Residence, Dusk

Dumont followed Paeter through the gates of the governor's complex into the inner courtyard. The two guards at the gate recognized Paeter as he approached and came to attention while he passed. Even though Paeter had no official standing in the province, the Thoron family was obviously still respected for the contributions it had made in prior generations. The guards glanced at Dumont, but said nothing to challenge him. Dumont took the guards' silent support as a good sign of things to come.

The shade of the residence entryway was a welcome relief as Dumont and Paeter stepped under the peaked overhang and out of the sun's bright heat. The front doors were propped open, and Paeter walked through them without hesitation. Dumont followed him inside to discover a waiting room with wooden benches and a clean, empty fireplace. Coat pegs, bare of garments this time of year, lined the walls to the left and right.

The main hallway door opposite the entrance also stood open to let the fresh summer breeze flow into the residence. Paeter started to walk through the doorway into the hall beyond, but he halted abruptly and took a step back into the waiting room with a hiss of frustration. Gripping the knot of a thick red cord that hung to the right of the inner door, he pulled sharply. A bell clanged, echoing down the dark wooden panels of the hallway.

Within seconds, a woman peered around the corner of the hall. She squinted at the two visitors standing back-lit in the entryway. A brief exclamation escaped her lips before she slipped around the corner and came toward them in a swift walk that turned into a gliding run.

Paeter held out his arms as she neared and she practically leaped into them. They kissed deeply, and Dumont discreetly stepped back a pace to give them a moment of semi-privacy. This woman could be none other than Paeter's wife Uriel. "Welcome home," she said to him breathlessly when their kiss finally ended.

Uriel Thoron was a beautiful woman. She hid her middle-aged figure under a loose-fitting, blue velvet dress, but nothing detracted from her sweet face and long, curly, dark brown hair that showed only a few random grey strands. Her large brown eyes wandered lovingly over Paeter's face, and she gave him another quick hug before releasing him.

She turned to Dumont and looked him up and down. Folding her hands together demurely at her waist, she waited patiently for an introduction.

"Dumont, this is my wife Uriel. Uriel, this is Headmaster Dumont Fortenz."

Dumont took Uriel's proffered hand and bowed over it while Uriel curtseyed. "A pleasure to meet you. Paeter speaks of you often," he said.

"I'm happy to meet you at last, headmaster," Uriel replied. "Especially if this visit means Paeter will be coming home for a while." Her pleasant smile never slipped, but her tone communicated an undercurrent of displeasure at Paeter's long absence.

Paeter looked down and his face flushed with embarrassment. "Please, Uriel. You know it was necessary for me to be away."

Dumont waved away Paeter's reaction. "Relax Paeter. It is perfectly reasonable for your wife to have missed you." Bowing slightly to Uriel again, he said, "And I apologize for keeping him so long, madam."

"No apology necessary, headmaster. I'm sure it was time well spent," she added with a raised eyebrow.

Dumont smiled at the implied question and nodded. "Indeed it was. And please, call me Dumont. Headmaster is a rather useless title when I'm away from the college."

Uriel tilted her head back in an appraising manner and said, "I'm sure you are headmaster wherever you go, Dumont. But thank you for the courtesy, and please do call me Uriel."

At the other end of the hallway behind Uriel, a thin, brown-haired, young maid turned the corner and paused when she saw the two men. She hesitated, apparently wanting to speak with Uriel, but not wanting to interrupt. Uriel noticed Dumont's shift in attention and looked over her shoulder at the girl. "I'll be back shortly, Temma. Whatever it is will have to wait a few minutes."

The girl curtseyed and mumbled, "Yes, ma'am," before scurrying off with her head down.

"You seem to have a great deal of authority here," Dumont observed.

Uriel nodded and said, "Since the governor's wife died, he increasingly relies upon me to help run the household. I don't think he's truly a spiteful man, but I do believe he secretly likes having a Thoron to order around. The townspeople have not been quick to embrace his rule, and it galls him that they miss the days of Thoron leadership."

Paeter curled his lip into an ugly smile of appreciation for the governor's difficulties, and then he narrowed his eyes at his wife. "As long as running the household is the *only* wifely duty he expects of you."

Uriel laughed. "Don't worry Paeter. I've seen that look in his eyes a time or two, but I've never encouraged him." After a quick glance down the empty hall, she leaned toward the two men and said in a low voice, "Perhaps we should continue this conversation somewhere more private."

Paeter stared down the hallway for a moment with an inscrutable look on his face before taking a deep breath and huffing it out. "One would think I could find a bit of privacy in my own ancestral home," he said before abruptly turning and marching out of the waiting room into the sunny courtyard.

Uriel's face softened with pity as she watched her husband walk away, and then it hardened again with determination. She turned to Dumont and said, "I assume that you are here with a solution to this problem?" Dumont nodded slowly and let his mouth curve up into a small, reassuring smile. Uriel shook her head and breathed, "Finally," before exiting the foyer to follow her husband.

Dumont decided right then that he liked Uriel. Paeter had chosen a good mate. Her part in their plans had been to ingratiate herself into the Brachus household, a task she seemed to have accomplished admirably. She was strong, decisive, and observant. Those qualities would be valuable when, with a little help from Paeter's amulet, the governor appointed her son to be his Heir Designate.

CHAPTER 27
THE OFFER

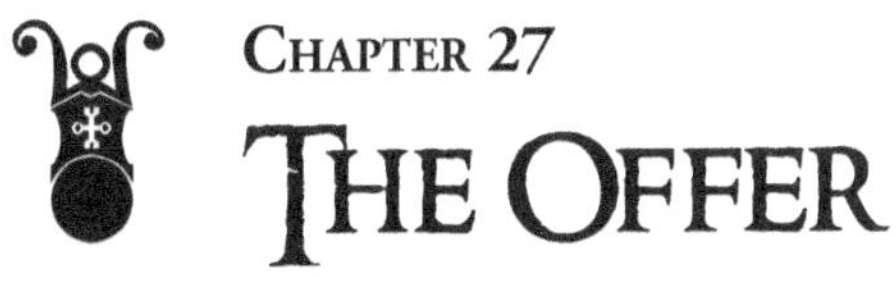

Sulana ~ The Courtyard, Thunderhead College

Sulana estimated that they had walked a little more than two miles when her captured team trudged through the main gates of the Thunderhead College courtyard. The college building was a wide, two-story mansion with a breezeway running through the center of the bottom floor. Two grooms ran out to retrieve the horses from the returning group. Sulana glared at them as her horse was collected along with all of the others, but the grooms never even looked at her.

A quick glance confirmed that her team was enduring their capture fine so far. Lohan had set a leisurely pace, so they had not been forced to jog. Daven's face was still a mask of suppressed anger, and his eyes rarely left Lohan.

Lohan sauntered over to stand in front of Sulana, circling the rope playfully so it swung back and forth between his hand and hers. She jerked the rope tight to stop the swing and got a little satisfaction out of seeing Lohan stumble a step before he tightened his grip and pulled back.

"You won't get away with this," she hissed at him.

Both of Lohan's eyebrows went up. "I won't? Well, let's think about that for a minute. Exactly who will the Archives send after me? I have their Sword Sorceress and their weaponsmaster right here. And both of you serve nicely as insurance for some good faith negotiating."

"Negotiating for what?" Sulana asked.

Lohan waved a finger at her. "Sorry, *Lana*. I don't want to spoil the surprise."

Sulana closed her eyes for a moment to let a spike of anger subside. In the future, assuming she had one, she and Lissy would have to be more careful about who they let overhear their private names for each other.

Her thoughts turned from Lissy to Jaylan. When word of her situation got back to the Archives, she doubted anything would stop him from coming after her, regardless of how he was doing with his training. If he charged down here unprepared, he'd be captured like the rest of them, or worse. It was the "or worse" that concerned her. Lohan had been easy on them so far, but Jaylan would not be in a forgiving mood if he found out Lohan was holding her hostage. A confrontation between the two former friends could turn deadly, and Jaylan would be at an extreme disadvantage against an experienced sorcerer.

She had to find out what was going on at Thunderhead College, and then she needed to get her team out of here as quickly as possible. Hopefully, she could do both without getting anyone killed.

Lohan was watching her steadily when her brief mental journey ended and she opened her eyes again. "Scheming already, Sulana? Don't worry. I'm sure we'll get you and your team back to the Archives soon enough."

As Lohan finished speaking, a man with a hawk-like nose approached from the breezeway. He looked comfortable in his leather armor and his stride automatically accommodated the movement of the sword that hung from his hip. His dark hair was cut with sharp bangs across his forehead and fell along the sides of his head in loose curls to his shoulders. His dark eyes never rested in one place for long; they roamed suspiciously across everyone in the courtyard, friend and foe alike.

Lohan gave the man a tentative smile and said, "Ah, Peltor. Just in time. I have some visitors here who have come to try out the new guest room you've created downstairs."

Sulana went still. Peltor was a familiar name. She had never met the man, but Jaylan had told her about him. At Buckwoods, he had helped Paeter Thoron escape from the village. To hear Jaylan tell it, the man was a menace.

Peltor narrowed his eyes at the line of "guests." He took in Sulana's startled look of recognition, Daven's glare, Talon's relaxed stance, and Barek's size. His hand went slowly to his sword. "Who are they?" he demanded.

"This is the Archives Sword Sorceress, Sulana Delano and her team," Lohan answered. He pointed at Talon. "That one deserves special care. He is Talon Destry, the Archives Weaponsmaster."

Peltor pulled his blade from its sheath with a hiss of steel and a flash of reflected sunlight. Lohan cringed slightly and spoke in a measured tone. "There's no need for bloodshed. The headmaster was very clear about that."

Peltor gave Lohan a flat look and said, "Just being cautious." He turned to sneer at Talon. "Besides, a weaponsmaster without a weapon isn't much of a threat." Talon said nothing in response, but the bored look on his face showed he wasn't impressed with Peltor's people skills.

Peltor strutted over to stand in front of Barek. He straightened his posture as he approached, as if that would somehow make up the disparity in their heights. Looking up into Barek's impassive face, he asked, "And what would a Winterman be doing here?"

Lohan waved his hand dismissively. "He works for the Archives as a Guardian."

Peltor tilted his head to the side and stared into Barek's eyes. "Maybe. Wintermen are not known for their loving support of sorcerers. I'll bet there's more to his *work* with the Archives than you think."

Barek growled low and took a step toward Peltor, causing the smaller man to quickly back up and drop into a defensive crouch. Barek smiled at Peltor's reaction and stepped back into his former position. Peltor's face went red and he straightened slowly, glaring at the smug look on the big man's face.

"Please don't play with the guests, Peltor," Lohan said. Speaking to Barek, he added, "And the guests would be wise not to antagonize the host. Peltor is not known for his restraint."

Peltor's sneer came back and his eyes gleamed with the promise of demonstrating his lack of restraint.

The exchange between the men put Sulana's nerves on edge, but Peltor's comment did give her pause. She had never really considered why a Winterman would join the Archives and volunteer to help Sulana's team. Barek's people were strong supporters of the Accords and keeping sorcerers under control, but they also avoided dealing directly with sorcerers as much as possible. Barek had never acted hostile or nervous around sorcery, so Sulana never had reason to ask him about his feelings on the matter.

But that was a concern for another time. The situation at hand demanded all of her attention.

Lohan took out his wand again and pointed it at the line of prisoners. "Peltor, make our visitors comfortable in the guest room, but leave Sulana here. I'll take her down there myself in a moment."

Daven eased back as far as the restraining rope allowed and bent his knees. Sulana saw him preparing to strike anyone who came close to her, and she shook her head. "Save it," she said to him. "Lohan isn't going to hurt me. For now, just do as he says." Daven looked unconvinced, but he relaxed his posture.

Lohan kept his wand pointed at Sulana while Peltor freed her hands from the tow line. Her wrists were still tied together, but she was no longer tethered to the rest of her team. Peltor told one of the patrol guards to take the end of the rope and lead the way. He trailed a few steps behind the line of prisoners when they headed into the breezeway, his sword still ready in his hand.

Lohan dismissed the other members of the patrol, leaving Sulana standing alone with him in the courtyard.

She raised her wrists toward him and looked at the wand in his hands. "You don't need that. You have my team. I'm not going anywhere, and this rope is chafing. If you take it off, I promise to come with you peacefully."

Lohan chuckled and shook his head. "I don't think so, Sulana. I may have taken away all of your toys, but I know you're still a physical threat to me." Angling his head toward her departing team members, he said, "You were trained by one of the best swordsmen in the empire, and I have no reason to take risks."

Sulana lowered her hands. After the embarrassment of being captured so easily, Lohan's claim that he considered her to be a physical threat actually made her feel a little better. Unfortunately, it also meant that he would not remove the itchy rope that truly was chafing her wrists.

"Then what do you want?" she asked him.

Lohan looked her up and down with a considering look that made her skin crawl. "This may come as a surprise Sulana, but I like you, and I want to make you an offer. Join me here at Thunderhead College and leave the stifling

Archives behind. We can show you how to do so much more with your abilities."

What? It didn't matter what they could teach her. Thunderhead College stood for everything she was sworn to oppose. One thing was curious. Lohan had asked her to join *him*, not *them*. Was he really deluded enough to think she would be interested in any kind of relationship with him? She would sooner put a knife in him than ever touch him tenderly.

"You're insane," was all she could think to say.

Lohan shrugged and actually looked disappointed. "Have it your way."

"Just let me join my team," Sulana said as she turned and walked toward the breezeway. She heard Lohan hesitate behind her and then take a few hurried steps to catch up. It was a very small moment of control, but it was enough to let her enter the breezeway with a small bitter smile on her lips.

Chapter 28
Paeter's Offspring

Dumont - Thoron Residence, Dusk

Dumont followed Paeter and Uriel through the city square and down a lane that a freshly-painted wooden sign identified as Panorama Street. Large and well-maintained homes were lined up along the edge of the city's plateau. Each home had a wide view of the valley below, which was clearly the source of the street name.

Low stone walls ran along the road and between the homes, creating distinct property boundaries. The entrance into each front yard was through a wide break in the wall, none of which were gated. A narrow back yard set the houses away from the cliff edge. Some of the residents had added flower beds or pots to the top of the roadside wall, and summer flowers filled the air with sweet smells while treating the eye to colorful blooms.

The houses reflected the common Dusk design theme of timber construction on top of a tall stone foundation, but all of these houses had two stories above ground. Dumont imagined that the view from the top floor windows overlooking the valley must be spectacular.

Panorama Street was remarkably quiet compared to the rest of the town. The only other pedestrians were a well-dressed elderly couple walking arm-in-arm in the opposite direction. Uriel waved to them and bade them a good day. They smiled and inclined their heads, returning the courtesy.

Their eyes lingered on Dumont as he passed, and he returned their curious smiles with a nod.

Looking ahead, the curving lane eventually turned sharply away from the bluff, but the Thorons led the way through a break in the wall about half-way down the street. Dumont followed them into the front yard of what appeared to be the most beautiful home on the block. Their home was situated on a large lot with side yards that were more than just the narrow walkways the other houses had. Tall flowering vines on trellises rose above the side walls, adding a sense of seclusion to the property.

Although the Thoron family had lost the province governorship, they had not lost the wealth they had built up over several generations. Thoron Craftworks was by far the largest builder in Sunset Province, and few structures in Dusk had been raised without their involvement. Paeter left the day-to-day operations in the capable hands of his business manager, Red Falconer. Paeter's son Astin loved the family business and hoped to take it over one day, not knowing that Paeter had other plans for him.

The Thorons opened the front door and went inside. Paeter held the door for Dumont as he entered behind them. Windows were open at the front and back of the house, letting a cross-breeze flow through. The house was clean and well appointed with fine furnishings and unusual decorations that hinted at past associations with important visitors. Dumont looked around with interest, thinking that the heirlooms of a governor's line were of a different standard than those of most families. The meticulously-detailed, life-size carving of a bald eagle on the mantle would alone be worth a governor's ransom.

A maid appeared soon after they entered the house, and Uriel arranged for refreshments. Paeter welcomed Dumont to their home, offering him a seat at the dining room table, which he gratefully accepted. After the long, warm morning walk, he was ready for a rest. The table was at the back corner of the house in a light and airy space with big windows and a lovely view of the mountains on the other side of the valley. The back yard was landscaped with low shrubs and ringed with more flower beds.

Light footsteps danced down the stairs from the upper level, and a lithe young woman in a yellow summery dress appeared at the base of the stairwell, her dark brown hair bouncing around her shoulders. She glanced at Dumont, but her searching eyes quickly found her father. "Daddy," she squealed, and she ran to him, throwing herself into his ready arms.

While hugging her and patting her back, Paeter smiled at Dumont over the girl's head and said, "This would be my daughter Hayli."

Releasing her father, the girl turned to acknowledge their guest with a curtsey and stepped back to stand next to Paeter. Dark brown eyes that closely matched her mother's took in Dumont quickly and then met his gaze. She waited for an introduction with a polite smile on her round, sweet face.

Paeter said, "Hayli, this is Headmaster Dumont from Thunderhead College. He is visiting Dusk and will be staying with us briefly. While he is here, perhaps he will have time to speak with you about attending the college."

Hayli's smile turned to a frown, and she glanced sideways up at her father with an irritated expression. She pressed her lips together and shook her head once before turning her attention back to Dumont. "It's a pleasure to meet you headmaster, but I'm afraid I have no intention of attending Thunderhead College. I'm sure you run a fine institution, but I prefer to study at the Archives."

"Hayli!" Uriel hissed at her daughter. "Show some manners."

The girl looked down at the floor and said, "I don't mean to be rude, but I also don't see any reason to lie about it."

Dumont chuckled and came to her rescue. "I'm pleased to meet you too Hayli, and you are right. There's no need to lie to me about wanting to study at the Archives. They run a fine sorcery college and I'm sure you'll do well there." He was fairly certain that he even managed to make it sound like he meant what he said.

Fortunately, he was prepared for the girl's declaration. Paeter had warned him before their journey to Dusk that Hayli was showing distressing Isolationist tendencies and that she had romanticized her memories of the time when they had lived at the Archives. She was determined to return to the Archives and study sorcery there.

The problem was one of timing. If Thunderhead College got into a direct conflict with the Archives, he didn't want Paeter to be distracted by concerns for his daughter's well being. For that reason alone, Dumont had encouraged Paeter to delay his daughter's admission and keep her here in Dusk for as long as possible. It certainly wasn't because he wanted the misguided youngster to attend his college instead. In the meantime, they would have to be careful when discussing their plans around her.

Paeter had waited through their exchange with his jaw clenched. After Dumont assured Hayli that he was not offended, her father spoke. "My apologies, headmaster. Hayli, you may go back to whatever you were doing."

Chastised and dismissed, Hayli held her head high and swished between the adults to the stairwell. She lifted the front of her dress and ran up the stairs without another word or a look back.

The maid arrived with refreshments as Hayli's footsteps faded down the upstairs hallway and a door slammed shut. Uriel rolled her eyes at her daughter's histrionics and motioned for Paeter to sit down. The maid had brought mugs of dark tea and a decanter of liquor. She placed a delicate ceramic plate filled with tiny fragrant pies on the table and left the room.

Dumont was anxious to get on with their plans, but found himself enjoying a brief moment of normal home life. His home had been Thunderhead College for so long now that he'd forgotten what it was like to relax in an intimate setting with friends. The afternoon sun angled through the west-facing windows of the dining room and warmed his arms and chest. He accepted when Paeter offered him some of the liquor for his tea, willing to take a moment to enjoy the warmth it spread through him after his first sips of the tasty brew.

Just as his mind was starting to turn back to matters of business, the front door of the house opened and a young man burst breathlessly into the room. The boy was in his late teens but still had the gangly look of youth. Short, unruly dark hair topped his head, and he had the same hazel eyes as his father. In spite of differences in their physique, there could be no question that this was Paeter's son.

The boy's words came out in a rush. "Father! I heard you had returned. Will you be staying for a while? I have so much to tell you." He stepped further into the room and the maid closed the door behind him. She frowned at his dirty work clothes and the half-dried clots of mud his boots had tracked into the house. She tapped his shoulder and pointed down at his boots. He absently pulled them off and handed them to her as his father introduced him.

"As I'm sure you've surmised, this is my son Astin. Astin, come and meet Headmaster Dumont Fortenz from Thunderhead College."

Astin padded over to where Dumont sat at the table and held out his hand. "Pleasure to meet you, sir." Seeing the dirty state of his hand, Astin quickly wiped it on his shirt before holding it out again.

Dumont shook Astin's hand and smiled. "It's a pleasure to finally meet you as well, Astin. Your father speaks proudly of you." Dumont waved his hand up and down to indicate Astin's clothing. "What are you working on?"

Astin turned toward his father as he answered. "The Millers had a terrible washout from the high runoff this spring and I'm helping the crew rebuild their basement and fix the drainage. Red let me design the new drainage and he said I had a natural talent for it."

Paeter nodded soberly and said, "That's great son, but I hope you have been keeping up with your studies as well."

Astin rolled his eyes and answered, "Yes, Father. But I don't see what good studying history and statecraft is going to do me when I'm running Thoron Craftworks."

Paeter considered his son for a moment before answering. "You'd be surprised. Statecraft teaches you a lot about how to deal with people. If you plan to be a leader of any kind, that knowledge is useful. And everyone benefits from knowing a little history. It puts everything we do today into perspective."

Astin sighed and said, "Yes, Father. I'll do my best."

Paeter shrugged. "That's all I ask. Now go wash up and join us here for some tea."

Astin ran up the stairs, puffs of dust leaving his pants and sleeves as his feet hit the treads. The maid followed him up shortly afterward with a bowl of water and a towel over her arm.

"Astin seems like a fine and industrious boy, Paeter," Dumont commented. Lowering his voice, he asked, "He still knows nothing of your plans for him?"

Paeter shook his head. "He knows nothing, and I'd like to keep it that way for now. Astin has a good heart, much better than his father's, and he has it set on running Thoron Craftworks. I'm afraid that being named Heir Designate will be an unwelcome shock for him."

Dumont chuckled. "Not as much of a shock as it will be for the current Heir Designate."

Paeter's face grew serious. "Yes, the governor's son Malcolm is going to be a problem. Probably our biggest problem."

Dumont wasn't concerned. They had been over all of this before, but Paeter tended to worry over the same problems like a dog with an old bone. Dumont said confidently, "We have plans, and we have contingency plans. If Malcolm doesn't cooperate, we have many options for getting him out of the way."

Their conversation was interrupted by an upstairs door opening and footsteps coming down the hall toward the stairs. Astin joined them at the table, and talk turned to what had been happening in Dusk during Paeter's absence.

CHAPTER 29
INCARCERATED

Sulana ~ The Dungeon, Thunderhead College

Sulana looked down at her hands in the thin light afforded by the single, weak illuminator that was recessed high up into the wall at her back. The manacles that encircled her wrists were attached to heavy chains that connected to another pair of manacles around her ankles. The chain snaked under the wall-mounted bench she sat on and joined to a solid ring embedded in the wall.

How had it come to this? Why had it come to this?

Thunderhead College had competed with the Archives for the training of young sorcerers for years. They had been vocal about their Integrationist agenda as well as their disdain for the conservative positions of the Archives Council with regards to the Accords. But they had never taken any kind of aggressive action like this.

But really, they had, hadn't they? The pieces came together in Sulana's mind with a rush. Paeter Thoron and his accomplice had tried to steal a portal key and had enslaved Buckwoods to experiment with mind control amulets. Now there was little doubt that the accomplice had been Lohan, who had just successfully stolen a portal key from the Archives. Peltor fled Buckwoods with Paeter when Sulana's team arrived, and now he was here at Thunderhead College too.

It all kept coming back to the college. Which meant it all came back to Dumont Fortenz. Councilor Rissik had been right again. The headmaster was up to something that required portal keys. He needed to be able to move around the empire quickly.

If she ever got out of this place, she was going to have to sit down with Councilor Rissik and have a long talk about where he got his information. She couldn't keep operating blind, or situations like the one she faced now would keep happening.

Sulana felt a shiver run down her back as her mind replayed their capture out on the road. They had been surrounded by both soldiers and sorcerers. The sorcerers were not the passive, studious type that were so common at the Archives. These sorcerers were trained in physical combat. One had carried a short sword and another had a mace. Dumont was assembling his own *team* of Sword Sorcerers.

Across the room from Sulana, Daven sighed and said, "This is just embarrassing," and clinked his chains to emphasize his words.

Talon glanced at Sulana's downcast face and said, "Shut up, Daven."

Barek got off his bench and inspected his chains, apparently uninterested in contributing to the discussion. He turned around and sat on the floor, dipping his neck to look down the length of chain to where it connected to the ring in the wall.

Daven huffed, "What? I can't complain that we are stuck down here in a dungeon? Our mission was to recover the portal key and return with Lohan if we could. Now we are Lohan's prisoners and the portal key is nowhere to be found."

Sulana stared woodenly at Daven, and said with carefully measured words, "What's your point?"

Daven looked back at her and then at the manacles on his hands. "My point is that our mission has failed. We need to get out of here and get back to the Archives."

Talon snorted and sat back on his bench. "Good idea. I suppose you have a plan?"

Barek planted his feet against the wall under the bench and grabbed the chain with both hands. The big man's back and shoulder muscles strained as he pulled hard on the unyielding ring.

Daven glared at Talon and said, "Well, somebody needs to come up with a plan. The one we've been using so far hasn't worked out very well."

"What's that supposed to mean?" Sulana asked, her eyes narrowing dangerously.

Daven seemed to realize he might have gone too far. In a conciliatory tone he answered, "I'm not blaming you, Sulana. You couldn't have known they'd be waiting to ambush us."

But maybe I should have, Sulana thought. Thanks to Councilor Rissik, she had come prepared with enough knowledge to at least suspect they might be walking into a trap. If she and her team had moved forward with more stealth, they might have avoided the ambush. But they still would not have recovered the portal key.

Barek tried pulling on the chain from side to side in an apparent attempt to loosen the ring, but it remained solidly planted.

Talon spoke up again. "It doesn't matter how we got here. What matters is what happens going forward. We may not have recovered the portal key and we may not have captured Lohan, but we did uncover a conspiracy that has alarming implications."

So Talon had been thinking along the same lines she had. Daven was right that they needed to get back to the Archives so they could warn the Council about what they had learned.

Sulana nodded at Talon. "I've been thinking the same thing. Headmaster Fortenz is creating an army of sorcerers here, and he will undoubtedly use the portal key to coordinate their efforts around the empire."

Barek abandoned his attempts to pull the ring from the wall and sat back down on his bench, his chest rising and falling from his efforts. "Mortar too new?" Talon whispered, and the Winterman nodded.

Daven blinked a few times at Sulana. "But why?"

Sulana shrugged. "I wish I knew. They have Integrationist supporters in sanctuaries around the empire. Maybe they plan to intimidate the other sorcerers into adopting their policies. From what Lohan said, their objective may be to take control of the Archives."

She looked at Talon for confirmation, and he nodded his agreement with her train of thought. Then he added his own conclusion. "Emperor Tanes will never tolerate Integrationists controlling the Archives. He will see that as a failure to uphold the Accords, and he'll respond accordingly."

A cold weight settled in Sulana's stomach as she realized Talon was right. If Emperor Tanes "responded accordingly," every sorcerer would end up in a dungeon. Or worse.

Maybe that's why Paeter was refining the amulets. They could be used to influence mundane leadership around the empire, putting pressure on the emperor to make decisions a certain way. Would they dare try to put an amulet on Emperor Tanes himself?

Impossible. No mundane leader would be seen consorting with sorcerers after the Battle of Riverview and the Grassgate Incident. The risk was too great. But still, the amulets had to fit into this somehow.

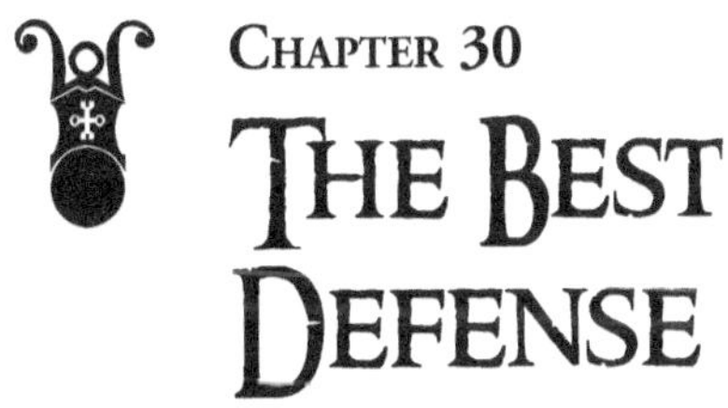

CHAPTER 30
THE BEST DEFENSE

I had just sat down in Professor Delano's classroom with my new spell book when Benjamin leaned over from the next table and said, "Congratulations, Jaylan. I hear you can cast." Daisy, sitting on his other side, glanced over at me but said nothing.

I waited a moment for the snarky comment that usually accompanied compliments from the twins, but none was forthcoming. "Thanks, Ben," I finally said.

Thankfully, the twins had eased off on their rudeness since Lohan left. Lohan's reactions to their teasing must have been more satisfying than mine. I mostly ignored their attempts to bait me, and I tried to treat them respectfully even when they were being annoying. In the end, I think they decided I was harmless.

Ben and I had even started forming a tentative friendship during our sparring sessions. With Talon gone, all of us who practiced swordsmanship were on our own for finding partners and scheduling practices. The young man was thin but wiry and he had the edge over me in speed and stamina. I had the edge over him in experience and reach. We made good sparring partners because he kept me on my toes and I helped him learn a few new tricks. However, he tended to fall back on immature behavior once he was here in the classroom with his sister at his side.

I'd noticed the same thing in Daisy: when she was away from Ben, she was serious and focused. But when they were together, she reverted to a sharp-tongued and rebellious teenage girl. As much as they seemed to love each other, they had very different personalities and were much more productive when apart.

My musings were interrupted by Ebnik walking into the room. He came over to where I sat, and I stood to shake his hand.

The old sorcerer held a blue, soft leather bag in his hand that was stretched into a teardrop shape by a heavy round object inside. He held the bag out to me and said, "Congratulations, Jaylan. I'd like to present you with your first casting orb. It's one I've had for years but rarely use any more. It has reliably manifested many a spell for me, and I hope it does the same for you."

I accepted the bag from him with reverence. It was heavier than it looked, and I could clearly feel the orb through the soft leather of the pouch when I cupped it in my hand. "I'm honored, Wizard Vlastorus. Are you sure you can part with it?"

Ebnik chuckled and answered, "I have a collection of them. Over the years, many friends have felt compelled to give me orbs as gifts. I've decided it's time I started doing the same before the shelf they're stored on breaks and I'm crushed in an avalanche of the things. Go ahead and take a look at it."

I set the pouch on the table and untied the leather string that held it closed. The twins both craned their necks to watch. Daisy got tired of bobbing her head around her brother to see, so she got up and stood next to me. I lifted the bottom of the pouch and let the orb roll out into my hand.

Daisy cooed, "It's beautiful."

"That's a monster," Ben added.

Ebnik blushed and ducked his head, "Yes, sorry about that. Truth be told, I prefer to carry a smaller and lighter orb myself now. But I figured you are young and strong, Jaylan, so the weight won't bother you."

The orb was about two inches in diameter, a little bigger than a plum. It was made from some kind of polished crystal. As far as I could tell, it was almost perfectly spherical. Striations wove through the interior in arcing and intersecting lattices. The striations were mostly white, but some had a pinkish cast to them. Hefting it in my hand, I could see where Ebnik might prefer a lighter orb, but I liked how it filled the palm of my hand.

Ebnik traced his finger across the surface of the orb and said, "Crystal orbs are a little more challenging to use than glass ones, but after you work with it for a while, you can use those striations to your advantage. One thing is for sure: your spells will never be limited by that orb."

Daisy snorted. "And if all else fails, you can hit your opponent over the head with it."

All of us laughed. Daisy went back to her seat, and I put the orb back into its pouch. "Thanks again. I'll use it proudly," I said to the old wizard.

Ebnik nodded. "Good luck with your training. I've done what I can with the amulets, and I need to return home to Plains End soon. But if you need anything, send word and I'll do my best to help."

I shook his hand and said, "I'll do that. Have a safe journey home."

A few moments after Ebnik departed, Professor Delano entered the room carrying a woven bag with rope handles. She spotted the orb pouch on the table in front of me and said, "I see Wizard Vlastorus has delivered his gift. It was kind of him to give you Froth, although you may want to stick with one of the classroom orbs for your training."

"Did you say Froth?" I asked her.

"Yes. Crystal orbs require a great deal of effort to make, so some smiths name them. When Wizard Vlastorus created that one, he named it Froth because of the patterns within it. He intended to create a smaller orb, but said Froth was meant to be the size it is."

I had no idea that Ebnik had worked so hard on the orb or that it was precious enough to be named. He had made it sound like it was an unwanted gift he once received from someone else. I felt unworthy of such a treasure. "I wonder why he didn't say anything about that," I mused, looking down at the bulging pouch.

Professor Delano shrugged. "He didn't want to make it seem like giving it to you was too big a deal. He was worried that you wouldn't accept it."

And I might not have. Ebnik and I had been through a lot together, but he didn't owe me anything. I was humbled by his generosity, and I swore right then to one day be worthy of Froth.

The professor set down and unpacked the bag she carried, extracting two books and placing them onto her desk. "Now," she said, raising her voice to address the room, "I've been asked to step up your defensive training, so we are all going to work on shielding today."

The twins groaned. "Can't we do something more fun? Shields are boring," Ben said. "And painful," Daisy added with a cringe.

Professor Delano grew stern and said, "Shielding is only boring and painful because you aren't very good at it. Both of you need to spend more time practicing the basics and stop trying to find creative ways to torture one another."

Ben glanced at his sister, and she giggled. The twins were evidently guilty as charged.

The twins fidgeted while Professor Delano went over basic shield theory. She occasionally shot a question at them to keep them focused. Their answers were right only about half the time, so she got across her point that they both still had a lot to learn.

My attention was not fully on Professor Delano's description of shields either. I wondered why she had been asked to step up our defensive training. Did the Council have reason to think we would need to defend ourselves in the near future? Were we preparing for some threat? I didn't much like that line of thinking with Sulana out in the field.

I wondered if we would be learning offensive spells too. It doesn't make sense to go into battle with a shield but no weapon. As we used to say when I was with the Imperial Guard, sometimes the best defense is a good offense.

I raised my hand, and the professor stopped to acknowledge me. I didn't want to alarm the twins, so I didn't give voice to my concerns about the Council having identified a threat. All I asked was, "Will we be studying offensive spells as well?"

Professor Delano looked at me intently. The extra tightness around her eyes and mouth told me that she knew I would read into what she was doing and that she herself was worried. She glanced at the twins before answering me. "Yes, but it's not a good idea to move on to offensive spells until we learn to shield ourselves from them."

Daisy took the professor's answer as a joke and giggled. I held the professor's gaze and nodded, accepting her oblique answer to my real question.

Shoving aside my worries about Sulana and what might be going on, I forced myself to concentrate on what Professor

Delano was teaching us. I've always found that the threat of practical application helps me give my full attention to the theory of how things work.

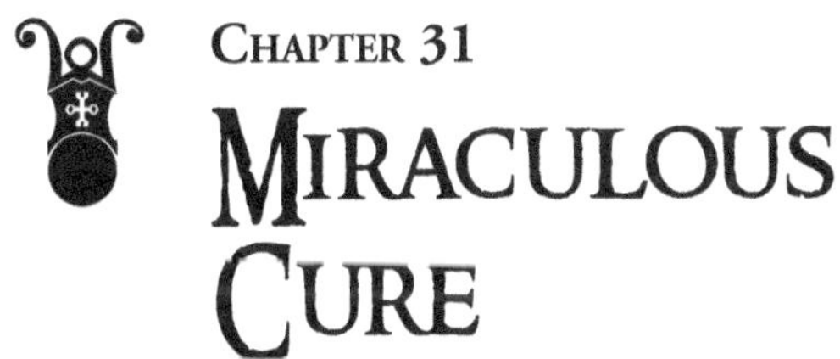

Chapter 31

MIRACULOUS CURE

Dumont ~ The Governor's Residence, Dusk

Housemistress Uriel Thoron carried the governor's morning tea into his bedchamber, leaving the door ajar behind her. Dumont listened at the narrow opening. The heavy, musty odor of a long-occupied room wafted out of the door. Frederick Brachus, Governor of Sunset Province, was suffering from gout, and the painful condition had kept him in his bed for the past two days.

"Ah, there you are, Uriel." The remark was followed by the rustle of bedclothes and a grunt of effort, most likely from the governor rearranging his bulk to sit up in his bed.

"Good morning, Governor. How is your knee today? I have your tea here, and I added a tincture that the healer said will ease the swelling."

Dumont smiled to himself. The tea did indeed contain an anti-inflammatory tincture, but it was also laced with a sedative that would help the governor relax when it came time to meet his surprise visitor.

"You would have made a fine governor's wife," the man quipped.

Dumont frowned. Pointing out that she was married to the man that he had replaced as governor was unkind to say the least.

"Don't be rude, Frederick," Uriel responded. "I earn more from running your household than a wife would, and my husband's business is doing better than ever."

The governor harrumphed and said, "That's the woman I know. Feisty as ever."

Dumont suppressed the urge to laugh at Uriel's return barb. When the Thorons left the governorship, they took their construction business and affluence with them. For the first time ever, the people of Sunset Province had to start paying taxes to support the Ruling Family. Consequently, the Brachus family was not as popular as the self-sufficient Thoron family had been.

Uriel chatted with the governor about household business while he drank his tea. She had cooled it before bringing it up to him so he would be able to consume it quickly. After a minute or so, Dumont heard him put down the cup and exhale a relaxed sigh. Uriel wasted no more time.

"I've brought someone to meet you, Governor," Uriel said. Dumont moved back from the opening when her footsteps approached the door.

"Woman, I've told you I do not receive guests in my room," he growled.

"Well you can't very well receive guests in the main hall right now," she responded as she pulled the door open and revealed Dumont waiting outside the room.

The governor straightened the bedclothes and adjusted his nightshirt while Dumont came forward to the foot of the bed. With a frustrated sigh, the bulky man sat back against his pillows and stared impatiently at Uriel, waiting for an introduction.

"Governor Brachus, may I present Dumont Fortenz, Headmaster of Thunderhead College."

The governor's posture went rigid. Dumont bowed to the man and said, "It's a pleasure to meet you, Governor."

The governor's eyes darted around the room as if looking for an escape or a weapon, but nothing was within reach and his swollen knee trapped him in the bed. Accepting his helplessness, the governor's fear turned to embarrassed anger.

"To what do I owe the pleasure of this visit?" he said with a sharp tone.

Dumont held up a hand in a gesture of peace. "Relax, Governor. I'm not here to do you harm. In fact, I think I can help you."

The governor stared at Dumont, suspicion tightening his face and his voice. "What kind of help?" He glanced over at Uriel, but she stood with her hands folded in front of her waist and an innocent smile on her face.

"We have talented healers at Thunderhead College, and one of them believes she can help you with your ailment," Dumont explained, keeping his voice calm and reasonable.

The governor shook his head. "I have healers of my own. My knee will improve in a day or so. It always does. Tell your healer thanks anyway."

"Not that ailment, Governor. I'm talking about the illness that has been weakening you for the past several months and has shown no sign of improvement. In spite of your healers' best efforts."

The governor's eyes went wide and his mouth dropped open at Dumont's words. Then his neck and face turned red and he glared at Uriel. "What rumors have you been spreading?" he accused.

Uriel went to his side and put a hand on his arm, which he pulled away from her touch. "There's no use pretending, Frederick. You are very ill. The gout will pass, but your stomach ailment is making you weaker with every passing month. Your healers have been able to do nothing. I asked Dumont if his people could help somehow."

The governor snorted. "His people. You mean his sorcerers."

Dumont's voice grew insistent. "Yes, Governor. Sorcerers. With access to power your healers lack. Your healers have already failed you. Would you reject a little sorcery if it could save your life?"

A brief flash of hope flickered across the governor's face. He sat quietly for a moment, considering Dumont's offer. Finally, the stress of the encounter and the sedative in the tea overwhelmed him; he closed his eyes with a sigh leaned his head back against his pillow.

Dumont dared to look over at Uriel and gave her a wink. Her mouth drew into a disapproving line and she cautioned him with a subtle but negative turn of her head.

Snapping his head forward and opening his eyes, the governor asked, "And what is it you want in return for this miraculous cure?"

Dumont had expected this demand. The governor would not believe he was offering to save the man's life out of the goodness of his heart. "I would like permission to open a school here in Dusk, Governor."

The governor looked confused. "A school? There's already a Sanctuary. Do you mean to expand it?"

Dumont shook his head. "No, Governor. The Sanctuary is run by the Archives, and their methods are often different from ours." *To say the least.* "I would like to open a separate school that would be chartered with finding ways to make sorcery more useful to everyone, as we do at Thunderhead College."

"What do you mean by *more useful?*" the governor asked, and then covered a yawn with his hand. The sedative was doing a good job of draining his tension. And his resistance.

Dumont wasn't sure he actually *would* set up a school in Dusk, even if granted permission by the governor, but he couldn't help warming to the subject anyway. "Our school would focus on ways sorcery can be safely integrated back into society. For example, we might be able to find ways to increase the yield of your crops, or to control the spring floodwaters."

The governor's brow furrowed and it looked like he might argue against the idea, but after a moment he ran a hand down his face and shook his head. "Whatever. As long as you finance the construction and operation of the school, I've no objection."

Dumont bowed slightly in acknowledgement and said, "Thank you, Governor. You are most kind. I will of course see to all the financial needs of the school."

The headmaster reached into his pocket and palmed the amulet Paeter had worked so hard to create. The governor's eyes warily tracked his hand as he handed the device to Uriel. The pendant's heavy gold chain slithered out of her palm to dangle and gleam in the lamplight. The amulet itself was a work of art—truly a gift fit for a governor. A large, square-cut amethyst was mounted in the center of a gold backing, bordered by rolled golden filigree.

Uriel's eyes brightened with admiration for the handiwork even though this was not the first time she had seen it. She was undoubtedly proud of her husband's skill, but knew better than to mention that Paeter was the artist who had produced it. The governor did not trust Paeter in the slightest, and had even banned him from entering the manor. Dumont was certain he would refuse the gift if he knew Paeter was involved in its making, regardless of how much he might desire it.

The governor smiled as he stared at the pendant, but the smile faded when Uriel came toward him and reached forward with the loop of chain held open. He leaned away from her on the bed, and she stopped.

"What is this?" he demanded.

"I know you are uncomfortable with sorcery, Governor, but the pendant was designed specifically for you," Dumont reassured him.

Tentatively leaning forward, the governor allowed Uriel to put the amulet's chain over his head. She rearranged the gold chain around his neck and set the sparkling pendant on his chest. "It is lovely," he breathed, looking down at it with equal parts wonder and apprehension.

Dumont came around from the foot of the bed and placed his hand on the governor's chest, covering the amulet. The governor grabbed his wrist with a surprisingly strong grip and stared directly into Dumont's eyes.

Dumont nodded toward the amulet and said, "I must activate it, Governor. Right now it is just a pretty piece of jewelry."

The governor's eyes reflected an internal debate that went back and forth between fear and hope. His expression finally settled into one of wary acceptance, and he slowly released his hold on Dumont's hand.

Dumont kept a sober look on his face, suppressing the excitement that tightened his stomach and rose into his chest. He opened a channel to the amulet and spoke the trigger word, "Protector." He then removed his hand. The amulet instantly began to glow. The glow deepened the beauty of the amethyst and flashed up the chain as it established a link to the governor's own well of vaetra.

The governor's eyes widened as the enchantment took hold. "That feels…extraordinary," he muttered.

Dumont nodded. "You have been given a great honor, Governor Brachus. You are not only the protector of Sunrise Province, but of Thunderhead College as well. It is your duty to see to the well being of all in your care. It is also important that you wear your amulet at all times, but you should hide it from those who might covet it."

The governor looked down at the amulet with uncertainty for a moment, but then his hands fumbled with tucking it into his nightshirt. He looked up at Dumont and opened his mouth to speak, then closed it again. He shook his head once to clear it and said, "I thought you said this would make me get better."

Dumont's excitement turned to wary caution. Perhaps the enchantment wasn't strong enough after all. Paeter had been concerned that subverting too much of the governor's normal behavior would reveal their manipulations. But the risk of discovery was equally great if the enchantment was too weak to control the man.

"It will, Governor. Don't you already feel it working? With my support, you can take better care of all your people." As he spoke, Dumont reached into his pocket and gripped his casting orb in case the amulet failed them and it became necessary to employ the backup plan. Dumont watched the governor's reaction carefully. If the amulet was working correctly, the man should be feeling a sense of well being and purpose, as well as camaraderie with Dumont, the amulet's activator.

The governor took a deep breath and his eyes wandered as he evaluated himself. "You're right. I feel stronger and more relaxed."

Dumont smiled and withdrew his hand from his pocket. The enchantment was working its subtle influence on the man, but they had to give it time to worm its way into his psyche. In the meantime, he would lay some groundwork for the next phase of their plan.

"I have to return to the college soon, but Uriel will act as my representative and convey a few ideas I have to improve quality of life for you and the people of Sunset Province. At the same time, I think we can improve your relations with your constituents."

The governor glanced at Uriel and then asked, "Must you leave? I would prefer to discuss your ideas directly with you."

"I'm afraid I have many responsibilities I must attend to, Governor."

"Of course, of course, I didn't mean to impose," the governor said, waiving his hand in apology. Dumont was pleased to note that the enchantment's influence was strengthening with each passing moment.

"It would be no imposition, Governor. I would like nothing more than to stay here and help." *But a sorcerer must not be seen at the governor's side during the changes to come.*

The governor yawned and patted his chest where the amulet lay. "Thank you for the treatment and the assistance, headmaster. I hope you can find an opportunity to visit again soon."

Dumont bowed to the governor in acknowledgement of the implied dismissal. "Have a good day, Governor."

The sedative was still at work in the man's system, and a nap would give the amulet time to work unhindered by conscious distractions. In any case, Dumont had done everything he'd needed to do.

Uriel opened the door to the governor's room and said, "I'll be right back after I escort the headmaster out,

Governor." The governor nodded once as he stifled another huge yawn with his fist.

Walking back to the entrance of the manor, Dumont could see that Uriel tried hard to keep a smug expression off her face as they passed a couple of servants. But finally, when they were alone again, she could stand it no more and looked up at him with a big grin. "That went extremely well, headmaster."

Dumont kept his expression sober in spite of the excitement he felt at the successful launch of their plan. "Time will tell, Uriel. But I agree. Indications are very hopeful."

The smile slipped from Uriel's face and she said quietly, "It's a shame Paeter couldn't be the one to direct things. It would have given him a great deal of satisfaction to win back some control over his province."

"Paeter understands that could never happen," Dumont replied. "No one here would believe that the governor had changed his feelings about Paeter, and having a sorcerer close to him while he made momentous decisions would raise undesirable suspicion. Besides, Paeter is going to be far too busy making more amulets."

Uriel waved her hand and shook her head. "I know, I know. It's risky enough just having me be so close to the governor, but everyone here knows I'm no sorcerer."

They reached the entryway to the manor and stopped in the reception room. A warm breeze floated in through the front door, ruffling Uriel's skirt and bringing with it the scent of dry pine needles mixed with road dust.

Dumont was beginning to like Dusk. He was almost disappointed to leave, but this was only the first step of many, and he had to prepare for his next move.

He looked at Uriel and waited until her eyes had locked onto his. He spoke quietly but forcefully. "Be very careful,

Uriel. When the governor starts acting out of character, suspicion will turn to you. You must distance yourself from his pronouncements as much as possible, and do what you can make his actions seem reasonable. It's no small challenge."

Uriel nodded and held Dumont's gaze. "I will be successful, headmaster." Her next words came out with a quaver in her voice, "As of today, I have no other choice."

Uriel was right. They had all passed the point of no return today. It was one thing to force the Minister of Riverview to be a lookout, it was quite another to manipulate a province governor into changing his appointment of Heir Designate from his own son to the child of a sworn enemy. Their plans were an egregious violation of the Sorcery Accords that would have serious consequences for all involved if they were found out.

Dumont put his hand on her shoulder and squeezed gently. "Paeter has a great deal of faith in you Uriel, and so do I. We'll both support you in every way we can."

Uriel sighed and looked down. "I know. That's what makes the burden bearable. Will you be heading back to the college today?"

Dumont looked out of the entryway to the sunny courtyard beyond and took a deep breath of the warm air that swirled around in the reception room. "I think I should. As much as I've enjoyed my visit here, a lot more work awaits."

After final goodbyes, Uriel returned to her duties in the manor and Dumont strode through the courtyard toward the Thoron residence. Passing back through the mostly quiet streets of Dusk's highest plateau, Dumont marveled once again at the relaxed nature of the town and the astounding views of the surrounding mountains and the valley below. It was easy to see why Paeter loved his home so much. If

Dumont were looking for a place to settle, Dusk would be high on his list.

But Dumont had bigger plans, and resettling to Dusk was not an option. As beautiful as it was, it was too far from the heart of the empire.

Chapter 32

Petition Hearing

Jaylan ~ Council Hall, The Archives

I'm not easily intimidated, but standing alone in the cavernous Council Hall before the full assembly of Archives Councilors made cold sweat drip down my back. I had to remind myself not to fidget, to breathe normally, and to keep my knees flexed to avoid passing out from standing at attention.

The five councilors looked down upon me from their comfortable chairs on the raised platform of the Council Seat. The long table they shared had a wood privacy panel across the front, with the Symbol of Sorcery carved into the center, right below the seat of Senior Councilor Boris Underwood. The councilors' expressions ranged from interested, to suspicious, to bored.

Senior Councilor Underwood shifted his sharp gaze from the paper in his hands to me. "You are Jaylan Forester?" he asked.

It seemed like a silly question. He had my petition to become a Sword Sorcerer in his hand. Who else would I be? But I could see by the set of the dark bushy eyebrows above his serious grey eyes and the scowl on his face that a flippant response would be a mistake. I simply bowed my head slightly and said, "Yes, Councilor."

The councilor stared into my eyes as spoke again. "Entering the Sword Sorcerer training program is a serious commitment, Mr. Forester. We do not accept candidates lightly, and we will not allow you to enter the training unless we are convinced of your sincerity to honor your commitment."

I wasn't sure what to say to that. I wouldn't beg them for the honor, but I would not have submitted my petition unless I was certain of my decision. Well, *certain* might be too strong a word. Since the day Sulana left on her mission, I had struggled with the decision to submit my petition to become a Sword Sorcerer. In the end, doing so seemed like the best way to demonstrate to everyone, including myself, that I wanted to be a long-term, contributing member of the Archives. I had accepted that my past would remain my past. Learning that I could cast had been the final argument in favor of moving forward with the petition.

"I understand, sir," I responded.

He stared at me a moment more, as if he might question my understanding. At length, he set my petition down on the table and said, "We shall see. It seems to me that you have only been with us a short time, Mr. Forester. Is that right?"

I didn't know where he was going with that question, and I couldn't help being a little defensive. "I'm not sure I understand the relevance of the question, Councilor. Is there a residency requirement associated with becoming a Sword Sorcerer?"

My question got the attention of all five councilors, and not in a good way. At the far left, Junior Councilor Maris Torlon looked disapproving. Next to her, Senior Councilor Gregor Rissik sat back and folded his arms, his expression inscrutable, but certainly not supportive. In the center, Senior Councilor Underwood's eyebrows rose in surprise. At the far right, Junior Councilor Rikard Shepherd shook his head and looked down at his hands. Next to him, Junior Councilor Velna Asher sat back and observed me with a smirk.

After a moment of silence, Councilor Underwood said, "Mr. Forester, please allow the Council to determine the relevancy of our questions. You will be given an opportunity to ask questions *upon acceptance* of your petition."

His words implied my petition would be accepted, but the way he stressed "upon acceptance" suggested the opposite. Professor Delano had warned me that the Councilors could be a prickly bunch and that I'd need to choose my words carefully. It was good advice, but so far my follow-through was lacking.

"I apologize Councilor. I have been here for about two months." I was briefly taken aback by the truth of my own words. So much had happened since I had come to the Archives that the time seemed much longer. In answering the Councilor though, I realized how short a period it really was. I felt my cheeks redden.

Councilor Underwood smiled, but it wasn't a friendly smile. "That long, Mr. Forester? I had no idea. By now you've surely had time to learn the mission of the Archives and understand the gravity of your request."

All five of the councilors had a chuckle at my expense. Even Councilor Rissik was amused, and he was the one councilor that Professor Delano had told me would be my most likely ally in the proceedings. My face burned as my embarrassment deepened. I longed to defend the value of the time I had spent at the Archives, but I had the sense to keep my mouth shut this time.

Councilor Asher's smirk carried into her voice. "Perhaps the time he has been spending with Miss Delano gives him an advantage."

According to Professor Delano, Junior Councilor Velna Asher was my most likely opponent. The woman had opposed Sulana's petition and confirmation. She looked down at me now with beautiful green eyes that held a dangerous glint. She wore her long, wavy, auburn hair in a cascade that rested on her shoulders. Crisply-cut bangs kept her hair out of her oval, perfectly-proportioned face. I had been warned that her beauty caused men to underestimate the sharp steel that lurked within. She and her crony Rikard Shepherd were the youngest of the councilors, and both were strongly Integrationist.

I did not see the relevancy of her remark, but I did not question it this time. I chose not to respond at all, since she didn't exactly ask a question.

Councilor Underwood ignored her interruption. "Mr. Forester, Sword Sorcerers have a great deal of responsibility. You will owe your allegiance to the Archives Council, and no one else. You will also be obligated to serve the Council for a minimum of five years." The councilor leaned forward at this point and emphasized his next words. "However, we do not confirm candidates who see the position of Sword Sorcerer as a job with a five year contract. We seek candidates who are willing to commit their life to the role and to the well-being of the Archives. Are you willing to make that kind of commitment?"

The councilor wasn't telling me anything I didn't already know. I'd been over it with Sulana and then later with her mother. Both had impressed upon me the seriousness of entering the training, and I had spent most of my free time ruminating on the subject since Talon had brought it up. But now, with the entire Council staring at me and waiting for my answer, I imagined it felt like that last moment at a wedding ceremony before you say, "I do." This was it.

My hesitation was brief, but Councilor Asher took advantage of the pause. "Don't let us rush you into anything, Mr. Forester. If you'd like more time to consider your petition, you are welcome to come back another time."

This time, Councilor Underwood shot an annoyed glance over at Asher for her interruption. She caught the glance, rolled her eyes, and sat back with her arms folded.

I decided to speak before anyone else had a chance to interject. "I do understand the commitment, Councilor. I have considered it at length. I believe in the goals of the Archives and I'm grateful for the training I'm getting here. Becoming a Sword Sorcerer is exactly the kind of opportunity I've been looking for, and it would be the best use of my skills."

Asher and Shepherd both suppressed a snort. Underwood looked at me through his eyebrows. "You've figured all this out in two months, Mr. Forester? That's extraordinary."

Asher sighed and inspected her fingernails. Shepherd actually drummed his fingers on the table. I was certainly getting no support from that quarter.

On the other side of the table, Rissik continued to sit and observe me. I couldn't get a read on his thoughts at all. Torlon mostly looked down at the table in front of her, but she lifted her round, owl-like eyes to look at me occasionally. Her doughy figure hardly moved, and like Rissik, her round face revealed nothing about her opinion either way.

I concluded that I was getting nowhere and turned my attention back to Councilor Underwood. "Are you rejecting my petition, Councilor?"

The fidgeting on the right side of the table ceased while Asher and Shepherd waited for Underwood to speak.

Councilor Underwood looked down at the petition for a moment and then back up at me. "No, Mr. Forester. Not yet. We don't know you, and I'm sure you would agree that you do not know us either. We will take some time to conduct an investigation into your circumstances here. When we meet again, you will be given a chance to withdraw your petition, and we will have made a decision whether or not to accept it."

Asher slapped her hand to the table. "You can't seriously be considering this petition."

Councilor Rissik leaned forward and looked past Underwood toward Asher. He spoke up for the first time, saying blandly, "We are all seriously considering this petition, Councilor. A petition to become a Sword Sorcerer is a serious matter. We would be doing a disservice to ourselves, the Archives, and Mr. Forester here to respond hastily."

Asher turned in her chair to face Rissik and opened her mouth to respond. But Underwood, who sat between them, held up a hand to forestall her reply. "Councilor Rissik is correct. We must give the petitioner his due." When Asher started to speak anyway, he spoke firmly over her. "The Council will discuss it privately later." Asher closed her mouth and clenched her jaw. She turned her glare back to me, as if daring me to say anything more.

I did not accept her challenge.

It was obvious that someone or something had poisoned Asher's opinion of me. I found it hard to believe that such prejudice could be inspired by a difference in political leanings, but I didn't know what else it could be. She probably assumed that my relationship with Sulana made me Isolationist, or she may have heard somehow that I generally agreed with keeping sorcerers separate from the mundane. Whatever her reasons, Councilor Asher was unquestionably antagonistic, and Councilor Shepherd was following her lead.

But I still had a chance. From what Professor Delano had told me, the three Junior Councilors represented a single vote. Even if Torlon approved my petition, she would be outvoted by Asher and Shepherd, so the junior vote was lost to me. However, the majority vote from Asher, Shepherd, and Torlon would be tallied with the two Senior Councilor votes.

That being the case, I needed both Rissik and Underwood to vote in my favor. Councilor Rissik was an enigma, but he had defended my right to fair consideration. Councilor Underwood seemed to doubt my sincerity, but he was willing to learn more about me before making a decision either way. I felt the odds were against me, but there was still a chance.

I probably should have waited to submit my petition until after I had been at the Archives for longer and established myself. Councilor Underwood was right. I didn't know any of them, and they didn't know me. I was asking them to put their faith and trust in a stranger. My relationship with Sulana had eased my introduction into Archives society, but her influence extended only so far.

While I engaged in mental wrangling, Councilor Underwood had taken a deep breath and waited a moment for some of the tension to fade. He finally looked at me and said, "I believe our business with you is concluded for now, Mr. Forester. You may go."

I bowed low toward the councilors and returned to attention. "Thank you for your consideration. If you need anything more from me, I am at your service." I turned on my heel and walked calmly toward the main door.

As I walked away, Councilor Asher mumbled just loud enough for me to hear, "Not yet, Mr. Forester. Not yet."

CHAPTER 33
MESSAGE TO THE ARCHIVES

Dumont ~ Headmaster's Office, Thunderhead College

Returning from Dusk through the Portal Keep, Dumont had just passed through the gates at Thunderhead College when Lohan hurried across the courtyard to meet him. Peltor trailed behind at a more leisurely pace.

Lohan stopped in front of Dumont with a proud grin on his face. "Master, I'm so glad you've returned. While you were gone, we intercepted an Archives team on a mission to recover the portal key. We captured their Sword Sorceress and their weaponsmaster!"

Peltor caught up and came to a halt just behind Lohan, glowering over folded arms. Dumont didn't bother reading much into Peltor's body language: the man was perpetually in a bad mood.

After the taxing journey from Dusk, Dumont mostly wanted to wash off the road dust and relax in his chambers for a while. He was too tired to think about the implications of what Lohan had just told him, and he wasn't in the mood to deal with whatever disagreement was obviously brewing between Lohan and Peltor.

Dumont raised a hand with a sigh. "That's good news, Lohan. We'll discuss it in my office later. Give me some time to freshen up and we'll go over it in detail."

Lohan's face fell in disappointment, but he bowed and stepped aside. "I understand, Master. Should I come to your office in a half hour or so?"

Tomorrow would be better, but Dumont could see that Lohan was excited about his victory and the situation did merit immediate consideration. "That would be fine," Dumont answered as he walked past Lohan.

Exactly a half an hour later, Dumont leaned back in the comfortable chair at his desk savoring a sip of brandy. He smiled to himself and lifted his glass to the Thunderhead College banner that decorated the wall opposite him. His trip to Dusk had gone better than anticipated, and a moment's celebration was well deserved. Although he had come home to a new problem, he had already formed the beginnings of a plan for dealing with the Archives prisoners.

A rapid knock on his door brought him out of his reverie. He sighed and drained the last of his drink before sitting forward and calling out, "Enter."

As he expected, Lohan and Peltor came into the room. Both men kept a distance between them, practically circling one another. Lohan bowed and said, "Welcome back, Master. I tried to explain to Peltor that we did not need him for this meeting, but he insisted on accompanying me." The complaint almost came out as a whine.

"Peltor is welcome to attend," Dumont responded. "If Paeter thinks he should be our new guard captain, we should include him in any discussions about our guests."

Lohan glanced at Peltor and pressed his lips together. He salvaged a small victory by scurrying over to the only empty chair in the room and seating himself next to Dumont's desk. Peltor gave Dumont a small nod in acknowledgment of his support, and then he folded his arms, seeming content to stand.

Dumont turned to Lohan. "Tell me more about our guests. Who exactly was in Sorcerer Delano's party?"

Lohan explained that she had been accompanied by the Archives weaponsmaster, a Winterman, and an archer. Their belongings had been confiscated and they were locked in Peltor's new dungeon. He went on to describe the ambush along the road to Riverview.

Dumont had been expecting the Archives to go in search of the missing portal key, but he had also expected it to take longer for them to make their way here. Thinking through the timing, it was unlikely that the Sword Sorceress could have followed Lohan's false trail to the south, discovered it was a dead end, and then made her way back here by way of the Archives.

Knowing that the Archives Council moved about as quickly as that glacier of a mountain they huddled upon, he figured Sorceress Delano probably hadn't left the castle more than a couple of days before she was captured.

In a musing tone, he said aloud as more a statement than a question, "I wonder why she decided to come this way first?"

A clunk and rattle brought his attention to the item Lohan had just dropped onto his desk. "This," Lohan said in a satisfied voice.

Dumont picked up the unremarkable glass rod and chain and inspected it closely. "A seeker," he concluded.

Lohan nodded vigorously, "That's what I thought too, Master. Someone must have created a seeker for the portal key before I left with it. My money is on Wizard Vlastorus."

Dumont looked intently at Lohan and asked, "Vlastorus is at the Archives?"

Lohan nodded and answered, "Yes, Master. He apparently went with Sulana's team to Buckwoods, and when they returned to the Archives, he participated in their investigation into the amulets and the portal key theft."

Dumont frowned. None of his sources at the Archives had seen fit to pass on that bit of information. Wizard Vlastorus was a crafty old adversary, and his presence at the Archives could complicate matters. Dumont had hoped the old man would enjoy his retirement at Plains End indefinitely.

At least he had an explanation for how Sorcerer Delano had known to go this direction first. She must have picked up the location of the portal key just before he and Paeter had left with it. Although he had considered the possibility of there being a seeker, he was surprised to discover it was true. However, the odds were extremely low that his enemies had created a second seeker, so the portal key that rested comfortably in the wand pocket of his vest was probably untraceable now.

He closed his fist around the Seeker and was tempted to shatter it on the fireplace hearth, but he restrained himself with the thought that it might still be useful. He could always destroy it later. He opened the top drawer of his desk and dropped the Seeker into it before shoving it closed with a thump.

"Good work, Lohan. Now, tell me more about this Winterman," Dumont said.

"His name is Barek Hunter," Lohan started to say.

"He's a barbarian," Peltor interjected. "We should get rid of him. We should get rid of all of them."

Lohan frowned and shifted in his chair. "I don't think killing them is a good idea, Master."

Dumont began to see the nature of the conflict between the two men. He had a simple solution. "Of course we aren't going to kill them. It would be a waste to destroy such valuable hostages."

Peltor looked unconvinced, but said nothing further.

Lohan actually breathed a sigh of relief. "I agree, Master," he said.

Before Lohan could say more, Dumont added, "On the other hand, if they become more trouble than they are worth or they lose their value in our impending negotiations with the Archives, I may revisit that decision."

Peltor slowly smiled at Lohan, who blanched and looked down at the floor.

Dumont could not seriously imagine killing the four Archives representatives. Doing so would have far-reaching consequences and most likely undermine his plans. Still, he found it amusing to keep his two underlings off balance and alert.

Peltor was right about one thing though. Keeping a Winterman hostage was a bad idea. He couldn't guess what this Barek Hunter was doing in Sorcerer Delano's team, but Wintermen were not known for their wanderlust or for swearing allegiance to anyone other than their own tribal chiefs. If he was at the Archives, he was probably representing his people in some capacity, and holding the man here was asking for trouble.

The last thing Dumont wanted was the attention of the Wintermen. They had created difficulties for him years ago at the Battle of Riverview, and he would not invite their interference again.

"I have a better use for our Winterman," he declared. "I need to send a message to the Archives, and he would be the perfect messenger. He has little value as a hostage, and killing him would have ramifications I would prefer to avoid."

Lohan stood to leave. "I'll get his horse ready while you write the message, Master," he suggested.

Lohan had latched onto the suggestion quickly, and Dumont began to wonder what it was that made him resistant to the idea of dispatching their prisoners. The man certainly wasn't known for being squeamish. His attitude was something worth watching.

Dumont shook his head. "Who said anything about a horse? The barbarian has legs. He can walk. We need all the horses we have."

Peltor harrumphed, and Lohan blinked in confusion. "But...it might take days for your message to reach the Archives," Lohan said.

Dumont opened a drawer of his desk. Pulling out a piece of parchment, he shrugged and said, "It won't take him that much longer on foot, and I'm in no hurry. The trip will keep him busy for a while. I'm sure the Archives is not expecting their team back for some days yet. We might as well keep them guessing a while longer."

Lohan stared at the parchment in front of Dumont with a frown. "What message will you send to the Council? Are we going to ask for a ransom?"

"In a manner of speaking. However, as much as we could use some extra funds, I think keeping the Council confused and out of our way has more value. I'll propose a merging of our colleges and ask for representation on the Council."

Lohan's expression changed from puzzlement to incredulity. "They'll never agree to that. And why would you want them to?"

Dumont grinned. "I don't. But just imagine the distress and distraction such a suggestion will cause."

Lohan nodded his head with a thin smile of appreciation. "They'll think this has all been a power play to gain control of the Archives."

"Exactly. The Council is just arrogant enough to think this is all about them and their precious Archives. While we go back and forth with them in negotiations, their attention will be distracted from our other activities around the empire."

Lohan snorted and gave Dumont a slight bow. "I am honored to serve under you, Master."

Dumont slid an ink pot closer and removed the lid. Selecting his favorite quill, he bent to the task of writing a note to the Archives. Looking up through his eyebrows at the two men who were still standing in his office, he said, "Lohan, accompany Peltor to the dungeon and see to the release of the Winterman. Then come back up here for the message." He pointed his quill at Peltor and added, "Do not harass the man. Keep him in chains and walk him to the courtyard. Remain there until Lohan returns with the message. Then you may give him the message and release him."

Peltor bowed with a smirk and said, "As you wish, headmaster."

He's going to antagonize the Winterman in spite of my orders. The fool.

By the time Lohan returned to his office to retrieve the message, Dumont had sanded the ink, rolled the parchment, and tucked it into a tube. He was just applying the wax seal when Lohan knocked twice and opened the door without waiting for an invitation. He eased the door open just enough to slip into the room and quietly sat in the chair next to Dumont's desk. The headmaster handed the message to him and waved him off. Lohan slipped out the same way he arrived, closing the door softly behind him.

Dumont got up from his desk and poured himself another brandy. He went over to an office window that overlooked the courtyard below. Peltor stood behind the big Winterman with his sword drawn, the tip practically touching the giant's back. This was as close as Dumont ever hoped to be to another Winterman for the rest of his life.

As if he felt Dumont's scrutiny, the big man turned his head and looked up at Dumont's window. Dumont was just raising his glass to his lips, and he involuntarily froze in place. The Winterman's gaze had the distant look of a predator sizing up the best path to its prey. Dumont shivered in spite of himself. He doubted that the barbarian had a clear view of him, but the man's stare unnerved him just the same.

Peltor poked the Winterman in the back, and the spell was broken. The Winterman glared over his shoulder at Peltor, and his big hands closed into fists. Dumont thought the man might make a move, but saw the tension in his shoulders ease when Lohan ran out into the courtyard with the message tube.

Lohan said something to Peltor, and Peltor tossed Lohan a set of keys while he kept his blade at the Winterman's back. Lohan looked down at the keys in his hand and hesitated. He said something to the Winterman and bent down to unlock the shackles on the prisoner's legs. Glancing nervously at the Winterman's face, he released the shackles on the man's wrists as well.

The freed prisoner rubbed his wrists where the shackles had been, and stared stonily at Lohan when the much smaller man held out the message tube toward him. Lohan straightened his shoulders and said something, shaking the message tube once for emphasis.

The Winterman slowly reached out and accepted the tube. Then, with no warning, he pivoted his body, knocked Peltor's sword away with a sweep of his arm, and drove a hard punch straight into Peltor's face. Peltor stumbled backward and toppled to the ground. His sword flew from his grasp and landed in the dirt a few feet away. Two guards moved into the scene from below Dumont's window with their swords drawn, but they kept their distance from the barbarian.

Lohan looked down at Peltor with his mouth agape. Peltor was out cold. Dumont could see that Peltor's nose would need realignment, hopefully before he regained consciousness. When the Winterman turned back toward Lohan, the sorcerer took several steps backward and fumbled with his jacket pocket to retrieve his casting orb. But by the time he got his hand untangled from his pocket, the barbarian was already jogging toward the gate on his mission to the Archives.

Dumont chuckled to himself and turned away from the window. *Better pace yourself, big man. You've a long way to go.*

He doubted that Peltor would learn anything from the encounter, but one could always hope. His hostility made him a poor choice for a guard captain, but he was their only real option at the moment. Eventually, Peltor would make one mistake too many. Hopefully they'd have a better candidate for captain by then.

CHAPTER 34
DESPAIR IN THE DUNGEON

Sulana ~ The Dungeon, Thunderhead College

Sulana took two clanking steps and her chains stopped her from taking another. She turned and took a few more steps in the opposite direction before she once again reached the limit of her chains. Sitting down with a sigh, she accepted that pacing was impossible under the circumstances. Sulana knew that the steady sound of the clanking chain would just annoy her fellow prisoners anyway. But she was concerned about Barek, and movement helped her think.

A couple of hours had passed since Lohan and Peltor had entered their cell and ordered Barek to get to his feet. Sulana and the others protested, but the two guards that accompanied Peltor kept everyone else seated while Barek was alternately led and pushed out of the room.

Barek glanced at Sulana on his way out. She returned his look and shook her head once to negate any plans he might have for trying to be heroic. So far, no one had harmed them, and she thought they should wait to find out the reason for his removal. As Lohan led the procession out of the room, she demanded that he tell her where they were taking Barek, but he ignored her completely.

Now, two hours later, she was about ready to scream unless someone came down here and gave her some answers. "What can they be doing to him?" she asked aloud for about the tenth time. "We've answered almost every question they've asked. There's no need for torture."

"Yeah, but that Peltor guy seems like the type who would enjoy torture for its own sake," Daven said with a droll tone.

Sulana grew quiet and wrinkled her brow. Daven was right.

Talon broke the silence. "That's not helpful, Daven." Daven shrugged a shoulder as if to say that the truth wasn't necessarily helpful.

Talon then said to Sulana, "Peltor's not in charge here, and I'm not sensing much cooperative spirit between him and Lohan."

Sulana didn't see his point. "So? Peltor does seem to be the person responsible for this little prison. Who knows what authority he's been given?"

Talon's tone grew more pointed. "Lohan is interested in you. While I agree that he doesn't have much use for the rest of us, I doubt he'd want to hurt you or earn your hatred by harming one of us."

Sulana snorted and said, "But I already hate him."

"Not the way you would if he hurt or killed one of us," Talon insisted.

"I guess," she responded with a shrug. She couldn't imagine liking Lohan any less, but she could imagine getting a lot more angry at him.

"Besides," Talon went on, "the fact that they don't work well together says to me that they are following orders. Someone else sent them down here to retrieve Barek, and specifically Barek."

Sulana considered Talon's words. *Specifically Barek.* But why Barek? She blew out her breath in frustration. If Talon was using this situation to teach her another strategy lesson, she was going to get annoyed with him. On the other hand, she thought, looking down at her manacled wrists, her strategy skills obviously needed more work. "You think his being a Winterman has something to do with it?" she asked.

Talon sat back on his bench and nodded once in satisfaction. But his reply was less conclusive. "I don't know. But you would have been the person to go if someone wanted to negotiate with us. If torture were the plan, Daven would be the most likely to break under pressure."

Daven scowled and protested, "Hey!" but Talon held up his palm in a gesture of peace and continued speaking.

"What I'm getting at is that Barek is a Winterman and holding him has political considerations that our host must be aware of."

Sulana bit her lip and thought for a moment. "What political considerations?" she finally asked. "Barek left his people years ago and works for the Archives Council now."

Talon nodded. "That's true. But you know what they say..."

"Once a Winterman, always a Winterman," Daven supplied.

Talon nodded and pointed toward Daven.

Sulana rolled her eyes. "You're making this too complicated. I appreciate the distraction, but I'm not going to feel better about the situation until they bring Barek back in the same condition he was when he left."

She jumped when a key rattled in the lock and the door swung open, as if on cue. Peltor swept into the room and marched over to Sulana. "Get up," he ordered.

Sulana stood and almost gasped when she saw his face. His nose was swollen and red, and a drop of blood leaked from one nostril. His eyes had red shadows that promised to bloom into a stellar pair of bruises. She had no doubt as to who was responsible for the mess his visage had become. At the thought of Barek punching Peltor, she almost giggled and had to look down to hide the smile that tried to escape from the corners of her mouth.

Peltor's breathing was shallow and fast. His face grew red when he saw her reaction, and he slapped her hard before she could collect herself.

Daven and Talon both jumped to their feet as Sulana fell back down to the bench clutching her face with her hand. Her cheek burned and she tasted the coppery warmth of blood from where the inside of her lip had been driven into a tooth.

"You'll pay for that, you son of a goat," Daven swore. He pulled at his chains in futile frustration.

Talon spoke no words, but his narrow-eyed glare said volumes.

Sulana gathered herself and stood again to face Peltor. Her tongue explored the inside of her lip while she stared boldly into his eyes, daring him to hit her again. He stood back just out of retaliatory range, but if he moved close enough to hit her again, she'd be ready to defend herself and strike back.

"That was for failing to maintain control over that animal you brought with you," Peltor hissed.

"I think the animal is standing in front of me," Sulana retorted.

Peltor's eyes went wide and he snarled. He reached for the knife at his belt just as Lohan stepped into the room behind him.

Lohan drawled, "Stop harassing the prisoners, Peltor. That broken nose was the result of your own idiocy. You need to learn to follow orders."

Peltor went still and his eyes swiveled to the side in Lohan's direction, but he didn't turn away from Sulana. His hand remained on his dagger. Sulana thought Peltor might actually draw his blade and attack Lohan. But Peltor couldn't see that Lohan had his casting orb ready in his hand.

"Paeter isn't here to support you, so you should think twice before you make too much trouble here at the college," Lohan warned him.

Peltor growled through a clenched jaw. He released his dagger, turned, and stormed out of the room, bumping his shoulder against Lohan's on the way out.

Upon seeing Sulana's face clearly for the first time, Lohan took a couple of involuntary steps forward. "Are you alright?" he breathed.

Sulana didn't doubt that Peltor's open-handed slap left a bright red mark on her cheek, and that was what brought alarm to Lohan's face now. Her lip was beginning to swell too. "I'm fine," she answered. "It's no worse than the bruises Talon has given me during training."

She sat back down on her bench and looked up at Lohan while he glanced over to check on Daven and Talon's condition. The encounter with Peltor had made her feel better. If Peltor was taking his broken nose out on her, then Barek wasn't around to receive the punishment.

With a tinge of smugness in her voice, she said, "I suppose Barek escaped? Is that why Peltor is here giving me grief?"

Lohan shook his head slowly and smirked. "He didn't escape."

Sulana heart rate spiked and all of the worry that had accumulated over the past two hours threatened to break free as angry tears.

Before her emotions could escalate into action though, Lohan added, "He was released."

Sulana's shoulders slumped. She closed her eyes and shook her head once. "Thank the spirits," she said with a sigh.

"The spirits had nothing to do with it," Lohan retorted. "The headmaster sent him to deliver a message to the Archives. He's on foot though, so it could take a while."

Talon sat back down chuckling. "Then you don't know much about Wintermen."

"What do you mean?" Lohan asked, genuine puzzlement in his voice.

"Wintermen don't usually travel on horseback," he answered.

Lohan shrugged once. "So? They probably have trouble finding horses big enough."

Talon shook his head and laughed. "No, it's because they're *faster* on foot."

Lohan narrowed his eyes at Talon and said exactly what Sulana was thinking. "You seem to know a lot about Wintermen."

It was Talon's turn to shrug. "I've been traveling with one for some time now, so I've picked up a few things."

That much was true, Sulana thought. Her team had only been working together for a few months, but Talon and Barek had been working together since Barek came to the Archives a few years ago. It made sense that Talon and Barek would have gotten to know one another pretty well in that time. They certainly had worked effortlessly together when her team was attacked by a troll on a return trip to the Archives.

Lohan looked deep in thought when she returned her attention to him. "I need to go," he said absently and left the room. As the door lock clicked into place, Sulana wondered if maybe Talon should have held back that bit of information about Wintermen and horses.

CHAPTER 35
THE PROPOSAL

Gregor ~ Council Level, The Archives

Senior Councilor Gregor Rissik sat at his desk reading through the latest reports from the Archives Sanctuary network. The content of the reports was as varied as the individuals who wrote them. Some were mostly dry recitations of financial status while others included insightful recounts of local political maneuvering. He took notes as he read, translating his conclusions into a collection of resolutions and initiatives that he would later present to the other Council members.

A loud knock on his office door interrupted his thoughts and he absently invited the visitor to enter. The door opened to reveal guardian Juli Farmins, who leaned in and said, "Barek Hunter is asking to see you, Councilor."

Barek Hunter? Was Sulana's team back already? They must have found what they were looking for rather quickly. We can probably thank Ebnik's brilliance for thinking ahead and creating that Seeker.

"Please show him in, Juli," the Councilor responded. He set aside his quill and was covering the ink pot when a panting and tousled Barek rushed past the guard into the room and firmly shut the door. The crisp scent of the outdoors wafted over to Gregor's desk along with the musky odor of heavy sweat.

Barek nodded to him and said between deep, even breaths, "Thank you for seeing me, Councilor."

"Of course," Gregor said. The man's winded condition and the urgency with which he moved set off alarms in Gregor's mind. If Sulana's team had returned, she would be the person reporting the status of her mission, and she probably would not come directly to his office to do so. Something else was going on here.

"What is it, Barek? Where is the rest of the team?" Gregor asked.

Barek responded by untying a message tube from his belt and thumping it onto the councilor's desk. "The rest of the team has been imprisoned at Thunderhead College," he answered. Pointing to the message tube, he added, "That message is from the headmaster."

Gregor sat back as the shock of Barek's news sent a chill down his neck and into the pit of his stomach. *The Headmaster.* Dumont Fortenz was holding Sorcerer Delano and her team. Gregor's mind shot through several possible scenarios and courses of action, and none of them led to a pleasant conclusion. After all these years of sly maneuvering, Dumont had finally taken a decisive step.

He frowned at the message tube on his desk with foreboding. That tube undoubtedly represented dark times ahead for the Archives. But before he would open that seal and take the first step down into whatever abyss Dumont had prepared for them, he needed to learn more from the Winterman.

"How did this happen, Barek?" he asked.

Barek explained how Lohan had ambushed them at the base of the mountain. Gregor's eyes closed in distress when Barek described how the team was chained in a basement room of the college.

When Barek paused to take a breath, Gregor asked, "Do you think they'll be safe?"

Barek nodded somberly. "For now. They fed us well enough. The biggest danger is the guard captain. A pig named Peltor."

Gregor knew nothing of this man Peltor. "Why is he a danger to them?"

Barek snorted. "He is psychotic."

While Gregor worried over that bit of news, he was struck by the oddity of getting this information in private and directly from Barek, who had obviously come straight up to his office from the trail.

"While I appreciate being first to learn of this situation, I'm wondering why you chose me," he said, watching Barek's face closely.

Barek nodded once and returned Gregor's stare. "Thunderhead College has declared war on the Archives." He angled his head toward the message tube. "I do not know what that says, but it brings trouble. Using our team as ransom, the headmaster will demand something the Archives does not want to give."

Gregor waited for Barek to say more. When he didn't, Gregor prompted him with, "I suspect you're right."

Barek lowered his voice and stepped closer to the councilor's desk. "My people will not accept Integrationist control of the Archives. Neither will the emperor."

Gregor nodded slowly, silently agreeing with the Winterman. Gregor knew that Barek was aware of his responsibilities to the emperor, just as he was aware of Barek's responsibilities to the Winterman tribes. Each of them were charged with verifying that the Archives continued to enforce the Sorcery Accords, as was its imperial-mandated duty.

"Well, let's see exactly what the headmaster has in mind," Gregor said, picking up the message tube. He used a knife from his desk to pry off the wax seal at the end of the tube and removed the parchment that was inside. He unrolled the parchment and bent forward to read Dumont's even, slanted lettering. His heart began to pound faster with every word he read. As Barek had surmised, it was in effect a ransom note, and in spite of the careful wording, the demands put control of the Archives at stake.

When he finished reading, he dropped the note in disgust. The parchment curled in on itself, rocking back and forth on the desktop. "It's exactly as we suspected. Dumont is demanding that the Archives and Thunderhead College join forces. He expects us to restructure the Council to accommodate Thunderhead representation. He cites the ease with which the Sword Sorceress was *detained* as evidence of how the Archives is no longer up to the challenge of enforcing the Accords."

Barek's hands tightened into fists, and his complexion turned ruddy. "Sorcerer Delano could have chosen to fight, but we were out-numbered and did not know what they were planning," he said in a steely voice.

Gregor held up a restraining hand. "There's no need to defend her to me. None of us saw this coming. If anyone is at fault, it's the Council. We should have been keeping a closer watch on what Dumont has been doing down there at the college."

"There's more," Barek said. "According to Sulana, this man Peltor helped Sorcerer Thoron escape Buckwoods."

Gregor saw the connection immediately. "So, Paeter Thoron, Lohan, and the headmaster are all in this together." When Barek nodded, Gregor continued, "Somehow, the amulets and the portal keys play a role in all of this too." At this, Barek shrugged.

Gregor tried to assemble the clues floating around in his head into a complete picture, but they stubbornly refused to fit together. The amulets would be useless against other sorcerers, and the distance between the Archives and Thunderhead College was not far enough to justify using the Portal Keep. He couldn't see how the amulets or the portal key would be useful in a plan to threaten the Archives. Either two separate plans were afoot, or one of them was a feint. Regardless, the curled parchment on the desk in front of him and the fact that the Sword Sorceress was being held against her will suggested that the headmaster's ultimatum had to be taken seriously.

The first thing they needed to do was convince the headmaster to release Sulana and her team. Their imprisonment was unacceptable. Interestingly, the ransom note did not specify a deadline or a specific consequence of inaction. The headmaster must expect the Archives to act quickly to secure the release of the Sword Sorceress. Or else he didn't care how quickly the Archives responded. It was hard to tell.

It would take time to gather the Council, craft a response, and get it down to Thunderhead College. In the meantime, every day that Sulana's team was incarcerated increased the odds that something bad would happen to them. How much time had they already lost?

"How long ago did they release you?" he asked Barek.

"Yesterday afternoon," Barek replied.

Gregor added that information to the timeline he was forming in his head, and then stopped as the implications sank in. "You left yesterday afternoon? You made it up here in less than a day?"

Barek shrugged. "It got too dark to see the trail last night, or I would have arrived sooner."

Gregor shook his head. "Your horse must be nearly dead."

"No horse. I ran," was Barek's reply. "Faster that way."

Gregor sat back in surprise. He knew Wintermen were supposed to have legendary stamina, but Barek would have had to jog or run virtually the entire way to reach the Archives in less than a day. "That's...remarkable," he stammered.

Barek blushed faintly and said, "I'm out of shape. Been spending too much time on horseback."

To Gregor, this was good news; not much time had been lost yet. Getting the Council to act would take time enough, he thought bitterly. Also, he would somehow have to find a moment when he could slip away to pass this disturbing news on to the emperor.

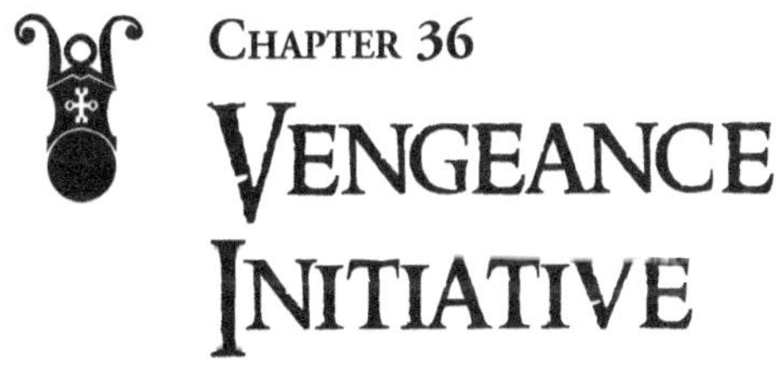

CHAPTER 36
VENGEANCE INITIATIVE

Jaylan ~ Alchemy Class, The Archives

I stared intently at the dozen or so herbs and flowers sitting on the work bench in front of me. Some were dried and some were fresh, depending upon which were currently in season. I wiggled on the hard wooden stool and grimaced, even though it wasn't really that uncomfortable. It was the quiz that was the source of my distress.

"I still think it would be better if we did this outside, so I could see the plants the way they really look," I said.

"No whining," Lissy replied. "We'd have to hike all over the mountain to find some of these, and others don't even grow here. I know this isn't the ideal way to learn plant identification, but it's the best we can do. Try that first one. It's easy."

I sighed and picked up the sprig of plant she indicated. Easy, she said. Any question is easy if you already know the answer, and not so easy if you don't. I considered saying as much, but she didn't seem to be in the mood for commentary.

The plant had a sturdy stem and long frilly leaves that looked like tiny fern fronds. The main stem branched into many thin, short stems at the very top, and each of the smaller stems ended in clusters of tiny white flowers. The clusters were so close together that the flower petals interwove to form a half dozen white platforms.

"That one was brought up from the valley yesterday. How would you describe the leaves?" Lissy asked me.

The leaves branched off the stem a few inches apart from each other. Lissy had taught me that leaves were described as "opposite" when they paired up together on either side of the stem, "whorled" when several leaves ringed the stem, and "alternate" when they branched off separately from each other and alternated down the stem. "Alternate?" I answered.

"Right. Now, crush the tip of a leaf and sniff it," she instructed.

I did as she suggested. The smell was strong and grassy. It reminded me of carrot greens and celery. "Smells like a weed," I said.

She rolled her eyes at me. "Very funny. Remember that aroma because it is one of the best ways to identify the plant when it hasn't flowered yet. Not that the leaves aren't distinctive in their own way. Can you tell me what it is?"

Actually I could. This question *was* easy because I *did* already know the answer. "It's yarrow. You used some dried leaves of it in your first potion demonstration. I've seen the Imperial Guard healers use it to treat bleeding wounds, and I've even harvested it myself for a healer I know in the valley."

I once spent some time collecting firewood for a healer who had helped one of my injured friends. While I was searching for wood, I gathered yarrow and a few other herbs as I ran across them, which I then gave to her to use in her potions and salves. She appreciated my thoughtfulness and gave me a jar of salve to take home when I was done helping her.

"That's right," Lissy confirmed. "Now, here's something I'll bet you've never tried. Tear off an entire leaf and hold it in your palm." I did what she suggested. "Channel some vaetra into it, and pay close attention to how it makes you feel."

I tried opening a channel to the leaf in my hand, not sure what I was doing exactly. The flow of vaetra seemed blocked until it came in contact with the torn end of the leaf. There it found some residual moisture and trickled into the stem. A faint tone came from the leaf, indicating that it was manifesting something using the vaetra I provided. Following Lissy's instructions, I paid close attention to the effect it had on me.

The first thing I noticed was that the tension associated with taking the quiz faded and I started to feel confident that I would do well. The second was a sudden awareness of Lissy's closeness and a desire to give her a hug to let her know how much I appreciated her. I blushed when I thought about how inappropriate it would be to act on that impulse.

I was about to cut the flow to the leaf when a strong feeling of foreboding came over me, like a stiff wind blowing dark clouds my way. A vision of heavy steps tromping down a hallway echoed through my mind. When the vision slipped away, I dropped the channel, but the foreboding remained.

"What did you learn?" she asked. She wore a mischievous half-smile, as if she knew the path my thoughts had briefly taken.

"It made me feel more confident about taking the test," I answered.

She nodded, that smile still playing at the corner of her lips. "What else?"

I was sure she knew what else, but she wanted to hear me say it. "I felt rather...friendly toward you."

Benjamin, who was working at a bench on the other side of the room, snickered and spoke to his sister, but he made sure he was loud enough so Lissy and I would hear him. "I think Jaylan has a crush on Lissy," he said.

Daisy gave him a shove and retorted, "Every man has a crush on Lissy. Including you."

Well, at least I wasn't the only person in the room who was blushing now.

Lissy patted me on the shoulder and ignored the twins. "That's good. Not that you felt friendly toward me, although I'm glad to hear it. You were able to pick up on a few of the lesser-known magical properties of yarrow: courage and camaraderie, or love as some would have it. Yarrow is not only used for healing potions, but also in love philters and strength potions. Some people even report psychic visions, although I've never had that experience myself."

Some people report psychic visions. Is that what just happened to me? A psychic vision?

"I think I just had one. Just before I dropped the channel," I said.

Her eyes brightened. "Really?" She leaned closer to me, looking me directly in the eyes as if she would be able to see an echo of the vision there. "What did you see?"

"It was pretty vague. I just saw and heard booted feet walking down a hallway. But it gave me a bad feeling, like a storm coming." As I spoke, I realized I was hearing those same booted feet again. I glanced at the yarrow leaf in my palm, but it just sat there looking a bit limp from the warmth of my hand.

I looked up at Lissy to tell her what was happening, but she had turned toward the door of the lab. Barek came through the door and sound of booted feet stopped. I looked down and saw that he wore the boots I'd seen in my vision. I knew before he said anything that he did not bring good news.

I tossed the yarrow to the work bench and got to my feet. "What is it Barek? Has the team returned? Is Sulana okay?"

He had been about to speak when my outburst interrupted him. Both of his eyebrows went up, and after a glance at the twins, he took another couple of steps closer to Lissy and me. The twins watched him with curiosity before getting up from their bench and joining us, unwilling to miss out on whatever was about to transpire.

"Sulana and the rest of the team were in good health the last time I saw them," he rumbled in his deep voice.

"What do you mean? Did Sulana send you back for something?" I asked.

"Not exactly." He looked down at the floor. "I am sorry to bring this news, but Sulana, Talon, and Daven are being held hostage at Thunderhead College."

I stuttered in confusion. "Held hostage? As in, for a ransom?"

He nodded. "More or less. The headmaster sent me back with a message for the Council that states his demands for their release."

Lissy broke out of her shocked silence. "What is it? What does he want?"

Barek shrugged and wouldn't make eye contact. "I am not allowed to say. The issue must be put before the Council first."

"Who told you to keep the demands secret?" Lissy asked.

He looked at her for a moment, as if deciding whether or not to answer her question. "Councilor Rissik."

Lissy stood straighter and some of the tension left her hand where she had been clenching her folded arm. "You went to him first," she concluded, and Barek just nodded, still looking into her eyes.

Some secret communication was going on between Barek and Lissy here, and I didn't like being left out. Lissy seemed to be friends with Councilor Rissik, so I was sure she'd figure out a way to pry the truth from him. I was less sure she'd share that knowledge with me.

I asked Barek about the conditions under which Sulana was being held. All of us grew somber when he described the chains and the dungeon. A slow burn started in my chest as he spoke, and by the time he had finished his description, my hands were clenched into fists at my side.

I pelted Barek with questions about the layout of the college and the number of men they had protecting the place. My anxiety for Sulana's safety demanded that I do something immediately, but my training as a guard captain forced me to first gain all of the intelligence about the situation that I could. I started to debrief him, without consciously thinking of it that way.

Lissy interrupted my interrogation and said, "Jaylan, wait. The Council needs to authorize any rescue mission."

"I don't work for the Council," I said coldly.

Her voice became urgent, "Not yet, you don't. But you said you thought your petition for Sword Sorcerer training is on shaky ground as it is. Going on an unauthorized rescue mission will kill the petition for sure."

"I don't care about that!" I shouted, startling her. She blinked and stepped back a pace. I softened my voice and said, "I'm not going to let Sulana rot in chains while I sit up here waiting for the Council to make a decision."

The truth was that I did care about my petition. Becoming a Sword Sorcerer would be a worthy challenge, and if I did a good job, I'd get back a measure of the respect I had as an Imperial Guard captain. It would give my life purpose, and I looked forward to being part of a team again. Since leaving the Guard, and then the mercenary ranks of the Raven Company, I'd felt adrift. Sorcery training was interesting, but I wasn't sure where it was leading me.

However, compared to Sulana's safety, none of that mattered. The thought of her being locked in a dungeon made my muscles twitch with the desire to leave now and get her out. The afternoon we made love had opened the way for new threads of commitment and trust in our friendship. The Council had good reason to worry that I might place my allegiance to Sulana before my allegiance to the Archives. Maybe they would be right to deny my petition. Right now, I didn't care.

"Just give them two days," Lissy pleaded. "Give *me* two days. I might be able to find out what's behind this, and we might be able to get the backing of the Council."

I closed my eyes and tried to calm my breathing. The rage and anxiety coiled up inside me like a snake. It rested, but it was ready for the right moment to strike. I opened my eyes again and looked at Lissy. "I'll give you *one* day. If the Council doesn't take action immediately, they aren't taking this situation seriously enough. I'll go by myself if I have to."

Barek harrumphed in amused agreement. "You will not go alone," he said.

Lissy's eyebrows went up and she rounded on Barek. "You can't be serious. You *do* work for the Council. Do you want to lose your position in the Guardian Corps?"

Barek folded his arms and shook his head. "I will not lose my position. I do exactly what I was ordered to do: protect the Sword Sorceress and support my team members."

Lissy looked doubtful. "But they'll probably give you new orders to wait here until they decide what to do."

Barek glared at her and said, "They would have no reason...unless someone told them I intend to leave with Jaylan." His look swept across the twins as well, the unspoken warning evident in his eyes.

Benjamin gave him an injured look. "I'm not going to tell anyone. In fact, I'm going with you. Talon and Daven are there too, and they're pretty much the only friends I have around here."

This was getting out of hand. I had secretly hoped that Barek would join me, and since he had, my confidence that I could succeed went up substantially. But while I could use Benjamin's skill with a sword, I didn't want to be responsible for the safety of someone else's sixteen-year-old boy.

Before I could open my mouth to object, Daisy did it for me. "Forget it, Ben. Mother and Father would strangle me if I let you run off into such a dangerous situation."

Ben drew himself up and puffed out his chest. "You aren't *letting* me do anything. You aren't my keeper. I've been trained by the weaponsmaster himself and I have more experience with sorcery than Jaylan. He needs my help. You can't stop me from going."

Daisy squinted at her brother and clenched her jaw. She exhaled a short breath and said, "Fine. If you won't stay behind, then I'm going with you." She tilted her jaw up and stared at him, daring him to object.

Ben was taken aback by her declaration. I could see him rethinking his decision now that he would be putting his sister in danger as well as himself.

Lissy saw Ben's indecision and took advantage of the moment. "This is a job for experienced fighters and sorcerers. Both of you need to stay behind this time."

Ben frowned, but didn't respond. Daisy nodded at Lissy and watched Ben's face closely for his reaction. Ben threw an annoyed glance at Daisy and then sullenly responded to Lissy, "Fine. We'll *both* stay behind."

I was glad to hear his decision, but Daisy looked unconvinced, and that concerned me. I trusted her instincts when it came to her brother. I didn't see what more I could do about Ben, so I looked at Lissy and asked, "We?"

She took my question as a challenge. "Hey, I'm an adult and I have experience. You could use a sorceress who knows what she's doing." The implication being that I *didn't* know what I was doing, which was not completely unfair.

I didn't doubt that Lissy's sorcery skills would be a valuable addition to the rescue team, but we might face physical danger as well as sorcery. I tried to reason with her. "Lissy, this mission is not just about sorcery."

She interrupted me before I could say more. "I know that. I'm competent with a dagger as well. Right Barek?"

Barek tilted his head to the side and shrugged, conceding the skill she claimed.

I rolled my eyes and was about to object again when she put her hands on her hips. "This had *better* not be about me being a woman. I can hold my own, and you need my help. Now give me one good reason why I shouldn't go." She stared into my eyes, watching for even a hint of condescension.

I could see that this battle was lost, and to tell the truth, I didn't really care to fight it that much. Sulana was in danger. I was going to do something about it, regardless of who offered to help. But there was one thing I needed to get straight first. We needed to work in concert, which meant someone had to be in charge. I hardened my gaze and said to her, "If you go, I need you to follow my orders without question."

She seemed startled to have won the confrontation without further argument. When my words sunk in, she stammered, "Yes...of course."

Barek sighed and seem to deflate a little. His haggard condition suddenly registered with me. The man was exhausted and still dirty from the road. He didn't smell that great either.

"You look like you could use some rest and a chance to clean up," I said. "Can we meet tomorrow morning for an early sparring session and do some planning?" He nodded and left the room. The sound of his retreating boots in the hallway was still haunting, but now that I knew the source of my foreboding, the dirge of his footsteps only served to underscore my resolve.

I had taken a bold step by declaring myself the leader of this expedition. I arguably had the most leadership and tactical experience, with the possible exception of Barek. But Barek seemed content to be taking action and not particularly interested in being the one to orchestrate it. Lissy was a powerful sorceress, but she had never led a team to my knowledge.

So the quest was mine. I did feel responsible for Barek's and Lissy's safety, but I would use them to the best of my ability and theirs. All of our lives might depend upon how well I did that.

CHAPTER 37
THWARTED

Gregor shook his head while Lissy paced back and forth. His office wasn't large, so it was just a few short steps in each direction, making her agitation seem all the more frantic. His cozy office was decorated with heavy tapestries, a tall bookshelf on one wall that represented most of his wealth, and thickly-padded chairs, but all that did nothing to relax his guest.

"Lissy, please sit down. You're making me dizzy," he complained.

She stopped and put her hands on the back of the chair that faced his desk on the other side of the wide wooden surface that was his shield against the world. She didn't sit down, but at least she had quit pacing.

"So there's no way the Council can meet tomorrow?" Her eyes were wide and her breath was quick and shallow.

"I'm afraid not," Gregor answered. "Senior Councilor Underwood is away visiting family at the capital. We can't hold a vote without him."

She slapped a hand on the chair back. "We have to find him and get him back here. Jaylan is going to take matters into his own hands if the Council doesn't act quickly."

Gregor leaned back and peered at Lissy over steepled fingers. "So you said. Does he realize that meddling in a politically-charged Archives concern without Council direction will jeopardize his petition to become a Sword Sorcerer?"

She hung her head. "He does. But he doesn't care. All he's thinking about is Sulana sitting in chains in some dank dungeon at Thunderhead College."

Gregor looked down at his hands and mumbled, "Can't say that I blame him."

Lissy abruptly straightened her back and her hands gripped the chair tightly. "I can't either. That's why I'm going with him."

Gregor leaned forward and placed both of his hands flat on the desktop in front of him. "You most certainly are *not* going with him. Get that out of your mind right now."

Her lips pressed into a thin, bloodless line. "I can make my own decisions. I have done everything you've asked of me and I'm a capable sorceress." Her voice took on a pleading tone. "Sulana is my friend, and Jaylan needs my help. We can't let her remain in the hands of the Integrationists."

Gregor folded his hands, but kept firm eye contact with her. "We *will* get Sulana back. The safest way to do that is through negotiation with Thunderhead College, not some half-baked rescue mission run by man who is letting his emotions overtake his common sense."

Lissy leaned forward over the back of the chair. "I might agree with you if I thought Thunderhead College would negotiate in good faith, but the fact that they opened the dialogue by capturing Sulana's team suggests otherwise. Something else is going on here, and we can't just let her sit down there in chains while we figure it out. We need to do something now."

Gregor shook his head. "A hasty reaction will only escalate the tension of this situation and increase the danger to Sulana and her team. She is the Sword Sorceress. She knows the risks of holding that title. She is doing her duty, and you must do yours." He unfolded his hands and drummed his fingers on the desktop briefly. "Besides, Barek tells me that the team may not be comfortable, but they are being cared for well enough."

He seemed to be getting through to Lissy. Her face was still pinched with worry, but she appeared to be genuinely considering his words. Her shoulders hunched and she looked down at her hands with an unfocused stare. Then she straightened up again and shook her head.

"Jaylan gave the Council until tomorrow, and then he's leaving. I can't let him go without someone stronger in sorcery to back him up." Her words were strident, but Gregor could tell that her confidence was wavering.

Gregor had had enough. The muscles in his jaw worked to hold back his growing anger, but he was rapidly losing patience with this discussion. "I will not be bullied by the ultimatum of a student," he said. He pointed a finger at Lissy. "You are not going with him, and that's final." An offended look came over Lissy's face and she opened her mouth to speak, but he overrode the beginning of her stuttering objection. "You have duties here. More important duties than getting yourself captured or killed in an ill-conceived mission that has little chance of success."

Lissy's shoulders slumped and she hung her head. After a moment, she murmured, "I understand."

But Gregor wasn't certain that she did. He decided to give her a reward for capitulating. "Jaylan is a good man, and I'm under no illusion that I can say or do anything to dissuade him from this reckless course of action. However, I think I can offer something that will help."

Lissy looked up at him, her eyes showing a glimmer of hope. She watched as he opened a drawer of his desk and removed a small wooden box. He tilted back the lid of the box and frowned as he removed a rather ugly ring with a wide, blue gem mounted on it. He handed the ring to Lissy, and her brows knitted as she looked it over.

"It's broken," she said, noticing the gem had a crack that marred the flat top surface.

"Yes and no," Gregor replied. "It was designed to be a variable-strength shield ring, but it never worked correctly. Then the crystal was cracked and it became even more useless for shielding."

Lissy looked at him in confusion. "You want me to give Jaylan a broken shield ring?"

Gregor chuckled. "If what I've heard about Jaylan is true, his uniquely low resistance and the flaws of that ring will work well together."

"I don't understand," Lissy said.

"I'd give you something better for him, but access to the armory is restricted because of the portal key theft, even for Council members. Also, I think it's best if the other Councilors remain ignorant of Jaylan's plans. Retrieving anything from the armory would result in too many questions."

Lissy nodded. "You think they would try to stop him? Or reject his petition out of spite?"

"Yes, those are possibilities, but I'm more concerned about word of Jaylan's mission preceding him to Thunderhead College," he answered. "If I can't convince him to wait, I'll do what I can to help him succeed."

Lissy stared at him for a moment and he could see her thinking through the implications of what he had just said. When she spoke, the words were hesitant, as if she were trying them on for size. "You think we have a spy at the Archives. And you suspect it may be a Council member. Councilors

Asher and Shepherd may be in collusion with Headmaster Fortenz."

Gregor gestured in her direction and said, "You see why I can't risk letting you go on this mission? Your insight does you credit, but you must be cautious about revealing your suspicions. I expect you to sit on the Council one day, and involving yourself in clandestine, unauthorized missions with serious political implications is not the way to get there."

Lissy looked down and fidgeted. "I appreciate your confidence in my potential, Councilor. But I want to do something to help my friends."

Gregor nodded toward her hand. "You are doing something. Give Jaylan that ring. It may give him the edge he needs to succeed."

She looked at the ring and frowned. "You still haven't explained how a broken shield ring will help him."

Gregor waved a hand in apology. "The ring may not work as it was originally intended, but it still has value. Most shielding devices are designed to perform at a certain strength and require a specific amount of vaetra to operate. This ring was supposed to let wearers adjust the strength of the shield by increasing and decreasing the amount of vaetra they channeled into it."

Lissy looked at the ring with new respect. "That's ingenious. You could keep the shield active at a low level for minimal protection, and increase the strength of the shield when you needed it, using up only the vaetra necessary at the moment."

Gregor smiled and nodded. "Exactly. In theory, it was a great idea. But that's not how it ended up working." Lissy raised an eyebrow at him, and he went on. "The ring accepts a variable amount of vaetra, but the shield doesn't form until about five seconds have passed. The resulting shield has the same characteristics as a normal, static shield, except its strength depends upon how much vaetra was being provided at the time it formed. So while the shield is indeed variable, the strength can't be adjusted once it forms."

Lissy pursed her lips and said, "That's disappointing."

"Indeed. The smith who created the ring must have spent months researching the runes necessary to power it and several days, at least, making the ring itself," Gregor said. "But that's not the end of the story. Somewhere along the way, the gemstone was cracked, and that changed the behavior of the shield. We don't know exactly where the crack came from. One legend has it that its creator threw the ring across the room when it failed to perform correctly, which is easy to imagine."

"How old is it?" Lissy asked, leaning over and holding the ring closer to the lantern on Gregor's desk to get a better look at the cracked blue gem.

Gregor shrugged one shoulder and said, "We aren't sure. The first mention of the ring is from about one hundred and fifty years ago, but it could be much older than that. I discovered the ring in the armory and decided to learn more about it. We have so many artifacts down there that have never been properly researched and documented."

"How did the crack change the shield?" she asked.

Gregor leaned forward. Researching artifacts was one of his favorite hobbies. He enjoyed sharing the history he uncovered, and while Lissy did not completely share his passion, she was always a good audience.

"The crack causes the shield to detach," he said. "At the moment the shield forms, it drains all of the vaetra offered through the sorcerer's open channel, detaches from the ring, and launches forward." He made a quick forward pushing motion with his hand to emphasize his description.

Lissy leaned back. "That sounds scary."

Gregor nodded and raised an eyebrow. "I can attest that it's quite an uncomfortable experience. That brief moment when the shield forms is like pushing on a door and having someone open it from the other side. Whatever vaetra you've been channeling into the ring at that moment gets sucked in as fast as your resistance allows."

"So, what happens to the shield?" she asked.

"It dissipates fairly quickly, but until that happens, it moves forward, pushing or crushing objects in its path. It's like a moving wall of force. We normally think of shields as defensive, but that ring creates a shield that can be used as an offensive weapon."

Lissy held the ring at arms length toward Gregor and bobbed her hand to indicate that he should take it back from her. "I don't think this is a good idea. You said it works with the sorcerer's resistance and the open channel. Jaylan has the lowest resistance anyone has seen, and his control over his channel isn't that precise yet. It would be dangerous for him to use this thing."

Gregor raised his palm toward Lissy, refusing to take back the ring. "Yes, I know it's dangerous, but it's all I can give him right now. Just tell Jaylan about how it works and caution him to use it only as a last resort. He may never need it, but if he does, you'll be glad he had it with him."

Lissy's brow creased as she looked down at the ring. "If this ring falls into the hands of the Integrationists, they may turn it against us."

Gregor sat back in his chair and wove his fingers behind his head. "Don't worry too much about that. Headmaster Dumont has had years to prepare for his assault on the Archives. I'm sure he has far more dangerous tools at his disposal than that ring."

She frowned at the ring and then gave Gregor a wry smirk. "Thanks for that comforting thought."

Chapter 38

Unknown Illness

Sulana ~ The Dungeon, Thunderhead College

Sulana stared moodily at the empty wooden bowl and cup next to her on the bench. The guard had brought their meal down a while ago. The food wasn't particularly good, but at least their captors weren't starving them.

When the guard came to retrieve the dishes, she would be expected to place them on the floor at the center of the cell as far away as her chains allowed her to reach. There was always a second guard too, making sure that no one made a move toward the man who collected the items.

Daven picked up his bowl and used a last crust of bread to clean off the residue of the simple stew they had been given. "At least they feed us well enough," he said, echoing her thoughts.

Sulana stretched and replied, "I wish they would let us out of here once in a while for some fresh air and exercise. I'm going crazy just sitting here doing nothing all day. And I hate that the only way we know whether it's day or night is by when these bastards come to feed us. Or when Peltor comes to taunt us."

Talon followed her lead and leaned forward, stretching his arms out with a groan. "It's sleeping on this bench that gets to me," he said. "I'd rather sleep outside on the ground."

"I agree with both of you," Daven said. "I'm just saying it could be worse."

Sulana narrowed her eyes at him. "I'm glad you find captivity so cozy. I'd personally like to get out of here and teach our hosts a painful lesson in manners."

Daven shrugged. "They are just using us for leverage. Taking hostages is a time-honored tradition for gaining an edge in negotiations. They'll let us go when they get what they want from the Archives."

Sulana put her hands on her hips and raised her voice. "You've got to be kidding me. This is not a negotiation between nations. This is a rebel sorcerer who threatens the Accords and is trying to subvert or destroy our home and our livelihood."

Daven rolled his eyes. "Don't be so melodramatic, Sulana. Look at what they've built here. It's practically another Archives. They have different politics, but they accomplish a lot of the same things. Just because you don't agree with them doesn't make them wrong."

Sulana turned her head and looked at Daven out of the corner of her eye. Was he being serious, or was he messing with her? He just stared back at her and raised both eyebrows. He *was* being serious. "I can't believe I'm hearing this. We sit here in chains and Thunderhead College uses our lives to threaten the Archives and you don't think they're wrong?"

Daven held up a hand, conceding her point. "I agree that what they are doing is wrong, but if the Archives had been willing to work with them sooner, and in good faith, it might not have come to this."

Sulana shook her head, paced to the end of her chain, and waved her arms as far as her chains allowed. "Have you lost your mind? Thunderhead College has never expressed any interest in working with the Archives. The only thing we exchange is students, and that only happens when someone with Integrationist views gets tired of the Archives policies or a student with Isolationist views gets expelled from here. The headmaster is famous for his intolerance of anyone who doesn't share his vision of reintegrating sorcery into mundane society. His sudden interest in portal keys and in negotiating with the Archives came out of nowhere."

Daven seemed a bit cowed by her tirade. He pressed his lips together and refused to meet her eyes. "Maybe," he said. "And maybe the Council *has* known this was coming and just didn't bring you in on it."

Sulana went still as she considered Daven's conjecture. It was true that the Council didn't tell her everything that was going on, but when it came to the security of the Archives and its residents, she had the right to know. Now that she thought about it, Councilor Rissik *had* been the one to suggest that she be wary of Thunderhead College. Did he know something more that he hadn't shared? Of course he did, but did he actually *expect* Thunderhead College to make a move like this? It seemed unlikely. She didn't believe he would let her go on this mission with such a vague warning if he truly expected something bad to happen.

She looked at Talon to see what he thought about all this, and was startled to see him lying on his side clutching his stomach. He coughed a couple of times and a little foam drooled out of the side of his mouth. She stepped forward without thinking and was brought up short by her chain.

"Talon? What's wrong?" she asked. Daven stood as well. Although he was closer, he couldn't reach Talon either.

Talon coughed again and sat up, wiping his mouth. "I don't know. I don't feel well. Must have been something bad in the food."

Sulana looked at his bowl, which was empty. It seemed like they had all gotten the same food, but she felt fine and Daven seemed okay, except for being an idiot.

Sulana shouted "Guard! We need help in here."

No one answered her call, so she tried again a few times. In the meantime, Talon vomited his dinner into his chamber pot. The stink of bile filled the room and she sat down, feeling a bit nauseous herself. She couldn't tell if she was just reacting to the smell or if she was starting to have the same problem as Talon.

Eventually, the door opened and Peltor entered, followed by two guards. Peltor saw Talon hunched over his chamber pot and smirked. "So, the mighty weaponsmaster couldn't keep his dinner down." He turned to one of the guards and ordered, "Get this man a wet towel so he can clean himself up. And replace the chamber pots."

Sulana stood up and said, "He needs a healer."

Peltor snorted and said, "Why? Because he threw up his dinner? I'm not going to bother the healer for that."

Sulana started to argue, but could see that Peltor had no interest in helping Talon and was just waiting for another excuse to put her in her place. The manacles on her wrists were enough of a reminder that she was at a serious disadvantage here, and arguing with Peltor would achieve nothing except possibly bring them all more grief. She sat down and said nothing.

"Good girl," Peltor said with another snort. He turned and left the room, leaving one guard to watch the proceedings as the other guard brought in fresh chamber pots and waited for Talon to clean himself up.

After Talon returned the towel to the guard, he laid himself down on his back with his arm over his forehead and one knee raised. The weaponsmaster looked miserable, but seemed to be recovering. Maybe Peltor was right and he didn't really need a healer.

After the guards left, Sulana realized that Peltor had not been surprised at Talon's condition, and he hadn't asked Sulana or Daven how they were feeling. On the one hand, he undoubtedly didn't care enough about them to be concerned, but on the other, he might have already known what to expect. She looked down and put her hand over her face, suppressing the urge to cry.

Daven saw her distress and tried to be comforting, his earlier bantering tone gone. "Don't worry Sulana, I'm sure we'll get out of here soon."

She wished she could agree with him. If they *weren't* released soon, they might not survive to the end of the negotiations with the Archives.

CHAPTER 39
DUPLICITY DISCOVERED

Gregor ~ The Archives

Gregor Rissik escorted a subdued and preoccupied Senior Councilor Boris Underwood out of the journey room. He nodded to the guard, who closed and locked the door behind them. The two senior councilors continued down the hallway that led back toward the main hall of the Archives council level.

Gregor spoke quietly to the somber man at his side. "I'm sorry about your brother and that I had to take you away from your family at such a sad time, Boris."

Boris sighed and shook his head. "That's all right Gregor. I understand the urgency, and I had already paid my respects. My family understands my obligations, and there really was nothing more I could do there. I'm sorry you had to come and collect me."

"Think nothing of it. I visit Cassandria frequently, so it was no problem," Gregor said.

A woman's voice interrupted their conversation. "Yes, you do visit Cassandria frequently, don't you? I wonder why that is."

A man and a woman stepped around a turn in the hallway to stand before Gregor and Boris. It was Junior Councilors Velna Asher and Rikard Shepherd. Velna had been the one to speak.

Gregor narrowed his eyes at Velna and answered, "That's none of your concern, Junior Councilor. What brings the inseparable team of Asher and Shepherd into our midst?"

Rikard glanced at Velna and hid a smile. Velna lifted her chin and glared. She chose to ignore Gregor's comment. "It *is* my concern if I believe the integrity of the council has been compromised."

Gregor wasn't sure where she was going with her vague accusation, but he doubted he would like it. This would be a bad time for her to stir up trouble with the council, which was of course, exactly why she was standing here now.

"You would know all about compromising the integrity of the council, wouldn't you?" Gregor retorted. Velna's biggest weakness was her temper. It routinely sabotaged the effectiveness of her arguments in council. But Gregor could see that his barb failed to take hold. The woman was on a mission.

Next to Gregor, Boris took a deep breath and shook off his grief for his lost brother. Focusing on the situation at hand, he demanded, "What is it you want, Councilor Asher?"

"I want Councilor Rissik to explain why he felt it was necessary to visit the emperor while he was in Cassandria," she answered.

Gregor was stunned into momentary silence while all eyes turned toward him. Rikard watched him slyly, carefully gauging his reaction, Velna's eyes gleamed in triumph, and Boris frowned with uncertainty.

Gregor was always careful when he went to Cassandria to "visit family." Most of the time, he actually did go to his family home in the Nobility Quarter before stopping at the palace. He watched his back the entire time to make sure he wasn't being followed. On this trip, however, he didn't have time to be cautious. He only had a small window of time to report to the emperor before he retrieved Boris from the Underwood home for the emergency council session. Someone *had* followed him this time, and his bet was on Rikard.

"What is she talking about, Gregor?" Boris asked.

Gregor didn't have time to make up an elaborate story. The longer he hesitated, the worse it would look. He decided that a partial truth would have to do. "I did visit the palace. I'm concerned that our problems with Thunderhead College could descend into an armed conflict, and I wanted to know if the emperor would be willing to assist us should that happen."

Boris' face and neck grew red, and his brow furrowed deeply. "Councilor Rissik, aren't you the one who keeps telling us that we must appear strong and confident to the emperor? Doesn't running to him for help at the first sign of trouble destroy that impression?"

"I'd say we are well beyond the first sign of trouble," Gregor answered. "Thunderhead College is holding our Sword Sorceress and our weaponsmaster hostage, and they are trying to undermine the Council's ability to uphold the Sorcery Accords."

Velna interjected, "That's a bit of a leap, don't you think? Thunderhead College has expressed an interest in merging their efforts with that of the Archives, and the reason you don't like it is because there's a possibility that the Council could end up with an Integrationist majority."

Gregor faced Velna and his voice grew in intensity and volume as he responded, "You make them sound like peace-loving, cooperative citizens with all the best of intentions, but you are skipping over the fact that *they are holding our people hostage.*" By the time he reached the last words they were nearly a shout.

Boris held up both hands and said, "Stop. Both of you. A hallway is no place for us to have this conversation. We will meet in session this afternoon." Boris took a step away from Gregor and turned to face him. Looking down his nose at his fellow councilor, he added, "I want to know more about any other trips you might have made to visit the emperor, and I'd like for you to explain how your involvement with him does *not* constitute Imperial influence in Archives affairs."

Gregor tilted his head in acceptance and said, "I understand your concerns."

Boris sighed and his shoulders slumped before he turned and continued down the hall on his own. The two junior councilors remained behind.

Velna took a deep, satisfied breath and said, "This should be interesting. I can't wait to see what being exposed as an Imperial spy does to your standing in the Council." When Gregor just stared at her and didn't reply, Rikard held his arm out to Velna. She put her hand in the crook of his elbow. They turned together and left Gregor standing in the hallway by himself.

A few moments after the others left, Gregor slowly started walking back toward his office. The meddling of the junior councilors would not normally be difficult to manage. But times were precarious, and he needed the support of Senior Councilor Underwood more than ever. His fellow Councilors operated under the belief that the Archives was completely independent of the emperor and had full responsibility for managing the affairs of the sorcery community and upholding the Accords.

But that belief was a delusion. The emperor granted the Council the powers it had, and the emperor could take those powers away. Sorcerer or mundane, they were all Imperial citizens, subject to Imperial law. Emperor Tanes certainly saw things that way, even if the Council did not. The timing was bad, but Gregor thought that it might become necessary for him to shatter the illusion so they could move forward.

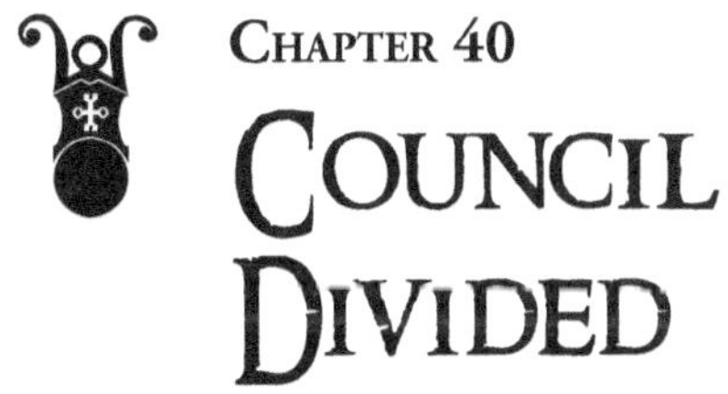

CHAPTER 40
COUNCIL DIVIDED

Jaylan ~ Incantations Class, The Archives

I struggled to clear my mind and concentrate on the incantation. It was a tough one. I knew I wasn't ready for such advanced spellwork, but I had limited time to learn something I could use on my mission.

Professor Delano stood just behind me and to the side, as was her custom when she helped me work a spell. I wasn't sure if she chose her position so she could more easily see what I was doing, or because she had a better chance of avoiding the unpredictable results of my efforts.

I had learned a few things about the people of the Archives over the past day since Barek had given me the news about Sulana's capture. One thing I learned was that secrets flowed through these halls like floodwaters. The furtive look of hidden knowledge floated in just about every pair of eyes I met. I also learned who supported my plan and who did not. Those same eyes clearly relayed approval or disapproval. But most importantly, I learned about loyalty. Those who supported me took what steps they could to help out. Those who did not support me stayed out of the way, and as far as I knew, had not yet reported my intentions to the Council.

Professor Delano had not broached the subject herself, but when I asked for special instruction in something I could use in a fight, she had not hesitated. In fact, I think she had anticipated my request and was just waiting for me to ask.

So here I was, trying to learn how to cast lightning. It was a spell that normally took a week or more of study to get right because the incantation required unusual and difficult vocalizations. I had to learn it in an afternoon. And it wasn't going well.

"Try again, Jaylan," the professor said. "If you get this at all, it's going to take the rest of the day. It's not too late to start over with something simpler, but another spell might not be as effective for...your purposes."

From the first moment that I began practicing the vocalizations for this spell, the strange lassitude I'd experienced before flowed through my consciousness and interfered with my ability to concentrate on anything in my surroundings, including the spell book on the table in front of me. This trance, or whatever it was, was beginning to annoy me. It got in the way of every spell I tried to cast. Professor Delano had dismissed it as fatigue back when we first started my spell casting lessons in earnest, but she was at a loss to explain why the condition persisted.

Daisy came over to my table and looked over the spell instructions. "Wow, that *is* a hard one," she said. "Are you sure you don't want to try something easier? If learning this one doesn't work out, you'll have wasted the whole afternoon."

I looked up at her and saw genuine concern in her light blue eyes. Her strawberry blonde hair cascaded around her delicate features, which were marred by a furrowed brow. Ever since I declared my intention to free Sulana, Daisy's attitude toward me had changed. She had stopped with the teasing jibes and tried to be helpful. It could be that she was just grateful I had not sided with her brother when he tried to join my quest to free Sulana.

I half-turned in my seat to look at Professor Delano. "Didn't you say this spell was the best fit for my abilities and that anything else would be nearly as hard to learn and less useful in a fight?"

"Yes, I believe so. Most *defensive* spells are easier to learn, but they aren't what you wanted. You could try to learn a different attack spell, but most of them aren't much easier than this one, and many of them don't give you fine control over targeting, which you said was important."

I nodded. "If it comes down to a fight, it could get chaotic. I don't want to accidentally hit one of our own."

Something I said caused Professor Delano to gasp and open her mouth slightly while her eyes went unfocused. When she came back to herself, she smiled and said, "I have an idea. There's a variation on this spell that is much simpler. I apologize for not thinking of it earlier, but we don't put much emphasis on attack spells around here. There's a spell called Shocking Hand that might serve you better. It's good in a close fight. The down sides are that you have to be close enough to touch the target and you can only use it on one target at a time.

I could tell that she chose the word "target" deliberately. She wasn't comfortable with the fact that I was prepared to use the spell I learned on another human being. The Archives sorcery training program focused on spells that were constructive or defensive. They didn't want to send sorcerers back out among the mundane with frightening powers of death and destruction that might be perceived as precursors to an abandonment of the Sorcery Accords.

I couldn't afford such delicate sensibilities. I had a mission, and I needed every advantage I could get.

I pushed the spell book away from me with some relief. I'd be happy to save the lightning spell for another time. "Sounds good to me. Where can I get the spell instructions?"

She pursed her lips and thought for a moment. "That spell book is in the library. I think I know where it is. I'll be right back." She bustled out of the room, leaving me behind with Daisy and Benjamin.

While Daisy had warmed up to me, Benjamin had withdrawn. He ignored just about everyone, including his sister, and rarely initiated a conversation. I had invited him to train with Barek and me thinking it would cheer him up, but he refused, saying there wasn't any point if he wasn't going to be traveling with us. Although he gave every indication of having accepted his sister's demand that he stay behind, Daisy continued to send worried glances in his direction and was careful to keep him in sight.

Daisy gave her brother that same worried look now. He was hunched over his work table with his back to us, pretending to be reading a spell book. I was pretty sure he was just sulking.

Daisy called over to him, "Ben, I think we should see if Professor Delano will let us learn this one too."

I thought she was just trying to distract him from his dark mood, but a serious note in her voice hinted at a deeper concern. Like she was thinking they might need to use the spell themselves one day soon. She could be right. Who knew how the conflict with Thunderhead College was going to turn out?

"Learn what?" Lissy asked as she rushed into the room. She came to a halt in front of my work table, breathing deeply through her nose, her dress settling back into place around her. She picked a loose lock of dark hair out of her face and tucked it behind her ear. It was the most disheveled I'd ever seen her. Lissy glanced down at the spell book and then up at Daisy. "You are learning to cast lightning? That's ambitious."

I answered for Daisy. "Actually, we've given up on this one. Professor Delano is going to find something called Shocking Hand for us to try. She said it would be easier to learn."

Lissy nodded thoughtfully. "That makes sense. Touch spells are almost always easier to learn than distance spells." She gave her head a brief shake and refocused her attention on me. "I have news," she said.

That got my full attention. She had promised to let me know as soon as she had any information from the Council. "Has the Council decided what they are going to do?"

"Yes." She paused for a moment, and I was about to urge her on when she continued with a grim twist to her lips, "As you suspected, they are going to do nothing."

I had hoped for better news, but like she said, I wasn't surprised. The councilors were in a difficult position with many considerations to juggle. I, on the other hand, had only one consideration: getting Sulana back.

"Well, I shouldn't say they are doing nothing. They just dispatched a courier to Thunderhead College with a message saying they are willing to negotiate for the release of the hostages and they will consider the headmaster's demands. The next step is to decide on a location for the parley."

That was unexpected. While I did expect the Council to react slowly, I never imagined that they would seriously consider any of the headmaster's demands. "Are they sincere, or do you think they are just buying time?" I asked.

Lissy shrugged. "A little of both, I think, depending upon who you are. The Council is divided at the moment, and entering negotiations is a compromise that delays a direct conflict between the councilors themselves."

The councilors were more concerned with avoiding an internal confrontation than with getting Sulana's team back?

My hand slapped the table before I could think to stop it. "Useless politics!" I shouted. Both Lissy and Daisy jumped and took a step back from me. I waved my hand and said, "Sorry. But this whole Integrationist versus Isolationist thing is starting to wear on my nerves."

Lissy stepped forward again and lowered her voice. "I know. And I agree. You and Barek need to leave as soon as possible." She glanced at the open doorway. "Too many people know how you feel about this situation, and it is only a matter of time before word reaches the Council that you might take action on your own. The Council has the means to stop or delay you."

I noticed that she said "you and Barek," and I cocked my head at her questioningly. She knew exactly what I was thinking and said, "I won't be going with you after all." She looked down at the floor and sighed deeply. Reaching into her pocket, she pulled something out and set it on the table. It was a rather large and gaudy ring with a blue stone.

I reached out and picked up the ring, turning it around to catch the light from the illuminators. The stone had a short crack across part of the surface, otherwise it would have been a lovely gem.

"By the spirits, that's ugly," Daisy said from my side, and I couldn't disagree. She looked up at Lissy. "Did you know the stone is cracked?"

"Of course I know." Lissy snapped. Daisy's hurt look made her close her eyes and take a deep breath. She looked at Daisy and said, "Sorry. It's kind of a sore subject." She went on to explain what the ring was and how it worked.

A broken shield ring. Somehow, it seemed fitting given how many other difficulties I had encountered lately regarding sorcery. I have big hands, but the ring had been made for hands even larger than mine. I slipped the ring onto the middle finger of my left hand. It was a snug fit. I tried to pull it off again but had trouble getting it back over the first knuckle, so I just left it in place. I commented, "Well, I won't lose it anyway."

Lissy put her hand over the ring to get my attention and looked into my eyes. "I want you to be very careful with that ring, Jaylan," she said. "I've been thinking about how it works. I was told it was a good fit for your unique abilities, and now that I've figured out what that truly means, I'm concerned."

"What unique abilities?" I asked with a wry tone. So far, my unique abilities seemed more like unique disabilities.

Lissy tone became insistent as she went on. "The moment before the shield separates, the ring drops its own channel resistance and drains all the vaetra it can. If you were to open your channel fully, the only limiting factor on the drain would be *your* resistance."

Ah. My infamous resistance. That was the unique disability she was talking about.

"So you are saying the ring could drain me completely in an instant." She nodded. "Do you know what that would do to me?"

She patted my hand before taking hers away. "Nothing good. It would probably knock you unconscious. But that isn't what concerns me."

"Then what?" I asked, genuinely puzzled.

"The ring projects a powerful shield. Even at low power, it knocks stuff over and breaks things. No one knows what would happen at its maximum strength. For your safety and that of everyone around you, it might be best if we don't try to find out."

I nodded. "I agree. Still, if we are pursued, leaving a powerful shield behind us could be very useful. Thanks for loaning it to me."

I didn't quite understand how long the shield would last or how it moved when it separated, but Lissy's description made it sound like those aspects would vary according to how strong it was at the time of separation. I imagined dropping a shield behind me to temporarily block a narrow part of the trail while we rode away.

But Lissy wasn't finished yet. She glanced over her shoulder at the door again and pulled a few small bottles out of her pockets and put them on the table. She arranged them in a tight cluster and positioned herself between them and the open doorway. "These are mostly healing potions, which I sincerely hope you won't need. The purple one lets you see in low-light conditions."

I picked up the violet bottle labeled "Night Vision." Being able to see in darkness could come in handy. "Thanks Lissy, this is generous of you."

She shrugged. "It's what I do. I'm sorry it's the best I can offer, but I'm convinced now that I can be more useful here. I know you get impatient with the politics around this place, but you can't just ignore them. I'm volunteering myself to run interference while you get Sulana back for us."

Lissy was right. I did get impatient with politics. And ignoring them had been the source of some of my life's most bitter lessons. I seemed destined to have to learn those lessons over and over again. "Thanks again, Lissy. I appreciate your help more than you can know."

Taking her lead regarding keeping the bottles a secret, I collected them and stuffed them into my pockets.

Footsteps in the hall heralded the return of Professor Delano. She came into the room with a fat, leather-bound tome under her arm. Upon seeing Lissy, she smiled and said, "Hello Lissy. What brings you to our class?" She glanced at my chest pocket, which bulged from a couple of the potion bottles, and her gaze lingered on the ring Lissy had given me. The woman didn't miss much.

"I just came by to see how you and Jaylan are doing since we got the news about Sulana," Lissy answered.

The professor's face fell, and she bowed her head for a moment. When she looked up, wetness ringed her eyes. "I'm worried for her of course, but she's a strong girl and I have faith that things will turn out all right."

Lissy put her hand on the professor's arm and said softly, "We'll get her back, Marlene."

The smile returned to the professor's face, and she squared her shoulders. "Yes we will." She shifted the book under her arm and said, "We'll all contribute however we can."

After Lissy left, Daisy and I worked side-by-side learning the Shocking Hand spell. Daisy picked it up much faster than I did, and she even managed to get Benjamin out of his funk by trying it out on him. His outrage turned to laughter when she made a face at his grumpiness, and for the rest of the afternoon, the three of us worked on the spell together. By the end of the day, we had mastered it well enough for all three of us to have rather frightening hairstyles.

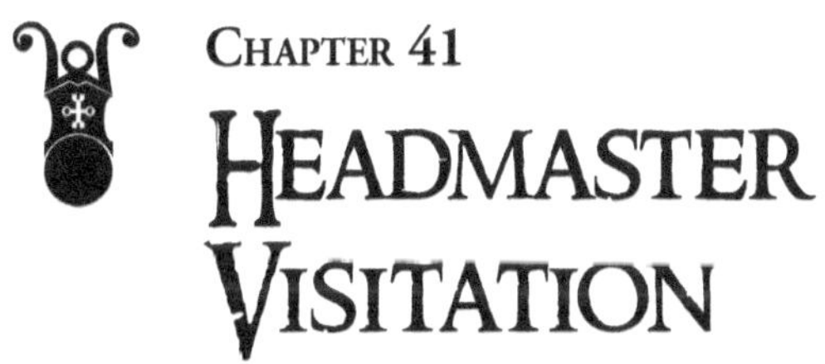

Chapter 41

Headmaster Visitation

Sulana ~ The Dungeon, Thunderhead College

Sulana awoke from a nap but didn't bother opening her eyes or sitting up. The flat, hard bench that kinked the muscles in her back told her everything she needed to know about the humiliation and hopelessness of her current situation. She didn't need a visual to reinforce it. The desire to leave this airless, uncomfortable basement room and use a wash basin was nearly unbearable. She wanted to feel the sun on her skin and breathe in some fresh air. How much longer were they going to be held here? Hours? Days? Weeks?

The metal restraints at her wrists and ankles added literal weight to her feeling of helplessness. A single tear leaked out of the corner of one eye and rolled along the side of her face until the tickle made her wipe it away with an impatient rattle of chains. All of those years she had dreamed of becoming a Sword Sorceress, and now it had come to this.

A key rattled in the cell's lock and the door opened to let in a welcome breath of air from the hallway. Sulana was prepared to ignore the guards who occasionally came to give them food and replace the chamber pots, but when an unfamiliar scent came in with the waft of air from the doorway, she turned her head and opened her eyes. Someone new had arrived. She quickly sat up to get a better look.

The guard who opened the door stepped aside to allow the two strangers and Peltor to enter the room. Peltor stood back against the wall and let the other two men come forward.

The first man was big and richly dressed. He wore a dark blue cape over a tooled black leather vest and white shirt. His fine black pants were made from a lightweight hide of some kind, possibly deerskin. Blue-grey eyes set in a pale, craggy face scanned the room.

Daven sat up on his bench as well, but Talon remained flat. Talon's color was much better now, but his breathing was still labored and his movement was often accompanied by a groan.

The big man's eyes settled on Sulana, and he said, "So this is Sulana Delano, the Archives Sword Sorceress. It's a shame we are meeting under such unpleasant circumstances, Agent Delano. I am Dumont Fortenz, Headmaster of this facility."

Sulana jumped to her feet, her pulse quickening and her hands clenching into fists. "You have no right to keep us here. Let us go now. The Archives won't let you get away with this."

The headmaster didn't immediately respond. He just stared at her, absently rubbing at a scar on his chin that showed through his closely-trimmed beard. His eyes took on a distant look for a moment before he finally focused on her again and chortled.

"We'll see about that, Agent Delano." He took a step closer and looked more intently at her face. Sulana narrowed her eyes at him and frowned. "Yes, I see the resemblance now. That dour, self-righteous frown is just like your father's."

"What do you know of my father?" Sulana demanded.

"Oh, I had the misfortune of being present at the Battle of Riverview. Your father was a force of nature. He was prepared to make an example of all of us, but fortunately, cooler heads prevailed."

Sulana knew that Headmaster Fortenz was one of the sorcerers from the Riverview Sanctuary who had been cleared of violating the Accords after the battle. The Imperial Tribunal had determined that the head of the sanctuary, Housemaster Montok, was behind the takeover of the Riverview ministry, but the old sorcerer refused to submit to Archives authority. The resulting fight destroyed half of the Riverview Sanctuary and ended in a final duel of sorcery that killed both Montok and Sword Sorcerer Lorn Delano, her father.

Their sanctuary in ruin, the remaining Riverview sorcerers were homeless. Minister Bogard demanded that they rebuild elsewhere, and he decreed Riverview to be a sorcery-free town. The people of Riverview rejoiced and tore down every remaining stick and stone of the Riverview Sanctuary.

Dumont Fortenz and the other surviving Riverview sorcerers moved into an abandoned manor about a dozen miles away from Riverview, and refurbished it to serve as their new sanctuary. That sanctuary eventually became Thunderhead College, and now, Sulana's prison.

Although the headmaster and his cohorts had been cleared by the tribunal, Sulana had never believed they were innocent. The old Riverview Sanctuary had always been an Integrationist stronghold. Thunderhead College was simply their new lair.

Sulana tilted her head back. She couldn't exactly look down her nose at Headmaster Fortenz because he stood head and shoulders taller than her, but she tried her best. "So, it seems my father was right all along. The whole lot of you were subversives who deserved to be put away."

Peltor growled at her disrespect, but his forward motion was arrested by the headmaster's outstretched arm and open hand. "Relax, Peltor," he said. "The poor girl lost her father. It's only natural for her to place blame on the survivors of the battle that killed him.

"If you are saying that we still believe in and fight for the Integrationist cause, Agent Delano, you are correct. It's time the Archives stopped wallowing in the past and started looking toward the future."

Sulana tried to fold her arms, but the chains interfered. She held her manacled hands out toward him as evidence and said, "And you think kidnapping us is an acceptable way to move your agenda forward?"

He waved a hand at her chains dismissively and said, "You haven't been hurt. And I don't intend to hurt you or your team. I've even allowed one of you to go free as a sign of good faith. I'm sure your team will be released early in our negotiations with the Archives. Holding you here ensures that the Archives takes us seriously and prevents them from using you against us at the same time."

Sulana looked over at Talon, who was still lying flat on his bench. "But you *have* hurt one of us. Something has made Talon ill," she said.

"That is why I brought our healer down here with me," the headmaster said. He stepped aside and waved the second stranger forward.

The healer was a stooped older man in a simple brown tunic and loose black leggings. His robe had a healer's red dot centered on the chest and back, and he carried a tan leather satchel that also bore a red dot. He shuffled over to Talon's bench and kneeled next to the weaponsmaster. Talon allowed the man to check his eyes and mouth, and to place a thin, bony hand across his forehead. The healer mumbled a few questions to Talon, who responded with nods and shakes of his head.

Finally, the healer rose slowly to his feet, using the bench for leverage. He came back to the headmaster and said in a gravelly voice, "He claims he is feeling better now. There's really nothing more I can do for him, although I recommend that he receive plenty of water. Was that all you needed, headmaster?"

The headmaster nodded once and said, "Yes, thank you."

The healer slipped around the headmaster and exited the room.

The headmaster came toward Sulana and positioned himself uncomfortably close to her. Refusing to be intimidated, she resisted the urge to step back and coldly stared up at him with her lips pressed tightly together. He was so close that she could feel his body heat, which was an annoyingly welcome sensation after days in the chill of this underground room. Peltor fingered his sword hilt and moved closer as well, apparently uncomfortable with the headmaster's proximity to Sulana.

Headmaster Fortenz spoke in a carefully measured tone. "Let's hope that you can learn to be more flexible than your father, Agent Delano. It's possible we will be working together one day. A new day for sorcerers is coming, and those who can't adjust will be left behind."

Sulana's jaw clenched and her hands closed into fists again. Out of the corner of her eye, she saw Peltor's hand grip his sword hilt firmly and he pulled the blade out of its scabbard a couple of inches. Although her desire to push the headmaster away from her was intense, she stared up into his cold eyes and said, "This is hardly the way to begin a working relationship, Headmaster Fortenz. And I wouldn't count on every sorcerer stepping out of the way of this *new day* you have planned. You do not control the Archives."

The headmaster snorted and abruptly walked away from her. As he went out the door he said, "Not yet, Agent Delano. But time will tell."

Peltor sneered at her as he slammed his blade back into the scabbard. "Get him some water," he told the other guard, gesturing carelessly at Talon as he followed the headmaster out of the room.

Sulana realized that the confrontation had left her shaking, and she slumped down to her bench. So all of this was really about taking over the Archives? The thought of Dumont Fortenz making decisions as part of the council made her stomach knot. Her father would be screaming in whatever place his spirit existed now. If Headmaster Fortenz was trying to drum up support from the other sanctuaries, the need for a portal key also made sense. Thunderhead College had no journey room that she knew of, so the Portal Keep would be the best alternative for getting around the empire quickly.

Her musings were interrupted by Daven, who had been completely silent during the entire episode. "I don't like that guy," he declared.

Sulana forced out a laugh, but the tension in her chest made it come out so loud that she startled herself. She took a few deep, calming breaths, and then she nodded at Daven. "I couldn't agree with you more."

CHAPTER 42
DOUBLE TROUBLE

Jaylan ~ Campsite, Eagle River Trail

I took Lissy's warning about leaving as soon as possible seriously. That afternoon, Barek and I saddled our horses and left "for an overnight hunting trip." The Archives courier had raced off with the Council's response to Thunderhead College only a couple of hours before we arrived at the stable with our gear in hand. I don't think our story fooled the groom. The normally effusive man helped us prepare our horses with quiet and efficient speed. Just before we left, he clapped me on the shoulder, looked me in the eye, and wished me good luck.

I wanted to give the messenger plenty of time to get to Thunderhead College, deliver his message, and return to the Archives, preferably without running into us along the way. Barek knew of a good camp site about two-thirds of the way down the mountain that would let us watch the trail without being seen. We could wait there until we saw the courier come back up the trail on his return trip the following day and proceed after he passed.

We hurried our horses down Eagle River Trail as quickly as was safe and arrived at the camp just before the last light faded from the sky.

The next morning, I watched closely while Barek drew a crude map in the dirt showing the layout of Thunderhead College and the surrounding grounds. The manor was a long rectangle. The courtyard around the manor was protected by a stone wall. Barek estimated the wall was about six feet high.

Getting over the wall would not be a problem, which was good since I didn't think walking in through the front gate was much of an option.

Barek and I had already discussed the manpower at the college. He didn't know exactly how many people lived at the manor, but he estimated at least a score of sorcerers and maybe a dozen guards. However, unlike the Archives, the college trained many of its sorcerers in arms as well as sorcery, so the line between sorcerer and guard was vague. It sounded to me like they were creating their own little cadre of Sword Sorcerers.

The only good piece of news was that the enemy wasn't particularly skilled at physical combat. At least not yet. Until fairly recently, they lacked serious training from an experienced soldier. When Barek broke the news that they had hired Peltor to train and lead their guards, I felt as if the ground had fallen away from my feet. Imagining Sulana at Peltor's mercy sent shivers down my spine and intensified my determination to get her out of there as quickly as possible.

Barek was drawing the position of the stable and explaining what he remembered of it when he went still. At the same moment, Patches and the horse that Barek had borrowed both nickered softly. Barek cocked his head to listen and I did the same. Was it the courier? No, we heard at least two voices, and they came from direction of the Archives. Had someone been sent to intercept us?

Our camp was positioned well off the trail and slightly above it. The clearing connected to an outcropping of rock that overlooked the trail. Barek and I crept to the overlook, but stayed back from the edge. By unspoken agreement, we chose to listen first, rather than peek over the rocks and take the chance on being seen.

A young woman's voice came to us first. "Are you sure this is the right trail? Maybe we should have taken one of the other turns."

She was answered by a young man. "Those other turns were game trails. This has to be the right trail. It's taking us down the mountain and it's better traveled."

Barek and I looked at each other. He rolled his eyes and shook his head. Both of us had recognized the voices of Daisy and Benjamin Morrison.

Now what? We could remain hidden, but Daisy and Ben would probably go all the way down the mountain looking for us, and a Thunderhead College patrol would promptly capture them. Would they give away my plans if that happened? Possibly. Either way, letting them go down the mountain alone was a bad idea.

I stood up and waved down at them. Ben saw me first and his hand went immediately to his sword. When he realized it was me, he grinned and pointed. "See. There they are. I told you we were on the right trail."

Pointing my arm toward the narrow, half-hidden side trail that led up to our camp site, I directed them to join us.

While the twins tethered their horses next to Patches, I was pleased to see that they had picked their mounts well. Both animals were large and strong. Having more horses to share the burden of our escape would be helpful.

I mentally started adjusting my plans. Barek and I hoped to liberate the horses that were captured along with Sulana's team, but if that proved to be too difficult, we could have Sulana and Daisy switch off riding double with the men. Barek had already proven that a horse was optional, so we could give his mount to Talon.

Riding double was okay as a back-up plan, but I still hoped we'd be able to get the other horses. If we had to leave in a hurry with pursuit close behind, having everyone on their own horse might make the difference between a successful escape and recapture. Besides, I knew Sulana loved her mare Stardust, and she would be sad to leave the animal behind.

Once their horses were secured, Ben and Daisy came over and looked at Barek's crude drawing. Ben kneeled down to examine it closer. Barek stood silently on the opposite side of the diagram with his arms folded, watching me and waiting to see what I would say to the twins.

Daisy and I locked eyes. "I thought you agreed to stay behind," I said.

Daisy twisted her lips into a sardonic smile. "So did I." She waved her hand at Ben. "Until I caught Ben sneaking out of his room to follow you."

"You were waiting for him, weren't you?" I guessed. She sighed. "Yes. He gave in too easily when I threatened to go with him. I had a feeling he would just leave without telling me." She stretched her leg out and pushed on Ben's shoulder with her foot. He toppled over into the dirt with an exclamation of surprise.

Ben chose to ignore her. He righted himself, bushed off the dirt, and moved a few feet further away before going back to studying Barek's diagram.

"We should send you back," I said.

She shrugged. "Fine by me. But if Ben stays, I stay. We're here now, so you might as well let us help. Ben can dispel manifestations better than either of us, and I'm better at shielding than either of you. You can use us both."

She was right. Daisy was growing into a competent sorceress, and Ben had a mix of martial and sorcery skills that could be very helpful on this mission. But they were still just kids. If I could not send them back to the Archives, I had to figure out a way to take advantage of their help without putting them directly into the line of fire.

I held Daisy's gaze for a moment more, and I could see within her eyes the strength of spirit that had driven her to place herself in danger to protect her brother. Her fine hair was bright red and wispy in the sunlight, contrasting with her light blue irises which practically glowed with determination. The close-fitting outfit she wore emphasized her thin and small-boned figure, but I knew in that moment that she was not as frail as she looked.

I nodded once. "If you are going to join us, you must agree to follow my orders. This isn't a game. We could all get captured or killed, and I need to know that you won't jeopardize the mission by doing anything unexpected."

Ben stood with a big grin on his face and said, "Yes sir, Captain Forester. Just tell me what to do."

Daisy rolled her eyes at Ben and then said to me, "I understand, and I agree. But I want to be in on the planning. I need to know what to expect and what our roles will be."

I chuckled and said, "I wouldn't have it any other way."

Ben immediately started asking Barek questions about his drawing and the four of us got down to the serious business of planning what we would do when we reached the valley.

As concerned as I was for the safety of the twins, adding their skills to our team gave me more options than I had before, and the strategist in me rejoiced. Now, all I had to do was figure out a way to get Sulana, Daven, and Talon out of Thunderhead College without getting any of us killed in the process.

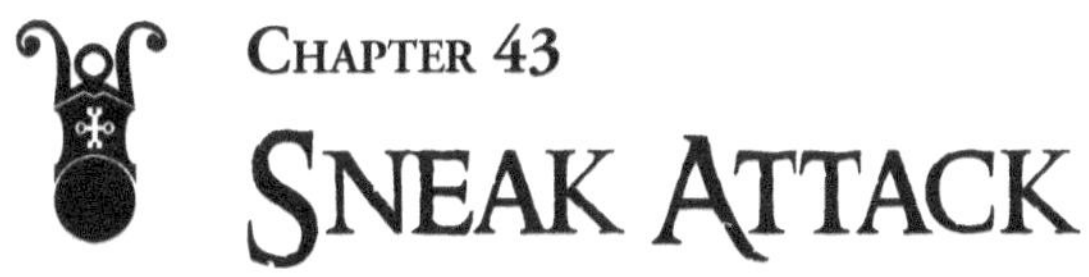

CHAPTER 43
SNEAK ATTACK

Jaylan ~ Thunderhead College

Crouched in the deep shadow at the edge of the forest, my team and I watched the evening activities at Thunderhead College. Torches cast a flickering light across the courtyard. Their uneven illumination made the manor seem to grow, shrink, and shift. A guard yawned at his post near the front gate, but snapped to alertness when rustling sounds came from the shrubs along the edge of the pond just outside the walls of the compound.

Earlier in the day, just a short while after Daisy and Ben had joined us, the Archives courier cantered his horse up the trail. The horse must have smelled our mounts or me, because he shook his head up and down and snorted as he went below the overlook where I was crouching. The courier looked around with concern, but I ducked before he looked my way. I stayed down and out of sight until his horse's hoof beats faded up the trail. We left the camp within minutes of the courier's passing.

When we reached the bottom of the mountain, Barek scouted ahead and found a clearing far off the main trail where we could hide our horses and safely leave them behind while we spied on the college. I left the twins in charge of the horses while Barek and I carefully picked our way forward through the forest until we found a good vantage point. The position let us keep track of what the guards were doing and gave us one of the shortest stretches of open meadow between the forest and the courtyard wall.

We made plans throughout the late afternoon. The place was too well guarded for a daytime sortie. We decided to wait until dark, hoping the sky would remain clear for a few more hours.

Luckily, the spirits were with us. A bright moon rose above the treetops and cast a pale light across the open areas while darkening the curtain of shadow along the tree line. A night bird made whooping noises over the pond. A large owl called who-who-whooo as a warning to the small furry denizens of the area.

"It looks like we're down to two guards," I whispered to Barek. I felt more than saw his nod. "And there's still a groomsman who never left the stable," I added. Again, Barek nodded.

Benjamin and Daisy squatted right behind us. Benjamin eased closer to me and asked, "Should I try to get the horses, then?"

Daisy whispered harshly, "No. It's too dangerous."

I turned my head toward the twins and said, "Quiet. Both of you. Follow your orders."

Activity on the college grounds had slowed to almost nothing as the residents moved indoors and settled into night-time routines. I smiled to myself. Routines are helpful when you plan to do something unexpected.

When I had been captain of the Northshore Imperial Guard, I instructed my guards to vary their patrol rounds and I frequently rotated their schedules. It kept the guards more alert and less predictable. I try to apply the axiom that you can't plan for the unexpected, but you can expect the unplanned.

Barek had explained the layout of the building to the rest of us, at least the small part of it he had seen. He and I had the job of getting into the manor undetected. We would head immediately downstairs and figure out how to free Sulana, Talon, and Daven from their shackles.

I tasked the twins with providing backup. Daisy would stay here and be prepared to use those spell-casting abilities she bragged about to slow down any pursuit. If I decided the risk was low enough, Ben would try to retrieve the horses that were taken with Sulana's team. As things stood, the stable did not have a guard assigned to it.

I figured Ben could handle a single stable hand, so in spite of Daisy's misgivings, I handed him Lissy's night vision potion. His wide, excited eyes reflected the torchlight as he took the bottle from me. He would wait until our plans were in motion before drinking it, because we weren't sure how long it would last.

Barek and I had been over the plan and the contingencies several times, and I had impressed upon the twins that they had to be prepared for anything. We might be completely successful and sneak out with the prisoners without raising an alarm, or we might all be running for our lives. We might even be captured or killed.

I watched the guards intently, waiting for our chance. When the two men met at the gate, they engaged in a brief conversation, and I signaled that it was time for us to make our move. Barek, Benjamin, and I skulked as quietly as possible across the open space between the forest and the wall. We followed a line of tree shadow cast by the pale moon for most of the distance.

This was one of the most risky moments in our plan because the wall around the courtyard wasn't particularly high. My guess was that the builders had originally designed it to keep domestic animals inside and wild animals outside rather than as a barrier against an armed attack. The short wall was both an advantage and a disadvantage for us; we could easily climb over it, but at the same time, the guard who wandered the inside perimeter was tall enough to see over it. We had to time our crossing for a moment when both guards were distracted.

We reached the wall without raising an alarm and hunkered down at the base, waiting for the two guards to stop speaking. Eventually, we heard the perimeter guard head off on his next trip around the wall. When I signaled Benjamin to go, he drank the night vision potion and started moving along the base of the wall toward the back of the college. He would have to sneak in the darkness all the way to the opposite side of the compound before he reached the stables. Meanwhile, Barek and I crept closer to the front gate.

Barek eased up slowly and peered over the wall. When the perimeter guard went behind the stables and out of view, he crouched back down next to me. He patted me twice on the shoulder to signal it was time for our next move. He crept further toward the gate while I stayed in position.

Barek's job was to distract the guard at the front gate and lure him away from the gate opening. As soon as I heard Barek use a rock to make scratching sounds on the wall, I climbed up onto the wall and flattened myself along the top. Verifying that the guard had left his post at the gate to investigate Barek's noise, I quietly lowered myself to the ground inside the wall.

I glanced toward the manor, feeling completely exposed. If someone happened to be looking outside, they would see me sneak up on the guard. However, the exterior torchlight was dim enough that the competing light from inside a room would make it difficult to see outside unless the viewer stood right at the window. We had been watching the manor for quite a while, and no one seemed inclined to stand at the window and stare into the courtyard.

I crept through the gate opening with my dagger out and ready. I nearly bumped into the guard, who had gone forward only a couple of steps to investigate Barek's noises. He must have seen my shadow in his peripheral vision, because he spun around and drew his sword in one smooth movement. His grin gleamed in the half-light of the torch when he saw that I was armed with just a dagger to his sword.

But that that was the last thing he saw before Barek rose up behind him and knocked him unconscious with a blow to the neck. I caught the guard as he slid to the ground, and Barek helped me remove the cloak he wore to protect himself against the cool night air. I donned the cloak and went back to stand at the gate opening with my back to the courtyard. *Nothing to see here. I'm just the gate guard standing at my post.*

Our luck had held so far. We'd managed to take out the gate guard without alerting the other guard, who was still around the back of the manor on his rounds.

An itch began to grow between my shoulder blades as I stood there with my exposed back toward the enemy. Several times, I had to arrest the urge to look behind, but I couldn't let the second guard or anyone else catch a glimpse of my face. Meanwhile, Barek tied up and gagged the gate guard using short leather bindings we'd brought for the purpose.

I fingered the hilt of my dagger and fidgeted while I waited for the second guard. My heart started to race when I heard his footsteps approach. I eased forward into the gateway and faced out into the night until he was within a few yards. Exclaiming as if I had seen something, I stepped forward out of his sight.

The perimeter guard called out and ran through the gate opening just as we anticipated. As he came through the gateway, I grabbed his arm and used his own momentum to slam him head-first into the wall. He hit the wall a little harder than I intended and went down with a grunt. As the guard rolled to a sitting position, a dark stain of blood dripped down his forehead. I knelt next to him to see if he was still alive while Barek held his sword point against the man's chest. I was relieved to find that he was still breathing, although I imagined he'd have a nasty headache when he awoke.

Barek took the larger patrol guard's cloak and we left the man bound next to the gate guard. I went back to my post at the gate, and Barek started off along the perimeter guard's route. We wanted the situation to appear as normal as possible until we were ready to go into the manor.

I stole glances at Barek's progress along the wall. When he reached the stable, he paused briefly, and his low whistle carried to me across the courtyard. Ben slipped smoothly over the wall and went behind the stable. Barek turned away from the wall and walked across the courtyard in front of the stable doors. He stopped when he reached the corner of the manor.

That was my signal to begin the next phase of our operation. I turned around and strode from the gate toward the breezeway of the manor, keeping my head tilted down the whole way. When I was about half-way across the courtyard, Barek started toward the breezeway as well, timing it so we arrived at the same moment.

I half expected another guard to be waiting for us, but the crunch of our footsteps in the gravel echoed against empty walls. The light from the torches on the front of the building didn't penetrate into the passage very far, so we both paused while our eyes adjusted to the dark.

Each wall had a door at the center. The left door opened into the south wing of the manor and the right into the north wing. Our destination was in the basement area below the south wing, but we had to enter through the north wing to reach the basement stairwell. I listened at the north door while Barek watched the other.

The door was made from thick, rough timber, so it was hard to hear anything through it. Positioning my ear at the lock only helped a little. I couldn't be sure, but the other side of the door seemed to be clear.

I was about to try the latch when we heard a commotion and a cry of pain from the stable. I debated running over to the stable to help Benjamin, but Barek put a restraining hand on my shoulder when I stood up. His message was clear: *stay focused on our own task*. After a moment, we heard a low whistle, and we knew Ben was doing fine on his own.

I put my hand on the latch and lifted. The door opened silently about an inch. Barek pulled his sword, the blade hissing free with a ring as it left the scabbard. I was about to reach for my own sword, but stopped and considered getting out my casting orb instead. It was the first time I ever had to make a decision between using a sword or sorcery in a potential conflict. Just having that choice gave me a brief thrill of pride, but this mission was too important to trust it to my fledgling sorcery skills. I decided on the more familiar option and drew my sword before opening the door.

The heavy door creaked loudly as the opening expanded, and I cursed silently to myself. There was nothing I could do about the noise I'd already made, so I moved into the hallway beyond the door expecting guards to rush at me from every direction. But the hallway was silent, and I encountered nothing except cooking smells. We had managed to arrive at dinner time.

To my immediate right, a stairwell descended into the basement. I went down a few steps and gave Barek room to come through the open door. Thankfully, the hinges were a little quieter when he closed it behind us. We descended the steps together.

The stairwell dropped into a practice area for the men at arms. When I reached the bottom of the stairs, I peeked slowly around the stairwell wall. No one was in the room. We both moved slowly across the wide practice area toward the hallway that ran under the south wing.

The entire basement was lit by illuminators set in the stone walls. At first, I was alarmed that they were already on before we started moving through. But the illuminators in both of the hallways leading out of the practice room were on as well. Did they stay on all the time? Or had someone recently come through here? I couldn't tell, but again, there was nothing I could do but move forward.

According to Barek, Sulana was imprisoned in a room at the end of the south hallway. I was so close now that I wanted to run the rest of the way, but caution held me back. We had been incredibly lucky so far. Everything was going according to plan, which was unusual in my experience. I had this theory that the longer a plan progressed smoothly, the more difficult the obstacle would be when you eventually ran into it. Encountering small obstacles along the way would have actually made me feel better about our chances for success.

The next phase of the plan was probably the most dangerous. Peltor had the key to the prisoners' shackles. Barek wasn't certain, but he believed that Peltor's office was across from the prison room. We had to overpower Peltor quickly and get the key without letting him call for help.

We crept down the hallway. I followed the left wall and Barek the right. At each door, we stopped and listened, but none of the rooms seemed to be occupied. As we passed the last room on the right, which was well before the end of the hallway, I paused and nodded toward the door, placing my free hand around my sword wrist to mimic a shackle. Barek nodded to confirm that I was looking at the prison door.

When I arrived at the last door on the left, Barek came across the hall and stood next to me. I listened, but heard nothing. I squatted and looked through the keyhole. There was light, but no movement. I couldn't tell if Peltor was inside.

One of a thousand things could go wrong now. Peltor might be upstairs eating with everyone else. The door might be locked and trying to open it would alert him to our presence. We might not get to him before he could call the guards, although it didn't seem like any guards were close by at the moment.

I put my hand on the door latch and looked at Barek. He hefted his sword and gave me a curt nod to show he was ready. I raised the latch carefully and the door shifted slightly under the pressure of my touch. It was not locked. I shoved the door all the way open and burst into the room, angling to the right. Barek was close behind me and he went to the left. But we both faced an empty room.

"Look for keys," I said, keeping my voice low. I left the room and went back across the hall. The prison door was wider than the others and it was reinforced with metal bands. My guess was that the room had been used as some kind of root cellar before it was converted to a dungeon. I had a lock pick with me, but I wasn't exactly skilled at using it. I got out the pick and tried anyway.

As I worked on the lock, I regretted not having the time to learn a lock opening spell before I left the Archives. Professor Delano said the spell not only helped you open the lock, but it gave you insight into the lock's construction, so manually picking it would be easier in the future too.

The lock stubbornly refused to budge, and I became increasingly aware of how long I was taking. The sweat dripping into my eyes didn't help. I was about to give up and evaluate whether or not we could break down the door when the lock made a loud click. I pushed on the heavy door and it started to open, but the bottom scraped along the floor with a gritty groan that made me cringe.

I glanced down the hall toward the training room and thought I saw movement. I froze and stared intently with my heart pounding in my throat. Nothing. Perhaps I was mistaken. Not wanting to make any more noise, I squeezed through the narrow opening I'd already made.

There she was. Sulana looked toward the door with a bored frown until she saw me standing there, and then she jumped to her feet with a grin. I placed my finger to my lips before she could say anything. Daven saw me too and sat up quickly, hope flaring in his eyes. Talon stayed lying down; he was not looking too good.

I went to Sulana and hugged her close. She tried to return the embrace but her chains stopped her. I stood back and held her cold little hands in mine. A knot settled into the pit of my stomach when I knelt to inspect the manacles on her wrists. The locks were simple, but strong.

A special kind of outrage started to build within me as the reality of her confinement sunk in. It was a quiet rage, and it was patient. The only outward signs of the suppressed fury were a slight tremor in my hands and a certain calculating set to my face, and only people who knew me very well would recognize them. I looked up at Sulana and her eyes told me that she understood exactly what I was feeling. She looked troubled by what she saw in my face, but she gave me a reassuring smile and squeezed my hand.

I got out my lock pick again and started to work on her manacles. As I worked, I glanced over at the other two agents and whispered, "What's wrong with Talon?"

"We don't know," Sulana whispered back. "We think he may have been poisoned. He needs medical attention."

I nodded, mentally adding another mark to the payback tally for Thunderhead College.

I was being as careful as I could, but the lock mechanism was too heavily built. A metallic *tink* from within the lock made my heart sink, and I removed the broken pick from the hole. The pick just wasn't heavy enough to lever the mechanism, and it was the only pick I had.

I was considering alternatives when footsteps sounded in the hall. I barely had time to rise to my feet and draw my sword before the door scraped open the rest of the way and Peltor walked into the room with a guard. The march of at least two other guards continued down the hallway toward Peltor's office where Barek was looking for keys.

Peltor looked at the broken lock pick in my hand and laughed. He patted a pocket and said, "That would be a lot easier if you had a key."

"I'm sure you're right. Thanks for bringing it to me," I said.

Peltor chuckled again. "Still the same old arrogant Jaylan. So sure of yourself." He waved his sword around the room and added, "Looks like we'll have to install more chains."

Peltor's confidence gave me pause. He knew I had the edge on him when it came to blade work, so I shifted my attention to the guard who was with him. The young man held a short sword in one hand, but the other hand had slipped into a pocket where he no doubt had a casting orb, and his lips moved as he started an incantation. Barek had warned me that many of the guards here were sorcerers as well as swordsmen.

With Peltor in the way, I doubted I could get to the sorcerer guard before he fired off his spell, so I did the only thing I could: I reached for my own casting orb. As soon as my hand closed around the heavy orb Ebnik had given me, I started a shielding incantation, hoping I could complete it in time.

Over the centuries, shielding spells had been refined so they could be cast quickly. Speed was essential because they were usually cast in reaction to an offensive spell that was already in progress. The incantation was short, but difficult. Daisy, who had a natural talent for spell vocalizations, could fire off a shield spell in about half the time it took me.

At the same moment I started my incantation, shouts and the ring of steel on steel came from the hallway, distracting Peltor. When his attention returned to me, his face went blank with shock when he realized that I was casting a spell. He started toward me to interrupt my incantation, but he was too late.

The low hum of my shield started at nearly the same moment as the high-pitched sound of whatever spell the sorcerer guard was casting. My shield sprang into existence just in time to deflect the spell he had cast. However, my hurried and inexpert casting let some of his spell get through, and my left arm went slightly numb. If I had not managed to get the shield in place, I would have been completely immobilized.

Fortunately, my right arm was unaffected. I raised my sword to deflect the flat-bladed strike Peltor aimed at my head to knock me out. While we exchanged blows, he tried to maneuver me into a position where the other man could either attack me with another spell or engage me with his own blade. In turn, I worked to keep Peltor between me and the other guard.

The battle in the hall continued as well, dropping in volume after a man screamed in agony before going silent. I was relieved that the scream wasn't Barek's, but I had a feeling his opponent had been mortally wounded.

Peltor heard the scream as well and pressed his attack with a flurry of quick blows, his eyes narrow and his lip curled in his habitual sneer. He kept his eyes on me, but shouted over his shoulder at the other guard, "Do something!"

The sorcerer guard shifted his position and brought up his sword, looking for an opening. Then he stepped back and held forth the casting orb he had taken out of his pocket. The man couldn't seem to make up his mind whether to cast a spell or step into the fray with his sword, and his indecision worked to my advantage.

Growling with frustration, Peltor renewed his efforts to swap our positions, putting me between him and the sorcerer guard. I resisted, but my movement was limited. I had Sulana at my back and didn't want to move deeper into the room lest a stray blow hit her or one of the other agents.

With full freedom of movement on his side, Peltor succeeded in his goal, and a sickly grin spread across his face as I stumbled into his former position in front of the other guard.

But Peltor had miscalculated. By moving into my position, he placed himself directly in front of Sulana. She raised her hands over her head and brought her manacled wrists down onto the back of his head, striking a thudding blow that echoed in the room. A brief look of surprise went across Peltor's face before his eyes closed and he collapsed to the floor. Sulana immediately dropped into a crouch and started rummaging around in Peltor's pockets for the keys to her bindings.

I turned and faced the remaining guard, who was looking at Peltor with an open mouth. Sulana would soon be free, and the fight in the hall was reduced to just Barek and one other swordsman. He looked at me, taking in my ready sword and the orb I had unconsciously removed from my pocket during my battle with Peltor. The feeling was returning to my arm, and I rotated my wrist to unknot the muscles that had tightened reflexively to grip the orb.

His wide eyes met mine. I raised one eyebrow and smirked. Before I could think to block his exit, he ran. Cursing myself for letting him escape, I went out the door after him, but I realized it was too late when I saw his retreating back go around the corner at the end of the hallway. If I continued the pursuit, I'd just end up following him right into more guards. Our best chance of getting out of here now was to stay together and move fast.

Barek was still trading blows with one of the guards in the hallway. The other guard who had intercepted him lay dead on the floor in a pool of blood further down the hall. Barek showed no signs of offering mercy to the second guard he was fighting, so I made a quick decision and took a calculated risk.

My casting orb was still in my hand, so I began an incantation. The guard glanced fearfully over his shoulder at me when he heard me start to chant behind him, and he tried to angle away from me, but Barek's attacks took all of his attention. As I finished the incantation, I slid my sword back into its sheath and reached out to grip the back of the guard's neck.

My hair stood on end as a tingling sensation shot from the orb across my shoulders and down my arm. It entered the guard's neck as a jolt that made his body go rigid for a second, shudder, and then collapse. His sword tipped toward the floor and slid from his unconscious grasp.

The Shocking Hand spell was my first use of sorcery as a weapon. I couldn't help but look at the hand that had done the deed and snigger.

Barek stood panting with his sword still raised in a defensive pose. He watched the guard to make sure the man was really down and slowly lowered his weapon. He glanced at the orb in my hand. "You probably saved his life," he said. "I was having trouble disarming him."

I was glad to learn that Barek wasn't actually *trying* to kill everyone here.

I put away the orb, pulled my dagger, and knelt next to the fallen man. He was unconscious, but still breathing. A distant shout from the guard who had escaped came down the hall from the building above. We had to get out of here soon or we'd be trapped in the basement.

"I'll be right back," Barek said as he headed toward Peltor's office. I nodded and returned to the prison cell.

While I was in the hallway, Sulana had freed herself and Daven. She was kneeling next to Talon with her hand on his forehead. He was still lying on his bench even though his chains had been removed. Sulana looked up at me and said, "He's really sick again. I don't think he can walk out of here without help."

Daven quickly went to her side and helped her raise Talon to a sitting position. "I'll help him," he said.

A wheezing snort caught my attention, and I looked toward Sulana's bench to see Peltor, still unconscious and face down on the floor, with her bindings transferred to his wrists and ankles.

Barek clanked into the prison room with his arms full of weapons. "Found them in Peltor's office," he explained as he handed the blades back to their rightful owners. Seeing Talon's condition, Barek helped Daven get the weaponsmaster to his feet and gently affixed his sword belt around his waist, buckling it for him. Talon looked up at Barek, his face grey and beaded with sweat, and he nodded gratefully with a weak smile.

Sulana and Daven quickly armed themselves, and as they did, I evaluated the condition of the former prisoners. Several days of confinement had taken a toll. Their faces and clothes were smudged with dirt and they had dark circles under their eyes. They must have gotten enough food, because their movements were still energetic and deft. Except for Talon, of course.

I had not counted on Talon being incapacitated. Now that we were faced with fighting our way out of here, he was going to be a serious liability. He would slow us down and interfere with Daven's ability to defend himself.

Talon returned my critical stare with a grim smile of understanding. "I'll stay behind," he said.

Sulana gasped, but before she could say anything, I snorted and said, "Not a chance. We're all leaving together. Right now." With those words, I drew my sword with my right hand and pulled out my casting orb with my left.

Daven and Talon looked at Sulana expectantly. Next to me, Barek went still and watched her as well. Sulana was the Sword Sorceress, and this was her team. She had rank and authority, while I had neither.

"Do you want to take command?" I asked her.

Sulana was staring at the orb in my hand. At my question, she raised her eyes to mine. "Absolutely not. You're the one with the plan, and you're doing great so far."

She absently touched her face tenderly with one hand, and I realized that one of the smudges was actually a light bruise on her cheekbone. I looked down at Peltor, still unconscious on the floor, having little doubt about the source of that bruise.

With a growl, I went over to him and placed the tip of my sword on his back, right above where his black heart would be. One firm push would end his potential for creating future misery. If I didn't finish him now, I knew I'd just have to face him again in the future with no assurances over the outcome of the fight.

But then Peltor snorted again. I stepped back, realizing I couldn't kill him in his sleep. His damaged nose and bruised eyes told me someone had already given him reason to regret meeting Sulana's team. Even though I knew he'd make trouble for us all again one day, having him on the opposing side had advantages. If I killed him now, they might just replace him with someone more dangerous. *Better the evil you know*, I concluded.

Sulana seemed to understand my brief internal battle. She nodded once to let me know she agreed with my decision. Then she held her hand out toward the cell door and said, "Lead on."

Sulana was right. She had yielded command to me, and it was past time to go.

"Okay," I said. "We need to get out of the building first. Benjamin should be waiting somewhere nearby with horses. Once we reach the horses, we need to get back to the trail." I stopped and looked doubtfully at Talon.

Sulana gripped Talon's arm. "I'll ride with him," she offered.

I nodded to Sulana and then to Barek. "Let's go."

Barek led our procession out of the room and down the hall to the practice room. He had his dagger in his left hand and his sword in his right, ready for action. We got to the stairwell without challenge, and Barek ran up the stairs. As he emerged at the top, a voice in the hall above shouted, "There they are!" Barek charged in the direction of the voice, leaving the top of the stairwell and the door to the outside clear for the rest of us.

I started running up the stairs after Barek as soon as I heard the shout. I opened the breezeway door while Barek blocked the two guards in the hallway. The breezeway held no sign of opposition. A glance toward the courtyard showed Benjamin waiting with horses.

I waved everyone out. As he stepped through the doorway, Talon broke away from Daven and fell to his knees, vomiting noisily on the ground. Daven helped him back up, and they stumbled together toward the horses.

I went back into the hall to help Barek. One of the guards was already down, clutching a bleeding leg. The second was attacking furiously, but he was unable to get through Barek's defenses. Meanwhile, every blow that Barek landed rocked the man backward a pace. Barek finally managed to land a back-handed blow to the guard's head with the flat of his blade, and the man collapsed like a scarecrow cut from its stand.

Barek and I both turned and ran out to the courtyard while the remaining guard shouted for help from his position on the floor.

Benjamin was mounted and held the reins of three more horses. I was pleased to see that he had successfully located and liberated all of the Archives agent's mounts. Daven helped Talon get onto Sulana's horse, and then gave Sulana a boost so she could ride behind the half-limp weaponsmaster.

Daven and I jumped into our saddles at the same time. As previously agreed, I rode Barek's horse while Barek remained on foot. As soon as he saw that all of us were mounted, Barek threw one last look at the building and started running toward the courtyard gate.

Barek's enormous gelding was named Boulder. Barek claimed that he chose the name because the horse was dumb as a rock, but I'd ridden alongside them enough to know that wasn't true. The truth was more like the muscular charger was *solid* as a rock and could roll over anything in his way. It was reassuring to feel his strong bulk beneath me.

I had just gathered the reins and kicked Boulder into motion when several guards spilled out of the breezeway door. I had to put away my orb to get into the saddle, but I still had my sword in my hand. I considered wheeling around and making a run at them, but the rest of the group was almost to the gate. Only Benjamin rode near me, waiting to see if I needed his help. I waved my sword toward the gate and shouted, "Go, go!"

Something tugged at my sleeve and a sharp pain bit into my arm, almost making me drop my sword. I looked back to see one of the guards reloading his crossbow for another shot. A second guard had a casting orb in his hand and had begun an incantation. A third was running for the stables.

I urged Boulder into a run, folding my sword arm at my waist to ease the pressure on my torn bicep. I held onto the hilt as best I could while I concentrated on riding.

Behind me, the sorcerer guard must have finished his incantation because the squeal of a manifestation came from behind me. I directed Boulder to put me between the sorcerer and Benjamin, who raced ahead of me. I felt the static charge of an oncoming lightning bolt and gritted my teeth against the strike that would either kill me or hurl me out of the saddle. I glanced back just as the flash left the sorcerer's orb and flared uselessly against a shield that had been raised behind me.

Looking over the wall toward the forest's edge, I saw a lithe form slip back behind the safety of the tree trunks. Daisy had been the one to save me, and as annoyed as I was that she had exposed herself, I couldn't help but be impressed by her skill. Raising a shield powerful enough to deflect the full effect of a lightning bolt was difficult enough, but doing it at that range was nothing short of amazing.

As I cleared the gate, another crossbow bolt buzzed through the air near me, but then I was out of the courtyard and partially protected by the wall. Our horses pounded down the road toward the forest without further action from our enemies, and we charged into the relative safety of the trees.

CHAPTER 44
PURSUIT

Dumont - Headmaster's Office, Thunderhead College

Headmaster Dumont Fortenz mopped up the meat juices on his plate with the last chunk of fresh but rather flavorless bread. The meal was satisfying, but the preparation was completely unimaginative. He would need to find a better cook soon.

He was wiping his lips with a napkin when footsteps pounded down the hallway outside his room and someone hammered on his door with a fist. "Headmaster Fortenz!" shouted a voice. It was Lohan.

His visitor's agitation brought Dumont to his feet. He moved around his desk and shouted, "Come in."

Lohan burst into the room, looking like he had been chased by a bear. "The prisoners are escaping," he exclaimed.

"How is that possible?" Dumont demanded. "Where's Peltor?"

Lohan's hands clenched into fists and he shook his head. "The fool saw them coming and tried to be a hero. He took only three men and probably got himself killed."

Growling with frustration, Dumont grabbed Lohan by both shoulders and shook him once. "Start at the beginning. What happened?"

Lohan put his hand to his head and took a deep breath. "Sorry, Master. Peltor had a guard watching the courtyard from inside the building. The man saw two infiltrators take out the perimeter guard and then go toward the breezeway.

The watchman reported to Peltor, and they went with two additional guards to trap the attackers in the basement."

Dumont was aware of the competition between Peltor and Lohan, and he usually thought their rivalry was a good way to keep them both sharp. Perhaps he should have insisted on more cooperation, although it seemed doubtful that doing so would have resulted in better judgment from either man. Still, four men against two should have been adequate.

Lohan went on. "After Peltor and one of the guards were taken down, one man ran for help while the other fought the interlopers." Lohan paused for a moment to catch his breath, and then looked down at the floor. "The guard who went for help said that the Winterman is back, and he brought a sorcerer with him."

Dumont's breath caught in his throat. *The Winterman is back and he has a sorcerer with him.* Heat rushed to his face as he realized that he had been a fool. Just hours ago, a courier had assured him that the Archives was willing to negotiate. But they had been stalling. The Council planned this rescue all along.

Distant shouts came up the hallway from the lower level of the building. Dumont went behind his desk to retrieve his travel jacket. The jacket had many pockets, and those pockets held implements he could use to put a stop to this rescue attempt. He glanced out his window as he was slipping the jacket on and then paused. A young man waited in the courtyard below with several horses. Lohan came over to stand at his side, and together they watched while the prisoners and their liberators ran to the waiting horses and clambered on.

Looking down into the courtyard, Lohan snorted and said, "I should have known. It's Jaylan Forester come to save his sweetheart. He must be the sorcerer the guard was babbling about."

Dumont's hand automatically reached for his casting orb and closed tightly around it. "How powerful is he?"

Lohan laughed. "Not very. He just started his training recently. We took classes together, and he's a slow learner."

"What about the other man?" Dumont asked, pointing toward the rider who had been waiting with the horses.

Lohan stared intently down into the courtyard. His eyebrows went up and he said, "I think that's Ben Morrison." Lohan eased back from the window. "He shows promise, but he's just a kid. I'm surprised Jaylan brought him."

Dumont relaxed. He should have no trouble overpowering two untrained sorcerers and a weak Sword Sorceress. He was about to turn from the window and begin his pursuit when something caught his eye.

The riders had all mounted except the Winterman, who sprinted toward the courtyard gate. The man Lohan had identified as Jaylan suddenly clutched his sword arm and swayed in the saddle. Dumont smiled grimly with satisfaction. *Finally, the guards are earning their keep.*

Dumont also heard a faint incantation through the closed window and waited to see what damage his followers would inflict on the fleeing prisoners. It would be good to know what to expect when he caught up with them.

A flash of lightning arced across the courtyard toward the riders, and Dumont had to avert his eyes as it struck some kind of shield and deflected harmlessly into the ground. When he looked back again, his eyes searched through the riders to see who had raised the shield.

Lohan pointed toward the forest's edge and said, "Look. They have a sorceress with them too."

Dumont looked toward the forest but only caught a flash of pale skin as the woman stepped back into the trees. She would have to be fairly powerful to raise a shield like that over such a distance. So much for an easy recapture. "Do you know who she is?"

Lohan shook his head. "I couldn't tell from here. Since young Ben is here, I would guess it's his twin sister Daisy, but I don't think she could have managed that shield. It might be Lissy Aragon, and she could give us some trouble."

As soon as the prisoners cleared the gate, Dumont hurried out of his office with Lohan right behind him.

CHAPTER 45
UNDER FIRE

Our horses pounded away from Thunderhead College and followed the road into the forest. I could see that Sulana was having trouble keeping Talon in the saddle in front of her, while keeping herself from sliding off the back of the horse. Stardust wasn't too happy about the load either and bucked a couple of times trying to unseat her. The horse nearly succeeded, but Sulana managed to hold on. I looked back and saw Barek falling behind even though he was running full out. Shouts of organizing pursuers came from beyond the walls of the college.

As soon as we entered the forest, the moonlight dimmed to the point that we could hardly see where we were going. I hoped we wouldn't miss the trailhead turn. Sulana slowed her horse to a canter, probably concerned about the same thing, but it still felt like we were going way too fast. She suddenly reined back and turned, nearly sliding off the side of her horse in the process. Talon's head was lolling, so he must have passed out, making her job even more difficult. Shifting her butt back into position on the horse's croup, she got a firmer grip on Talon and urged Stardust up the trail at a fast walk.

The rest of us had to get into single file behind Sulana. Daven was right behind her, Ben followed Daven, and I took up the rear. I took advantage of the moment to put my sword away, hissing in pain as I raised my punctured arm to guide the sword point into the scabbard. I took one last look down the road as I entered the trail and saw Barek already catching up to us. The Winterman's stamina was astounding. I could not yet see torches or any other indication of how close our pursuers were.

Within the narrow, tree-lined confines of the trail, Boulder was inclined to follow the other horses, so I extracted one of Lissy's healing potions from a side pocket of my leather vest. Holding the reins loosely with the hand of my damaged arm, I pulled the cork free with my teeth and swallowed the entire potion. Seconds later the hum of the healing manifestation spread from my stomach out to my extremities, and the sharp pain in my arm weakened to a dull throb. The wounded muscle remained stiff, but I thought I could wield a dagger in my right hand if necessary.

Up ahead, Sulana reached an open area along the trail where we were supposed to meet Daisy. Patches and the other rescue team horses were tethered at the far end. Sulana was nearly to the other side of the clearing when Daisy ran out into the open from a narrow side trail, returning to join us from the vantage point where she had cast her shield moments earlier.

Startled by the sudden appearance of the young sorceress, Stardust shied and reared. The horse's front hooves only rose off the ground a few inches, but it was enough. Despite a desperate reach around Talon for the pommel, Sulana slid off and Talon toppled after her. They both hit the ground and Sulana grunted as she absorbed most of the fall along with Talon's weight. She struggled to get out from under the unconscious weaponsmaster and wobbled to her feet. She bent over with her hands on her knees, trying to regain her breath.

Daven and I leaped from our saddles the moment we saw Sulana start to fall, and we both ran over to her. Daven asked if she was all right and she nodded breathlessly. I got down on my knees at Talon's side and saw that he was starting to foam at the mouth a little. I carefully turned him onto his side as Daisy knelt next to me. "What's wrong with him?" she asked.

"Sulana said something about poison. Do you recognize it?" Daisy probably had the most healer training among us, although Sulana had more practical experience.

Daisy took out her casting orb and uttered a short incantation. The orb lit up and we both averted our heads from the brightness. She adjusted the illumination to a more comfortable level and took a closer look at Talon's face.

"Would one of Lissy's healing potions help?" I asked.

Daisy shook her head absently. "No, those are for binding flesh wounds. Poisons are internal and work in a variety of ways. We need the right antidote." She closed her eyes for a second and then suddenly called to her brother, "Ben, come take look at Talon."

Benjamin came closer and bent over Talon's head. "I think we've seen this before," he said.

Daisy nodded excitedly. "I think so too. At home. It's some kind of poison. What did Mom do to fix it?"

Ben's brow crinkled, but he shook his head. "I don't remember. I wasn't there when she treated the worker who got sick."

Daisy's face fell, and she stared at Talon, absently pushing a lock of hair out of his face while she thought. "Charcoal," she finally said. "It was a special kind of charcoal."

Sulana had caught her breath and was stretching her arm to work out a kink she got from breaking Talon's fall. "Activated charcoal? I think I have some of that." She went to her horse and stopped. "These aren't my saddlebags."

Ben went to her side and said, "Sorry. I didn't have much time to look around in the stable. These looked familiar so I took them. Maybe I put yours on one of the other horses."

Sulana went to check the other horses. When she inspected the bags on Talon's horse, she called, "Found it." She walked back with her healer kit in her hands. "Do you know how to prepare it?" she asked Daisy.

Daisy nodded and rose to take the kit from her. She grabbed a water skin that was tethered to her horse.

While Daisy prepared the treatment, Sulana joined me at Talon's side. His breathing was a little labored, but he seemed to be holding steady for the moment. She took his hand in hers and said, "I think it's good that he hasn't been holding down his food. He'd probably have more of whatever is hurting him in his system. I think Peltor was poisoning him out of jealousy."

I should have eliminated Peltor when I had the chance. The man was a menace and wouldn't hesitate to kill every one of us. Sulana believed he had it in for Talon because of jealousy, but I knew from past experience that Peltor didn't need an excuse to be cruel.

I looked at Sulana to find she was staring back at me. She spoke quietly when she had my attention. "So, do you have something you want to tell me?"

I reached into my pocket and pulled out the heavy casting orb. The moonlight reflected off the milky swirl that was within it, sparkling when I shifted my hand. "Ebnik gave it to me after we discovered I could cast," I said. I looked down at Talon. "A lot of good it's doing me now," I added.

She shrugged. "You aren't a healer. But at least you can cast. You should be happy about that. I'd say your life just got a lot more interesting."

I reached across Talon's prone form to put my hand on her shoulder. "I've got you again. That's all I need."

She gave me a brief smile. "Thanks for coming. I didn't know if I'd ever see you again. I heard an Archives Courier came this afternoon and that the Council was going to negotiate for our release. I figured that might take weeks, and I honestly didn't know if we would last that long under Peltor's supervision. I can't believe the courier was just a ploy and they sent you on a surprise rescue mission."

She waited for me to respond, but I released her shoulder and took a deep breath.

Reading into my silence, her eyes went wide and she looked up at Daisy, who was coming back toward us with a cup in hand. Sulana glanced over at Benjamin and then her breath caught when Barek came jogging up to us. She looked hard at me and said, "This isn't an authorized rescue mission, is it? The Council would have given you more support, and they never would have sent Ben and Daisy."

Daisy sat down on the ground and avoided Sulana's eyes. She lifted Talon's head into her lap and encouraged him to drink the dark liquid in the cup. He coughed up the first bit, but was able to swallow the rest. Barek stood next to her for a moment, but then mumbled something about watching for pursuit and went back to the edge of the clearing.

I shook my head at Sulana's accusing stare and let out the breath I'd been holding. "I couldn't leave you there. You just said yourself that you could have died. The Council wanted to send help, but they were bogged down by political entanglements. I was not."

Sulana was silent for a moment, and then stood up. "You might have just ended both our careers. Not that mine was doing so great anyway." She walked over to Stardust and rubbed the equine's face, thanking her for getting them safely away from Thunderhead College.

I looked at Daisy to see if she needed any more help from me, but she subtly waved me off. I got up and followed Sulana.

"I don't think we have time for this," I said to her back. "Thunderhead College guards could be coming down the path at any moment."

She looked over her shoulder at me and said, "Then stop wasting time talking about it and get everyone ready to go."

Barek ran back to us and said, "We need to get moving. I hear horses on the road."

They were both right. I could hear several horses and the voices of their riders down on the road. They'd have to slow down when they got to the trailhead, but they weren't far behind us. We had a few minutes at most.

"Everybody mount up," I ordered. "Daisy, I want you and your shielding abilities at the back with me. We'll put Barek, Benjamin, and Daven in front of us." I looked down at Talon, who was conscious again and able to sit up. He was still too weak to get to his feet without help, but he would probably be less trouble for Sulana to keep in the saddle. "Talon will keep riding with Sulana for now, and she'll set the pace at the front. Sulana, I really think you should ride Boulder. He probably won't even notice the extra weight."

Sulana raised her eyebrows at the big grey gelding and blew out a deep breath. Fully four hands taller than her petite appaloosa, she would look like a child sitting on him. At least there would be plenty of room for her and Talon.

Catching Barek's and Benjamin's eyes, I added, "If they catch up to us, and they probably will, we may have to stay back and slow them down. I want Daven and Daisy to stay with Sulana." Daisy stepped forward and opened her mouth to protest, but her brother shushed her before she could make a sound. She closed her mouth and took his hand instead. He squeezed her hand back reassuringly.

Sulana jogged over to Talon's horse and started rummaging around in her saddle bags. "I for one still need implements if I'm going to be worth anything in a fight. Assuming those bastards didn't take them."

I was left to ponder a different problem while Sulana equipped herself. We now had too many horses. Benjamin had managed to get all four of the horses belonging to Sulana's team, so the four we rode down from the Archives made a total of eight horses for seven riders, and two of those riders would be on one horse.

Daven was helping Daisy get Talon on his feet, and I was about to ask him if he thought the horses would follow us without being tethered when a shout came from the trail toward the road, "They're just up ahead!" A second voice commanded, "Get out of the way."

At the sound of the second voice, Sulana froze. Daisy and Daven slowly lowered Talon to the ground again, and Daisy came toward me, taking out her casting orb as she moved to my side.

A big man came to the edge of the clearing and shouted, "Give it up, Sword Sorceress. You can't outrun us, and we outnumber you two to one."

Sulana shouted back at him, "I'm not going back there, Headmaster." She turned back to her urgent search for her implement case, which she pulled from the saddle bag with snort of triumph.

Having seen the headmaster's men in action, I was okay with two-to-one odds. However, it was possible that the men Barek and I had already encountered didn't represent the best of their forces. Having the headmaster here himself was certainly worrisome. By all accounts, he was a powerful sorcerer.

And he was a sorcerer who was beginning an incantation.

As soon as I realized what was happening, I started a shielding incantation. Hearing me start the chant, Daisy followed suit. Behind me, I heard Sulana quickly step away from her horse and come up behind us. With an implement in hand, she'd be able to strike back almost instantly, once Daisy and I blocked whatever spell the headmaster was sending our way.

The headmaster struck far faster than I would have thought possible. His lightning spell arced toward us just as my shield came up. Daisy had nearly caught up to me, but her shield was still forming when mine snapped into place. In nearly the same instant, the headmaster's strike slammed into my shield and sheared through it. It cut through Daisy's partially-formed shield as well, deflecting a little off both of them to pass between us. As our shields fizzled, we were thrown away from each other by the force of the passing bolt.

I opened my eyes to see the moon and stars. Some of the stars were shooting around the edges of my vision, and I shook my head as I sat up. Daisy glanced fearfully toward the headmaster and crawled over to me. "Are you okay?" She asked.

I was shaking and feeling a little dizzy, but otherwise I seemed to be fine. I nodded my head in response to her question and picked up my orb, which had rolled out of my hand when I fell. "What is it with these guys and lightning?" A sense of dread rolled through my mind as I realized how outmatched we were. On the other hand, casting a spell that strong had consequences, so surely the headmaster would not be able to do something like that again.

Daisy patted my shoulder and answered my question with a quip: "I guess now we know why they call it Thunderhead College."

When I looked toward the headmaster, I saw that a familiar figure had replaced him at the head of the clearing. Lohan. He raised a device of some kind in our direction, and then his arm slowly went down. At the same time, Daisy gasped and gripped my arm tightly, looking over my shoulder at something behind me.

I twisted around quickly to see what had caught her attention. Sulana and Daven were both down. Sulana was crumpled onto her side on the ground. The implement she had selected, a jeweled dagger, was stuck point-first into the ground a couple of feet away. Daven was flat on his back and moaned as he started to regain consciousness. The lightning bolt that had missed Daisy and I must have hit Sulana and Daven. Although our shields had taken some of the juice out of it, it still had enough strength to knock out those behind us.

I groaned to my feet and stumbled over to Sulana with Daisy right behind me. I turned Sulana onto her back and patted her face gently. No response. I put my fingers to her neck. A shot of adrenaline went through me when I felt no pulse. I put my head on her chest, but heard nothing. Next to me, Daisy held one of Sulana's hands and started to cry.

My mind shut down in that moment. I felt like I was floating away. Sulana could not be dead. Losing her now was unacceptable. I had come to rescue her, not get her killed. This was my fault. I blinked and a tear rolled off my cheek and landed on my hand. It splashed against the broken gemstone of a big ugly ring.

The cold knot of anger that had been coiled within me since I first heard of Sulana's capture flared into an inferno. I may have put Sulana in danger by rescuing her, but it wasn't me who kidnapped her and then killed her. My anger had a target now, and I had a tool that would let me strike back. Lissy's words of warning about the ring were incinerated in a blaze of fury. I was shaking from head to toe. I turned my head and glared in Lohan's direction, and I could swear he took a step back.

I stood and raised my hand toward Lohan. With cold precision, I opened up a channel to the ring and poured everything I had into it. Lohan realized what I was doing and raised his hand again to trigger his own device. But he was too late. When I spoke the trigger word, the ring instantly started keening so loudly that normally I'd want to cover my ears. But this time, the ring's manifestation noise was a song of vengeance.

I could feel the ring building a powerful shield with the vaetra I was feeding it. It was so strong that Lohan's form seem to waver through the visual distortion it created. Lissy's warning about the ring draining me completely had no significance. Sulana was gone. I didn't care if using the ring killed me too.

As the shield separated from the ring, it sucked the vaetra from me with such force that I involuntarily exhaled in a cough and my knees buckled. Lohan's spell struck the shield, sparking insignificantly on its surface. My hand fell to my side and my vision shrunk to a narrow tunnel, while the enormous shield roared away from me toward the enemy.

I could no longer tell what noises were from the shield ring's manifestation and what was true sound. I struggled to remain conscious as I slowly dropped to my knees. I had a surreal vision of Lohan turning to run just before the trees at the edge of the clearing burst into splinters or were ripped from the ground in a spray of soil and broken roots. Men screamed and the ground shook. Rocks were dislodged from the nearby slope and rolled into the clearing, making our horses shy and mill. One of the horses bumped me and I fell over. A small spark of regret flashed across my mind as I fully appreciated the destruction I had unleashed.

And then there was nothing.

Dumont ~ Eagle River Trail

Dumont awoke to searing pain in his legs. He was on his back, and his head was spinning even before he tried to sit up. A hand on his chest pushed him back to the ground, and his vision cleared enough to see that Lohan was leaning over him.

"Stay still for a moment, Master. We're still splinting your leg," Lohan said.

"What happened?" Dumont asked weakly. The last thing he remembered was Lohan turning from the edge of the clearing in a panic and charging straight into him shouting for everyone to run. A moment later, the forest seemed to explode around them. He turned his head to the side and saw some of the aftermath. The trail was littered with rocks and downed trees, their roots reaching uselessly into the air. The earthy scent of loamy soil mixed with crushed pine boughs was strong. Moans of pain came from all around.

"They used a spell I've never even heard of," Lohan answered, his voice tinged with awe. "It was a giant moving wall of force that crushed everything in its path."

Dumont coughed some of the dust out of his lungs and asked, "Who cast it?"

"Jaylan Forester did. He used an artifact of some kind. A ring, I think. After your lightning bolt took down the Sword Sorceress, he pointed a fist at us and struck before I could immobilize him." Lohan paused for a moment before continuing in a subdued tone. "I think you may have killed Sulana."

Dumont's mind was clearing, and the implications of their current situation started to sink in. "We have to stop them. Gather the men and finish this. Forester won't be good for anything after powering a spell that strong. The Archives has played us for fools, and we need to show them that was a mistake."

Lohan started shaking his head long before the headmaster finished. "There are no men to gather, Master. Everyone is injured, one guard may not live another hour, and one of our sorcerers is dead. The Winterman could take us all out by himself.

With a painful effort and loud groan, Dumont raised himself up onto his elbows so he could look around and fully evaluate the scene. Lohan had a bloody bandage across his forehead and his right arm was in a sling. Only one female guard was mobile and she was tending to the injuries of the others. She herself limped around with bandages on her arm and leg. The damage to the surrounding forest was appalling; they were lucky they hadn't all been killed.

Lohan was right. They were in no shape to pursue the prisoners. But at least he had exacted a price for their escape. He had seen his lightning bolt take two of their number down. If the Sword Sorceress was truly dead, the possibility of further negotiations with the Archives would be gone. However, her death would also temporarily paralyze them, which would serve his purpose just as well.

Young Sorceress Delano has followed in her father's footsteps a little too closely.

Dizziness and nausea forced Dumont to slowly lower himself back to the ground. "All right, Lohan," he panted.

"Get us out of here and back to the college. We'll figure out what this means to our plans tomorrow."

CHAPTER 47

LIGHTING STRIKES TWICE

Jaylan ~ Eagle River Trail

I woke to someone slapping my face. I put up a restraining hand and croaked, "Enough." I sat up, and my head spun for a moment before my vision cleared and I saw the twins standing over me. Tears streaked both of their cheeks.

"What are we going to do?" Daisy wailed.

I crawled over to Sulana and checked again for a pulse. There was none. The lightning had stopped her heart. My feeble shield had failed to protect her, and now she was gone.

They say lightning never strikes the same place twice, but I almost wished it would. Maybe that would bring her back to me somehow.

With that thought, an idea formed. I shouted, "Daisy, how long was I out?"

Daisy shuffled over to me, wiping the tears from her eyes. "Just a few seconds. You fell to the ground, but woke up again right away." Benjamin followed her over and stood above me.

I started unlacing the top of Sulana's jerkin and pulled the leather down and away to expose the shirt underneath.

"What are you doing?" Daisy asked as she sank to her knees next to me.

"I need your help," I answered. I unbuttoned the top of Sulana's shirt as well to expose part of her chest.

I put my hand on Sulana's exposed skin and tears blurred my vision when I felt nothing but stillness. No breath. No heartbeat. But she was still warm. I blinked away the tears and took out my casting orb. I tried to open a channel to it, but it was like turning a spigot on an empty barrel. My reserves of vaetra had been completely drained by the ring.

I held my hand out toward Daisy, with the orb facing downward. "Put your hand over mine."

Daisy hesitated and looked up at her brother. He shrugged and nodded, and then she did as I asked. Her cold palm settled the back of my hand and her fingers wrapped around mine. "I need you to open a channel to me. I need you to give me some vaetra."

"What are you going to do?" she asked.

"I'm going to see if I can restart her heart," I answered.

"How?" she asked with a confused tone.

"Just trust me," I said, and she nodded. Her eyes were wide as she glanced back and forth between me and Sulana's still form. When she opened a channel to me, I felt her power flow into me like rainwater filling an empty creek.

I started an incantation, but before I got very far, Daisy dropped her channel to me and took her hand off mine. She recognized the spell I was going to use. I stopped and looked her directly in the eyes. "Please, Daisy. I have to try. We have nothing to lose and not much time."

She looked down at Sulana and a fresh tear rolled down her cheek. She nodded and replaced her hand on mine with a tighter grip than before. Ben kneeled on the other side of Sulana to get a closer look at what I was doing. "Don't touch her," I warned him. He nodded and shifted himself further away.

I began the Shocking Hand incantation again and used Daisy's vaetra to power my spell. I felt the charge build just as it had when I attacked the guard in the basement. With an audible crackle, the charge surged into Sulana and made her back arch. After she slumped back to the ground, I put my ear to her mouth. She still wasn't breathing. But my hand, which was still on her chest, felt movement. A beat. And then another beat.

She needed to breathe. I pulled my hand away from Daisy's and set the orb down. I tried giving Sulana my own breath. Her chest rose a little, but most of the air went back out her nose. I pinched her nose closed and tried again. And once more. I still felt a weak pulse in her neck, so I kept trying. After about ten attempts, pressure pushed my own breath back at me. The pulse in her neck strengthened, and her chest moved slowly up and down on its own.

I grinned up at Benjamin who looked at me in astonishment. I gently gathered Sulana up in my arms and brushed her hair away from her face. She had never looked more beautiful to me as the color pulsed back into her cheeks. After a few moments, her body convulsed and she coughed a couple of times. Her arm twitched and then her eyelids opened. I witnessed the miracle of her eyes focusing on mine, and I smiled down at her through tears of joy.

Daisy moved closer to me and put her hand on the top of Sulana's head. "I don't believe it. You brought her back from the dead."

I smiled at Daisy. "I couldn't have done it without you."

We were joined by Barek, who supported Talon on one side and Daven on the other. Daven dropped to his knees across from me and looked from Sulana's face to mine with wide eyes and a pinched brow. "I think she's going to be okay," I said.

Daven nodded and whispered, "Thank the spirits."

Barek tilted his head in the direction of the carnage I'd invoked. "I think we are out of danger for now, but we have a long way to go to reach a healer."

He was right. Our group was pretty banged up, but we'd probably be able to make our way up the mountain if we traveled slowly.

It was not going to be the triumphant return to the Archives I'd imagined. The mission was technically a success, but it had nearly ended in disaster. I was suddenly quite sure that I had yet to pay the full price for this rescue mission.

Chapter 48

RESIGNATION

Sulana ~ Council Hall, The Archives

Sulana watched Junior Councilor Velna Asher's face break into a broad smile before she carefully folded her hands on the table in front of her and said, "That's very gracious of you, Sorceress Delano. We accept."

Senior Councilor Boris Underwood glared at Asher with obvious irritation, but it was Senior Councilor Gregor Rissik who contradicted his colleague. "Very amusing, Councilor Asher. Your opinion is noted."

Sulana stood before the assembled Archives Council and had just offered her resignation as Sword Sorceress. Her failure on the mission to retrieve the Portal Key and her subsequent capture by the Thunderhead College patrol were only a small part of her rationale. The real problem was that Dumont's lightning bolt had caused side effects that made her unfit for duty. She constantly felt the need for a nap, and her reflexes were terrible. She could barely finish a practice session with Talon, and the weaponsmaster was still recovering from being poisoned. She hadn't even attempted to channel vaetra since the attack. The healers recommended against it, and to be honest, she was afraid to try lest she discover that ability had been damaged too.

And now Jaylan could cast. He would make a great Sword Sorcerer, if the Council would give him the chance. After her father died, she had waited in vain for a new Sword Sorcerer to come forward, avenge his death somehow, and make the Archives safe again. When that didn't happen, she decided the responsibility was hers. Now she could step back and let Jaylan become the belated hero she'd been waiting for all those years.

Councilor Asher sat forward and looked down the table at Councilor Rissik. "What is there to discuss? Sorceress Delano has just made an excellent case as to why we should accept her resignation. Forcing her to complete her Commitment would be cruel. With her impaired abilities, she could be killed trying to fulfill her duties. She had enough trouble fulfilling those duties before she was damaged."

Councilor Rissik shook his head. "Sulana has been back for less than a week. She should still be resting, not pretending like nothing happened. The lightning damage may very well be temporary. As for her failure to anticipate such aggressive and criminal behavior from Dumont Fortenz, that is hardly her fault. The Council ordered her to go after the portal key thief, and the Council should have anticipated and prepared her for the difficulties she might encounter."

Velna huffed out a deep sigh and threw herself back into her chair. "Speaking of criminal behavior, it seems we have another problem. Jaylan Forester is our only candidate to replace Sulana, but he has proven untrustworthy and possibly dangerous. Headmaster Fortenz demands satisfaction for the death of his guards. We need to find another candidate for the training program, and do it quickly."

Sulana's pulse quickened and she felt a flush of heat. She spoke without thinking. "None of this is Jaylan's fault. I'd still be stuck in Headmaster Fortenz's dungeon if he hadn't taken action. The Council certainly wasn't making much progress getting us back." She wished she could take back the last part, but she couldn't help saying what she felt.

Councilor Underwood raised a hand to stop Sulana from continuing. "That's enough, Sorceress Delano. When we want your opinion, we will ask for it." He turned to Asher, who was taking his rebuke of Sulana as support and was smiling smugly. "And you, Councilor Asher, will stop trying to make decisions for the entire Council." Her smile faded, and her neck and face colored as she looked down at her hands.

With Asher temporarily silenced, Rissik spoke again. "I think Sorcerer Forester has shown great initiative and ingenuity in rescuing Sulana's team. The Council would be foolish to discard his petition without serious consideration. His mission may not have been explicitly authorized, but the outcome was certainly in the best interest of the Archives."

Junior Councilor Rikard Shepherd had been silent up to now, his demeanor and reactions mirroring that of his compatriot Velna Asher. But after Rissik's remarks, he snorted and said, "The outcome of that mission was in the best interest of Jaylan Forester. The fact that he went forth in secret proves that he had no concern for the interests of the Archives."

Through most of the discussion, Junior Councilor Maris Torlon had been idly playing with her drinking cup, tilting it this way and that, and stopping once in a while to take a sip. Now, she sat the cup down with a thump and startled everyone in the room by opening her mouth and speaking with a strong clear voice. "None of this would have happened if representatives of Thunderhead College had not stolen the Portal Key, unlawfully imprisoned Archives personnel, used said personnel as hostages to negotiate damaging concessions from the Archives, and finally, attacked the rescue party. I see no way that Jaylan Forester is to blame for any of this. He is the only person so far who has had the nerve to take action. Dumont Fortenz is the criminal here, and we should be talking about what we are going to do about him."

Everyone in the room was silent for several moments after Torlon finished. Sulana was pleased and stunned by her show of support for Jaylan. It was unprecedented for Councilor Torlon to say much at all, much less launch into such a strong statement of opinion.

Councilor Underwood raised an eyebrow and said, "Thank you, Councilor Torlon. Your summation is a bit simplistic, but your point is well-taken." He then looked at Councilor Rissik and said, "I gather you are voting to reject Sorceress Delano's resignation?" Gregor nodded his head once. "Assuming that your position represents the interests of the Archives, and not the emperor, I agree."

Sulana had apparently missed something while she was gone. She had noticed extra tension among the Councilors, but she assumed it was because of the crisis with Thunderhead College. She wasn't sure what Councilor Underwood's comment about the emperor meant, but Councilor Rissik's eyes narrowed and his lips thinned. He looked like he might retort, but instead he took a deep breath through his nose and said nothing. Sulana made a mental note to herself to ask Lissy about it later.

Councilor Underwood steepled his fingers and looked over them at Sulana. "Sorceress Delano, I regret to inform you that we cannot accept your resignation at this time. You are required to continue your Commitment as Sword Sorceress until such a time as you are proven to be unable to continue your duties. We will grant you a convalescence period to be determined by the Council."

Sulana sighed in relief. She didn't want to resign, but felt it was the right thing to do given her impaired condition. And she greatly preferred resigning to the humiliation of being discharged.

She looked at each of the Councilors in turn. Maris Torlon gave her an encouraging smile. Gregor Rissik gave her a nod and a wink. Boris Underwood watched her with concern. Velna Asher glared at her through narrowed eyes and had a look that warned she was plotting her next move. Rikard Shepherd stared at his folded hands with a frown.

"I understand, Councilor Underwood," she finally said. "May I go now?"

The Senior Councilor nodded once. "Yes, Sulana, you may go."

CHAPTER 49
HEALING

I over-reached with my thrust and nearly dropped my practice sword when a sharp stab of pain shot through my bicep. I cried out and the tip of my sword drooped to the floor. Talon aborted the counter move he had started and stepped back.

"We're going to have to work on that," he said. "More stretching."

I nodded, massaging my sore arm. Lissy's healing potion had closed the quarrel wound I'd received during the rescue mission, but the muscle was still rebuilding in the damaged area. My practice sessions with Talon were slowly helping, but once in a while I pushed it too hard.

Talon grabbed an oiled rag and wiped down his practice sword, checking the blade over for damage caused by our sparring. "Let's call it a day," he said. "I've had enough too."

Thanks to Daisy's quick thinking at the fateful clearing, Talon was recovering well from the poison that nearly killed him, but he still tired easily and didn't have much of an appetite.

Sulana entered the practice room while I was putting away my gear. I turned to face her, but I couldn't read her expression. Did the Council accept her resignation? What was she going to do if they did?

We had discussed her decision to resign for hours, and I couldn't talk her out of it. Her ordeal at Thunderhead

College and the after-effects of the lightning strike that had nearly killed her had left her depressed and frustrated. When I tried to convince her that she would be fine with enough time to heal, she rightly argued that I couldn't know that. She was convinced that she was no longer capable of doing her job, and she was putting the Archives at risk by continuing her Commitment. She thought that I should take her place, which was not what I wanted at all.

"How did it go?" I asked her, still watching her face for an indication of what she was thinking.

She shrugged and said, "They rejected my resignation. At least for now. They put me on convalescent leave, but I don't know for how long yet."

I wanted to congratulate her, except the outcome was not actually what she wanted. "What will you do now?" I asked.

She smirked and said, "Convalesce, I guess. Maybe I need to get out of here for a while. Follow the healer's advice and get away from the politics and stress."

Her choice of wording put me instantly on alert. It didn't sound like she wanted me to go with her on whatever journey she had in mind. "Where are you thinking about going?" I asked with a sinking feeling in my heart.

"I haven't decided yet. Probably some place I've never been before that will distract me from all this," she said, rolling her eyes and waving an arm to indicate the whole of the Archives.

"Do you want company?"

She wouldn't meet my eyes. "I'm not sure. I think you'll be needed here, particularly if your petition is accepted. They'll want you to move forward with your training as quickly as possible."

That made me laugh. "I seriously doubt they'll accept my petition now. I'm surprised they haven't expelled me from the Archives already."

Every day since my return, I expected the Council to call me into session and tell me to leave the Archives forever. I figured the odds of my petition being accepted were less than zero. I had been quietly worrying about what would happen between Sulana and me if I were expelled. Part of me had hoped her resignation would be accepted so we could leave the Archives together. But now we were stuck without a clear way to move forward.

Sulana shook her head and finally looked at me. "You're wrong. The Council is still seriously considering your petition. They'd be foolish not to." Her voice took on an adamant tone. "You would make a great replacement, especially now that you can cast."

The news that the council still considered me a candidate was unexpected, and I blinked at her a few times in surprise. "That doesn't make sense. The last I heard, Thunderhead College was demanding my arrest for killing one of their guards."

"Two, actually," she said.

"What?"

"Two guards. A second guard died due to injuries sustained during 'the incident,'" she clarified.

I shook my head. "I'm sorry that happened, but they were the ones who started the attack with deadly force."

Sulana snorted and spread her arms. "You certainly don't have to tell *me*. But you also don't have to convince the Council. They know that the headmaster is posturing. They've abandoned the negotiations with Thunderhead College, but no one is sure what that means for what happens next. No one thinks we've heard the last of Dumont Fortenz."

"I'm sure they're right." I mused. But my thoughts had turned back to her earlier statement about replacing her.

"I wish you wouldn't talk about me replacing you," I said. "Just because I can cast doesn't mean I know what I'm doing. You have years more experience with sorcery. I need your help, and I still think we should work together." We were repeating the argument we'd had earlier, and having just as much luck convincing each other.

She knew that I meant we should work together in more than just a professional sense. The conversation was starting to get personal, and she glanced over at Talon, who was politely ignoring our conversation while he put away his practice gear.

She lowered her voice, although in the confines of the practice room, it didn't make much difference in terms of privacy. "Maybe it's best if we keep our personal relationship separate from our professional relationship anyway." I started to object, but she interrupted and spoke over me. "We can figure it out later. Right now, I'm too tired and confused to argue about it." She turned and started toward the door.

Her abrupt end to our conversation and walking away spiked my temper. "That's it? We can't even talk about this?"

She looked over her shoulder at me and glanced at Talon again. "I said later."

I felt like she was just using Talon's presence as an excuse to avoid the subject, but pushing the issue would only antagonize her more, so I let her walk out of the room without saying anything else.

I gritted my teeth and started changing out of my practice clothes. Sulana was slipping away from me and it seemed there was nothing I could do to stop it. If it came to a choice between being with her and being a Sword Sorcerer, it was no contest. I would choose her, and I was sure she knew it.

Was she using my petition as a way to get out of what we had started together? Maybe the lightning injury had changed her somehow.

Whatever happened, I knew that I didn't want her to leave and go somewhere to heal without me. I wanted to help her, and I was afraid of what she might decide while she was away from me and away from the pressure of her responsibilities at the Archives. I kept telling myself to trust her. She had to decide for herself what would make her happy, and if that didn't include me, there was nothing I could do about it. But those rational thoughts did nothing to ease the pain in my heart.

Talon came over to me and put a hand on my shoulder. "Have faith in her, Jaylan. She'll come around. But you can't push her back to you. She has to come back on her own. Be supportive and just keep moving toward a future here with her. Assume it will happen. Show her it will work."

I wasn't sure I could do what he suggested. When something went wrong, my inclination was to "fix it" somehow. But I was at a loss as to how I could fix this particular situation, and Talon's suggestions were sensible. I thanked him for his advice, and he left me standing alone in the practice room.

I shook my head and sat heavily on a bench. Discovering my ability to channel and making the decision to come to the Archives had been the most significant event in my life. Petitioning to become a Sword Sorcerer committed me to this new life as a practitioner of the vaetric arts. But my motivations all circled back to Sulana. I told myself that I didn't make any decisions *because* of her, but had to admit that I would not have made the decisions I did *without* her. I no longer wanted to go back to my old life, even if I could. But I also didn't want to go forward without Sulana by my side.

Maybe Talon was right. I would try to be supportive and let Sulana work out what she needed to do to be happy. Realistically, I didn't have much choice anyway, and the last thing I wanted to do was drive her away.

Besides, I had other things to worry about. I'd managed to make several enemies in the short time I'd been involved with the Archives and its representatives. I had no doubt that Lohan and the rest of Thunderhead College would continue to complicate my life. Paeter Thoron, who was markedly absent during my latest confrontation, was still out there somewhere as well. And I had a score to settle with him.

Feeling better now that I had a plan of sorts, I got up and stretched. I would take things one day at a time and help Sulana as best I could. If the Council approved my petition, I would train as hard as possible to make myself the best Sword Sorcerer I could be. The next time Thunderhead College made trouble, I'd be ready to face them.

I had to have faith that Sulana would be at my side when that happened.

THANK YOU FOR READING

Thank you for dedicating some of your reading time to the Vaetra Chronicles. I hope you are enjoying the adventures of Jaylan and Sulana and that you are looking forward to *Vaetra Unleashed*, the climactic conclusion of the trilogy.

If you would like to be notified by email when I release a new book, you can sign up for my New Releases email list at the series website, Vaetra.com. The signup form is right at the top of the home page.

I know that not everyone likes to write book reviews, but if you are willing to spare the time to write a sentence or two about what you thought of *Vaetra Untrained*, I encourage you to post a review at your favorite book vendor site or share a message with your social networking friends.

If you would like to share your thoughts with me privately, you can reach me through the contact page on Vaetra.com. Those messages go straight to my inbox. I look forward to hearing from you.

Happy reading,
Daniel R. Marvello

Acknowledgements

Writing is often a solitary affair, but publishing a book benefits from the support of many people besides the author. I first want to thank my wife for her love and for her support of my writing career. She is my anchor and my muse in this crazy and unpredictable "real" world.

I also give thanks to the readers of the first Vaetra Chronicles book, *Vaetra Unveiled*. Their patronage and feedback inspires me to keep writing and to keep improving.

I received excellent feedback on this book from my beta readers. Special thanks go to Susan Daffron, Cynthia Daffron, Paul Sheriff, and Ken Rahmoeller for helping me make *Vaetra Untrained* a better story.

Finally, I'd like to give a shout out to the writers and readers who post at the Writer's Café on KBoards.com. Their advice, support, and perspectives have been an invaluable part of my publishing education. Thumbs up to the forum moderators Harvey, Ann, and Betsy for maintaining discipline in an often unruly crowd.

About the Author

Daniel R. Marvello writes fantasy adventure stories from his log home on forty acres of forest and meadow in the North Idaho panhandle. The setting for his Vaetra Chronicles book series was inspired by the scenic beauty of his surroundings. Daniel shares his home with his loving wife of 20 years and several wonderful animals.

Visit the Vaetra Chronicles Web site at:

www.Vaetra.com

Visit Daniel's blog at:

www.DanielRMarvello.com